GW00319641

AOIFE MANNIX

Heritage of Secrets

flipped eye publishing
manchester

Published by flipped eye publishing, Manchester 2009
www.flippedeye.net

First Published in the United Kingdom by
lubin & kleyner 2008

Copyright © Aoife Mannix 2008
Front cover Image © iStockphoto.com/inhauscreative
Cover Design © Petraski for flipped eye publishing 2009.

All Rights Reserved. No part of this publication may be reproduced,
stored in a retrieval system, or transmitted, in any form or by any
means, electronic, mechanical, photocopying, recording, or otherwise,
without the written permission of the appropriate individual author,
nor may it be otherwise circulated in any form of binding or cover
other than that in which it is published and without a similar condition
including this condition being imposed on the subsequent purchaser.

This book is typeset in BaskervilleMT and Palatino from Linotype GmbH
Printed in the United Kingdom.

ISBN-13: 978-1905233243
ISBN-10: 1905233248

British Library Cataloguing in Publication Data
A catalogue record for this book is available from the British Library

The publication of this book was made possible
thanks to a grant from Arts Council England
Printed in the United Kingdom

For my mother, Joan Mannix

Acknowledgements

With many thanks to my editor Nii Parkes and everyone at flipped eye publishing. A very special thank you to my mentor Geraldine Collinge for all her support and invaluable suggestions. Also to Sarah Ellis, Kate Morgenroth, Les Robinson and Heather Tyrrell for their inspiration, encouragement and faith.

"Yet each man kills the thing he loves,
By each let this be heard,
Some do it with a bitter look,
Some with a flattering word,
The coward does it with a kiss,
The brave man with a sword!"

- Oscar Wilde, *The Ballad of Reading Gaol*

1

THE SMALL CONGREGATION OF MOURNERS shuffled their feet nervously as Bernard O'Connell made yet another attempt to speak at the funeral. He stood like a scarecrow of the man he had once been, at the front of the nearly empty church, swaying slightly beside the priest. He seemed to have forgotten the occasion or where he was.

"It was too much love that killed her," he began.

Jack felt embarrassed. He knew his mother would not appreciate this public discussion of her life - and death. Luckily, his father again lapsed into silence and, after a few more torturous moments, returned to his pew.

The rest of the ceremony passed in a surreal blur. Few of his father's family had deigned to come and, from his mother's side, only his cousin Brendan.

"She was a good woman, no matter what anyone says," Brendan mumbled before hugging Jack so hard he thought he felt his ribs crack.

That was nearly two years ago. Jack and his father had moved from Derry shortly afterwards. Their hometown may have been the second largest city in Northern Ireland but when it came to scandal, it was one of the tiniest villages on the planet. Jack's father made it clear he wanted to shake off the ghosts of the past, or if that proved impossible, at least his haunted reputation. He found himself as obscure a post as possible as headmaster of a tiny school on the west coast of Ireland. His son he packed off to college in Dublin to study medicine.

Bernard O'Connell now lived alone in a rather dilapidated cottage right beside his school.

"It's a bit of a come down to go from five hundred boys to a few dozen, but at least I'm still in charge. And I know you'll make something of yourself. You're the main reason I keep myself going now your mother's no longer with us."

The place was tiny, but it had a spectacular view of the wildness of the Atlantic Ocean. At night you could hear the waves crashing with a savage loneliness. It was a far cry from the cramped streets where he and his son had grown up but he insisted it suited him.

"Less than five minutes walk to the beach," he informed Jack. "Not that I have time for sunbathing mind you. Or indeed that there's much in the way of sunshine."

Given that his mother had drowned, Jack couldn't help wondering if this decision to move to the seaside wasn't some kind of masochism.

Jack wanted to ask his father what he'd meant by his thwarted speech at the funeral, but he didn't dare. His father never mentioned it again yet it left Jack with a deeply unsettling feeling. Perhaps why at the age of nineteen he'd never had a proper girlfriend.

It wasn't as if he didn't get offers. With his black hair, blue eyes and cheekbones you could slice yourself open on, he cut a mysterious and deep figure to girls, who regarded him with fascination. He braved the occasional date but could never bring himself to arrange a second. He just wasn't interested.

But now all that changed. Jack had fallen in love.

Father O'Brien slapped him so hard on the back that he nearly fell flat on his face. "Are you not dancing?" the priest roared.

The school dance at St. Michael's Parish Hall was hardly the most romantic of settings. With its crumbling plaster and low hanging ceiling, Jack thought it was probably more suited to exorcisms than declarations of undying love. Music droned from a hi-fi. Rainwater dripped from the leaking roof.

"I said, are you not dancing?" Father O'Brien repeated.

For a horrified moment, Jack thought it was an invitation. He stared into the older man's flushed face and stammered, "No. No, just watching."

Father O'Brien was tapping his foot, swaying his considerable bust and mouthing, 'Well, since my baby left me, I found a new place to dwell…' He paused mid-phrase. "Young fella like yourself, haven't you all your life to be watching?"

Jack wondered what had possessed Father O'Brien to become a priest. In another life he could have been a rock-n-roll superstar; maybe not the King himself but more of a minor royal.

"Will you have an orange juice, Father?" Jack asked, turning uncertainly towards the drinks table.

Out of the corner of his eye, he could see his own father making his way across the dance hall towards them. At the last hop, someone had spiked the punch with enough vodka to knock out an entire regiment, so this time his father had put him on police duty. Really he was too old to be at these school dances. Everyone knew he was the headmaster's son, there to guard their sobriety.

Bernard O'Connell had spent most of the evening patrolling the

8

dance floor and interrupting couples that were getting overly amorous. As the night wore on, he became swollen with moral indignation. Now he demanded an orange juice from Jack and downed it in one, holding out his paper cup for another. Clearly, protecting the youth from their lustful urges was thirsty work.

"A kiss is one thing. I have no objections to a kiss, have you, Father?"

"No, no Bernard. Sure there are plenty of kisses in the Bible."

Jack wondered how he'd managed to miss them all.

"But I tell you that O'Flaherty boy had his hand right up her top and I swear to God, there was spittle dripping from his mouth."

Jack coloured with embarrassment. This was turning into the longest evening. Why, oh why, had he agreed to come?

The answer to this question just at that moment walked in the door.

It was so typical of her to turn up when the dance was finishing, practically for the last set. He had been determined not to waste any more time. He would screw up his courage and walk over to her the moment the first needle scratched the record. Whatever the song, it would be perfect. Whether anyone else was on the floor or not. He would sweep her out under the lights before she even had the chance to think about saying no. That was the fantasy nearly four hours ago. Since then his confidence had popped along with the few remaining scraps of balloons stuck pathetically to the walls.

The first time he saw her, he knew his life was over. That life where he got up in the morning, washed his face, ate breakfast, and headed off into the blankness of his every day routine. He'd had no sense of purpose or direction, only a dull ache that had settled into his bones since his mother's funeral. He was so used to feeling numb that meeting Kate was like touching the end of a raw nerve. The shock of it was to stay with him for years.

It wasn't that she was pretty. Mary Horan, with her long blond hair and round, dimpled cheeks, was pretty. Kate, on the other hand, was beautiful in a way that caused him physical pain. She had eyes the colour of absinthe and a smile you could get drunk on. She was tall and slim with small, elegant hands that never stopped moving. There was an energy about her that crackled and threatened to burst into flames.

That first time they met was only a little over nine months ago, but it felt like centuries. It was Christmas eve, the night after Jack got back for the holidays, and his father insisted on dragging him down the pub to show him off. The place was jam packed with ex-locals reunited for the holidays. Few people over the age of consent and under the age of fifty

9

still actually lived in the town. Unemployment, emigration and boredom made sure of that but they had come flooding back to celebrate the birth of our Lord. With all the shouting and cheering and cries for drinks, Jack could hardly hear himself think.

He offered to get a round in to escape his father's insistence on introducing him to total strangers with the words, "This is my son I was telling you about. The one studying medicine in UCD."

It was mortifying that this piece of information came even before his name. He would shout 'Jack' in each ear as they pumped his hand before turning back to talk to his father. Still he was pleased for his father that he'd managed to get to know so many people, far more than Jack had succeeded in meeting in Dublin.

He found himself pressed up against the counter, fumbling in his pockets for money as the girl behind the bar yelled, "What can I get you?"

When he looked up into Kate's face, his mouth opened, but no words came. He tried again. Again nothing.

He was elbowed aside by a gruff voice shouting, "Four pints of Guinness, a Jameson's, and a gin and tonic there, love."

Jack found his face crushed up against a huge inflated Father Christmas that hung against the wall. The Santa exploded suddenly with a sound like a rifle shot and the bar fell silent. Everyone stared at him as if he were a terrorist.

Only Kate saw the funny side. "He's only after blowing up Santa." She laughed with delight.

To Jack's relief, the buzz of the bar returned. He apologized profusely and offered to pay for damages. Kate's eyes were lit up with a mixture of amusement and puzzlement. "You're not from round here, are you?"

"I'm Jack. Jack O'Connell. Bernard O'Connell's son."

"Ah the one doing medicine."

His face flushed red as she turned back to her other customers.

"You were an age," his father complained on Jack's return with the drinks. "What were you doing? Brewing it yourself?"

Kate O'Rourke. He managed to elicit her name. That was one good thing about a small town; it wasn't hard to find out who anybody was.

"Talk about exploiting your own children. She's barely old enough to be in here. Certainly not to be serving drinks, never mind consuming them. She should be in school."

"It's Christmas Eve, Dad. Even you're not in school."

"Ah you know what I mean." This was an expression his father often used when he was making no sense whatsoever.

Just before closing time Jack introduced himself to the owner of the pub, Kate's father, Cathal O'Rourke. He was a small man, sort of folded in on himself, and he spoke very quietly and quickly.

"It's been a real blessing having your father take charge of the school. Putting a bit of order on the place at last. Those young lads were running wild altogether. But they don't stand for that nonsense up North, do they Bernard?"

"No, indeed not. They save all that delinquency for chucking stones at Orangemen. Gets it out of their system."

"Suppose they could do with more than a few rocks. Even up the odds a bit." Mr O'Rourke's voice fell even lower. "There's plenty round here be keen to help."

Jack's father took a deep sip of Guinness. "I wouldn't know about that, I'm not a political man myself."

Mr O'Rourke raised his eyebrows. He looked from Jack to his father as if trying to gauge if there was any chance they'd come south of the border to further the glory of the nationalist cause. Jack felt himself withering under the shrewdness of the gaze. He was pretty sure that Kate's father could tell just by looking at him that he was a million times more interested in his daughter than he was in the reunification of Ireland.

"I've yet to meet a Northerner that wasn't obsessed with politics. Unless maybe he were a Protestant, I don't know much about what they think."

Mr O'Rourke managed to make this sound like an accusation and Bernard O'Connell shifted his weight uncomfortably. Jack knew this kind of conversation was exactly what his father was so keen to avoid.

Jack's father cleared his throat. "Education is my game and I've never been afraid of applying discipline. Routine, regulations and a strict diet is what keeps boys from getting into trouble. The Blessed Virgin Mary herself would agree with me, I'm sure."

This reference to the Virgin seemed to appease Mr O'Rourke somewhat. He laughed, an odd rattling sound, "Ah sure you're right, she probably had occasion to take a leather strap to baby Jesus himself."

This struck Jack as bordering on blasphemous but his father just chuckled and patted his stomach. Something about his smugness seemed slightly fascist to Jack. He was being too harsh again he knew. He should be pleased that his father had set up a whole new life so quickly. He still missed Derry terribly himself, even if everyone in Dublin said it was a shit hole.

Even Brendan said this, and he'd only left a year ago to move in with Jack. "We're well shut of that God forsaken whore of a city," he declared on the night he arrived at 3 a.m. in a small battered car with an equally battered suitcase. "What did it ever bring us but trouble and heart ache."

Jack was taken aback by his cousin's sudden appearance but glad of the company. He found Dublin a snobbish place, full of unfriendly people who acted as if Northern Ireland were a barbaric alien planet they'd rather not think about. His father claimed they'd fit in better in a proper Catholic country but Jack still considered Derry his home, the place where he'd lived with his mother. He didn't care much for university life but he knew his father would never forgive him if he dropped out.

"So you're going to be a doctor?" Mr O'Rourke looked Jack up and down as if he were a new breed of cattle. "Your father says you're on a scholarship?"

Really; had his father told everyone his life story? In this case it turned out well, because he'd also said his son was looking for holiday work and Jack found himself being offered a job.

"We always need a bit of an extra hand round the holliers with all the students coming back and what have you."

Jack made an effort to hold himself a bit straighter. He needed the money and suddenly O'Rourke's Pub seemed like an exciting prospect.

"Have you ever pulled a pint?" Mr O'Rourke stared at him with small, rat-like eyes that seemed to pierce the depths of his soul.

"Ah no Sir, I haven't," he mumbled.

His father gave him a jab in the ribs for the stupidity of his honesty. "He's a very fast learner, Cathal," his father smoothly reassured.

"Well with the headmaster for his father, I suppose he'd want to be. You can start tomorrow. Be here for six sharp. I can't stand lateness."

Jack stammered his gratitude, but Mr O'Rourke was already halfway back to the bar.

His father was rather pleasantly surprised by his enthusiasm for the new job as Jack had always turned his nose up at the thought of working in a country pub.

But Jack offered no explanation for his sudden change of heart. He came home to work over Christmas, and Patrick's Day weekend, and Easter, and he even accepted a job for the summer.

"Thought you might want to go to London with your mates and work there a bit," his father remarked when he told him he'd be home for three months.

"Do you not want me around?" Jack had learned that the best form of defence with his father was attack.

"No, no sure I'm delighted to have you, you know that."

And indeed the irritation of having to live with his father again seemed a small price to pay for the privilege of working every day with Kate. She was just about to go into her last year of school, but that summer she was working full time in her father's pub.

The pub itself was divided into two sections, neither of which were much bigger than a sitting room. The bar with its battered wooden high stools, and the lounge with its tiny, prized snug. Even at the height of August, it remained dark and cool inside. The cloud of smoke was so thick you could hardly see in the evenings and in the afternoon, the ghosts of nights out hung like mist in the air. Kate's family lived above and Jack always arrived early in the hope that he might get to see a little more of her. Mr O'Rourke admired his dedication to his work, but his wife was wise to Jack's real motivations. Mrs O'Rourke was still a handsome woman herself and she always made him feel at home, insisting that he ate plate loads of her homemade biscuits. She said that her daughter Caitriona would never touch them and was fading to nothing before their very eyes. Not that she particularly reminded him of his own mother, but it was nice to be fussed over. His father largely ignored him at home and there was never much to eat in their house. The man seemed to have given up food along with all the other pleasures in life.

The only thing that made Jack uneasy was that Mrs O'Rourke was very religious and often asked him if he'd been to mass. He always said that he had, which wasn't a lie, as his father wouldn't hear of them not going when Jack was home. Jack never mentioned he no longer believed a word of it. He suspected his father didn't either, but just wanted to keep appearances up. Maybe he was right, why give people an excuse to find fault with you?

While Jack found it easy to chat away to Mrs O'Rourke, once Kate appeared he often found himself at a loss what to say. There were so many things he wanted to tell her, but it never seemed the right moment. Not that he didn't feel he was making progress. The afternoon shifts were the best. In the evening there were always too many customers and he didn't like the way men looked at Kate after they had a few drinks in them. But in the afternoons, it was quieter. While he polished the black wood of the bar, she would ask him about life in Dublin. She seemed so desperate to hear tales of parties and dances that he found once he'd run out of ones he'd been to, he started making them up. In fact, he much preferred the Dublin he created for Kate while she was washing up the glasses and putting out the ashtrays, to the one he actually lived in.

It wasn't like he had to say much; she provided most of the detail. She had an older sister, Pat, who worked in a shop on the north side of the city and she'd been up to visit her a few times. Pat was always telling her Dublin was the place to be. Though – Kate confided to Jack – America was where she was headed. He could just imagine her on the silver screen and never stopped to ask himself how these plans would fit in with her being a doctor's wife. He didn't care for medicine much any way. The sight of blood made him feel rather sick. It was his father who had pushed him into it and at the time he was too confused to offer any resistance.

Jack's main problem was that Mr O'Rourke never gave them the same time off. Otherwise Jack would have invited Kate to the pictures long ago. And so the whole summer had flown away from them. He pretended he missed his exciting life in the big city and was only working in the pub because he worried about his father on his own. But in truth he'd never been happier than those long summer evenings he spent learning how to pull a decent pint of Guinness and watching Kate charm her way with all the customers. She never seemed to stand still.

"You're like a hummingbird," he told her.

She just smiled and shook her head at him.

It was true though; there was a lightness to her that Jack envied. She had a beautiful singing voice too. Sometimes the pub fiddler persuaded her to sing while he accompanied her. She'd only agree to this when her father wasn't around as Mr O'Rourke disapproved of her 'making a spectacle of herself' as he put it.

The fiddler's name was Flynn Joyce and he'd turned up out of the blue one afternoon when Jack was washing the front windows of O'Rourke's. "I'm looking for work," he announced.

Jack took him in to meet Mr O'Rourke who was initially dismissive until the small man took out his fiddle and began to play. Kate's father listened in silence, then when Flynn stopped, he pronounced with distaste, "Tinker music."

Flynn looked furious and turned to leave.

"...but the place could do with a bit of atmosphere. You can start tomorrow if you want."

Kate adored Flynn's playing. And the fiddler quickly worked out that Jack adored Kate. He said to him with a wink, "You two were made for each other. Only a matter of time before you're walking out together."

Jack wasn't superstitious. Still, he couldn't help hoping the musician was also a fortune teller.

But the time passed far too quickly. September arrived out of nowhere and Kate stopped working the afternoons. She was back at school and, as she had exams coming up, she only helped out one night a week in the pub. Jack had to go back to Dublin as college was starting but he couldn't leave without having some idea what she thought of him.

The dance was the first one of the school year and even though his father was going to be there, it was still the last chance he was going to get. He should have said something back in June when there was still all that time in front of them. Anyway, it wasn't as if Dublin was that far away. If he saved his money he could still come back for the odd weekend. He wondered what she'd say if he asked her to marry him. Probably pass out with the shock. He knew they were meant to be together, he just wasn't so sure if she'd realised it yet. But what was the use if he couldn't even bring himself to ask her to dance? His stomach felt like there were eels trying to wriggle their way out of it. He took a last sip of orange juice and strode over to where she was sitting with her friends.

He would've preferred a slow set rather than a fast one, but it was now or never. "Would you like to dance?"

Two of her friends burst into giggles and he nearly turned on his heels and ran.

But Kate got up out of her seat and took his hand. "Sure why not?"

He'd never been much of a dancer, but he made an effort to keep up with her. Normally at work she had her dark hair tied back, but now she wore it loose and free. She had on a blue dress with small white flowers on it.

"You're gorgeous," he said.

"What?" she shouted back at him and twirled around, his words lost forever in the beat of the music. He would've been happy just to watch her dance for the rest of his life.

"You're so lucky to be able to leave. I'd give anything to get out of this kip." She spoke with a desperate intensity.

Later on Jack wondered: If he had offered to take her away there and then, would it have all turned out differently?

The music cut with an abrupt silence and all the lights came back on. There was a chorus of groans and pleading to at least finish the song. He cursed his father who was already shooing people towards the exit. Jack could see in his face that his father loved the power of being able to ruin people's good time. Students stumbled around blinded by the sudden strip lighting. It was pretty obvious that some of them hadn't had to rely on Jack's orange juice, but sneaked their own supply in despite his father's thorough frisking at the door. All the magic had evaporated from the evening. The hall was once again a tired, broken place with church community fliers pasted to the wall. One large poster read 'Jesus is watching you.' And he's probably laughing, Jack thought bitterly.

"Well I best be getting home," Kate said. "My dad has a conniption if I'm out after twelve."

He couldn't bear it. To have worked himself up like this and then to say nothing. "Do you fancy a stroll on the beach?" he blurted out, amazed at his own daring.

"My dad'll kill me. And he's likely to shoot you, even if you are his star barman." She walked over to pick up her cardigan.

Jack felt utterly deflated.

But then she was back. "Well come on then."

"What about your father?"

She was laughing now. "I'll just blame you and sure you'll be gone before he catches you."

She even took his arm as they were walking out the door. He looked up at the stars, feeling more positive towards the heavens than he had in a long time. His father came running after him complaining that part of his job was to help with the clearing up.

"I promised Mr O'Rourke I'd walk Kate home. I'll be straight back."

His father cursed, but turned to go back inside.

"God but you're a good liar." Kate looked at him in admiration. It was the first compliment she'd ever given him.

They had the beach completely to themselves and soon left the lights of the small town trailing behind them. Jack had brought a small pocket torch and shone it in front making a tiny path for them to follow. The air had a bite to it, a warning that the softness of summer was leaving. He insisted on Kate wearing his coat. It was huge on her.

"I look ridiculous." She put her hands in the pockets and spun around.

Suddenly she lay down on the sand and started waving her arms in a circle above her head. "I'm making an angel," she explained. "Like they do in the snow in America. It doesn't work so well in the sand."

"Kate, I need...." he began, but she wasn't listening.

"I'd love to see real snow. Not just a bit of hail and a few flakes that cling to the bushes and are gone the next day. Proper mountains. Big banks of it that you could throw yourself into. I'd love to go skiing. When we get snow, it's barely enough to make a snowman out of."

He put his hand out and pulled her to her feet. Then he kissed her. Swallowing her little cry of surprise. Nothing in his life ever again was to have the passion of that moment.

She stepped back, staring at him quizzically. "You're a dark horse, aren't you, Jack O'Connell?" She laughed. "I was beginning to wonder how I'd ever get you to kiss me." Then she pulled him close.

If only he could have taken a photograph of that warm embrace and lived inside it the rest of his days.

They only stopped when they heard shouting. For a confused moment Jack thought Mr O'Rourke had tracked them down. But the man racing towards them was a stranger with an odd accent, like he'd stepped out of a film. He was wearing a sailor's outfit that was dripping wet. He was so panicked and incoherent they thought he'd been washed off a boat. Something about his friends in trouble. They ran down the beach after him. Right by the water's edge, two young men were standing over another who lay flat out on the wet sand.

One of them had tears running down his face and cried out in an American accent. "I told him not to get into the water."

The smell of whiskey mixed with the salt of the sea slapped Jack in the face. He suddenly remembered he was supposed to be a doctor. He sank down beside the unconscious man and shone his torch in his face. He didn't appear to be breathing. His skin had a plastic whiteness that reminded Jack of the only other dead body he'd seen outside of a lab. When the sea finally decided to give his mother back, it was Jack who had to identify her. His father refused to go into the mortuary. As if, as long as he didn't see it, he could pretend it hadn't happened.

Jack put his hands on the sailor's chest and began to pump hard. He breathed into his mouth. The man's lips were cold and he had stubble. For some reason Jack found himself crying and pleading with a God he was sure wasn't there. Suddenly the man gave a loud cough and vomited water and whatever else he'd swallowed at the bottom of the ocean all over Jack.

The sailors treated him like a hero and insisted on plying him with whiskey to express their gratitude. They kept slapping him on the back and calling him 'man'. They were American seamen on leave from their ship. Kate's eyes shone with sheer joy at the adventure of it all. Jack wondered what kind of crazy people would be tempted to go for a midnight dip in the Atlantic Ocean in September. He stared out at the black unfriendliness of the water and shivered. The nearly drowned man was at first unable to speak much, but after a while he shook Jack's hand

and introduced himself as Troy.

He explained, "I tried swimming back in, but I just kept getting sucked further out. I kept thinking, I don't want to die like this."

Kate was thrilled to hear all the gory details of Troy's story, but Jack turned away from them both, thinking of his mother. It had been her choice to walk into the waves. If he lived to be a hundred, he would never understand it. Had she changed her mind and tried to swim back but found it was too late? If he'd been there, would he have been able to bring her back to life? This was the beginning of Jack's feeling that he'd saved the wrong person.

Troy was saying to Kate, "And then I opened my eyes and there was just the most beautiful girl I'd ever seen looking down on me. You know, I thought you were an angel."

By the time Jack got home, he felt like he was drowning himself. His head spun from the whiskey and the whole night had become a bizarre blur. He wasn't even sure if he had kissed Kate. He struggled to get his key in the door, but his father flung it open.

He was in his nightshirt. "It's four in the morning. You're drunk." He angrily poured Jack a glass of water in the kitchen.

Jack felt accused and blurted out the whole story in his defence. He thought his father would be pleased by this tale of his medical proficiency. He would be able to dine out on it for the next six months at least. But his father just patted him awkwardly on the head.

"Well at least it wasn't you in the water. You best get to bed," he said softly.

2

JACK OPENED THE DOOR TO the tiny bed-sit he shared with Brendan to discover the whole floor submerged under two inches of water. Brendan was spending the weekend in Derry and wouldn't be back till tomorrow. Jack flicked through the phone book looking for a plumber in despair. After he found one – who spent the whole time complaining about not being in the pub and charged him nearly a week's wages – he called Brendan to tell him what had happened. His cousin clearly had a few pints on him. When Jack told him the news, he laughed hysterically. "Ah fucking hell, the roof will fall in on us next."

By the time Jack got into bed, he was numb with tiredness. He dreamt he was in a small rowing boat at sea with Kate. She was laughing and messing about and he kept warning her to sit down. The boat tilted dangerously and Kate lost her footing and fell overboard. He woke in horror as she hit the water.

The clock read half past four in the morning and the street lamp outside was reflected in the water on the floor of the flat. Jack had woken the day before with the most horrible hangover. Like a little man was tapping at the inside of his skull. As the bus lurched its way along the windy roads back to Dublin, it'd taken all his concentration to hold on to the contents of his stomach. He'd hoped to pop round the pub and say goodbye to Kate, but his father was so paranoid about his lateness that he practically manhandled him on to the bus. It was a beautiful, sunny morning and he waved to O'Rourke's pub as he passed it. The shutters were still down and there was no sign of life. Jack felt he'd found an even more painful form of homesickness and vowed he would return very soon. But the plumber's bill didn't help. And Mr O'Rourke wouldn't need him now until Christmas. He'd have to find an evening job in Dublin to pay for his weekend bus fare.

He thought about ringing Kate, but was put off by the possibility of Mrs O'Rourke answering and asking him which church he went to in Dublin. He'd never been to mass in the city and with no one to pass judgment on his burgeoning atheism; he had no intention of going. He had a superstitious belief that Mrs O'Rourke was like his mother in always knowing when he was lying. He wondered if all mothers were like that, or just Irish ones. As he lay in the semi-darkness watching the lights from passing cars throw prison bars across the ceiling, he decided writing was the answer. In his head he composed a letter so perfect in its declaration that Kate was bound to realise that their walk on the beach was a sign they were destined to be together forever.

As the birds started singing in the trees, Jack got up, pulled a piece of paper out of the drawer and cleared a bit of space for himself on the kitchen table. Brendan hadn't washed a dish or wiped a surface the entire time Jack had been away. There was a quarter of a bottle of milk that had entirely solidified, and the remains of a loaf covered in a greenish fuzz. The white grease of at least three different breakfasts clung to plates that had been slung into the sink. But Jack was determined not to be distracted. He chewed the top of his pen. *Dear Kate...*

Two hours later he'd got no further. The blankness of the page seemed as impossible to fill as the facts of his future. He scrunched it up in frustration and threw it into the slimy festering water in the sink.

Brendan didn't turn up till after eleven that night. Not even able to make it from the bus stop home without dropping into the pub. He looked slightly cleaner than usual; probably his mammy had made him take a bath. His red hair still stuck up in big clumps behind his overgrown ears. Ears that looked like that was how the doctor had lifted him into the world, Jack's mother used to say. Jack didn't mind Brendan really, he was grand to go for a pint with, but living with him was a health hazard.

"How was Derry?" Jack asked, keen to hear news of his hometown.

"What a shit hole. I'm telling you, boy, we're lucky we escaped while we still could."

A week passed in an agony of indecision and in the end Jack went back to the idea of phoning. It would take him years to write a letter and, the more time went by, the more unreal the kiss seemed. Perhaps he had dreamt it. Or perhaps she'd only kissed him because she knew he was leaving the next day and felt sorry for him. Maybe it meant nothing to her at all. Just one of hundreds of kisses on beaches she'd had.

He found it increasingly difficult to concentrate on his studies. The lecturer droned on about the circulation of the blood, while Jack's seemed to be burning through his veins. One afternoon they all got introduced to the body they were expected to dissect. The professor fancied himself as a morbid comedian and slapped the corpse cheerfully on the back like they were old friends. Several students turned very pale and had to leave the room. Jack felt oddly superior, as if knowing what death looked like were something to be proud of.

But that night he dreamt he was cutting open a body on a slab, only it turned out to be his mother. He woke up screaming and Brendan came running. They'd divided the room by means of a bed sheet strung up. Brendan was not a pretty sight in his Y fronts and grubby T-shirt, but he insisted on making them both a cup of tea with a liberal dash of whiskey thrown in.

"Get that down you," he instructed Jack. He wasn't a bad sort really.

The next day Jack phoned O'Rourke's. Her father answered. Jack made a few pleasantries and then asked if Kate was there.

"She's not in," yelled Mr O'Rourke and put the phone down on him.

Maybe he was still angry about Kate getting home so late. He was the kind of man who wouldn't think saving a drowning victim was any kind of excuse. Apparently he'd been even stricter on Kate's sister Pat, not wanting to let her out of the house at all.

Jack hung up in defeat. Maybe it would be better to see her face to face. He wasn't great on the phone anyway. He could never think of any news to tell his father when he rang and they always ended up talking about the weather or the football. He decided to ask Brendan to lend him the money to go home. He told him his father wasn't well and he was worried about him.

Brendan looked at him suspiciously. "I'm down to my last few shillings and I don't get paid till Tuesday."

Sadly this was true and most of his wages would be drunk by Wednesday.

Brendan worked as a bouncer for a dance hall in the city centre. He told Jack he didn't think the work would suit him, but if he was that desperate for cash he could get him a trial evening on Friday. All going well, Jack would have the money to go home the weekend after.

"Think your Da will last that long?" he asked Jack with a wink.

Brendan wasn't exactly an intellectual, but he wasn't stupid either. "You've been moping round here like a long streak of piss ever since you got back. Are you in love or something?"

Jack's blush gave him away as usual.

The dance hall was called 'The Palace.' A name that proved the owner, Jimmy Byrne, had a greater sense of irony than most people gave him credit for. Jimmy shook Jack's hand so hard, he thought he could feel the bones cracking.

"Brendan's cousin, are we?" Jimmy bellowed. He'd spent so much time trying to make himself heard over loud music; he no longer knew how to speak in a normal tone.

"Not first cousins like. His mother and my mother..." Jack stumbled over his explanation but Jimmy just put his arm round him and led him down the steps into the bowels of the cellar. The walls were lined with bottle after bottle of spirits and huge fat kegs of beer hulked together in the dark.

"This is where I keep my babies," Jimmy explained. "To be honest with you, I don't like hassle, but as long as folk don't puke or bleed on my floor, they can fucking kill each other for all I care. First sign of trouble, you grab them like this." Jimmy lifted Jack up effortlessly by his collar. "And you chuck them out the side door and down the steps. After that, they're not your problem. But if you catch any little fecker trying to break into my drink, you let me know and I will personally snap every bone in their body. And that goes for staff as well."

Jimmy put Jack back on the ground and he attempted to straighten his shirt. "Anyways people do know not to be messing with Ulster men. Isn't that right, Brendan?"

"Yes Mister Byrne, you're spot on there, Sir." Brendan nodded sagely at Jimmy's words of wisdom. "There's a war on and we're all soldiers in it. Until we get our country back, we've no choice but to be tough as nails."

"Very well put lad. Not just a pretty face, eh?" Jimmy winked at Jack who smiled uncertainly.

Jack got changed into the penguin suit Brendan had lent him. It was at least two sizes too big and he was swimming in it.

Brendan creased up when he saw him. "Don't worry about it. You look grand," he said when he'd stopped laughing. "It's nothing to do with size anyway. It's all a question of attitude. As long as you act intimidating, you'll be fine."

As he rolled up the sleeves of his jacket, Jack reminded himself this was all so he could see Kate and that was the only thing that mattered.

Himself and Brendan took up their positions just outside the door. There wasn't a soul in sight. Brendan yawned and lit a cigarette.

"Just relax." He blew a large smoke ring over their heads. "Be totally dead until the pubs close."

Jack watched a very elegant woman in a fur jacket being helped out of a taxi by a man. They crossed the street quickly and headed into the theatre. The lady wore impossibly high red shoes and moved with the grace of a gazelle. The man kissed her lightly on the cheek just as they went through the large wooden doors. Jack imagined putting his arm around Kate like that. Taking her to plays, and cocktail parties, and dinners. She would love it.

It began to rain a fine mist. Brendan turned his collar up. "He's a character Mr Byrne, don't you think?"

He offered Jack another fag which he gratefully accepted. They both stamped their feet in an effort to keep the blood flowing and stave off the chill.

Jack lowered his voice. "He seemed a bit dodgy to me."

"Ah no, he's sound enough. Just don't let him start talking to you about politics."

"I never talk to anyone about politics."

"Wise man." Brendan blew on his hands and rubbed them together. "But he thinks what with being from Derry and all..."

"What's his problem with that?"

"Ah no, he's all for it. He knows a lot of people like."

"What kind of people?"

"Well the RA has to get its money from somewhere. All I'm saying is don't let him start going on to you about The Cause."

Jack sighed. His suspicions that Jimmy Byrne was a total gangster seemed to be confirmed. He'd never asked Brendan why he got out of Derry so quick because he didn't really want to know. "Don't be asking questions you don't want to hear the answer to," his mother used to say.

A queue began to form and snaked its way around the corner. Brendan instructed Jack to stand on the other side of the cordon as he began to wave people through. He paid no attention to the girls unless they were attractive; in which case he looked them up and down admiringly and said, "Now make sure you behave yourselves ladies. No doing anything I wouldn't do."

The girls generally laughed, but their boyfriends looked less pleased. Jack felt wholly irrelevant to the proceedings, just standing there like a fool. He wondered if he was destined to spend all his life in this role. He avoided the girls' eyes as he waved them through. Some of them were pretty enough, though they wore a bit too much make-up. But none of them was a patch on Kate.

A young man in drainpipe trousers and a bright red shirt shouted at Jack in a London accent. "Let us in, mate. It's bloody freezing out here."

Brendan looked him up and down with contempt. "Not unless you sing us the Irish National Anthem."

Several people in the queue laughed.

"Go on. Let's hear it."

To Jack's amazement the bloke stepped out of the line and began to sing, "Sinne Fianna Fáil A tá fé gheall ag Éirinn…"

There wasn't a trace of an English accent in his Irish and he had a fine tenor. People began to clap before he had finished.

Brendan smiled. "For that boy, you can go in for free."

Jack wasn't so sure if he approved of Brendan's door policy, but he said nothing. The hall reached maximum capacity remarkably quickly. With the music booming inside, and the audible shouts and laughs of people having a good time, the mood of those still queuing quickly turned sour.

A couple of blokes began to chant, "Why are we waiting?"

"Cos we're fucking full, you morons," shouted Brendan.

The rain began to come down in earnest.

"Here, I'm dying for a pee," said Brendan. "You hold the fort."

As Brendan turned to go inside, Jack felt suddenly nervous. Two rather big lads began to plead with him. "C'mon we're regulars. We come here every week. Give us a break. It's probably half empty in there."

Jack clutched the cordon as if it were an impenetrable barrier. A girl with peroxide hair and a mini skirt shouted at him, "Hey young fella, I'll give you a kiss if you let us in."

"You'll have to give him more than that," another female voice replied.

Their laughter pounded in Jack's ears as he turned bright red. A wave of self-loathing engulfed him.

Suddenly he heard a familiar voice. "Hey man, is that really you? Hey, I know this guy."

Troy looked so much healthier than the last time Jack had seen him that he would never have recognised him if it wasn't for the American accent. He wasn't wearing his sailor's uniform either, but a leather jacket. His jet-black hair was shaved practically to the bone, which made his brown eyes look even bigger. He slapped Jack on the back and gave him a huge hug before turning to inform the queue, "This guy saved my life."

Jack shifted on his feet uneasily. At that moment, Brendan stepped back out.

"Some eejit giving you trouble?" Brendan leered at Troy.

Troy moved back nervously. Jack had never quite realised how menacing Brendan could be. He always saw him as a kind of bumbling, gentle giant.

"No, no," Jack explained quickly. "He's the sailor, the one I told you about."

"The nutter what drowned?"

"That's me. Back from the dead." Troy grinned. He had perfectly straight, white teeth.

"Well any friend of Jack's is a friend of mine. In you go, boy."

Troy slipped through with delight. A number of the crowd booed this decision. Jack felt like telling his cousin that Troy wasn't exactly a friend; he'd only met him once before.

"We're chocker in there. Be at least an hour before we can let anyone else in," announced Brendan.

With much groaning and hurling of abuse, most of the crowd dispersed in search of other pleasures. Another bouncer offered to take their place outside.

"That's typical, Mick. Offer to take over when there's no one left to worry about," Brendan grumbled.

Jack was comforted to see that Mick was even scrawnier than himself, and very happy to get inside at last. He felt as if the cold had entered the marrow of his bone.

"Just patrol the outside of the floor and keep your eyes sharp. First sniff of anything that might be trouble, start making your way over, but if it looks like a fight, make sure you get me first. There's no place for heroes in here." Brendan instructed.

Jack had never been to a dance as big before. The music flowed through him and he admired the girls' skirts twirling under the lights. He drank in all the details so that he would be able to recreate it perfectly for Kate. He wasn't just lonely, hanging around the edges, he was working. By next weekend he'd have earned the money to go home and surprise Kate by turning up with a huge bouquet of flowers. Roses. Girls liked roses.

His reveries were interrupted by Troy punching him playfully on the shoulder. "I can't get over you being here, man. Let me buy you a drink."

"Thanks, but I'm not supposed to."

"Not while on duty, hey?" Troy swayed slightly on his feet. He shouted to the barman. "Jack Daniels and Coke."

The barman looked blank.

"Whiskey," Troy yelled. "Whatever you got." He knocked back the shot in one go. "It's so hard to get a decent drink in this country. That black stuff you all consume by the barrel load is vile."

Jack looked around uneasily in case Jimmy Byrne saw him slacking on the job. Brendan had told him they were not supposed to consort with the customers, especially the girls. Although Jack could see, out of the corner of his eye, his cousin on the far side of the room chatting up the peroxide girl from earlier.

Troy saw him looking. "Are you searching for the lady love of your life?" he asked with a wink.

"No," said Jack. "I'm working."

"Me neither," sighed Troy. "But that's because I've already found her. I feel like the luckiest guy alive and I got you to thank for it, man."

Jack felt his stomach lurch, but was sure he was being paranoid.

"You know what they say, don't you?" Troy draped his arm over Jack. "If you save someone's life, their soul belongs to you forever."

Jack wasn't sure he liked the sound of that. He had enough trouble trying to take care of his own soul.

"And that's why, in addition to being one of the few people I actually know in Dublin, I'd be proud, indeed just thrilled, to have you as best man at my wedding."

Jack felt relieved. "You're engaged?"

"Yes sirree, to the most beautiful girl you ever clapped your eyes on."

"Is she American?" Jack asked.

Troy burst out laughing. "Nope. But she will be." Troy sighed happily. "You know her, man. The girl on the beach. Kate. Kate O'Rourke."

The whole hall swirled around and Jack thought he would fall dead to the floor. He felt as if the bottom had just dropped out of the universe.

"Surprised you, didn't I?" Troy continued, oblivious. "I know it's sudden. And people will think we're plain stone crazy. But you know when you meet someone and you realise you've been waiting all your life for this to happen, but you just didn't know it. You saved me from death, but when I saw her, I'm telling you man, I was reborn."

Troy's words rushed over him filling his ears with unspeakable horror. How after Jack left, Troy had gone into O'Rourke's to catch another glimpse of his 'angel.' He'd only two weeks leave, but by the end of it, he felt like he'd known her for years. On his last evening they went for a walk on the beach. He got down on his knees in the wet sand and begged her to be his wife. At first she insisted he was joking, but he protested his seriousness and refused to get up until she said 'yes.' In the end she agreed, she said, because his trousers were getting ruined.

This was far worse than the nightmares Jack suffered from. He found he'd lost the power of speech, but Troy didn't seem to notice. He was lost in the tale of his romance.

"So will you be the best man?"

Jack opened his mouth like a fish gasping on a hook. Just then Brendan walked over and gave Jack an elbow in the ribs.

"You're not being paid, boy, to stand around chatting." He shoved a mop into Jack's hand. "Some arsehole's after puking in the jacks. Clean it up, will ya?"

Jack stumbled away. His own stomach was in his toes.

The gents were down a steep set of stairs. The smell of vomit mixed with urine assailed Jack before he even opened the door. He stepped in cautiously. Troy's words bounced off the walls of his skull, but refused to stay still. He clutched at the sense of them. Maybe Kate had taken the proposal as a joke. She was probably laughing about it with her friends right now. Some crazy Yank getting his trousers soaked. But even as he tried to reassure himself, he couldn't forget the way her eyes shone whenever she talked about America.

Suddenly Jack heard a strange, gurgling noise. It was coming from one of the cubicles. He banged on the toilet door but there was no response. He crouched down and peered underneath. He could see black, newly polished shoes and drainpipe trousers. Whoever was inside was not sitting on the toilet, but lying curled up on the floor.

Jack shouted, "Hey, you all right?"

The only answer was a muffled groan.

"Open the door!"

The groans became louder. At a loss what to do, Jack reached under and tugged on the man's shoe. It came off in his hand. Scared the man was dying, he ran out still clutching the shoe to find Brendan.

"He'll be dead soon enough if it's him what's after puking up all over the place." Brendan moved at considerable speed through the dance floor. Jack hurried to keep up with him.

Brendan took one look and seeing no signs of life, he gave the door a massive kick. It sprang open instantly to reveal the anthem singer with the red shirt. He was no longer groaning.

Jack put his fingers to his neck. "He's got a pulse," he informed Brendan with relief.

27

"He's also pissed himself. Let's get him out."

Brendan dragged the man out by his legs. Jack made a clumsy effort to get the shoe back on, but Brendan's withering look made him give up. Between them, they managed to hoist the man to his feet. Brendan put him over his shoulder and carried him up the narrow steps. Jack followed and could see the man's eyes were now open. They swirled red and crazy glaring at Jack.

"Coming through," shouted Brendan attempting to cut across the dance floor towards the exit.

Suddenly the man seemed to come to life. He kicked and screamed and slithered out of Brendan's hold. "Let go of me, you fat bastard."

With these words he switched in Brendan's mind from irritating, but essentially passive, victim to active troublemaker. He pinned his arm behind him and frog marched him towards the exit. The singer howled blue murder the whole way. Jack rushed ahead to push open the emergency exit. There was a brief struggle in the doorway as the man desperately tried to claw his way back in as if he were about to be tossed overboard. Brendan gave him one last hard shove. The singer lost his footing and toppled down the stairs. They were not particularly steep, but Jack noticed with horror how the young man's head hit the last step with a sickening crack. He lay there in a crumpled heap. Brendan made to close the door.

"You can't just leave him there," Jack cried. "He could have a fractured skull."

He ran down the steps and cradled the man's face in his hands. A smudge of blood and dirt covered one half of his face.

"You could've killed him." Jack took some tissues from his pocket and tried to see where the wound was. The singer began to shake his head vigorously like he was trying to dislodge something from his ears.

Brendan stood at the top of the stairs. "See he's grand. Come back inside."

Whether it was the sound of the voice of his assailant set him off, Jack never knew, but suddenly the injured man reared back and loafed him in the head. Jack's nose exploded with blood.

"Jesus Christ, boy." Brendan came running.

The singer swayed off into the night as Brendan used his handkerchief to stave the flow of crimson.

"I reckon it's broken," Jack mumbled. He felt slightly dizzy and sick.

"When are you going to learn there are some people not worth the bother?" With a heavy sigh, Brendan helped Jack back inside.

Jimmy Byrne was not a man known for his empathy. When Brendan informed him he needed to take his cousin home, Jimmy laughed.

"You're having me on right? You know I can't be two bouncers down. There'll be a riot."

"He's still bleeding and he says he feels dizzy."

Jack resented the way they were talking about him as if he wasn't there. He was sat in a chair in the cloakroom and although he felt a bit unsteady, he was conscious.

"Well he can go, but you're staying." Jimmy slapped Jack on the back so hard the room spun. "Don't normally pay for trial nights, but here's your taxi fare." He put a couple of coins in Jack's hand and sauntered out of the room.

"Prick," Brendan observed. "Hey, I've got an idea. Be back in a sec, you sit tight."

Jack carefully removed the handkerchief from his face to see if the blood had stopped. The red splash on the white hanky made him feel faint. For a second darkness rushed in at him, but he managed to hold on. He really hated the sight of blood, especially his own.

Brendan came back in. "C'mon. The taxi's outside."

Jack stood up quickly and had to lean on his cousin for support. He didn't know why he felt so awful; it was only the one blow after all. But when he saw Troy holding open the taxi door, he remembered it wasn't only his nose that'd been broken that night.

"Real sorry to hear what happened. Your cousin's asked me to take you home." Troy's sympathy and concern was nearly more than Jack could bear.

"I'm fine." Jack threw himself into the back of the cab and attempted to pull the door closed behind him, but Troy was too quick for him.

"Seriously man, it's the least I can do. And to be honest I'm staying in this fleapit of a hotel. Brendan says you've got a sofa and I'd be really grateful for a bit of home comfort."

Jack wanted to tell Troy that it was actually a large armchair with the stuffing coming out of it. And that the worst hotel in the world couldn't compete with the desolation of their bed-sit, but Troy was already giving the driver instructions.

"You and me gotta look out for each other," Troy informed Jack as he slammed the door of the taxi.

3

WHEN THEY GOT IN, JACK managed to convince Troy that what he really needed was sleep. He pulled one of Brendan's old blankets out of the press and threw it at Troy secretly hoping it was infested with some kind of fatal disease. Jack crawled into bed with his head pounding and his whole body aching, as if the pain in his nose was travelling through his bones.

Troy picked up a framed photo on the mantelpiece. "She's cute. She your girlfriend?"

"No, she's my mother. Now put her back." Jack felt like strangling Troy.

"Hey, no offence. But she sure is a looker." Troy kicked his shoes off and eased himself into the chair with a sigh. He pulled the blanket up to his chin. "Sweet dreams," he whispered. Five minutes later he was snoring like a small motorcar.

Jack turned over with his back to Troy and drifted off. He woke up when he heard curses outside the door and recognised the depressingly familiar sound of Brendan struggling with the lock. There was a knack to twisting the key that was hard enough to master when sober. Jack heaved himself up and opened the door. Brendan stumbled in.

"When I get my hands on that English bastard," he informed the room. "I'll kill him... I'll tear his head off and puke down his throat. That'll teach him.'

This rant woke Troy who stretched and yawned. "You tell 'em, Big Guy."

Jack glared at Troy like he was the one who'd assaulted him. "I don't think he was English. Remember he sang the anthem? In Irish."

"So what? He still spoke like a Brit. Probably a spy. Yeah, sent by the British government to assault innocents."

All Jack wanted was to go back to sleep, but Brendan insisted his cousin's face needed to be cleaned. It stung like hell. Brendan with his large, callused hands that suffered from a visible tremor would never have made a surgeon. More of the disinfectant ended up on the floor than on the cotton wool. Jack flinched with the pain and Troy squeezed his shoulder supportively.

"You know I hate to say this, but I figure your nose's broken pretty bad," said Troy. "Gonna be a bit crooked from now on. It's cool though, makes you look tough – like a boxer."

Jack stared up at the perfect symmetry of Troy's handsome face and clenched his fist. Brendan mistook this for an effort to contain the pain.

"Hang in there, boy, nearly done. I'm terrible sorry, Jack. I never should have put you up to working in that kip. You who's going to be a doctor. I mean what would your mam say? And to think I promised her I'd look after you."

Jack glared at Brendan in surprise. He thought they'd a tacit understanding that they never discussed family business, most particularly Jack's mother.

"Reckon she'd be horrified. She told me she hated doctors." Jack had had enough of Brendan's brutal attempt at nursing and pushed him away.

"Ah don't be saying that. She'd be fierce proud of you."

Troy chuckled. "I joined the navy because my Mom told me once she thought the uniform was real sexy. Funny reason to choose an occupation I know, but I'm sure there's worse."

Jack closed his eyes. Was that the reason his whole world had collapsed? Because women were more turned on by silly stripes than a stethoscope?

Brendan wasn't impressed by this either. "You damn pervert Yanks. You wouldn't catch my mam admitting to a uniform fetish. Don't reckon I've ever heard her utter the word sexy."

Troy laughed. "You guys are gonna think I got a thing about mothers. I already made the mistake of admiring Jack's Mom. In the photo I mean." Troy pointed to the picture. "Obviously I never met the woman."

"That would be difficult seeing as she's dead," Jack remarked bitterly.

Troy instantly became subdued. "I'm real sorry to hear that. I didn't realise. I'm always putting my foot in my mouth. It's a wonder I haven't choked yet."

Jack couldn't help thinking how much he wished he would.

Brendan was taking a bottle of whiskey from the press. "Well a lot of women have a weakness for men in uniform."

Jack looked at his cousin sharply. He was unsure how much Brendan knew about his mother's shame. Maybe it was his way of saying he didn't hold it against her. The evening was getting out of hand altogether.

Brendan slapped down three glasses on the table. "C'mon lads, we'll have a night cap."

Troy rubbed his hands together happily. Jack made a feeble protest, but Brendan didn't even pause, pouring him a large measure.

"Well here's to absent mothers," Troy declared.

Brendan was slightly taken aback by this toast and raised his glass uncertainly. Jack felt so sad and furious; he knocked back the whiskey in one. He instantly regretted it; the pain in his face actually intensified.

"Is your mam still back in the States?" Brendan asked.

Jack wondered how they'd managed to get on to one of his least favourite topics of conversation.

"Probably, I couldn't say for sure. We're not exactly in touch on a regular basis."

"Ah now you should write to your mam, she'll be worrying. I'm terrible for not ringing mine. It makes me feel fierce guilty."

"Well she ran away from home when I was four so I don't figure I'm the one who should be making the effort."

That Troy was now expecting sympathy only made Jack hate him more. He didn't want to know about Troy's troubles, which couldn't possibly compete with his own. He'd never told Kate what happened to his mother. He didn't have to. His father explained to everyone how she died after a short fight against cancer. Maybe his father didn't consider this a lie. Maybe he saw it as a kind of cancer. But he'd left Derry to put the more complicated truth behind him and it wasn't for Jack to shatter this precious new identity.

He knew how it felt to be whispered about. To see people half crooking their fingers at you and turning to stare before busying themselves in their own lives, pretending they weren't enjoying raking over the sordid details of yours. He often wondered: was it just that their neighbours were deeply bored or did they derive a certain morbid smugness from the close observation of the misery of others?

Kate had tried to broach the subject a couple of times with a few murmurings of sympathy, but Jack had cut her short. He'd become paranoid that questions that seemed honest expressions of concern were actually the sly weapons of the gossip. Their curiosity a kind of cruel hunger fuelled by superiority and an insatiable need to judge. He thought it wiser to suffer in silence. But he could just imagine Troy pouring his heart out to Kate. Bleeding his tale of abandonment into her caring ears. Everybody loves a sob story, an orphan boy in need of love.

"Suppose you didn't miss her if you were too young to remember her," Jack said as he poured himself another drink. It came out almost like an accusation.

"I remember a couple of things. None of them good." Troy looked suddenly deflated and held his glass up to the kitchen light as if his scattered memories were dissolved in the alcohol.

"You seriously remember her telling you sailor suits were sexy?" asked Brendan.

Not for the first time, Jack admired how on the ball Brendan could be even when he'd been drinking. As if, at his core, he was always sober. Troy had been caught out Jack thought with satisfaction. He was clearly a bullshit artist. Kate mightn't realise it yet; she might've been swept off her feet by all his Yankee swagger and his fancy lies, but she'd see through him soon enough. He had made up tall stories himself to impress Kate, but they were different. There was a sincerity behind his exaggeration. He wanted to tell her the truth about himself, how lost and afraid he'd felt until he met her. How there had even been times when he'd questioned whether life was worth all the trouble. Not that he would ever have put his father through all that again knowing how much it hurt. But he struggled with the symptoms – as if, in some strange way, suicide was contagious.

But Kate had given him a purpose, a reason to draw breath. From the swirl of shadows in his brain, he'd finally found a destiny for himself. He was meant to love and look after her. If that wasn't the plan, what else was there? Troy was just a temporary setback. He had come out of the sea and he could be put back there. Jack's mind swirled with whiskey and the desperation of his determination. All this was obviously some kind of test. He would prove to Kate how much he loved her. She'd discover what she felt for Troy was just a romantic crush, like she'd had for that fella in 'Gone with the Wind.' He wasn't angry with her. She was wonderful, but like most women, she needed to be protected from her own feelings. Look at what happened to his mother.

Jack stumbled through these thoughts as Troy explained to Brendan he'd discovered what his Mom considered to be sexy when he tracked her down when he was eighteen. She'd left him to be raised by his grandmother because she wanted to follow her career as a singer. She was in love with some club promoter who'd promised to make her a star.

"Funny thing is, she actually hadn't gone that far. She was singing her heart out in some little dive just off 42nd street. She claimed she wanted to come see me loads of times, but my grandma wouldn't hear of it. Told her it would only be confusing for me."

"Jasus you must have been well pissed off with her just leaving you like that." Brendan shook his head sympathetically.

"Yeah I guess I was for a long time. Like most of the time I was growing up. But you know when I saw her, she just looked so... well so tired. She had a lot of make up on, but you could still tell. And she had a real sweet voice. I went to hear her sing and I remembered how she sounded. Like I was hearing my favourite music for the first time since I was a baby. It was hard to hate her after that. Though like I said, I don't see her that much."

Jack wanted to dismiss all of this as just more American sentimental nonsense. But Troy didn't seem so loud and brash any more. He had a look of deep concentration on his face as if he were trying to work out something that puzzled him.

Brendan said sadly, "Jack's mam was a beautiful singer. Wasn't she, Jack? Had a voice like an angel."

Jack poured himself another glass. The only way to cope seemed to be to aim for total obliteration. He didn't remember passing out, but he'd the vague sensation of Brendan carrying him to bed as gently as if he were a small child who'd stayed up past his bed-time.

Troy tucked him in. "Take it easy, man," he told him.

Jack could hear the hushed murmuring of Troy and Brendan continuing their conversation behind the hanging sheet. He felt a twinge of betrayal at how his cousin seemed to have warmed to Troy before he sank once more into the black relief of a dreamless sleep.

He woke a couple of hours later. It was still dark, but the small lamp by his bed was switched on. Troy was lying on the ground beside him. Jack wondered what on earth he was doing until he heard the scratching of a pen on paper. The American was writing furiously. He stopped and looked up as he felt Jack scrutinizing him.

"Listen I got a big favour to ask you. But first I'm gonna make us a cup of coffee."

Jack tried to speak, but his tongue stuck to the roof of his mouth. The pain of his hangover was already beginning to seep in. He touched his nose very gently and the swelling felt enormous. He wanted to tell Troy that himself and Brendan only drank tea, never coffee, and that he was the last person on earth Troy should be considering asking for help.

Troy came back in with the teapot and two mugs on a tray. "No coffee huh? I'm telling you first thing I do when I get back to New York is go down to Ronnie's and order myself a decent cup of coffee and a big slice of blueberry pie."

Why couldn't you have just stayed in America in the first place, Jack thought.

"See the problem is this. Well Kate's dad... It's just complicated." Troy sat himself on the edge of Jack's bed. Jack considered pulling the blanket over his head and ignoring Troy, but curiosity got the better of him.

"He kind of found out about me. And for some reason, God only knows, he don't approve. I said to him, listen old man, this is none of your business."

Jack tried to picture Mr O'Rourke's face at being told this. It'd be funny, if it wasn't so awful.

"Anyway I'm not meant to see her any more. Of course I'm not gonna let some old codger stop me. But that's why I had to come up to Dublin to set the date for the wedding. I tried telling that priest what's his name..."

"Father O'Brien," offered Jack.

"Yeah that's the one. Big, fat guy. But he kept saying I needed the parents' permission cos she's under eighteen blah blah... I reckon he was just too scared to stick his neck out."

Father O'Brien prided himself on his wedding ceremonies. He always got a bit carried away by the romance of it all and invariably had prospective mothers-in-law sobbing in the aisles. He'd told Jack with a wink that as soon as he found the right girl just to let him know; he was the man for the job. Jack recalled the priest's round, good-humoured face with bitterness. At least he'd had the sense to turn this impostor down.

"But I've managed to find a priest up in Kilmainham that's not such a stickler for the rules. I told him the pickle I was in and that there'd be a couple of bottles of whisky in it for his trouble, and he's agreed to marry us in six weeks. That's the soonest I can get leave again."

So some alcoholic clergyman was about to destroy all Jack's hopes.

"But I've got to go back to my ship tomorrow. And I can't seem to get in touch with Kate. I figure her dad isn't letting her near the phone. I was getting kind of panicky about the whole thing. But then Brendan told me last night you're going home next weekend and I'd a brain wave."

Troy thrust an envelope into Jack's hand. "I've written her a letter. I don't trust the mail cos I'm sure that ogre of a father of hers checks it. But I know I can count on you. You been a real friend to me man, and if you could deliver it for me, I would appreciate it even more than when you got me breathing again."

Jack turned the envelope over and over in wonder.

4

ONCE TROY HAD LEFT, JACK put the letter on the kitchen table and stared at it as if it might bite. Brendan crawled out of bed and set about making breakfast. Soon the kitchen was full of the comforting smell of sizzling bacon.

Jack hid the letter in his dressing gown and drank his tea moodily. Brendan insisted on examining his smashed nose before announcing, "You want to see a doctor about that."

"I am a doctor," Jack snapped.

"No, you're not, boy. You're a long way off being qualified for anything."

Brendan said he had to hurry as he had a meeting. Jack never asked what these meetings were that Brendan was always scurrying off to. He figured it was none of his business. In his medical opinion the only meetings his cousin should consider attending were AA, but he never dared to say this.

As Brendan turned to go out the door, he handed Jack a brown envelope. Good God, thought Jack, surely Brendan hadn't spent the night writing as well? When he opened Brendan's envelope, he found a small bundle of money. His exact fare home.

With Brendan safely out of the way, Jack heated up the kettle. He used the steam to unseal the envelope and, pulling out the bulk of pages, he began to read.

Angel,

> *I keep calling you, but you never answer the phone and I don't dare say anything to your father for fear of getting you in more trouble. Not hearing your voice is like a kind of torture for me. Especially when I'm scared your silence means you've changed your mind. I worry that without my being there, all the heavy ropes of rationality will be tugging you back down to earth. That you'll start to consider you hardly know me and I'm asking you to leave all your friends and family and come away with me to a strange country you've never been to before. But you have to trust me. I know you worry that marriage is just another trap, but real freedom lies in making a choice. To me our meeting was a kind of miracle. Something that only God could have planned. You're everything I ever wanted and without you my life has no meaning. I think what has happened between us is a once in a lifetime opportunity and if you let this pass you by, you may*

spend the rest of your life regretting it. I know I will. I also know I haven't got a lot of money and I can't offer you security, but as I keep telling you, in America, everything is possible. People don't care about where you come from; they care about where you're going to. I really believe that with you beside me I can achieve anything I want. You may think this arrogant, but it's not. It's just because I love you as I've never loved anyone before in my life and will never love anyone so much again. I have total faith in this love and I know that we are meant to be together forever…

Jack put the letter down and lit a cigarette. For a moment he considered setting fire to the whole thing so he wouldn't have to endure the rest. He held the match close to the paper, watching the flame edge close to the painful words. How could Troy, some dumb Yank, manage to say so effortlessly the very things he'd been longing to tell Kate for months? He wanted to believe this ease was a sign of insincerity, but as he finished the letter he found himself persuaded by Troy's arguments. If he was Kate he would go, he thought, sinking into despair. He carefully put the pages back in the envelope and resealed it.

Two days later he went home. His father looked even thinner than Jack remembered. He shook his hand vigorously and didn't ask him how come he'd turned up at such short notice. For a change his father made him dinner. He wasn't much of a cook; the only thing he really knew how to do was steak. Jack watched him poking a fork at the red meat.

For the first time in as long as he could remember, Jack wanted to ask his father's advice. But he didn't know where to start and it would be difficult to discuss his own heart trouble without the shadow of Jack's mother hanging over them. Jack wondered if his father regretted his handling of the whole thing. Everyone said he was a saint to be so forgiving, but Jack wondered if his mother had seen it that way. She'd suffered with her nerves since Jack was a small child. One of his earliest memories was finding her in bed in the afternoon with the curtains closed. She was sobbing and held him tightly as if she'd never let him go. He'd overheard his Nana talking about some kind of breakdown after he was born, but she shut up the moment he walked into the room and he never managed to find out more about it. He often wondered if it was having him that had been the start of her problems. Maybe she'd never wanted him and wasn't able to cope when he was born.

Then when he was fifteen, he came home from school one day to find his father systematically smashing every plate in the kitchen. He stood and watched in amazement, until his father saw him and strode out of the house. No one heard sight nor sound of him for the next two weeks. Jack's mother was in bed and he wasn't allowed to see her. He was sent to his Nana's where he lived for the next month. No one actually sat Jack down and told him anything, but he pieced the story together from whispers he heard here and there.

His mother had done an unspeakable thing; she'd been caught kissing a British soldier in an alleyway. Two days later a masked gunman walked into a pub where the same soldier was having an off duty drink and shot him at point blank range. Maybe it was bad luck or maybe the IRA didn't appreciate Catholic women, particularly married ones, consorting with the forces of occupation. Jack's father may have forgiven his wife but her family, die hard Republicans and staunch Catholics every one of them, never spoke to her again.

As his father slapped the meat on to the plates and urged Jack to tuck in, it occurred to Jack for the first time that perhaps his father had known about the affair, that perhaps he'd been involved in the soldier's death. It sent a deep chill through him. Surely not. His father might be a bit set in his ways, but he wasn't a murderer. Jack had often heard him describe the IRA as a bunch of thugs. But he was beginning to understand that jealousy did strange things to a man. He'd known his father all his life, but what did he really know about what went on inside his head?

These new suspicions kept Jack awake all night. He sat on his bed peering out the window at the dimly lit street for hours. He wanted to penetrate the darkness and understand what was happening to him. Apart from one old drunk who stumbled by, singing incoherently, and a few stray cats, he saw nothing. The letter burned inside his jacket pocket but he resisted the temptation to take it out. A hundred times he'd considered tearing the paper into tiny shreds and feeding it to the wind. He had become obsessed with the idea that if he'd known what was going to happen, he would have let Troy drown. Now he asked himself, if he could have him shot, would he? Maybe if he'd never met him, maybe if he'd never read the letter, but he was finding it harder to hate Troy with any real conviction.

The next morning he went down to O'Rourke's pub. Mrs O'Rourke greeted him warmly as if he were a long lost son, insisting on making him breakfast despite his protests that he'd already eaten.

"I'm glad you're here, Jack," she said to him. "Maybe you can talk some sense to Caitriona. God knows she doesn't pay a blind bit of notice to what me or her father try to say to her."

He found Kate out in the tiny back yard hanging up clothes. She had a wooden peg in her mouth and was struggling with one of her father's white shirts as it flapped wildly in the breeze. Jack grabbed one of the sleeves and helped her pin down the other shoulder.

She laughed and gave him a big hug. "Ah Jack, you're always here in my hour of need."

She was wearing a perfume he didn't recognise and the smell of it made him feel slightly dizzy. She looked even more beautiful than he remembered, something he hadn't thought possible. The yard really only had space for the clothesline. Kate pulled down two old crates and offered Jack a seat. He felt uncomfortable being so close to her and looked down at his feet in confusion. She got up to check the back door to the pub was shut.

"I don't want my mother listening in on us," she explained. "She never gives me a moment's peace."

Jack took a deep breath. "I wanted to come sooner but I didn't have enough money," he began to explain. "I tried ringing but your dad didn't seem very happy about that."

"Oh sure all men are the enemy these days. Even you, Jack."

Jack had a certain sympathy for Mr O'Rourke's paranoia. Still he'd planned what he wanted to say and for once nothing was going to stop him. He took a deep breath. He wasn't going to hide his feelings any more. He wanted to be honest. If Troy could say all those things to Kate, then he could too.

"I want you to know that since I left, you're all I've thought about. That I've been in love with you since the moment I met you."

Kate jumped up in state of agitation. "Oh Jack, don't tell me that. You can't mean it. You can't be serious."

Jack tried to assure her that he'd never been so serious about anything, but she cut him short.

"I've... I've met someone else."

He told her he already knew, that he'd bumped into Troy in Dublin. Kate looked confused but then he pulled out the letter. He was doing the decent thing; he was giving Kate the opportunity to choose. He handed it over feeling like he was signing his own death warrant. Kate pounced on it and ripped it open. The look of sheer joy on her face as she began to read was nearly more than Jack could bear. Catching on to herself, she put the letter down.

"I'm terrible sorry, Jack. But you're too late. Troy and me are getting married."

Any glimmer of hope Jack had that Kate would choose him over his American rival was snuffed out. He stood up to go. He felt tears stinging his eyes and the last thing he wanted was Kate's pity. He struggled for a moment to get the door open, and then rushed through the pub and out the front gasping for air. Kate called after him, but he stumbled blindly up the road.

What was the point of anything any more? He was always too late. Too late to save his mother, too late to get Kate to fall in love with him. He didn't blame Kate, he blamed himself. He remembered a story his mother had read him as a child called "Deirdre of the Sorrows." It was about a princess who was so beautiful it was prophesised she would break men's hearts and lead to a civil war. To prevent this, her father hid her away in the forest where no ordinary man could reach her. But of course there's no escaping destiny and everything that had been predicted came to pass. It wasn't Deirdre's fault; her only crime was to have the wrong people fall in love with her. The story struck Jack as deeply unfair.

He remembered he'd asked his mother if people really did die of broken hearts. She'd replied, "I'm afraid it happens all the time."

Maybe she was right.

5

"O'ROURKE'S," AISLING SHOUTED, GASPING FOR breath as she answered the telephone by the bar. She'd run all the way down the stairs from her bedroom cursing her father who was too busy watching the hurling match on the pub's small telly to acknowledge the phone's insistent ring.

The voice on the other end sounded amused. "Jasus, Angel, you'll frighten the life out of the customers picking up like that. They'll think they've got through to a sex line."

She was so surprised to hear from her brother that, for a moment, all language deserted Aisling.

"Hello? Are you there?"

"Where are you?" she demanded.

"Dublin of course." Cathal's tone had the same dry warmth as always. Like he was trying to suppress a fit of giggles. Or something worse. "I'm coming home tomorrow."

About bloody time she nearly said, but she didn't. Because she knew she would sound like her mother and Cathal would hate that. Instead she told him how excited she was, how much she'd missed him.

Her brother sounded bemused by this, like he'd only been gone a few days. "Has it been three months? God how time flies."

Aisling didn't know if he was taking the piss or not. Maybe he was aiming for a casualness that would pass over the need for any explanations. He hadn't even rung at Christmas and now here he was, turning up out of the blue in the middle of February. Her brother lived by his own calendar. Although he was only three years older than her he acted as if there were decades between them. Ever since he'd moved away to college in Dublin last September,.

At breakfast the next morning Aisling peered out the window and was surprised by the daffodils. They had spilt their yellow overnight. Pouring his tea, her father pronounced that winter was finally turning the corner. The sun shone for the first time in weeks and weeks and Aisling could feel the grey heaviness in her stomach dissolving into the excitement of anticipation.

At school, she thought the day would never end and cycled home at top speed through the rain that had begun once more to pour down relentlessly.

She rushed into the pub. "Is he here yet?"

"Get out of those wet clothes before you catch your death of cold," her mother instructed. "Your brother is upstairs watching television," she added grudgingly,

Aisling frowned at her mother, not sure if she believed her. Cathal never watched TV except maybe the odd travel programme.

In fact Cathal had the telly on, but he wasn't looking at it. He was staring out at the rain with that peculiar intensity he had. She had the odd feeling she was interrupting him. Then he turned to face her. And the next moment he was hugging her close.

He looked paler than he had a few months ago. Thinner too. The blueness of his eyes was shocking. Their mother believed this proof of the evil malnourishment of city life, but Aisling thought it made him more heroic looking. He'd grown his black hair and had it tied back in a pony-tail.

He switched the TV off. "C'mon, let's go for a walk."

"It's pouring rain, Cathal."

"Trust me, the storm out there is nothing compared to the storm there's going to be in here if we don't make a run for it."

As they slipped out the back and headed up the street at a fast pace, Aisling allowed herself to imagine that Cathal had come back to get her to run away to Dublin with him. She was dying to know all about university life, the parties he'd been to, the girls he'd met. She had so many questions bursting inside her that she didn't know where to start. Cathal was strangely silent. She peered up at the patchy stubble on his face and wondered what was going through his head.

When she was little, he had told her he could read her mind and she'd believed him. He said it was just a question of tuning in, like with a radio. Her thoughts were songs he could sing along to. But hard as she tried, she never could hear what he was thinking. Just static.

Like now, she thought they were headed for town, but instead he took the track that led down to the beach.

"I don't want to bump into anyone." He seemed to be answering her unspoken question.

The path was muddy and overgrown. She had to pay attention to avoid sinking into the damp grass. There was no protection from the wind, which beat down on them, making conversation impossible. Aisling stumbled along behind her brother. The waves crashed with the power of loneliness. The beach was entirely deserted and the rain had pockmarked the sand, but because of the dunes it was more sheltered than the road.

Her anxiety made her come out with the wrong question. "Why didn't you come home for Christmas?"

Cathal picked up a stone and hurled it into the sea. "Now don't you start guilt tripping me as well."

Suddenly she felt like slapping him. These past few months she had listened to her parents ripping him to shreds while she attempted to elaborate defences on his behalf. She had smothered the whisper of disappointment she'd felt on Christmas Eve when the last bus from Dublin had brought in a whole mob of drunken students piling into the pub. She had stood at the bus stop in a kind of shock. He really wasn't coming. But she had never until that moment blamed him for it. She had always believed he'd have a reasonable explanation.

He clearly wasn't in the mood to give one. He took off his socks and shoes, and, dropping them behind him, ran off down the beach weaving his way closer to the water. For a horrible moment she thought he was going to run into the sea. But he stopped just on the edge with the spray licking his toes. She chased after him. He was shouting now, great whoops that battled to be heard over the thud of the waves. He began to splash her, laughing with a kind of desperate enthusiasm, and she knew she could forgive him anything.

On the walk back, he put his arm around her and they shivered together all the way home. He told her he'd decided to drop college. In fact he hadn't been to a lecture since November. He was working as a waiter, saving money. He hadn't come back sooner because he couldn't face the grief. Aisling felt strangely protective of him.

Dinner was even worse than they feared. The weight of the silence was enough to give them all indigestion. Her father managed to make 'Pass the butter' sound like a death threat. As the knives and forks clinked off the plates, Aisling sat huddled over her meal waiting for the inevitable explosion. Perhaps Cathal couldn't take the tension any more and decided to give his father the opening he was looking for; he took a piece of lamb off his plate and leant down to feed it to the dog.

"Don't feed her at the table, Cathal. It only encourages her to beg." Their mother must have said this fifty million times in the dog's short life.

Her father growled. "That's right, you just throw away good food. It's not like you've had to work for it."

"Come off it Da, the famine finished hundreds of years ago." Cathal had a special sneering tone he reserved for his father.

"Don't get smart with me." If there was one thing their father couldn't cope with, it was the suggestion he was stupid. "You think you're so bloody clever. Too know-it-all to even need to go to college. Reckon you've got all the answers already." He wasn't shouting yet, but his face was already flushed.

Cathal rolled his eyes insolently.

"Just tell me this Mr I-Don't-Need-A-University-Education. What exactly are you planning to do with the rest of your life?"

Cathal sat back in his chair. "Thought I might do a bit of travelling," he replied calmly.

This was news to Aisling. She'd been so happy at the prospect of him being around for a while she hadn't considered he might have other plans.

"Travelling?" Her father made it sound like it were a criminal offence.

"You know... see a bit of the world." Cathal yawned as if they were all boring him to tears.

It was more than their father could take. He reached across the table and grabbed his son by the scruff of his jumper and began to shake him. A glass fell over and crashed to the floor and the dog ran for cover.

"You useless little bastard. Can't you see what you're doing to your mother?"

And indeed their mother was crying, making little effort to stop the tears chasing each other down her cheeks. Aisling was on Cathal's side of course, but she couldn't help feeling he wasn't going about this the right way. Cathal pushed his father off and, knocking over a chair, stormed from the kitchen.

Her father made to follow, but her mother snapped, "Just leave him be."

Like a wounded bull that doesn't know where the next spear is coming from, her father spun around. "You've always spoilt him, that's the problem. You wouldn't let me knock some sense into him."

He was clenching and unclenching his fists as if he'd love to be able to knock some sense into the whole world. Aisling wished she could join the dog who'd retreated deep under the table, but she was afraid any movement would only draw attention to herself.

"Don't you ever call him a bastard. Not ever. Do you understand me?" Her mother's face was white with an anger Aisling had never seen before.

"Oh for God's sakes, Pat." Her father swept from the room.

In the sudden quiet, Aisling wanted to say something reassuring, but she was too afraid it would come out wrong. The silence stretched between them until eventually her mother stood up and said, "Make sure you do those dishes," before following her father.

Aisling could hear them continuing their argument in hushed tones in their bedroom. A door slammed downstairs as Cathal went out into the night. Aisling was left to sweep up the broken glass.

That night she lay in bed wide-awake waiting for her brother to come back. The rain swept against the window in huge torrents. She could hear water running along the roof and then dropping into the gutter. The wind shook the glass and it seemed to her all the badness in the world was trying to get in. Where could he be? There wasn't really anywhere to go. Apart, that is, from another pub. He'd never had many friends when he lived with them. Or not any that he ever brought round. Eventually she heard the side door creak open and the soft sound of footsteps on the stairs. Then a stumble and a whispered curse. She hopped out of bed and ran on to the landing. Cathal was sitting on the bottom step. She hurried down to him. He hadn't had the sense to take a hat and his hair was plastered to his face. She carefully pushed it out of his eyes.

When he saw her, he started to sing quietly. "On Raglan Road on an autumn day, I saw her first and knew, that her dark hair would weave a snare..."

"Quiet, you'll wake them," she hissed, though she would have bet money that her mother was already straining to hear their every word.

She put her arm under his and heaved him on to his feet. He leant on her and started to chuckle. The smell of beer and smoke was momentarily overpowering, but somehow she dragged him up to the bathroom. He sat on the edge of the bath and let her remove his shoes as if he were a small child.

"You know Aisling, I don't feel so good."

In one swift movement she had the toilet seat up and his head thrust into the bog. She held his hair back as he puked.

"You're not called an angel for nothing, you know," he told her as she carefully washed his face.

His clothes were so wet she had to peel them off, but by the time he had pulled on a clean t-shirt, he seemed more sober.

He flicked on his bedside lamp and told her, "There's something I want you to see."

He reached deep under the bed pulling out an enormous black book. She recognised it at once as a Christmas present from their mother. Cathal sat cross-legged on the rug with the atlas balancing reverentially on his knees. She scuttled down close beside him. As he opened it, he sighed with happiness. For a moment she forgot the relentlessness of the rain and her parents on the other side of the wall. She forgot everything but the slightly musty smell of the pages as he turned them.

"Here it is," he announced solemnly. "The United States of America." He said it like it was a magic spell. He opened up the pull out pages to reveal that he'd traced his route with a fine red marker.

"I fly into New York and then I'll work my way across the country. I got one of them Greyhound bus tickets. I reckon in six weeks I should reach Los Angeles." He said it proudly like Hollywood was waiting for him.

But Aisling felt her heart falling away. "You're leaving?" she whispered.

"Hey," he gave her a quick squeeze. "It's not forever you know. I'll be back before you know it."

"Mam'll go mad. She'll never let you go. She thinks Dublin is a cesspit of violence and madness, never mind New York."

Cathal slapped the book shut. "There's nothing she can do about it. I've already bought the ticket."

For a second she thought she saw something distant and cruel in his face. She knew there was nothing she could do about it either.

He was going in a week. She wished she could make time hold its breath, but the days seemed to eat themselves up. The day before his departure, they packed a picnic and he balanced her precariously on the cross bar of his bike as they headed off to the coast. They had to abandon the bike by the pigsty and make their way by foot along the steep, narrow path that led to the edge of the cliff. When she was little, he had told her this track strewn with rabbit droppings was a faery road that led up into heaven itself. They were only allowed to use it because he'd got their passports stamped. He had a special rubber that the faeries used for this purpose which read 'Not To Be Sold Separately'. She never got to see the workings of faery bureaucracy because their office was only open at midnight when she was sleeping. The passports she'd made herself by covering old Christmas cards in brown paper. Cathal filled in their names and dates of birth. Ridiculous kids' stuff, but she couldn't help wondering where the passports were now.

She had found Cathal's real one in the drawer by his bed. Running her thumb over the strange visa as if she could somehow rub it out. His hair was short in the picture and he looked surprised like he'd been caught in the act. His name was typed in small black letters: CATHAL BERNARD O'ROURKE. He'd been so triumphant when he got it a few months previously, just after his eighteenth birthday. Their parents were deeply offended that he used his mother's family name.

"That's what my real name is," he declared, slamming the door behind him.

Later Aisling had attempted to ask him what he meant by that but he refused to explain.

Cathal had brought a picnic blanket and he fluttered it out in the wind before spreading it on the ground before them. The wind had an edge to it, but the sun was shining. Aisling unwrapped the sandwiches their mother had made for them. Cathal wolfed his down like a starving animal.

One of the bananas had got a bit squished and Cathal threw it out over the edge of the cliff. "A gift for the faeries," he declared. "And I have a gift for the young lady too."

She was expecting a banana, so she was surprised when her brother pulled out a neatly wrapped package. It even had a red bow.

"Go on, open it."

Aisling carefully removed the paper to reveal a small cardboard box. She opened the lid and inside lay two bracelets made of leather. Cathal took them out and Aisling could see that on one of them was her own name and on the other was Cathal's.

"Got them in Dublin," her brother explained. "They're handmade friendship bracelets. They don't engrave the names in, they use a special kind of torch to burn them on to the leather."

Aisling thought they were beautiful.

Cathal tied the one with his name around her wrist and the other one around his own. "So we never forget each other," he said, which made Aisling smile, as such a thing was so utterly impossible.

Then her brother pulled a small bottle of Paddy's from deep in his coat. He took a large swig and offered her some. She hesitated, then threw her head back. The shock of the fire in her insides made her head spin. The sky had grown enormous and she watched seagulls dancing overhead. She divided a bar of Cadbury's Fruit and Nut between them and wished that the afternoon would never end.

The next day her father drove them all to Knock to say goodbye. The airport, small as it was, was packed with people. There must have been a match on because there were a lot of men in bright green shirts who kept breaking into snatches of song. She was hoping a thunderstorm would delay the flight, but there was only a persistent drizzle. Their parents looked awkward in the airport, like they were in a church that wasn't

Catholic and they weren't too sure what the form was. Cathal seemed dwarfed by his enormous orange rucksack. He kept up a flow of nervous chatter as if he was afraid of giving them a chance to say something to change his mind. Their mother kept telling him to make sure he ate properly; so many times that Aisling felt like screaming at her to shut up. She strained her neck to catch a last glimpse of him going through customs. A final flash of black ponytail and he was gone.

The last thing he said to her was, "Don't worry, I'll see you very soon."

Shortly after, it was her mother's birthday. Aisling bought her a card and a large brightly-coloured scarf and made her breakfast in bed. No one mentioned Cathal, but every time the phone rang, her mother couldn't help looking hopeful. God knows why; he'd never remembered to ring her on her birthday even when he was in the country. Besides, relations with his parents had reached something of an all time low just before he'd left. The night before his flight, his father knocked on Cathal's door and asked to speak to him. Aisling put her ear to the wall to listen. Her father told her brother that he hoped once he got this travelling out of his system, he'd settle down a bit and start making something of himself. Think about getting a trade or maybe going back to college.

Cathal didn't appreciate this career advice. "Well I'm not going to spend my life serving drinks and watching the clock on the wall, that's for sure."

Her father's voice suddenly rose. "This pub is what's put clothes on your back for the last eighteen years, you ungrateful brat."

It didn't take them long to start insulting each other, Aisling thought sadly. The truth was they'd never really got on. Cathal was totally hyper as a kid. He had all this energy and could never sit still. He was terribly accident prone and always seemed to be knocking things over. Their father was quick to lose his temper and Cathal's carelessness drove him mad. As time went on, they had less and less in common. Their father was a big hurling and Gaelic football fan and tried to get Cathal to go to matches with him. But Cathal had no interest in sports. He preferred to spend his time in his room reading. Her father was slightly hard of hearing and complained that Cathal spoke too quickly and mumbled his words. It was as if they spoke alien languages. "What's he on about?" was a refrain they both used.

Their father proceeded to tell Cathal he was wasting his life. That he'd never amount to anything if he didn't pull his finger out. Cathal let him carry on in this vein for some time. Aisling, crouched on the other side of the wall, wanted to run in and beg them to stop before someone got hurt. But it was too late.

Cathal started to shout. "Get the fuck out of my room. You're in my room."

Their father roared back, "Don't you dare speak to me like that. This is my house."

And then Cathal said it; "You can't tell me what to do. You're not even my father."

The words hung like poison in the air. Aisling was scared her father would hit him. When they were kids, he often took a leather strap to Cathal in an effort to make him pay more attention. But Cathal was now considerably taller. She heard the slow heavy step of her father's footsteps retreating and, after a couple of minutes, she slipped into her brother's room.

"You shouldn't have said that about him not being your dad. That's a horrible thing to say," she reproached Cathal.

"Well it's the truth."

"What are you talking about?"

"I don't know. I don't know what I'm talking about. I don't know who I am."

Aisling wondered if her brother was having some kind of nervous breakdown. He'd never been the most academic and had gotten into college by the skin of his teeth. To give it all up to go to traipsing across America struck her as taking teenage rebellion a step too far.

"What's going on with you, Cathal? You're being really weird."

"Listen Angel I can't bear it any more." Her brother looked as if he might cry. "I've got to get out of here. I need to find some answers."

"Answers to what?"

"Mam made me promise not to tell you till you're older."

"I'm fifteen for fuck's sakes. I'm not a child."

Cathal sighed. "I need to get away from this place. I need to get away from them and their stupid lies. Please, Angel, just leave me alone."

She tried several times to push him on what he meant by "their stupid lies" but he refused to discuss it further. It was as if he had already withdrawn into his own world where she wasn't welcome.

Thus it seemed to Aisling the chances of her brother remembering to send a card, never mind ring their mother on her birthday, were slim. Indeed they were all surprised, shocked even, when the flowers arrived. A huge bouquet of yellow roses. Her mother's favourite colour. The little card inside read, "Wishing you a very happy birthday. Much love from Cathal."

Aisling filled the big glass vase and helped her mother cut the stems. The flowers were placed proudly in the front window of the pub so that everyone would ask Aisling's mother where she got such beautiful flowers.

Even her father said, "Well at least he hasn't forgotten us completely."

As it turned out he had. They never heard another word.

After three weeks passed, her mother asked, "Aisling, you would tell us if Cathal called, wouldn't you? It's just I'm getting a bit worried."

Aisling told herself her mother was fussing for nothing. Cathal was notoriously unreliable. They were bound to hear from him soon. She overheard her mother talking to her father about getting in touch with the police.

"Don't be silly, Pat. He's just sunbathing somewhere. You know what he's like."

"But what if something's happened to him? We've no idea where he is."

"Well I don't see what use Inspector Kelly is going to be. He can't even track down stolen sheep. And I doubt if he's ever been out of the country."

Her mother started getting up early to check the post. As if she suspected Aisling of hiding something from her.

The 11th of August arrived. They hadn't heard from Cathal in nearly three months. But that was the day he had a return ticket for, so her mother insisted they all drive out to the airport to collect him. She kept saying things like she wondered if he'd have a tan, as if he'd just gone off to Spain for two weeks. Aisling and her father kept quiet. The flight was delayed by an hour. Aisling stood at the railing watching the people coming through. Her mother's hope was infectious. It would be just like him to turn up without a word of warning. But when the last passenger had been kissed away from Flight 507 from Dublin, connecting with Los Angeles, they turned around exhausted. Her father spent ages questioning the check-in desk trying to squeeze information out of them. No Cathal O'Rourke had boarded any flight from LA in the last two days.

"He could easily have missed the flight," her father said. "He's not the most organised. He's probably having such a good time he's decided to stay on a bit longer."

The fact her father was being so reasonable, instead of his usual blustering angry self, made Aisling aware he didn't believe what he was saying. Her mother looked very pale as she lit her cigarette in the car. She was supposed to have stopped smoking since New Year's Eve. Her father just rolled down the window and said nothing.

Soon the school holidays were over and another school year began. Aisling felt empty and angry and her classes seemed interminably dull. Nothing seemed worth the effort since Cathal had performed his vanishing trick. Miss O'Hanlon informed Aisling she was a troublemaker. This came as a surprise as she had never considered herself one before. Cathal was the one who got into trouble. She'd always been the one who did what she was told. But now he wasn't around maybe she was expected to take his place. Like in the story of how the Irish hero Cu Cuchlainn got his name, from a guard dog that he killed when it attacked him. He felt so guilty about the animal's death, he offered to take its place and protect Cuchlainn's house, hence Hound of Cuchlainn. Aisling couldn't shake the feeling that she should have done more to protect Cathal, to find out what was really troubling him. He'd said he wanted answers but he'd never explained to her what the question was.

Now Aisling had questions of her own. Was it true her father wasn't Cathal's father? She tried to ask her mother but she just turned white with anger and told Aisling not to be ridiculous.

"Cathal wasn't well when he left. He imagined all kinds of nonsense. Of course Martin is his father. I don't want to hear any more of this rubbish from you."

Aisling sat in her classes thinking about her mother's anger and what it was she wasn't being told while her teachers droned on in the background. Aisling's end of year report wasn't very impressive, but her parents barely seemed to notice.

Her father had gone to the police station and reported Cathal missing – as if he were a stray dog, Aisling thought every time she saw one of those hand written posters stuck to trees. Pleading for 'Lucky', or whatever the unfortunate pet was called, to be returned. The local guards just kept repeating the word 'America' like they had never heard of the place before. They put her father on to the section of the Department of Foreign Affairs that dealt with people who failed to return from their holidays. They seemed to think young people nowadays made a habit of forgetting to tell their families where they were. Aisling's father went up to Dublin to speak to one of their officers. They spoke to the embassy in Washington, promised to look into it and told him not to worry – Cathal would probably just turn up of his own accord. Her mother wasn't convinced. As the weeks slipped by, she started to talk about going over to the States to find him herself. Her father told her mother not to be ridiculous.

"I mean, people don't just disappear into thin air," her mother said.

"They do, Pat love. Apparently they do all the time," her father sighed.

Her father's resignation infuriated her mother so much that she moved into Cathal's room. She claimed it was because her husband snored really loudly and she couldn't sleep. But Aisling often heard her moving around late at night, even though she had a bed to herself to sleep in. She still worked in the bar, but seemed to spend all her free time in Cathal's bedroom as if searching for clues. She only came out at dinnertime and then she ate hardly anything. Aisling was initially reluctant to show them the atlas, but with Christmas nearly upon them and her mother spending more and more time in her brother's room, she guiltily handed it over. Her mother was really excited and announced a plan of contacting all the places marked in red.

"But Pat, you've no way of knowing if he stuck to this route." Her father closed the atlas like it was a book he had no intention of reading.

"You just don't care, do you?" her mother accused. "You don't want to find him; you're glad he's gone."

Her father smashed his hand so hard against the kitchen wall that it swelled up and Aisling had to wrap it for him later. She looked at the strange purple bruising around the knuckle. It reminded her of a map of somewhere.

"He'll come back," she told him.

Her father hugged her tight. "At least I've still got you," he mumbled.

Christmas was a muted affair. They hardly spoke at all over the turkey. Aisling kept getting up and peering out the window, as if she expected Cathal to arrive on a sleigh pulled by reindeer. The rain fell heavy and steady and dark. There wasn't even a hint of snow. Nothing was as it should have been. An icicle slid into Aisling's heart. Maybe he really wasn't coming back. Maybe he'd been lying.

The other possibilities were worse. Her father suggested he might have had an accident.

"He's not dead," her mother stated. "I'd know if he was dead. I'd feel it."

"No, no I just meant in hospital, you know, not able to get in touch with us..." Her father's words trailed off as they often did these days.

Her father wasn't a big man, but he was compactly built with broad shoulders and thick, strong arms. He had a loud, booming voice that could be heard above the din of a packed pub. A voice that people listened to – and a legendary temper. He had no qualms about throwing trouble-makers out of his pub and he was not a man who let his authority be chal-lenged. With the exception of Cathal, most people were slightly in awe of him. Aisling knew better than to disagree with him, but with her brother gone, her father seemed to shrink in on himself. He no longer spoke with the same certainty and often seemed to lose track of his thoughts, as if he was a man accused of a crime he didn't understand.

As a kid, Aisling's favourite part of Christmas had always been the lighting of the Christmas pudding. She loved tipping the alcohol into the small measure, pouring it carefully in a semi-circle over the top, and lighting the match. The blue glow of the burning whiskey seemed to her a pure form of magic. Cathal said the longer the fire burned, the longer you would live. This year she peered into the eerie flickering of the flame and wondered what he was doing right at that moment. As if by concen-trating hard enough she would see his face rising up before her. But the fire gave a final green flash and abruptly vanished. Her father turned the lights back on. The sudden harshness of the kitchen lamp was unkind on the flaking paintwork and the faded wallpaper.

A heavy knock on the front door of the pub made them all jump and stare at each other in confusion.

"Who in the name of God could that be?" Her father walked slowly to the stairs like he was moving under water.

Her mother grabbed Aisling's hand and held on so tight Aisling thought her fingers would break. "I knew he'd come back, I always knew he would," her mother whispered.

Then she sprang to open the door as her father led a stranger into the kitchen. Aisling peered behind the man still expecting her brother's handsome head to appear. But there was no one. Her mother let out a cry and fell back into her seat.

"I'm sorry to be bursting in on you like this, Pat." The man had a soft Northern accent and was in his late thirties. He was tall with a pale, drawn, elegant face. His hair was beginning to thin, although still a long way off bald. He wore a stylish dark suit and carried a heavy, woollen coat over his arm. He looked like one of those film stars from the fifties her mother loved so much to watch on Sunday afternoons. Only more tired, as if not being in black and white didn't agree with him.

"What the hell do you want, Jack?" Her mother's voice was colder than the Atlantic Ocean.

6

AISLING WOKE EARLY ON STEPHEN'S Day to the sound of pots banging around in the kitchen. As she turned over to try to go back to sleep, the night before came flooding back; the stranger in the kitchen and her mother ordering him to get out of their house. She reached to the side of her bed and yanked open the curtains. The room filled with sunlight.

Her room wasn't a proper bedroom. It was a box-room that had been used for storage until her brother complained about being too old to share with a girl, but she wouldn't dream of moving back into the room she used to share with Cathal. It would be like admitting he'd never return. Anyway it was her mother's room now, even though all her brother's things were still in there. His heavily patched denim jacket still hung on the back of the door and his faded Doctor Who posters peered down from the walls. His tape collection overflowed from a large cardboard box on the floor. Her mother preferred to step around The Cure and Joy Division. It was okay to sleep in the room, but she knew how much Cathal would hate her moving his things around. It looked as if he'd just popped down to the shops and would be coming through the door any second with a packet of fags and some chocolate for Aisling. He used to smoke his cigarettes leaning far out the window and then drown the room in deodorant to hide any lingering smell. Their father had promised that if he caught him smoking again he wouldn't wait for the cancer to kill him.

Aisling blinked her eyes in the shock of the dazzling light. She rubbed the frosted up window and peered out. She couldn't believe it. The back yard was covered in a brilliant whiteness. It shone with a startling clarity. A few birds had already made small tracks over this new wilderness, but otherwise it was as solid as a blanket. Aisling threw the cover back and jumped out of the bed. A strange joy made her press her nose against the glass. The world looked so new it took her breath away.

She couldn't even remember clearly the last time she'd seen snow. She had still been in primary and all the pipes in the old school had burst. There were no lessons for over a week and then, for a fortnight after, they had to have class in the gym. They had sat hunched at their desks still wrapped up in their coats and scarves as the flooding also meant no heating. Aisling remembered the excitement of learning in that odd echoing space and how dull it had seemed when they had to go back to their regular classroom.

She grabbed her dressing gown from its peg and rushed into the kitchen shouting. "Snow. Have you seen there's snow?"

She stopped so abruptly she nearly fell over her feet. It wasn't her mother clattering around, but the man from last night. He turned around at her sudden appearance and, for a moment, they just stared at each other.

Then the man held out his hand to Aisling. "I don't believe we've been properly introduced," he said. "I'm Jack. Your Uncle Jack."

"I don't have an Uncle Jack," replied Aisling. If she did, this was the first she'd heard of it.

"Yes you do." Jack spoke slowly. "I was married to your mother's sister Kate a long time ago."

That wasn't possible, but before Aisling could query him further Jack went back to the cooker and gave the pan a vigorous shake. "I'm making pancakes. You want one?"

With that he turned round with the handle in his hand and expertly tossed the pancake high in the air. It landed back in the melted butter with an impressive sizzle. The delicious smell assaulted Aisling's nose, yet she hesitated.

"It's all right," said Jack. "Your father invited me here."

Aisling considered this highly probable. Recently everything her parents did seemed to be in total contradiction to one another. As if they were two opposing nations attempting to start a war. Aisling felt she was the principal target of their propaganda. "Tell your mother not to be so childish," her father would say. "Ask your father, has his selfishness got no limits?" her mother would snap. Aisling wandered around in the no man's land between them.

Jack put a plate on the table and slapped a pancake on to it. He sprinkled it with sugar and then squeezed half a lemon all over the top. He carefully rolled it into a long sausage shape and pushed the plate in Aisling's direction. She sat down and picked up a fork warily. She checked over her shoulder to make sure her mother wasn't spying on her and began to eat.

Jack poured more batter into the pan and began to sing quietly to himself, "I'm dreaming of a white Christmas."

Aisling couldn't help but smile as she tucked in.

The pancake was delicious and she devoured it quickly before asking, "Why doesn't my mam want you here?"

Jack sighed. "I behaved very badly a long time ago and I don't think she's forgiven me."

Aisling sympathised. At least with her father, if he was pissed off, he would scream and yell and threaten to throw you out of the house, but once the storm was over that was the end of it. With her mother, she just went quiet, sort of slowly froze you out. It could take you weeks to discover what your crime was. She never shouted, she just let you know she'd expected better.

"But now I've come back to try to set things right," Jack continued. "I'm here to find your brother."

Aisling stiffened. "He's in America."

"I know but I think he might have got lost."

At that moment Pat strode into the kitchen and glared at the two of them sitting there. "Don't be filling her head with nonsense."

It was obvious she'd been listening at the door. Her mother was notorious for eavesdropping.

"Look Pat," Jack pleaded. "At least give me a chance. What harm can it do?"

Her mother's look was withering. "Martin should never have asked you to come here."

"I understand why you don't trust me," Jack said.

Aisling's mother glanced sideways at her with anxiety. It was that special look she had for when she feared one of her children was about to hear something she believed they would be better off not knowing. She stood up and grabbed her coat from the chair in a savage gesture.

As she buttoned up, she hissed, "It's too late, Jack, I don't want to hear it. I'm going to mass. I don't want you here when I get back."

There was threat in her voice. In her own oblique way, Aisling's mother could be more intimidating than her father. Since Cathal's disappearance, her mother had taken to going to mass every single morning. Her father said she was wearing herself out praying, not to mention the huge waste of money on special novenas pleading with God to return her son. He thought the nuns were guilty of robbery, taking bribes from a desperate woman.

"God cannot be bought," he declared time and again.

The response was always the same. "At least I'm trying."

It gave Aisling the odd feeling that perhaps God had put a price on her brother's head. If only she knew what was expected of her, she could get him back. She had given it a go in the privacy of her room. Her knees cold and stiff against the wooden floor. All she got for her efforts was a splinter. She seemed to lack the concentration for serious prayer.

"Dear God, wherever Cathal is, please send him back to us."

She wanted to say more, to dress it up a bit. Perhaps mention that she knew He was very busy and that the Department of Foreign Affairs in Dublin had told her father there were millions of disappeared people – her brother was a needle in a haystack. But every time she tried to build up the sincerity and desperation of her request, she was interrupted by the memory of Cathal's sniggering. Whenever they went to mass on Sunday, he used to pull funny faces at her in a deliberate attempt to make her laugh. Once he even put a large spider down the back of her jumper right in the middle of communion.

"God is evil," he told her. "If he cared anything at all about people, the world wouldn't be such a mess and we wouldn't be expected to sit here being bored to death. I just can't like a supreme being that has inflicted this dullness on us." Perhaps God was punishing her brother for his short attention span.

Her mother headed out of the door. "Make sure you clean up this mess," she said to Aisling as she slammed out of the room.

Jack poured water into the sink. Aisling could sense he was unwilling to continue their conversation. Sometimes she felt her whole life was made up of snatches of words left hanging in the air as she entered a room. She only caught glimpses of this other world with its hushed tones and odd secrets. Nobody told her anything. They just smoothed it over with offers of cups of tea and remarks about the rain.

Jack was drying his hands on a tea towel. "Well I suppose I better go, think I've worn out my non-welcome."

"You said you were going to find my brother," Aisling accused.

Jack reached into his pocket and pulled out an envelope. He handed it to Aisling. She opened it; an airline ticket to New York.

"That's where he flew into, so that's where I'll start."

Aisling suddenly saw Jack in a whole new light. Here at last was somebody prepared to do something.

"I've got something to show you." Aisling hurried to get the atlas.

She showed Jack the trail marked in red.

"Well at least this is something to get going on. Would you mind if I kept it?"

Aisling was flooded with doubt. Her brother had entrusted the atlas to her. She didn't know this man who claimed to be her uncle and whom her mother so clearly disliked. After all her mother was as desperate to get Cathal back as she was.

"Look," said Jack. "Why don't we go for a walk? We could go down to the beach. Then I can explain things a bit more without having to worry about your parents interrupting us."

Aisling quickly went to get dressed. Ten minutes later she and Jack were headed up the road. There wasn't a soul to be seen and the snow muffled all sound. The quiet was nearly eerie. Aisling spotted a robin sitting on a low wall. His red breast flashed against the white and she thought it was the closest thing she'd ever seen to a real live Christmas card. She rarely went to the beach in the winter and she had certainly never seen it with snow on it before. The sea had washed half the beach clean but where the wet sand stopped, the snow still held on. There wasn't a cloud in the sky and the blue vastness of the heavens reflected in the green of the ocean. The purity of the colours filled Aisling with a sense of enormous space. It was as if the world had ended and she and Jack were the only ones left. The light of the sun had a special quality, like they were walking through a painting.

"There's nearly enough to make a snowman," she said to Jack happily.

"You like snow hey?" Jack smiled at her.

"Cathal would love this. He'd make snowballs and fire them at the seagulls. They've loads of snow in America, don't they?"

"So I've been told," Jack replied softly

Her uncle led them down to where the beach gave way to rocks. Huge, black broken boulders that jutted out from the land. They were full of little pools where, in the summer, Aisling and Cathal hunted for crabs. They used a single line and put the crabs in a bucket with water. The crabs would struggle to climb up the plastic walls, their little claws snapping uselessly. At the end of the afternoon, Cathal always insisted they set the crabs free again. Aisling objected; it took so long to catch them in the first place, hours spent peering into the water trying to spot them among the seaweed and camouflaged against the rocks.

"It's like we're peering down on their world," Cathal told her. "I guess that's what God feels like."

Aisling and Jack took shelter behind one of the rocks crouching down out of the wind. Despite the threat of the waves splashing over, the rock still had snow on it. Aisling gathered up a pile and put some in her mouth. It was so icy it stung. She had to swallow quickly, her tongue numb.

Jack had his head thrown back and was looking up at the birds circling overhead. He pulled his coat tighter round his skinny frame. He took out a cigarette and struggled to light a match in the wind. They went out practically the moment they were struck and Jack sighed in defeat. Aisling took the box and the fag from him. Curling her hand around the flame, she lit the cigarette easily and handed it back to him.

Jack sucked on his cigarette and then asked, "Have you any idea why your brother hasn't come back?"

Aisling shook her head. She wanted to say more, but her tongue wouldn't move. If there was one thing her mother hated above all others, it was the idea that her private business was known to others. She'd told Aisling a thousand times not to discuss her brother's disappearance with anyone. Aisling had become an expert at deflecting questions – indeed keeping her mouth shut in general. As her parents' voices rose, Aisling found herself becoming quieter and quieter. She seemed to have far less to say in general. Life above the pub had become a field of eggshells and Aisling treaded as lightly as she could. There was no way of knowing which innocent word could turn out to be a mine exploding under her. At school she no longer put her hand up to answer questions, but had managed to secure a seat in the back row of every single class. Here she perfected the art of staring out the window and discovered she could tune out the voice of the teacher completely. Sometimes she felt, in her own way, she was disappearing too.

Jack opened his wallet and took out several well-worn black and white photographs. They were creased and slightly faded, like they'd been stared at too long. One was of a naked toddler in a giant sun hat standing on a blanket on a beach. Crouched down beside him and holding his hand was a beautiful woman in a swimsuit. She had a warm open smile as if she'd just heard a very funny joke. Jack passed the photos to Aisling.

"I took that here on this very beach. Back when I was still welcome to come and visit. That's Cathal as a baby."

Aisling peered at the photo. There were hundreds of pictures of her as a baby, but she'd never seen one of Cathal before. Her father said it was because he couldn't afford a decent camera back then, but Cathal told her it was because he was born deformed. He said he'd been the world's ugliest baby, that he came out all yellow and with his head partly flattened. He would do a grotesque impression of what this looked like that always made Aisling laugh. Cathal said their mother had burned all the photos out of shame and fear people would realise he was a monster. He claimed to have only taken a more human shape by the time he was five. The toddler in the picture looked like an angel. He had a round grinning face and a shock of black curls.

"I'd never have recognised him." Aisling ran her finger over the photo.

Cathal also claimed to be a changeling. These strange creatures were the offspring of faery folk. The faeries wanted human babies so they'd kidnap them and put a changeling in their place so the parents wouldn't notice. These changelings would miss their world and cry all night. They grew up to be mischievous and untrustworthy.

Aisling had been disturbed by this story and remembered asking her mother when she was six, "Am I a changeling?"

"Of course not," her mother reassured.

"Well how come Cathal is?"

She recalled the familiar feeling – even then – of having said the wrong thing. Like there was a rush of silence followed by a flurry of words to cover up whatever error had been committed.

"Cathal just likes to make up stories. You know you can't believe a word out of his mouth," her mother had snapped.

But recently Cathal's imaginings had begun to come back to Aisling. She remembered things he'd said with a burst of clarity, and his lies were beginning to seem truer than her parents' silences.

"How come my mam never told me I had an uncle?" she asked Jack.

Her father was an only child and her mother had just the one sister Kate who died when they were still kids. Aisling had been intrigued to know the details of this tragedy, but her mother would only say, "It was an accident. She didn't know how to swim. I don't want to talk about it."

"Your mother hasn't seen me in over fifteen years. Maybe she forgot.' Jack dug at the sand with his hands. He seemed reluctant to look Aisling in the eye. His words reminded her of what Cathal had said when he gave her the bracelet she still wore.

"You don't just forget about people." Aisling didn't want to sound angry and accusing, like her mother, so she hurried to explain. "I'm not forgetting my brother. I remember him better the longer he's gone."

"I think I know what you mean," said Jack as he held up a shell he had uncovered. He scooped the sand out of it and handed it to Aisling.

"A present for you."

It was actually half of a clam. One side was black and chipped while the other had a flaky white softness with a mother of pearl shine. Aisling put the shell in her pocket.

She handed Jack his pictures pointing at the beautiful woman. "Is that what my mother used to look like?"

Jack held the photo up to the light. "No, your mother wasn't bad looking at all. But it was her sister was the real stunner. That's your Aunt Kate."

Aisling didn't understand. "But it can't be. She died when she was my age. There was an accident and she drowned."

Jack stood up abruptly. "Is that what your mother told you?"

He shoved the photos back in his wallet and began to stride up the beach. Aisling had to run to catch up with him. She was amazed to see he was crying. She didn't think she'd ever seen a grown man in tears before and was at a complete loss what to do. He came to an abrupt stop just by the water's edge.

"I think it was here. I'm pretty sure it was right here." He appeared to be talking to himself and for the first time Aisling wondered if her mother wanted nothing to do with him because he was a lunatic. "There was a man who nearly drowned. He washed up on this spot and he wasn't breathing any more. But I saved him. I brought him back to life."

Jack stared at Aisling wildly. "She didn't drown by accident. Your mother shouldn't have told you that. I was married to Kate, I ought to know what happened to her."

Aisling was totally bewildered. She didn't know what to believe any more. Everything she'd once been sure of seemed to be melting away. Her mother wouldn't lie to her about something like that. Would she?

Cathal had said to her once, "That's the trouble with this family. We wouldn't know the truth if it bit us on the arse."

"I've had enough of all this," Jack announced. "I'm going to America and I promise not to come back till I find Cathal."

Jack put his hand on Aisling's shoulder for a moment to reassure her. Then he turned around and began to walk back the way they'd come with an air of determination Aisling admired.

7

AFTER HER UNCLE'S VISIT, AISLING found it increasingly difficult to concentrate. It was as if her soul were travelling with Jack in America and only the hollow shell of her body remained behind. She was trapped behind her school desk as the teacher mumbled on and on. The only subject that didn't bore her to tears was history. She had a book about 1916 and the Easter Rising and spent hours fantasising about being a sniper shooting at English troops against impossible odds.

She always went to her history class, even if she went to less and less of the others. It wasn't a conscious decision to stop going, it was just that she cut a few here and there and it grew like a habit. She'd smoke a joint behind the bicycle shed or, if the weather wasn't too bad, slip off to the beach for a couple of hours. She'd taken up smoking cannabis as a New Year's resolution.

Maths was a safe bet because the nun who taught it was practically blind. She had large double focus glasses that made her look like a small round owl. She mumbled away in what might as well have been double Dutch, only pausing every few minutes to peer at them and ask with great sincerity, "D'ye follow girls?" The rumble of assent seemed to reassure her and she'd carry on. As long as enough of the class showed up to make the answer audible, she had no way of seeing who was actually there.

Religion was also a piece of cake. A young priest from the boy's school was drafted in to cover when the old one, Father McKay, fell ill. This new priest had the huge misfortune of being good-looking. Facing a class of thirty girls who'd just hit puberty, this, combined with how easy it was to make him blush, was a serious problem. They all went out of their way to ask him embarrassing questions. Particularly Susan FitzSimon who had the best developed breasts in the entire year.

Opening another one or two buttons on her blouse and leaning over him in an alarmingly seductive manner, she'd ask, "Father, is it only a sin if you kiss a boy using your tongue? I mean if it's just your lips, is that all right?"

The poor priest who was the victim of this sexual harassment would stammer a response, including mention of Jesus and holy matrimony, that left the issue no clearer. Aisling disapproved of this carry on as she felt sorry for Father Doyle and embarrassed on his behalf. So embarrassed that she stopped going to his class. Father Doyle was, by this point, so terrified of the lustful stares of the girls in his charge that he rarely looked up from his Bible, so he never noticed Aisling's empty seat at the back of the class.

Aisling considered it a good omen when Jack's first letter arrived on a Thursday when she had double religion in the afternoon. She sneaked out during lunch break and headed straight for the beach. It was a cold, bleak February afternoon and she felt like all her senses were dulled. The letter in her hand seemed to glow with a special warmth as though the American dream had seeped into the envelope. She hadn't wanted to open it in the pub with her mother's needle sharp eyes trying to read over her shoulder. Just because they were barely speaking didn't stop her mother from watching her like a hawk. If Aisling was five minutes late home from school, she was bound to find her mother standing in the pub doorway peering anxiously up the road. She wasn't allowed out after dark, which these winter days meant four o'clock, and she had to account for her every movement. She found this constant supervision stifling. Jack's visit seemed to have shocked her mother into remembering her existence. Aisling wished fervently she could go back to being invisible.

Aisling had attempted to confront her mother over what had happened to her aunt Kate. She waited till Jack left, believing this gave her mother a fair opportunity to defend her own version of events. She chose her moment carefully when they were doing the dishes together. Her mother seemed distracted and Aisling felt a dramatic opening was necessary to grab her attention.

"Uncle Jack says you lied about your sister drowning when she was a child."

Her mother picked up a tea towel and studied it with great interest. It was a green one with a country cottage and the words 'May you be in heaven half an hour before the devil knows you're dead' emblazoned across it. She sighed deeply. Then picked up a plate and wiped it dry with the cloth.

"I ought to know what happened to my own sister," she said slowly as if the words caused her pain.

For a moment Aisling felt guilty. How could she ever have doubted her?

Then her mother continued. "Whether she drowned or not, the fact of the matter is she's dead. And the dead should be left in peace."

Aisling didn't know what to say to this. She opened her mouth like a fish that suddenly finds itself out of water, but before she could formulate her next question, her mother walked out of the room. Aisling felt a righteous anger at her mother's abruptness, as if she'd been slapped across the face.

That night as she lay in bed, she heard her parents having an enormous row in the kitchen. It wasn't the usual hissed whispers and violent silences; this was full blown shouting and yelling. Jack had lifted the lid on a boiling pot and now the water was bubbling over into the flames.

"You had no right to go behind my back," her mother roared.

"He rang me." Her father's voice boomed. "He said he wanted to help."

"You stupid man. If you'd just kept your mouth shut."

"Cathal had a right to know. You can't treat me like this, Pat. I brought him up as if he were my own. I did my best."

Aisling shivered. So her father knew Cathal wasn't his? Why had they pretended her brother was lying?

"You never loved him," her mother shouted.

Aisling hurriedly jumped out of bed. For once she wanted to be the one to silence her parents. They seemed to have lost control and it scared her.

"You drove him out of here. It's because of you that he left."

The accusation reverberated like a gunshot. It stopped Aisling in her tracks just as she reached the kitchen doorway. Afterwards she wished she'd stayed in bed. She arrived just in time to see her father pull back his hand and strike her mother full force across the face. Her mother screamed and kicked him hard in the shin. For all their bickering, Aisling had never seen her parents come to blows before. The sight shocked her to the core.

"Now look what you've made me do," her father cried and fled from the room, nearly knocking Aisling over in his hurry.

The look of terror on his face was something Aisling would find hard to forget. She heard the car engine starting up and her father roaring off into the distance.

Aisling turned to comfort her mother whose cheek was an angry red glow. But her mother shouted, "Get out of my sight," as if Aisling were the one who'd hit her.

Aisling turned and ran. When she got back into bed, her heart was banging against her chest. She hated both of them. Cathal had been right to leave. Who wouldn't want to get away from this mad house? It was only after she calmed down that she started to worry about her father. What on earth were they going to do if he didn't come back? Fear prevented her from sleeping. Could he really drive off into the night without leaving a trace?

Aisling had always viewed her family as a kind of immovable rock. In fact she found her parents rather dull. Their life seemed to be set in a routine of granite. The pub opened and closed like clockwork, and in between time, her father went fishing and her mother cooked, cleaned, and went to mass. Before Cathal's disappearance, it never occurred to Aisling to ask herself if they were happy. Over the past year, she'd become more and more aware of their misery. At first she thought if Cathal could see how unhappy his absence was making them, he'd come rushing back. But recently she'd been struck by the odd notion that Cathal running away was more of a symptom than a root cause.

The sun was beginning to rise when she heard the car pull up outside. The engine continued to purr for a minute then was shut off. She waited for what seemed an eternity before she heard the pub door's familiar creak. Then there was silence. Eventually Aisling plucked up the courage to sneak down the stairs. Her father was lying on one of the benches in the lounge, partly covered by his coat, which he had taken off to use as a blanket. Aisling could only half make out the hulk of his body in the gloom and couldn't see his face to tell if he was awake or not. She crept back upstairs to bed.

Aisling went to school the next morning without speaking to either of her parents. To her astonishment, when she returned both her mother and father acted as if nothing had happened. The pub was open and the regular afternoon customers, mainly old men in tweed caps, greeted her with their usual friendliness. Her mother asked how her teachers were and her father if she'd learnt anything. Dinner was polite and restrained and the fight or Cathal wasn't mentioned. The only noticeable change was that her mother moved back into the room she used to share with her husband. Aisling was mystified by the whole thing. She couldn't work out if it was a positive development or not.

From that day on neither of her parents would say Cathal's name. If Aisling mentioned him, she was greeted with such a painful silence that she quickly learned the subject had become taboo over night. In a way the semblance of normality was a relief. She no longer had to shut out the awful sound of her parents tearing each other to shreds. But this new careful politeness they had around her seemed slightly sinister. As if they were all in a show, but she was the only one who hadn't been given a script.

She hoped Jack's letter would shed some light on her parents' weird behaviour. Aisling sat herself down in the same sheltered spot on the beach where she'd helped Jack light his cigarette a few months previously. It felt like years ago already. Before Jack's visit, Aisling often held conversations in her head with her brother. But recently his responses had become so disturbing that she now found she preferred Jack. In these internal dialogues, Jack was a kind and sympathetic listener who understood how oppressed she had come to feel in this small town. He was an educated man of the world who'd never dream of wasting his life in a place with only one main street, two churches, three schools, and countless pubs. Aisling hated the way all the shopkeepers asked her how her mother was doing while the customers nodded with sympathetic murmurs. She hardly ever met anyone who didn't recognise her. She wanted to scream at them all that they didn't know her, they had no idea who she really was. She felt closer to Jack even though they had only met the once. Jack's character in her imagination was so fully rounded that it was a shock to read his letter and realise he was an actual person with a voice of his own.

Dear Aisling,

I hope this letter finds you in the best of health. I am writing to you from the balcony of a hotel in Greenwich Village, in the heart of New York City. I've yet to find your brother, but I have by no means lost hope. I'm following several leads and people have been incredibly helpful and sympathetic. It must be said that Americans are a friendly bunch, particularly in this part of the country. Practically everyone I meet seems to consider themselves Irish. I've hired a private detective, a man called Sean Brennan. Apparently he's got family in Clare, cousins of his great grandmother, that he tracked down a few years back. Tracing your roots the Yanks call it. It seems to be a national obsession. Sean thinks if he can find distant cousins thousands of miles away than a missing nephew shouldn't pose too much of a challenge. Besides he says it makes a pleasant change from the usual divorce cases. Apparently he spends a great deal of his time being paid to find out who's cheating on who. Not an occupation I'd enjoy, but he certainly has some good stories to tell.

I'm never alone here and yet I must confess I do feel lonely. I would give a great deal to be sitting in O'Rourke's pub, nursing a pint of Guinness and watching the afternoon sunlight making shadows on the wall. Isn't it strange that I can feel homesick for a town I lived in nearly twenty years ago? And yet I'm not unhappy here, I do believe I'll be able to keep my promise to you. Every day I feel I get a little closer to finding your brother. I hope you share my hopes.

Yours,
Uncle Jack

Aisling couldn't understand Jack wishing he was back in her father's pub. She felt she'd be happy if she never had to see the place again. Which was probably what Cathal felt, she thought sadly. But why did he have to include her in his rejection? It hurt, and while she was thrilled that Jack seemed convinced he would find her brother, she wondered, for the first time, if she'd ever be able to forgive him for abandoning them. Wasn't it the height of selfishness to have just left her behind like that? How could he care so little for her when she loved him so much? She felt irritated by her own self pity and folded Jack's letter carefully before putting it back in its envelope and hiding it in the depths of her coat pocket.

Aisling had a nasty shock when she got back to school. The head-mistress, Sr. Agnes, wanted to see her. Apparently Father Doyle had finally cracked under the pressure. Susan FitzSimon had asked whether God thought it was all right to give your husband a blowjob. Instead of answering, Father Doyle burst into tears and rushed from the room. The girls all sat there in stunned silence unsure what to do. Someone suggest-ed they should run after him to see if he was all right, but Susan said not to be ridiculous. They decided to pass the time in having a sing-a-long. When Sr. Agnes had accepted the tearful priest's instant resignation, she went down to his class to discover what they had done to drive Father Doyle into what she was to describe as 'a state of nervous exhaustion.' She walked into the room to find the girls in the middle of a swinging rendi-tion of 'Patricia the Stripper' and Susan FitzSimon on top of a desk with her skirt hitched up and swirling her school jumper around her head.

Susan was facing expulsion for this 'lurid display' but Aisling was also in deep trouble when it was discovered she wasn't there to witness it. Sr. Agnes rang her mother on the spot. Aisling sat hunched down in the uncomfortable wooden chair in the headmistress's office listening to her clipped tone as she explained over the phone that the school took a very poor view of students who preferred to go to the beach rather than to class. Aisling regretted saying where she'd gone as Sr. Agnes's sarcasm at her attempt to go sunbathing in February was scalding. Her mother took enormous offence that it was religion she'd skipped. Aisling knew that explaining there were many other subjects she often cut wasn't going to help. Her mother clearly believed she had another atheist delinquent on her hands.

"Just because your brother had no respect for God..." she started to say, but then stopped when she remembered that Cathal was never to be spoken of.

Whatever mistakes she had made with her son, she was determined

Aisling would turn out differently. As punishment, she made her daughter get up at six every morning for the next month to go to mass with her. Aisling felt like pointing out that this was likely to kill off any spiritual feelings she might have altogether, but bit her tongue.

She faced torturous hours of detention after school. The only saving grace was that, following Mrs FitzSimon crawling on her hands and knees and promising to knock the brazen hussy out of her daughter, Susan was not expelled, but shared Aisling's punishment.

"Just as well she walked in when she did," she told Aisling with a grin. "If it'd been a few minutes later, I might not have still had me knickers on."

Susan was small and this made her considerable bust seem even bigger. She had long, flaming, red hair and small freckles like light brown dust all over her face. She hung out with the smokers and had a boyfriend who was nineteen. Aisling looked down at her own flat chest and felt increasingly intimidated by Susan. But Susan didn't seem to notice and continued to chatter away nineteen-to-the-dozen. Father McKay had been forced to delay his retirement plans because of Father Doyle's nervous breakdown and he was in charge of watching over the two girls. He was a large man with a shiny baldhead which he compensated for with a big bush of a beard. They were supposed to be writing out passages from the Bible and he was supposed to be correcting religious homework, but often, after ten minutes he'd fall fast asleep. His large head would loll forward, and after bopping for a while, come to rest on his shoulder as he sprawled in his chair. Sometimes he would lean too far back and the chair would move, waking him with an unpleasant jolt. He'd sit bolt upright and stare around the room in wild terror like he had only just discovered what his lot in life was. Then he would excuse himself to the "little boys' room" and not come back for a good half hour.

"Probably gone for a wank," Susan told Aisling.

Aisling discovered that Susan was a mine of information. She had four older sisters – two of whom were married with kids – where Aisling had no one. Sex, a subject her mother avoided like the plague, Susan could quite happily chat about for hours.

Aisling was nearly sorry when the three weeks detention was up. On the last afternoon they whispered and giggled together as usual. Father McKay was snoring loudly; he sucked the air up his hairy nostrils and trumpeted it out again. Susan started doing an impression of him that had Aisling in silent hysterics.

Suddenly inspired, Aisling whipped Susan's bright red lipstick from her bag and approached Father McKay with great stealth. She wanted to colour his lips, but they were lost in the undergrowth of his beard and she was afraid to wake him up. Instead she wrote on his forehead in big, red letters - R.I.P. It wasn't that she intended to be morbid; it was the first thing occurred to her that would fit on the shiny canvas in front of her. Susan tiptoed up to observe Aisling's handiwork, but had to rush away with her hand over her mouth, trying to control her laughter. Father McKay didn't even twitch. If it wasn't for the snoring, you'd think he really was dead.

Aisling sat on a desk so that Susan could stand and braid her hair. Up until a few weeks ago, Aisling had always worn her long brown hair in a simple ponytail, but Susan had pointed out how boring it looked. Now she nimbly crossed the plaits in between whispered laughter.

"God Ash and to think I used to reckon you were a bit square. But, as me mam says, it's the quiet ones you have to watch."

Aisling basked in the praise. She wished she did have some dark secret to hide. She decided to confide to Susan that she'd never actually kissed a boy.

It was an incredibly painful and embarrassing admission, but Susan just laughed. "But sure there's nothing to it. You should practice on yourself first."

Aisling was bewildered, but Susan put the back of her hand against her mouth to demonstrate. She began to snog her own hand with exaggerated enthusiasm.

Aisling giggled until Susan said, "Go on, let's see you do it."

Aisling blushed and looked at her hand as if it were an alien object.

"Oh for God's sakes. It's no big deal." Susan grabbed her and kissed her full on the lips. It only lasted a second or two as Father McKay made a sudden movement in his chair and the two girls rushed from the room in a fit of hysterical laughter and fright.

Aisling was terrified Father McKay would have them both expelled, but to her amazement, nothing was ever said. He might not have seen the kiss and maybe he thought the RIP was a message from God because he retired a week later. He was dead by April. When her mother told her Father McKay had gone in the night, of a massive stroke, Aisling felt as though her lipstick prediction made her a murderer.

Susan acted as if nothing unusual had happened. Aisling supposed that, having kissed loads of other people, it meant nothing to her. Anyway did kissing a girl count? Aisling supposed that it didn't; she would just have to hurry up and find herself a boyfriend.

8

JACK WANTED TO GET THE next bus back to Dublin. He felt he was going mad. To stay any longer in Kate's vicinity was more than he could bear. He hurriedly began to repack his small bag. His father appeared in the doorway of his bedroom and asked him what he was doing.

"But you've only just arrived. What was the point of paying for the fare?"

Jack felt a prick of conscience; he could imagine Brendan thinking the same thing. "It's no business of yours how I spend my money," he snapped at his father.

He instantly regretted the harshness of his tone, especially as, for once, it wasn't his father who was setting his teeth on edge.

"Is it something I've done?" his father asked sadly.

Jack knew he was guilty of taking things out on his father, but he couldn't explain what had happened either. He turned away angrily.

His father refused to let it drop. "You know if there's something bothering you, you can talk to me."

"Look Dad," Jack replied more gently. "I just want to be left on my own."

His father turned to go, but then paused in the doorway and remarked, "That's exactly what your mother used to always say."

Jack couldn't meet his father's eye. In the weeks after his mother's death, Jack would go downstairs late at night to find his father sobbing in the kitchen. A nearly empty bottle of whiskey on the table in front of him. His grief was slurred and incomprehensible. Jack felt as if he were looking over the edge of a well and was in danger of tumbling in if he got too close.

One particularly bad night, his father had gripped Jack's hand and hissed, "It was me. It was all my fault. She'd be alive now if I hadn't been such an idiot…"

Jack didn't want to hear that. He thought his father wasn't any more to blame than he was, but Jack also felt crushed by a guilt he couldn't name. If only he'd said this, if only he'd done that, if only, if only… That way led to madness. Jack had insisted on dragging his father off to bed. He emptied the rest of the whiskey down the drain with grim determination. The next morning, when his father was feeling weakened by his hangover, Jack chose his moment of attack.

"You can drink yourself to death if you want, there's nothing I can do to stop you, but don't expect me to sit here and watch you do it."

His father nodded his head slowly, clearly in pain. "You're all I've got left to live for, Jack. All I want is to see you happy."

After that his father made a considerable effort to sober up. And since they had moved south and left Derry with its ghosts behind, Jack had never seen his father drunk –nor had either of them spoken of Jack's mother. As if the mere mention of her name might alert her spirit as to where they were and she'd start to haunt them again.

Jack didn't want to hear he was echoing his mother's words. In a rush of fresh bitterness from his own heartbreak, Jack spat, "And I wonder why she used to say that?"

His father looked as if he'd been punched and Jack instantly wished he could take the words back. His father stepped into the room closing the door carefully behind him. Jack half expected his father to hit him, but instead he sat himself on the edge of the bed.

"I don't know, son. I honestly don't know." His words sounded hollow. Jack knew he was looking at a shell of a man.

"All I know is I should I never have listened to her. If only I'd inter- fered."

Somehow having this conversation without a drink taken was far worse than when his father was pissed. His inebriated state had before always allowed Jack to keep a certain superior sober distance. Now Jack felt like his father's fragility was in the palm of his own hand.

"Dad, for the last time, there was no way you could've known what was going to happen, she wasn't well..."

His father waved his hand in a feeble dismissal of Jack's words. "I don't mean the day she died. I mean before that. Way before that."

Jack wondered what was coming next. He had the odd sensation that him and his father were always destined to have this conversation, and that he had been trying to escape it all this time.

"That soldier. I suppose you know about the soldier?"

Jack nodded in silent acknowledgment.

"I knew she was seeing him. For months I knew."

Jack drew his breath in sharply. This was what he had dreaded hear- ing.

"That night they were spotted together. I knew where she was going. I knew, but I didn't want to admit I knew. I thought as long as I said noth- ing it would all blow over of its own accord. I was so scared of losing her. So I just let her go."

71

His father paused as he struggled to put this memory into words for the first time. Jack waited for whatever was coming.

"She was in love with him you see. She was never really in love with me. If I hadn't been such a coward, she'd never have gone out that night. They'd never have got caught, he'd never have been shot. I used to dream about strangling the life out of him, but when he died, it was too late. Your mother never got over it. If I'd just been man enough to step in there at the beginning, to nip it in the bud. I thought I had to accept her choice, but I could've saved her from all that unhappiness. She needed my protection, and I let her down."

Jack didn't know what to say. He should've felt relieved that his father wasn't the murderer he'd suspected, but instead he felt deeply depressed that his father was a fool. An even bigger fool than Jack. He sat down on the bed beside his father. They said nothing for what seemed an eternity.

Eventually Jack turned to his father. "You weren't to know. You were trying to do the decent thing."

His father chewed his lips. "Sometimes I wish it'd been me that was shot."

Jack felt infinitely sorry for this man he'd never understood before. "Listen... There's no reason why I can't stick around for a few more days. I'm not really in that much of a hurry to get back."

His father claimed he didn't want Jack missing any of his study, but quickly gave in. Jack realised for the first time that he was needed.

The next morning when his father told him Kate was at the front door, Jack wasn't surprised. Part of his reason for wanting to leave the day before was his certainty that she would make an appearance. He'd read the end of Troy's letter, where Troy begged Kate to give Jack a message to bring back to him. To let him know if she could make it to Dublin for the wedding. Jack's only surprise was that Kate had the nerve to still ask him. They sat in the kitchen and, after a few pleasantries and inquiring about Kate's mother's health, his father made a tactful withdrawal. Jack peered at his own reflection in his cup of tea. He could see his face looked sullen when in fact he was numb.

Kate was stumbling through an apology. "I'd no idea you felt like that, Jack..."

He stared at her. Despair made him brutally honest. "What the hell did you think I kissed you for?"

Being humble didn't really suit Kate and she flared at Jack's words. "Well I didn't hear a word from you afterwards. I thought you'd only done it cos you were leaving in the morning and saw no reason not to."

"I tried to ring you, but your father hung up on me."

Jack didn't even know himself what he was accusing Kate of. One kiss on a beach hardly meant she owed him lifelong fidelity. The last thing he wanted was to have a row with her. He'd spent much of the previous sleepless night working through that his father's fatal error was to accept what destiny threw at him. Jack wasn't going to make the same mistake, he refused to simply lie down and roll over in the face of fate. He intended to bounce back fighting, but alienating Kate wasn't going to help. He had to be cleverer than that. All this waiting for the right moment just wouldn't wash any more. He needed to make his own moments. He already felt like a fool, so he hadn't even his pride left to lose. He was going to get Kate back whatever it took.

For an atheist, Jack had a strange confidence in what he took to be signs. He believed his dreams were trying to tell him something. When he'd finally dropped off to sleep at around four in the morning, his mother had come to visit him. It was a version of a dream he'd had many times before. Normally he would be with his mother in their old house in Derry and she would be telling him that Dr. Gordon's sleeping pills really seemed to be working – she was feeling much better. The details of this changed but the feeling was always the same. He'd be happy to see his mother looked less pale and drawn than usual, that she was up out of bed and seemed to be coming out of another dark episode. Then he'd remember that it was too late to be having the conversation, that she was, in fact, already dead. At this point he'd wake up, often with his face wet with tears. It was like he had to relive the moment he saw her body in the morgue and knew the awful truth. But last night they weren't in the house in Derry. They were on the beach where he'd kissed Kate. His mother was trying to tell him how much better she felt to be getting some sea air, but he cut her short.

"You're not really here," he said. "This isn't real, it's a dream, and I want to wake up."

He actually felt the sensation of rising to consciousness as if he were swimming up from under water. As he broke through, he found himself awake in his bedroom. He thought the dream meant he was finally taking charge of his own grief. Maybe there was nothing he could do about the past, but the future was still full of possibilities. That his father had told him the truth about his mother's affair, just at the moment when he was about to accept he'd lost Kate forever, struck Jack as more than a coincidence. It was a warning to him not to make the same mistake.

"Kate, I'm not blaming you, really I'm not. I just wonder if you're sure you're doing the right thing."

Kate was staring resolutely at the floor. "How can I possibly know that?" she replied. "I only know that I love Troy and I want to be with him. I'm really sorry if it hurts you to hear that."

What was the point in telling her it was like being stabbed in the chest?

"Well in that case, I wish you and Troy the best of luck." Jack struggled to keep himself together. "I hope you'll be happy Kate, I really mean that."

Kate gave him a quick hug. "I'd better get going. I'm barely allowed out of the house these days."

Jack realised he was being overly cynical in imagining she had only come to give him a message for Troy. Maybe she did have some feelings for him after all. Her half smile seemed full of genuine regret. She wasn't dressed for work or school, but instead wore jeans and a T-shirt with one of her mother's Aran cardigans over it. She looked like a child or a small elf. As she struggled to open the heavy back door, it seemed to him as if she were made of glass. He felt overwhelmingly protective. She reminded him of those Waterford crystal figurines his mother had been so fond of collecting. He didn't want anyone to drop and break her.

"Don't you want me to tell Troy anything? In response to the letter I mean."

For a moment she peered at him suspiciously.

"He asked me to make sure you gave me an answer. He didn't say what the question was."

Kate seemed to reach a decision. "What bus are you getting?"

"I was planning to stay around for a few days. I don't have to be back really till Thursday."

"Grand, that'll give me enough time to get some money together."

He looked at her in shock. "You can't come with me. Your father would never forgive me."

"Well one way or another I'm getting out of here before the week's over. I refuse to be made a prisoner in my own house. My dad can go to hell."

Jack didn't relish the role of chaperon, but he wanted to keep as close to Kate as possible. As long as he kept her in sight, his opportunity to change the awful way events were unfolding was bound to present itself.

KATE WAS AGITATED AND FULL of nervous excitement on the bus. She asked Jack lots of questions – about Dublin and the dancehall where he'd met Troy. She seemed deeply impressed by his tale of how he got his nose broken and for over an hour Jack managed to fool himself that she wasn't running away from home to be with Troy. She was coming to Dublin to live with him. But as the bus pulled into the grimy station, he had to face that she was serious about Troy. He insisted on carrying her bag and tried to crack a joke about how he'd be happy to take her to America any time she wanted, but she didn't laugh.

She simply said, "I love him Jack."

There wasn't a lot he could say in response to that.

Kate wanted to go straight to Troy's fleapit hotel It was early evening and Jack briefly considered trying to persuade her to stay with him and find Troy in the morning, but she was adamant. Troy had written the address on the letter. She said she could find her own way, but since she'd never been to Dublin before Jack insisted on them getting a taxi.

Troy's face was a picture of joy when he walked into the hotel reception to find them there. He gave a kind of whoop, then grabbed Kate and kissed her passionately. Jack concentrated on a crack in the ceiling and counted to ten.

Troy broke away to pump Jack's hand up and down. "You're something else, man. I ask you for a message and you bring the angel herself."

Kate had the grace to look embarrassed. Troy wanted to buy him a drink, but Jack mumbled something about needing to get home – early lecture and all that. Kate squeezed his arm with gratitude. They'd barely made it in time. Troy was due back on his ship the next day and wouldn't get leave again for another three weeks. But he had the wedding all organised with the priest lined up. Troy asked Jack if Kate could stay with him while he was away. He didn't want her to be alone in a strange city. Jack agreed although Kate glared at him as if this was the last thing she wanted. Jack left them staring intensely into each other's eyes. He stepped out into the darkened street and pulled his collar up against the chill. He'd never felt so alone in his whole life.

When Jack made it back to his flat, Brendan asked him how his father was doing. Jack looked at him, blank.

"Is he feeling any better?" Brendan repeated.

Jack couldn't even muster up the strength to keep up his tall story about his father's sudden illness. "He's the same as ever."

Brendan tapped him affectionately on the back of his head with his fingers. "Whoever she is boy, she ain't worth it."

Jack didn't agree.

The next afternoon he met Kate in Bewley's on Grafton Street as agreed. He could tell from the shine of her eyes that she'd been crying and felt mean for hoping it was because the evening before had been a disaster. He couldn't bring himself to imagine her in that grubby hotel room with some sailor. Not that his own bed-sit was in any way superior, but she deserved better. For the first time since he started his studies, Jack wished he was a qualified doctor with his own practice. Then he would be able to treat her like the princess she was. Instead he had to content himself with buying her a cup of tea and a sticky bun.

"God forgive me, Jack, I know I shouldn't be talking to you of all people about this." Kate looked like she might start to cry again but she pulled herself together. "But I've no one else and I feel like I'm going mad. I'm just so scared something will go wrong. Anything could happen in three weeks. What if he never comes back?"

Jack felt like telling her if she had that little faith in Troy, she shouldn't be marrying him.

Instead he said, "Well you can stay with me for as long as you like."

"That's hardly fair on you." Kate took his hand. "I'm not trying to torture you, Jack. I was thinking I could go stay with my sister."

"Won't she just tell your father where you are?"

"Oh, Pat won't approve, but she'd never betray me."

Jack figured that if Pat was her father's daughter there was a fairly good chance she would. "Why don't you give her a ring?" he suggested.

He didn't personally like Mr O'Rourke much but, to a desperate man, an enemy's enemy is a friend. If Kate's father were to suddenly appear in Dublin and drag his wayward daughter off, kicking and screaming, Jack knew he would stand by and watch it happen.

Unfortunately Kate looked mightily relieved when she came back from the phone box. "She says I must be out of my mind. Mam's been on the phone every five minutes going frantic with worry. But Pat's promised not to say anything and I can head straight over."

There was always the chance that her sister was lying, Jack thought as he flagged down a taxi.

Kate's sister, Pat, lived in a tiny flat above the shop where she worked on the north side of the city. When she opened the door, she looked Jack up and down and exclaimed, "Is this him? Well he's a fine thing. I'd nearly run off to America with him myself." She laughed loudly and gave Kate a huge hug.

Jack looked aghast at being mistaken for Troy. Kate hurried to explain. Pat slammed the door and ushered them upstairs into a sitting room. A large picture of the Virgin Mary hung over the mantelpiece. For the first time in his life, Jack found the presence of religious imagery somewhat comforting. Pat looked like a slightly older, not quite as pretty, version of Kate. She had the same warm open face but her features were less refined and her mouth was smaller. She was still, by anybody's standards, a very handsome woman.

Pat wasn't impressed to hear that Kate had spent the night in a hotel room with Troy. "I hope you didn't do anything you'll regret," she said and raised her eyes to heaven.

Jack shifted uncomfortably. He realised he'd have to leave soon as there was no particular reason for him to stay. Pat wasn't showing any signs of inviting him for tea. Kate looked relieved to see him go.

On the way out, Pat thanked him for taking care of her sister. But it was just an excuse to pump him for information. "So this friend of yours, Troy. What's he like?" Her tone was casual but failed to mask an underlying concern.

Jack wanted to say, "He's a total bastard and you need to get your sister out of his evil clutches." All he managed was, "I don't really know the bloke."

Pat sighed. "Neither does Kate, but she doesn't seem to be letting that get in her way."

Jack tried ringing Kate a number of times over the next couple of weeks and although she always returned his calls, she made excuses about seeing him. Eventually she agreed to meet him for a drink.

He got to the pub early so he could secure the snug. Kate arrived looking rather pale, but still extraordinarily beautiful. Far from changing her mind, she said she was counting the days till Troy's return. Only four more to go, thank Christ. Her sister spent the whole time trying to get her to put off the wedding, telling her she couldn't marry a foreigner who was virtually a stranger. Jack felt grateful for that, although the only result seemed to be that Kate had been suffering from a continuous headache.

"I just want to get away from them all," she told Jack. He was hurt that he was indirectly included in this.

Kate had a favour to ask Jack. Pat's objections included the fact she'd have to break the news to their parents that Kate had run off to America.

Kate had offered to write and explain once she'd left. But this still left the problem of where Kate had been hiding these past weeks. Pat claimed her father would never forgive her if she knew Kate was staying with her so she wondered if Jack would mind terribly if she said she'd been hiding at his place. Jack didn't feel like drawing the wrath of Mr O'Rourke down upon him, particularly when he was guilty of precisely nothing. If Kate was running away with him, he would have faced her father even if it was down the barrel of his shotgun. But to be hated by Kate's parents for his involvement, when he was the only person alive who objected more strongly than they did, was a bitter irony. He looked at Kate's tense anxious face and sighed.

"No problem," he said as he took a large sip of his Guinness.

How had things become so complicated since the last time he was in a pub with Kate? One minute he had his whole future worked out and now he was facing a complete blank. Once she got on that plane there was every chance he'd never see her again. Time was marching on and he'd still no idea how to prevent the inevitable. Short of kidnapping her himself, there didn't seem to be any options. He was so close to despair that he actually turned the idea over in his head. It was totally ridiculous of course, he could hardly lock her up in a tower forever and as soon as she got out, she'd find her own way to America.

Kate told Jack she was meeting Troy in O'Neill's pub at seven o'clock on Thursday as prearranged. The wedding was the next morning and they were catching an evening flight. Troy had organised time off for his honeymoon. Jack already knew all this and couldn't figure out why Kate insisted on running through the painful details.

Kate was staring at him intently. "Troy told me he asked you to be the best man? No offence Jack, but I don't think you being there is a very good idea. I talked to Pat about it and she said the whole set up was odd enough and your presence could only make things more awkward and painful for everyone. Especially for you, Jack. I can't imagine why you'd want to come?"

All this was explained so gently and carefully that it took Jack a moment to realise he was being uninvited.

"I... I just want to make sure you're all right," he stammered.

He felt like a total idiot. Of course she didn't want him there. He could tell she'd never told Troy about their kiss. She just wanted to pretend nothing had ever happened between them; Jack was being written out of the script. She no longer had any use for him.

"But, I mean, I'll see you again before you leave?" He hated the way he couldn't quite keep the note of desperation out of his voice.

Kate kissed him lightly on the cheek. "I think it's best if we leave things the way they are, don't you?"

She had her coat on before he realised she was going.

"At least say you'll write to me," he pleaded.

She looked at him with what could only be described as pity and he wished the ground would swallow him whole.

"I could say that Jack, and it's really not that I don't care about you. You've been a very good friend to me and that's why I don't want to lie to you. I will write if you really want me to, but to be honest, what's the point? Isn't it only going to make things harder for you?"

The fact she understood the agony he was in, sympathised even, filled him with rage. He couldn't speak and she opened the door of the snug and walked out of the pub. He remained seated, paralysed, staring at the space where she'd been.

10

AISLING HAD READ IN SOME teen magazine that over fifty percent of the population of Ireland got their first kiss in the Gaeltacht. So, despite the dismal level of her own Irish, she didn't resist when her mother signed her up. The Gaeltacht was essentially a kind of summer camp where it was forbidden to speak English, only Irish was allowed. Even if she'd had to speak in tongues, it would be worth it to get away from her parents for the summer. Aisling was looking forward to not having to speak at all. Just shutting herself up in incomprehension. Despite learning Irish in school from the age of four, she couldn't hold more than the briefest of conversations about the weather. And she could ask a teacher if she could go to the toilet. Her ineptitude was something that outraged her mother who railed about how Aisling's grandfather had been a native speaker and would turn over in his grave if he could hear Aisling murdering the beautiful language he'd fought so hard to keep alive.

Aisling remembered her granddad as a small, crumpled man with a stick. He spent hours staring at the fire and saying nothing. For years she'd believed he didn't speak English, but Cathal assured her it wasn't so. There was just nothing in English he wanted to say. He died when Aisling was nine and she felt bad that she hadn't been more upset about it. Especially as he was the first dead person she'd known. And he was always very generous to her, giving her sweets and money every morning as she was going out the door to school. Cathal he ignored, despite the fact that the boy had been named after him.

"Your grandfather always said the purest Irish was spoken on Inis Oirr," her mother told her. "That's why he sent us to the Gaeltacht there."

Aisling wasn't so thrilled to be walking in her mother's well-trodden shoes. But she took the 'us' to mean her mother and her aunt which was an admission that Aunt Kate had made it to being a teenager as you had to be at least fourteen to go.

"Is Jack my uncle or not?" she asked her father.

He was cleaning his Volvo. It was ancient, but her father treated it as if it was about to be entered for the Grand Prix. Washing it every Sunday afternoon seemed far more of a religious ritual for him than going to mass. Aisling knew how much he hated to have this tranquillity disturbed, but it was the only time she could safely speak to him without her mother overhearing.

He'd straightened up and wiped his brow wearily, the sponge still dripping in his other hand. "Of course he's your uncle. Just your mother doesn't like him very much. And I suppose she has her reasons. But just cos you don't like someone, you shouldn't go pretending they don't exist. He always seemed a decent bloke to me. Clever but not stuck up about it. I figured if anyone could find your brother he could. He's had a rough old time of it, sometimes your mother can be a bit harsh."

Aisling told him what Jack had said in his letter.

"Well don't tell your mother. There's no point in getting her hopes up for nothing."

Aisling figured he also didn't want her mother reminded that he'd encouraged Jack to look for Cathal. She promised she wouldn't say anything on the condition that her father agreed to send on any letters she received from Jack to the Gaeltacht.

Her parents drove her as far as Lisdoonvarna. The fair was on and the small town was full of middle-aged bachelor farmers in search of a wife. One or two even cast an eye in her direction, sending a chill down Aisling's spine. The whole notion of matchmaking seemed medieval to her.

"It's like they think they can pick out a wife the same way they pick out a cow."

Her father looked at her in amusement. "Sure they're just lonely, Aisling. Nobody wants to be on their own."

Aisling looked around at the balding men with their beer bellies and found it impossible to muster up any sympathy. Her mother launched into a familiar spiel about how much she was looking forward to Aisling's wedding day. How beautiful she would look in the white dress. How they would spare no expense, she wouldn't have to have it on the cheap the way her parents did.

Aisling was unsure why, but she knew this last comment was intended as a dig at her father. As always, he rose to the bait. "Well that'll be because you have a father prepared to pay for it. It's normally the bride's father who coughs up. But your granddad was too much of a tight old skinflint to give us a penny.'

Her mother said nothing in response, but Aisling could feel her seething for the rest of the morning. Her mother could give off waves of dangerous radiation, like a microwave, only stronger. No one quite knew what the damage from her mother's emissions might be. It amazed Aisling that her mother could harp on so much about how important it was for Aisling to marry when her own marriage seemed to bring her so little pleasure. Aisling had taken to stating ever more forcefully that there was no way she was ever tying the knot. Aisling didn't dare tell her shocked mother that it was because her parents were hardly a walking advertisement for marital bliss. Instead she resorted to legal arguments.

"I might consider it if divorce were to become legal in this country. There's no way I'm going to be stuck with someone I don't want to be with for the rest of my life."

Her mother was appalled by the lack of romanticism in Aisling's approach. She lectured her about the importance of making a commitment to God. Once you'd made a promise, you couldn't just go breaking it.

"We don't want to end up like them crazy Americans. Getting divorced at the drop of a hat. Marrying four or five times. You have to work at relationships, you can't do a runner at the first sign of trouble."

Aisling did think Cathal had been wrong to run away, if that's what he'd done, but she also thought it was wrong to just stick out unhappiness because you'd made a mistake. Surely people deserved a second chance?

It was a relief to finally board the ferry. She went on to the upper deck to wave goodbye to her parents. She fantasised that this was one of those tearful farewells of over a hundred years ago. Instead of going to a tiny island just off the coast for a month, she was emigrating to America and might never see her family or her homeland again. Her mother waved her hands furiously, but her father just raised his hat and swung it once like a flag – or a distress signal. She watched them retreat into black specks among the small crowd gathered at the harbour. They were just two more strangers in a horde of people she didn't know. Watching them disappear was like a weight lifting from her shoulders.

Her mother had said to her, "The place is going to be so quiet without you."

It made Aisling feel bad. Home was pretty silent even when she was there. She couldn't imagine what they would say to each other over dinner. At least it was the summer and they would have tourists for company. The Germans in their fluorescent coloured rain macs and the elderly Americans with green tweed trousers. Ripping the piss out of foreigners was the only thing that got her parents through the long, summer evenings when the Guinness flowed and the fiddle player went quietly mad in the corner. His name was Flynn and no one knew where he came from. That is, they said he was a Traveller.

Aisling's mother wouldn't hear of this. "He's not a Traveller, he's a very nice man."

Aisling just loved his music. It raced with a speed that made her heart want to skip and spin around the room. He had an incredibly soft-spoken accent that she'd never heard before. It wasn't from the city, but it wasn't country either. His whole demeanour was one of calm resignation, but he played the fiddle like a demon, like the notes were eating him alive. The tourists loved him. They would clap and cheer and buy him drinks. They never seemed to notice the edge in his music. A sort of desperation that Aisling had found disturbing since she was a child. He was only there in July and August and no one knew where he spent the rest of the year.

This summer he arrived the day before Aisling left for the Gaeltacht. In a sudden burst of honesty Aisling opened up to Flynn as she placed a pint down in front of a particularly obese Swiss tourist. "I'm leaving tomorrow and the only thing I'll actually miss is your music."

He cradled his fiddle under his chin and stared at her with his sharp green eyes. He winked and said, "Music's the one thing you never leave behind you. You'll still be able to hear me wherever you go. And don't be worrying about your brother. I seen it since he was able to walk; the boy has Traveller blood in him."

Aisling found Flynn cryptic, but at least his words gave her pause for thought. They seemed to cut closer to the heart of the matter than her mother's confused mixture of instructions. In between long lectures about the importance of consuming meat and veg, her mother chewed her lip and told her that boys were only after the one thing. She didn't actually say what this one thing was. Aisling tried to nod her head wisely in an attempt to stop her mother. But her mother felt she had to expand.

"It's supposed to be special, Aisling. You're meant to be in love. It's not like having your breakfast or shaking hands."

Why her mother thought either of these two activities resembled casual sex, Aisling would never know. Secretly she thought she would promise to become a nun if only it would shut her mother up. As she hadn't even so much as kissed a boy as yet, she found the whole conversation excruciatingly embarrassing – even her mother seemed to think she was more sexually advanced than she was.

There were eight girls in her dorm at the Gaeltacht, all her age from all over the country. Two of them were twins from Dublin with posh accents and tales of getting served in under age pubs. Aisling had lived in a pub all her life and she was often called upon to help out. She had learnt the art of how to pull a mean pint of Guinness from the age of ten, but apart from a glass of stout at Christmas, she'd never been allowed anything other than lemonade and coke. Her father had a fanatical attitude to the law and often asked people in their thirties to produce ID. Other drinking holes in the town took a much more lax approach and one or two had a room upstairs that was regularly crowded with teenagers, some of them boys still in their school uniform with only their tie removed. But all the publicans knew who Aisling's father was and were scared of him, so she had about as much chance of being served as a man lost in the Sahara.

Still, the twins, Paula and Jenny, were the only ones whose Irish was as atrocious as Aisling's. They also had a mischievous sense of humour and had, in the course of their short lives, perfected ways to torment and confuse with the sheer impossibility of telling them apart. They constantly pretended to be one another and claimed their mother had mixed them up a few times as babies and to this day even she wasn't sure which was which. Aisling had always wanted a sister, but she wasn't so sure if having one that was like looking into a mirror would be so comforting. She wasn't sure if her mother knew who she was, and this made her feel closer to the twins. She also admired their arrogant attitude to being forced to communicate in their native tongue. The rules of the Gaeltacht quite clearly stated that if you were caught speaking English, you would be sent home.

At first Aisling found it incredibly frustrating, but she adapted quite quickly as she was used to keeping her thoughts to herself. Also there was something about their illicit English conversations about boys late at night in the dorm when they were supposed to be sleeping, that gave them all a sense of camaraderie. That the words themselves were illegal made them infinitely more precious. It was like being part of the French resistance, Aisling thought. Indeed there were many aspects of the Gaeltacht that reminded her of fascism. There was far too much singing and marching for her taste. Her mother had forced her to join the Girl Guides when she was younger but all the skipping in formation and the tying unnecessary knots had bored her to tears. Now at the Gaeltacht she complained about the military nature of the exercises. She felt she was in training for a war. She hadn't really thought about her own patriotism before, but singing the national anthem every day struck her as excessive. She imagined what Cathal would make of the prayers in Gaelic before every meal. Yet, almost in spite of herself, her Irish did improve.

And the island was beautiful. It was so small it would take less than a day to walk around the whole of it. The Gaeltacht was up on a hill as far from the tiny village by the harbour as possible and they weren't allowed go anywhere unsupervised. But the sun shone nearly every day and they were taken down to the beach to go swimming. Aisling was a fine swimmer and something about being surrounded by water on all sides was comforting. She liked that the mainland seemed so far away. Aisling felt as if she were in a foreign country. There were no roads apart from one strip of tarmac that had inspired a couple of locals to bring over a car on the ferry. Apparently they tore up and down the strip for a few hours before becoming bored with the obvious pointlessness of the exercise.

The only real sounds were the cries of seagulls. Aisling imagined the people talked so quietly because they'd never had to raise their voices above the noise of traffic. Apart from the recent outbreak of B&Bs, the island looked much as it must have done for the past few hundred years. There was a wild peacefulness to it as if the land knew that the inhabitants had only got a foothold in the harbour, the rest of the broken green rock belonged to no one.

Aisling wrote to her parents far more often than any of the others. She knew if her mother didn't receive a letter every couple of days, she was likely to become hysterical. In the week leading up to her departure, Aisling noticed her mother becoming more and more nervous. Several times she walked into her own bedroom to find her mother staring out the window. On hearing Aisling, her mother would give a little jump and hurry from the room muttering about looking for something.

Aisling felt like saying, "Look Mam, I'm not going to New York." But she knew her mother wouldn't see that she was trying to allay her fears. She'd just think she was being grossly insensitive.

Her mother sent a note back straight away every time and her father added a few lines at the end. She wished they would write to her individually. She figured they were censoring each other as all they did was describe what the other one was doing. The letters were full of "Your mother has made new curtains for the kitchen," and "Your father has had to take the car in for repairs again." These domestic details were like the still water of a pond that only offered her own reflection.

Aisling had been at the Gaeltacht over a fortnight when a teacher came in one afternoon to tell her with obvious disapproval that there was a man claiming to be her uncle who wanted to see her. Aisling rushed down the stairs in excitement. Maybe her uncle had come to tell her he'd found Cathal.

Jack was standing alone turning his hat round in his hands. His skin was the colour of pale leather, but he seemed even skinnier and rather forlorn. He looked up sensing her presence.

The last of the day's sunlight fell softly through the window above the door lighting up the dust. Jack appeared to be standing in a stream of hazy light.

"Let's get out of here," he said.

Half an hour later they were sitting in the island's one pub. The walls were lined with bits of fishing tackle and a large stuffed swordfish took pride of place over the bar. There was no one there apart from the barman and an old man dressed in black. They stared at Jack and Aisling as they came in, but quickly returned to doing the crossword in the newspaper together. Jack had a pint of Guinness and Aisling a coke and a packet of Tayto crisps.

She'd known from the moment she saw Jack in the hall that he hadn't found her brother. His defeat was written all over him. He kept apologizing as if she'd hired him to do a job he'd proved to be useless at. He told her where he'd been, the hundreds of people he'd talked to, how sometimes he seemed to be within a whisker's breath of finding Cathal. He'd had several definite sightings as well as countless rumours. Then just when he felt sure he must be catching up with him, the trail went dead. At first he couldn't believe it and was sure another clue was bound to turn up. But there was nothing. Jack had hit a brick wall. He hung around aimlessly for a few weeks until the detective told him he was sorry; he couldn't go on taking Jack's money when they seemed to have exhausted all the possibilities.

Then the private detective had said to him with great sympathy, "You know some people just don't want to be found."

It hadn't occurred to Aisling before. She preferred to treat her brother's disappearance as a kind of kidnapping; they just had to locate him and set him free. Jack looked so weary and disappointed that Aisling couldn't bring herself to be angry with him for breaking his promise.

"The trail went dead." The phrase echoed around in her heart. As if she herself were on a path that didn't lead anywhere. She remembered once, when she was really small, she went for a walk with her parents in the mountains. The track got smaller and smaller until eventually it petered out all together. Her mother was irritated they had to turn back and her father announced, "It's a dead end." Aisling had never heard the phrase before and it struck her as oddly sinister. On the way back her father amused himself by telling her the story of a giant spider that ate little girls alive. That night she woke up screaming and her mother called her father a fool. Although she couldn't recall the nightmare itself, the memory was tinged with the emotion of a child's bad dream.

Jack said he'd felt he'd owed it to her to bring her the bad news himself. Also he couldn't face speaking to Aisling's parents. Jack gave her a card with his name and number on it, telling her she probably didn't think he could be relied on any more, but if she was ever in any trouble, she could give him a call. Aisling was surprised to see he was a doctor. In fact according to the card he was a senior cardiothoracic consultant and the head of department. She realised how little she actually knew about her uncle. Why did he go to America to look for a nephew he hadn't seen since he was a child?

She put Jack's card carefully in her pocket and got up to leave. "At least you tried," she said.

It was rather half hearted and not as comforting as she might have wished. She shook Jack's hand rather formally outside the pub. He said he wasn't staying the night, he would get the evening ferry back to the mainland. He looked at her as if she'd broken his heart. Aisling felt uncomfortable; she just wanted to get away.

"You look more and more like your Aunt Kate all the time," he told her softly.

"What happened to her really?" Aisling asked.

"I don't know how I could even begin to explain it to you," Jack replied with a catch in his voice.

She asked the question that had been niggling at her ever since her parents' argument. The time she'd overheard her father admit her brother wasn't his child.

"Are you Cathal's real father?" she asked.

Jack stared at her. "If only you knew how much I wish I was," he said.

Then he turned and walked back up the street.

11

AISLING ENJOYED HER LAST TWO weeks at the Gaeltacht, but it wasn't the same after Jack's visit. That her uncle was in the States looking for her brother had temporarily lifted Aisling's soul. She'd felt less worried because someone was actively searching for him. Now that particular illusion was shattered.

When she got home, she told her father about her uncle's visit as she'd promised Jack she would. She thought he would take it with the fatalistic resignation he seemed to have perfected in dealing with her mother, but his eyes filled with tears. He turned away from her, hiding his emotion behind a box of corn flakes. She had chosen breakfast to tell him because her mother was at mass. She realised guiltily that she had come to believe her mother's accusation that her father had never really liked Cathal and so wasn't that upset at his disappearance. Now she realised in some ways it was hardest on her father, precisely because they hadn't been close.

"Maybe I should go myself," he said.

Aisling just looked at him. They both knew he'd never go because it would be less than pointless. Her father had once attempted to emigrate to London before he was married, but had come back in six months because he said he couldn't follow the underground maps. All those lines in different colours had made him feel terribly confused and he longed for home. Besides, the pub never closed apart from Christmas Day and Good Friday. In her whole life the farthest Aisling had ever seen her father go was Dublin, though he apparently went to Belfast once, which was slightly further. She just couldn't see him wandering around America and it wasn't as if Jack hadn't tried. Her father finished his cereal crouched over the bowl, avoiding Aisling's eyes. He seemed to take Jack's failure on board like it was his own.

Aisling continued to wait, but she wasn't entirely sure what she was waiting for any more. She still thought of Cathal every day but it was more like a dull ache now rather than acute pangs. She threw herself into the distractions of being a teenager. She didn't set out to be a rebel but the world around her seemed so small and petty. She did feel sorry for her parents, but she couldn't help despising them a little. They had lost their only son, but you'd never think it to look at them. Instead they worried their way through hours of conversation about the increased tax on alcohol and cigarettes and the price of petrol. Their concerns struck Aisling as entirely irrelevant to the problems of the world.

She attempted to discuss global warming with her mother but all she said was, "Well if it brings a little more sunshine our way, it'd do wonders for bringing the tourists in."

Aisling despaired of their narrow-mindedness. The planet was crumbling beneath their feet, but all they cared about was whether they could afford new wellies.

When the morning of her sixteenth birthday arrived, her father proudly presented her with the stereo they'd bought her. She had insisted on accompanying him the Saturday before to pick out the one she wanted.

"Don't you trust your father?" her mother moaned.

"I want one with a CD player," Aisling replied. "I don't want to end up with a gramophone."

Her birthday was on a Friday and Aisling begged to have the day off school as a birthday treat.

Her father looked on the point of agreeing, but her mother cut in, "It's only five months now to your Junior Cert. Every day counts. Today could be the very day they cover something that comes up on the exam paper. Aren't we throwing a party for you tonight?"

Aisling found her mother's pessimism tiring but there was no point in arguing. She didn't even particularly want a party. It was her mother's idea but it was so long since her mother had seemed enthusiastic about anything that Aisling didn't like to discourage her.

Aisling arrived in school thinking of Cathal. Over the last few months she'd resigned herself to the idea that she might never see him again. But like a gaslight that had been turned all the way down, hope now flickered and flared up. It wasn't logical she knew, but some of the conviction of her childhood superstitions came back to her. She felt in her bones that Cathal wouldn't want to miss her official emergence as a young woman. Maybe he would feel that whatever it was he had thought her incapable of understanding before, he could confide in her now.

She was so deep in her reverie that she nearly jumped out of her skin when Susan pounced on her from behind. They had become very close although they remained outwardly worlds apart. Susan was going through a Wendy James vamp phase and had bleached her hair white-blond. She wore the palest pink lipstick and various tight pink outfits to match. She despaired of Aisling's weakness for flowing black skirts and deep black eye liner.

"For a pretty girl you do a remarkably good job of looking like something out of the living dead," she'd tell her.

Aisling was never offended by this, nor did she tell Susan that she'd always found the colour pink vaguely repulsive.

Susan dragged her into the ladies' loo. Her friend was even more hysterically excited than usual. "Cheer up Vampira," she laughed. "I've got something to chase those birthday blues away." At which she pulled out the largest joint Aisling had ever seen.

Aisling was momentarily puzzled. "But you only smoke fags."

"True. But sure there's a first time for everything and seeing as it's your birthday, I asked me brother to do me a favour."

Aisling couldn't help but feel touched as they huddled into a cubicle. It was fun to be showing Susan how to do something for once and Aisling sadistically enjoyed seeing Susan's eyes widening, and her desperate coughing as she held the smoke in for too long.

What happened next really was just bad luck. Susan and Aisling had been sharing a first-thing-in-the-morning ciggie in the toilets for months without getting caught so they were shocked when there was a bang on the door.

Miss O'Hanlon's unmistakable nasal piercing voice cut through them. "Who's in there? Come out this instant."

They were too stunned to move. Susan in her panic dropped the jay into the toilet. "I know there's someone in there. And unless you want me to get Mr Cleary to come and remove the door, I suggest you open up."

Mr Cleary was the school janitor – a horrible old man who was always trying to look up their skirts. Aisling nodded and Susan drew back the bolt.

Miss O'Hanlon looked delighted to see them. She took a big sniff and pronounced "Drugs" with considerable satisfaction. She even reached into the toilet bowl and pulled out the dripping remains of the joint.

Aisling couldn't help thinking that being sixteen couldn't have got off to a worse start. She was back in the hated wooden chair in Sr. Agnes's office. Susan was sitting next to her. She tried glancing sideways to catch her eye, but Susan was examining her nails with an air of deep concentration. She did this when she was really worried.

Aisling knew that her birthday would not be taken into account as a mitigating circumstance. In the headmistress's mind there was absolutely no difference between smoking marijuana and injecting heroin. Drugs were drugs and they did not exist in her school. Aisling could almost see Sr. Agnes drawing up battle plans in her mind in the face of this new threat. The war on drugs had finally reached her little backwater and she was not going to be conquered without a fight. Admitting that the joint was a birthday present was only going to cast Susan in the role of evil drug dealer corrupting innocents. The most likely assumption, already, was that the hashish was entirely Susan's idea. While Aisling was considered by her teachers to be troubled and disturbed, Susan was seen as an outrageous slut and full-blown degenerate. But Aisling could sense that trying to explain Susan had never smoked before, but was only doing it for her sake, wasn't going to help. There was this unbridgeable gap between reality and the official view of their behaviour.

Sr. Agnes was already on the phone telling Mrs FitzSimon that Susan had left her with no option but to expel her. Susan's face had turned an ashen colour. Maybe they'd laugh about this one day, but Aisling found it difficult to imagine. Her stomach had turned to mush and she'd lost all feeling in her legs. Her mother was going to hold this against her for the rest of her life. Sr. Agnes was even now calling the guards.

The girls had already been subjected to an hour's interrogation as to where the drugs came from. There was no way Susan was going to drag her brother into this. He was a married man with a small child and a respectable job in the post office. He was about as far away from Sr. Agnes's image of a drug pusher in a long leather coat hanging round playgrounds and destroying innocent young lives as it was possible to get. Aisling refused to crack under pressure. She'd often daydreamed masochistically about being interrogated by Nazis, but she now discovered it wasn't as easy to be a hero as she'd imagined. Plus Sr. Agnes could have easily worked with the Gestapo. She had a relentless way of breaking you down.

"But you must have got the drugs from somewhere?" she asked for the millionth time.

For once all Aisling wanted to do was go home. Or at the very least have a lawyer present. But the headmistress felt completely within her rights to torture them into confessing their drug addiction. Just when Aisling thought things couldn't get any worse, her mother arrived. Sr. Agnes must have rung her even before Aisling was settled into the interrogation chair. Her mother took one look at Aisling in her school uniform and burst into tears. She began a confused rambling about how she'd just been about to collect her birthday cake. Aisling couldn't help wishing her mother had more of a sense of dignity. Also she preferred the hard coldness of her mother's usual disappointment to this rare display of emotion.

Even as a small kid, Aisling often felt she'd much rather receive a good beating with the wooden spoon than have to face her mother's pained, "But why did you do it?" Aisling never knew why she did it or if she did, she couldn't articulate it.

Even Sr. Agnes looked as if Aisling's mother's tears had taken the wind out of her sails. Juvenile delinquents were always easier to deal with than sobbing mothers. Aisling glanced at Susan who clearly wished she could curl up and die. She wasn't used to this either – her own mother had a far more robust approach to disciplining her daughter. Mrs FitzSimon would be absolutely furious, but she wouldn't give off the worrying sense that she'd never get over it.

Aisling saw a way to at least get Susan off the hook.

"It was my joint," she announced. "Susan was just with me. She didn't smoke any of it I swear. She tried to tell me it wasn't a good idea."

Susan stared at her in open mouthed amazement. She was about to protest Aisling's version of events but Aisling glared at her so fiercely that she just closed her mouth.

As a result of this confession and her mother's tears, Aisling and Susan were eventually released and sent home in disgrace. They had a second alone as Aisling's mother opened up the car.

Susan looked tearful herself. "You didn't have to take the blame like that." Aisling shrugged.

Susan gave her a quick hug. "Well I doubt I'll be allowed come to the party, but happy birthday."

They both managed a half laugh.

Susan quickly turned away before hers became a sob. Sr. Agnes had darkly informed her that while she had yet again escaped expulsion by the skin of her teeth, if Susan were to put so much as a toe out of place from here on in, she would be out that door in a thrice and all her mother's pleading and begging wouldn't make an ounce of difference. Susan was forced to promise she would be a reformed character. Sr. Agnes sincerely hoped that Susan's brush with hard core drugs would make her reconsider where her young life was going.

Then she informed Aisling's mother that while she would like to be able to help Aisling, she couldn't be seen to tolerate drug abuse in her school. She was terribly sorry but she thought it might be for the best if her daughter considered pursuing her education elsewhere. Aisling's mother had started to shake ever so slightly and, without another word, she took Aisling's arm in a vice like grip and pulled her out of Sr. Agnes's office. She then marched off leaving Aisling and Susan to stumble after her.

Aisling assumed the party would be cancelled, but she'd underestimated, yet again, her mother's concern with appearances. Even if her daughter had brought shame on the whole family by being expelled from the local school, something even Cathal hadn't managed, there was no need to draw attention to the fact by turning people away at the door. Her mother's ability to carry on regardless to what she felt inside was impressive. Aisling tried to tell her she was no longer in the mood for a party, but her mother just glared at her in disgust.

"This party is happening whether you like it or not," she informed Aisling, making it quite clear that the aim was no longer to celebrate her daughter's birthday.

The party turned out to be a surprising success. People seemed to really enjoy themselves. Far more came than Aisling would ever have imagined possible. The news that Aisling and Susan had been caught smoking blow in the girl's loo had spread around the school like wildfire. Aisling had to cope with offers of sympathy and support from people who normally wouldn't lower themselves to speak to her. She'd officially become an admired rebel. Unfortunately she only had to think of her mother lying in bed in the next room with a supposed migraine while the music thumped from Aisling's new stereo to be reminded that being expelled wasn't cool. She was really in deep shit now. She locked herself in the bathroom and tried to rectify the damage tears were doing to her mascara.

She clutched the sink and found herself able to pray with total sincerity for the first time. "Please God, if you were ever planning to bring Cathal back to us, let it be tonight."

As she came out of the loo, a drunken boy in the year below her, whose name she couldn't remember, told her she was beautiful. Then he puked, splattering her shoes. She felt bad because, presumably, he'd been waiting to be sick in the toilet rather than all over her mother's prized rug. Aisling had sat in there for a good twenty minutes ignoring the banging on the door. She just wanted to be on her own for God's sakes. Was she expected to take the blame for everything that went wrong?

Aisling put on her coat and slipped out into the tiny yard. She really didn't feel like playing hostess. It was a freezing cold night but the sky was clear and she could see an extraordinary number of stars. As a kid she'd told Cathal she wanted to be the first woman to walk on the moon. He'd been very encouraging, but when she got to secondary and discovered that maths was her weakest subject, she'd adapted her ambitions. Somewhere after long division it all got far too complicated and moon walking no longer struck her as a possibility. For a while she'd thought she'd content herself with being a scientist on earth, but now peering up at the sky, she felt she was completely illiterate when it came to reading the heavens.

"Cathal, you bastard, where the fuck are you?" She said it out loud.

As if they were still children playing hide-n-seek and he was cheating again by going outside, using his superior strength to climb up the neighbour's tree. She heard a sound above her and looked up in fright, but it was only one of the many stray cats that haunted the yard. The neighbour had been an ancient old woman with a shock of white curly hair. Cathal was convinced she was a witch. She'd owned at least twenty cats and when she died a few years ago, the cats stayed on. Aisling's mother called the RSPCA who'd succeeded in taking some of them away. But the cleverer ones remained at liberty. The cat staring at her now was a huge black tom with round yellow eyes. He hissed at her and then turned away in disdain. She watched him elegantly leaping from the tree to the neighbour's roof and slipping shadow like into the night.

Cathal wasn't coming back and that was that. The finality of this realization made Aisling's teeth chatter. She put her hands in her pockets and took out her wallet. In it she kept a picture of Cathal and herself at her eighth birthday. He was blowing one of those silly paper party whistles into her face and they were both laughing hysterically. She considered tearing the photo into pieces. But it seemed ridiculously melodramatic. It was a nice photo. She folded it and put it back.

She pulled out Jack's card instead. She hadn't heard from him since they'd said goodbye on the island. She wondered if he knew it was her birthday. She didn't see what help he could be, but at least he didn't live in this nasty little town, and he might listen to her properly. Aisling checked she had enough change for the phone booth at the end of the road and let herself out the back gate. She could hear the sounds of the party in full flow, retreating behind her as she walked away.

12

JACK WAS DESPERATELY LOOKING FOR a way to stop the wedding, but he had no idea how to do it without making Kate hate him forever. He had spent the four days since she'd said goodbye to him in a kind of daze. He ate nothing. Brendan was convinced he was ill, but he refused to discuss what was troubling him.

It almost seemed accidental when Jack found himself outside O'Neill's pub that Thursday evening, the night before the wedding. He didn't dare go in. Instead he peered through a small side window at the warm, yellow interior. It was full of people. Mainly men in suits enjoying a pint after a hard day at the office. It seemed like the snuggest, most lovely place in the world but he couldn't go inside. It took him a while to spot Kate on a stool in a far corner. She still had her coat on and he couldn't see the expression on her face. He nearly jumped out of his skin when he felt a hand on his shoulder.

Troy was looking at him with a mixture of excited anticipation and apprehension. "What's going on, man?"

Jack stared at him and swallowed. The lie rolled off his tongue before his brain had even formulated the words. "Nothing. Everything's grand. Just Kate can't meet you tonight."

Troy was startled. "But the wedding's tomorrow? She can't have changed her mind?"

No such luck, thought Jack. "Course not," he replied. "But there's been a slight change of plan. Come on and I'll get you a drink and explain."

Troy was so worried that it didn't even strike him as odd that Jack didn't lead him into O'Neill's pub, but hurried across the road into another one. There were no seats apart from a stool at the bar. Jack insisted that Troy take it while he remained standing. This gave him a slight height advantage, and as he ordered Troy a double whiskey and a Guinness for himself, Jack's mind was working overtime on how he could convince Troy the situation was under control.

"It's Kate's sister Pat. She really isn't happy about this wedding. Kate was staying with her but yesterday she went and rang their father. Kate's had to go into hiding. Her sister knew you were meeting in O'Neill's tonight and Kate was scared her father would turn up and clock you one.'

Troy shook his head in despair. "Ah, man, if only she'd just stayed with you, she'd have been much better off."

95

Jack paused briefly. "Look don't worry about it. She's still going to be there, all in white, tomorrow. She just didn't want to risk coming out tonight. Only the three of us know which church it is. Everything will be fine."

Troy looked grateful for Jack's reassurance. "Yeah she's gonna be so beautiful." He took out a small box out of his pocket and opened it up. Inside lay two gold rings. "I kind of wanted to show them to her before-hand, but do they look okay to you?"

"Perfect," Jack managed to say.

Troy laughed nervously. "Knowing my luck I've probably got totally the wrong ring size. Have you noticed she's got the most incredibly slender fingers?"

Jack, who'd spent countless hours admiring the elegance of Kate's hands, drew his pint to his mouth to cover his emotions. "Don't be worry-ing," he told Troy. "Sure anyway it's bad luck to see the bride the night before the wedding."

"I guess so." Troy placed the rings in Jack's hand.

Jack was momentarily alarmed before he remembered that Troy had no idea Kate had asked him not to be the best man.

"Don't lose them. See I had them engraved on the inside with our names and the date we met."

The rings burned Jack's skin and he quickly placed them back in their box and inside his jacket pocket. "You can count on me," he said to Troy.

Troy was still quite nervous and thought maybe he should go back to his hotel room. Jack was seized with terror at the possibility of Kate spotting them walking out.

"Sure you won't be able to sleep anyhow," he convinced Troy easily. "And this is the closest you're going to get to a stag night." He ordered another round of drinks.

The more drunk Troy got, the more sentimental he became. It was torture to listen to, but everything he said about Kate was true. They were the last ones to be kicked out of the pub. O'Neill's across the road had already pulled down its shutters. Jack suggested Troy kip at his place. He wanted to keep an eye on him and make sure he wasn't drunkenly tempted to ring Kate's sister. Jack had said Kate was staying with a friend and he didn't have the number. Anyway the bride and groom were not meant to have any contact the night before the big day. Troy like most sailors was superstitious and accepted the logic of this, putting his arm around Jack as they stumbled home together.

Troy's speech was slightly slurred as he confessed, 'You know man, the only real fear I got, the one big thing that's scaring the shit out of me, is that I'm not good enough for her. I ain't got any money, I drink too much, I'm just not special the way she is. You know what I mean?"

Again Jack couldn't help but agree.

When they got back to the bedsit, Troy asked for some whiskey. Jack knew Brendan kept a bottle somewhere, but he wasn't quite sure where. Thankfully Brendan came stumbling in at that moment, his hair slick with sweat. Troy was delighted to see him and once Brendan heard about the impending wedding he insisted on toasting the groom. Troy explained that it was a very hush hush affair, but he was adamant that Brendan should be there.

"Jack and Kate's sister were going to be the witnesses but I don't think she wants to come any more. Be really great to have you instead."

Brendan looked chuffed. "Well I've only got me suit for work to wear like, but I do love a good wedding. There's nothing like people happy and in love to warm the heart."

The phone rang and Jack hurried to answer it.

It was Kate. Her voice sounded strained. "Have you heard from Troy?" she asked.

Jack hesitated. All Troy's drunken declarations of love hadn't made Jack feel as bad as the obvious desperation in Kate's tone. He didn't even know what he'd hoped to achieve by dragging Troy away from O'Neill's. He was only postponing the inevitable. But somehow he couldn't stop.

"No, I haven't," he answered.

"I waited and waited for hours but he never showed," Kate's voice cracked. "Just if he does get in touch, tell him to ring me. The wedding's tomorrow but I'm not showing up if I don't hear from him. Pat says he's making a fool of me."

With that she hung up. Maybe if she'd stayed on the line longer, he would have told her the truth. But he could always have rung her back. He didn't, and when Brendan asked him if that was his lady love calling, he just squeezed out a half smile that was more like a grimace. It was slowly dawning on him that he might be able to get away with this. He just needed to bide his time and pray that Kate didn't change her mind.

The next morning was bright and sunny. A perfect day to get married. Yet having to stand by Troy at the altar while he kept looking over his shoulder for his bride to be was the closest Jack felt he had come to experiencing hell. He was at least as anxious that Kate would turn up as Troy was that she wouldn't.

The church was empty apart from two old women at the back on their knees quietly reciting the rosary. The priest kept looking impatiently at his watch.

"I'm very sorry," he said after what seemed an eternity. "But I have a christening this afternoon and I do need to get the church ready."

Brendan looked deeply uncomfortable. "Ah now," he said, "She might get here yet. You know traffic's terrible."

The priest sighed but agreed to wait another half hour.

Troy hung his head like a man condemned. Eventually he gasped, "She's not coming." He stormed out of the church. Brendan ran after him.

Jack found himself alone with the priest. "I'm sorry to have put you to all this trouble for nothing, Father."

"Well," the priest said, "it's happened to me before. Sure the workings of the human heart are nearly as great a mystery as God Himself."

13

JACK SPENT MANY POINTLESS HOURS justifying his actions to himself. The fact that he couldn't tell anyone what he'd done meant his inner trial continued in an endless loop. Kate was too young to be running away to America leaving all her family and friends behind. She needed to finish her education. Troy was a sailor and a drunk. He would probably have abandoned her the moment they got there. Jack had saved her from a life of miserable loneliness and deprivation. He would nearly reach the point of convincing himself when the image of Kate sitting alone in O'Neill's would rise up to accuse him.

The whole thing seemed unreal. As if it had been another man who'd stood in that church with Troy, and Jack was only dealing with the consequences.

Back at Jack's flat, Troy asked if he could make a few calls. Jack tried to eavesdrop but Troy's voice was too low to make out the words.

When he came back up to the bed-sit, Troy said, "I rang Kate's sister. Looked up the number of the shop in the phone book."

Jack's heart was in his mouth.

"Some lady said Pat wasn't there. I talked to the guys on my ship. They set sail tomorrow. They told me I should forget about Kate and go with them."

"Listen, boy," said Brendan, "maybe you should try talking to your girlfriend. You know there might be a reasonable explanation. Like she got the date mixed up or…"

Jack could've killed Brendan

Troy looked desperate. "I don't even know where she is. Maybe I should go round to her sister's? I know she hates me but if she'd just get a message to Kate…"

Jack nearly choked at the thought of Kate finding out what he'd done. "I'll go round for you if you like. She might be more likely to listen to me."

Troy put his hand on Jack's shoulder and peered at him intensely. "Just tell her to let Kate know my train is at ten o'clock. Tell her I don't care about getting married, I only want to see her before I go. I need to understand why she changed her mind."

Jack borrowed Brendan's battered car and drove around the streets of Dublin for over three hours, thinking, "I can't go through with this, I'm going to have to tell Troy what I've done."

Somehow the idea of Troy beating him to a pulp was nothing compared to his fear of how much Kate would despise him when she found out. What had started out as a desperate time buying measure now looked like it might solve all his problems. But the more he thought about it, the more awful he felt. He told himself he wanted to save Kate from a marriage he was convinced would be a disaster. But deep down he knew he also wanted to have her for himself.

At half past nine he headed down to the train station. It was dark and the wind was damp and bitter. Troy was standing forlornly under a street lamp. He rushed towards Jack, but then faltered when he saw he was on his own.

"She's not coming, is she?" All the usual exuberance had seeped out of Troy. He looked utterly defeated.

This had gone far enough. Jack decided he couldn't really allow Troy to think Kate had abandoned him. It was too cruel. "Listen…"

"I should've guessed it when she didn't turn up in the pub. She doesn't give a damn about me. It was just a dream I was telling myself."

"Listen I'm terribly sorry…"

Troy shrugged angrily. "Don't be, man. She's just some dumb kid I went and fell for. I must be going crazy with homesickness or something. I'll get over her in no time, I got lots of other girlfriends."

Jack found himself hesitating. If Troy really loved her, wouldn't he insist on seeing her? Wouldn't he stick around to find out what really happened instead of getting on the next boat out?

"Hell I'm way too young to be getting married. I got lots of wild oats still to sow. As my skipper's always saying, 'That's the joy of the navy, meeting foreign women and screwing them.'" With that Troy picked up his bag and slung it over his shoulder.

Jack hated him for his crudity and for the idea that Kate was just one of many women he'd had.

Still Troy gave him a big hug. "Take care, Jack. Even though right now I kind of wish I'd just stayed at the bottom of the ocean, I'll always be grateful for all you've done for me."

Jack felt sick to his stomach. He spent the next two days in bed. He felt weak and feverish. Brendan insisted on feeding him big bowls of chicken noodle soup. Jack protested at first, but then he drank them down. He needed all the nourishment he could get, even if he didn't feel he deserved it.

He was desperately worried about Kate, but also unsure if he could face her. There was the added complication that he was meant to think she was on her way to America. He didn't want to have to admit that he'd seen Troy before he left. Claiming total ignorance of Troy's motivations seemed the wisest option. He hoped she might ring him again, but the days passed in silence. He couldn't stand it, he had to know if she was okay.

But it was a dream that absolutely convinced him he must see her. He was standing on the beach and Kate was further down by the water's edge. She turned to him and smiled, then proceeded to walk into the waves. He ran to stop her, but he seemed to be running and running without getting any closer. What if in the shock of Troy not showing up, she'd done herself harm? He didn't think that the end of her romance with Troy was likely to lead to any long term damage. After all, she was only seventeen, and they'd only known each other for a matter of weeks. She had her whole life ahead of her to forget about Troy. Quite why he was so convinced Kate was suffering a teenage crush, while he, who was only two years older, was in the grips of true love, was a question he buried in the back of his head.

Jack took Brendan's car and drove deep into the Dublin Wicklow Mountains to get rid of the rings. There wasn't another soul to be seen. The heather was in full bloom and he sprang through a field of gorgeous purple. He walked for hours drinking up the freshness of the air in an effort to get the fuzziness out of his mind. The day was far clearer than his conscience. He climbed until he could see far down into the valley below. It was mainly forest and there were no signs of human habitation – only half an hour outside of Dublin, and it was as if he'd found another planet.

Brendan had told him these hills were full of the undiscovered bodies of those who'd fallen foul of the Republican movement. "They stick them in the boot. Drive up into the Wicklow Mountains, get them to dig their own graves, bullet in the back of the head, and Bob's your uncle. Sure they'd never find you for another five hundred years."

Jack shivered as he took out the box with the rings. He'd planned to dig a small hole and bury them, but thinking of Brendan's words, he felt like a criminal about to destroy the evidence, like throwing them away would be an admission that he'd done something terrible. In the end he closed the box and put it back in his pocket.

He went back to the car, cold and exhausted, feeling like he had blood on his hands. He drove straight to Pat's shop. Although it was dark when he got there, the small grocery was still open. He sat in the car with the engine running unsure what to do, unable to think of a single believable excuse to go in. He wondered if Pat would be working. For over an hour he waited, feeling utterly paralysed.

In the end, he worked up the nerve to go buy a packet of fags. The bell on the door jingled as he opened it and gave him a fright. The small corner shop was overwhelmingly bright. There were no other customers. Jack's hands shook as he pointed to the cigarettes he wanted and he dropped his wallet when he reached for his money. Finally he glanced sideways at the cashier.

A pleasant looking woman in her mid fifties was peering at him curiously. "Can I get you anything else?"

He realised he was just standing there like an idiot and handed his money over quickly. He couldn't tell if he was more relieved or disappointed that it wasn't Pat. "Awful chilly night," the shopkeeper said conversationally.

Her friendliness gave him courage. "Was just wondering if Pat O'Rourke still worked here?"

"She does indeed. She lives above. Are you a friend of hers?"

"Sort of," replied Jack. Then realising this might sound odd, he hurriedly added, "She was at school with my sister."

"Well she's not around at the moment I'm afraid. She's gone home to the countryside."

"That's a shame," said Jack, wondering how he could get more information.

Luckily the shop assistant was only too happy to gossip. "She'll be back next week though. She was only taking her sister home. Poor girl was engaged to be married to some sailor fella and didn't he up and leave her. The sister Caitriona I'm talking about now. Not Pat."

Jack nodded.

"Course you know what they say about sailors. A different woman in every port. Mind you that's true of a lot of men." The woman sighed at this insight into the male gender.

Jack thanked her and turned to go.

"What's your name, love, and I'll tell Pat you dropped by?"

Jack didn't even pause. "Tell her Brendan says hello."

He rushed into the relative safety of his cousin's car. The engine cut twice on the journey, and at one point, he thought he might have to push the thing the rest of the way. But even this didn't bother him much. Kate had gone back home – he felt infinitely better for knowing where she was.

14

JACK ARRIVED AT HIS FATHER'S house in the early evening in the middle of the week. His father was alarmed to see him again so soon.

"I hope you're not feeling obliged on my account. Of course I'm delighted to see you, but your study is what comes first. I don't want you missing any more lectures." Coursework was the last thing on Jack's mind, but he couldn't tell his father that. Instead he gave his father the usual brush off before heading to O'Rourke's pub.

On the way, Jack ran over plausible reasons he could give Kate as to why he was home again so soon. He could say his father wasn't very well but his father drank in O'Rourke's and if Kate had seen him knocking back pints the night before, she would find his sudden illness odd. Maybe he could claim he hadn't been very well himself, he had the flu and thought he would return for a bit of home comfort to get his health back. Not that his father was any use at playing nurse, but Kate didn't necessarily know that. And saying he was ill wasn't so much a lie as an adaptation of the truth.

Jack prepared himself for being totally shocked to see Kate. He had to act as if until that moment he'd assumed she was in the States. But when he walked in there was no sign of Kate. Pat was working behind the bar.

Jack ordered a pint and asked as casually as possible, "So what brings you back here?"

"Can't I visit my own home without having a particular reason?" Pat snapped at him and walked off.

Jack wanted to ask her if she had any news from Kate, but he didn't dare, so retreated to a corner. His patience paid off eventually. As it turned out he didn't have to fake surprise at seeing Kate. She looked so different it was shocking. Her face had become pale and drawn and there were huge dark circles under her eyes. She was still beautiful, but now instead of a healthy, laughing, young woman, it was the fragile beauty of an invalid. She reminded Jack of a picture he'd seen of a singer in 'La Traviata,' which was his mother's favourite opera. The photo was on the sleeve of an album of the opera she'd loved to play despite the record being scratched from overuse. It had always struck Jack that the closer the heroine came to dying of consumption, the better she sang.

Kate was descending the stairs from the flat above and as she was looking at the ground, she didn't notice Jack. He half stood up out of his seat and she glanced in his direction. She didn't look remotely pleased to see him, but still she did come over. With her standing in front of him, the full reality of what he'd done finally hit him. If she ever found out the truth, she'd kill him.

"I thought... well em I thought..." He stumbled over the words and could feel himself flushing crimson.

Thankfully she interrupted him. "You thought I was in America. Well I'm not. It turns out you were right all along. It was just a crazy dream. Troy never had any intentions of going through with it. It was only a game to him."

The bitterness in her voice was so totally unlike her that Jack wondered if he hadn't underestimated what a blow Troy supposedly standing her up must have been.

"He was never good enough for you," he stammered partly in his own defence.

"He used to tell me I was an angel. But my wings are long gone now." With that Kate walked away.

What had he expected? He was hardly going to waltz in here and pick up where Troy left off. He hated to see her hurt like that and swore to himself that he'd give her a far happier life than she'd ever have had with Troy. He'd take her to Hollywood, round the whole world, to the moon and back if she wanted. It was for the best, she just needed a little while to realise that. Of course she'd miss Troy, but the memory would fade and soon it would be as if she'd never known him. She was never meant to meet him. It was all an unfortunate accident. A kind of drowning where he'd pulled her out of the water just in time.

Pat appeared beside Jack. She leaned in low, and with a voice full of threat, said quietly, "I think it's best if you leave my sister alone. She's been through a bit of a rough time."

Jack was taken aback. "I only want to help her," he replied.

"Well your friend the American certainly didn't do her any favours."

"He wasn't my friend. I barely knew him," Jack protested.

"No," said Pat slowly. "I don't suppose he was." She narrowed her eyes at Jack. A trick she'd clearly learnt from her father.

15

AISLING'S HEART WAS BEATING HARD in her chest as she put the coins in the slot. The phone rang into emptiness. It seemed in keeping with this horrible night that Jack wouldn't be in and Aisling was about to hang up when she heard "Hello?"

Jack had clearly run for the phone and sounded out of breath. Now that she'd got through, Aisling was at a loss what to say. How could she explain about the cat on the rooftops, smoking pot in the loo, and how because Cathal had failed to show for her sweet sixteenth, she'd been seized with the conviction she'd never see him again?

Jack repeated, "Hello? Anyone there?"

"It's me," said Aisling.

A pronounced silence followed.

"Aisling, your niece."

Jack's voice returned. "God for a second there I thought you were someone else. It's lovely to hear from you."

Jack spoke with such genuine enthusiasm that Aisling regained her confidence. She stumbled through the story of her expulsion and Jack listened intently, only asking the odd question. The pips on the phone went because she had no more money, so he asked for the number to ring her back. But some witless vandal had scratched it out and written 'Tanya sucks dick' in red marker underneath instead. The silence clicked in and Aisling found herself listening to the hollow ringing of a dial tone. She hung up the receiver in defeat. What could her uncle do anyway? He'd done his best to bring Cathal back and, apart from that, what was done was done.

Aisling wandered slowly back up the road towards home. She didn't know if she could face the dregs of the party. She had no money but she did have Jack's address. She considered trying to hitch to Dublin. It would take her most of the night but she'd get there eventually. She certainly didn't want to end up an unidentified body in a shallow grave, but her birthday was making her feel so bleak, she thought it might be worth the risk. She remembered that a girl two years ahead of her in school had gotten a lift home one night and had never been seen again. She was spotted getting into a blue car with a man with a beard and that was the last of her. Aisling had followed the story with great interest. Since her brother vanished, she had taken up following missing persons' stories practically as a hobby.

These thoughts were running through her head when, to her great surprise, she met her father walking in the middle of the empty street. She hadn't seen him since she'd got home from her school interrogation. As her mother explained what shame their daughter had brought on the family, her father's face had looked thunder, but he'd said remarkably little. Since then, he seemed to have been in hiding for the whole evening.

"Ah there you are." He stopped and stared at Aisling. "I thought I'd come looking for you."

He was wearing his battered old overcoat that her mother was always on at him to throw away. It was an odd shade of green, "The colour of pigeon shit," her mother would say, and was slightly too small for him. He'd had it for years and Aisling couldn't remember when it fitted him properly.

Aisling was all set for a lecture after disappearing in the middle of the night. "Well Squirrel," her father said, "that was a silly thing to do." He took her hand and they walked back to the pub together in silence.

Squirrel was the nickname her father had given her, apparently because as a baby she loved eating the pub's peanuts. He hadn't called her that for years. Not since she'd told him it was embarrassing.

She felt as if she was six years old again. It was rather comforting. She remembered how her father used to sit her up on the bar while he served drinks, as all the customers admired her pigtails. She loved watching her father at work. He seemed so strong and sure and efficient – the master of all he surveyed – and she was dead proud to have a father like that to look up to. It seemed like a hundred years since he'd held her hand.

When they got in, her father put his years of experience to use and had the place cleared inside fifteen minutes. His familiar cry, "Time's up. Have ye's no homes to go to?" struck Aisling as comical, but she realised the pub was her home. Running away wasn't going to solve anything.

Aisling's mother managed to get her accepted at the local technical college where students were more interested in pursuing a trade than academics. Aisling wondered if she was to be condemned to a life of plumbing. Or, worse still, nail polishing. Holy Faith Convent was a palace of luxury compared to the tech. The building itself was a Victorian hulk that looked far more like a prison than a school, and the students made Susan seem subtle. They nearly all wore their hair in what was known as a 'ripple' which basically involved bleaching it, perming it into scraggly curls, and scraping it back off their heads in a large banana clip. To them, Aisling was a suspicious convent girl, but when they learnt she'd been expelled and the reasons why, they figured she couldn't be all bad. Aisling had always been led to believe that the girls in the tech were thick, so stupid as to be bordering on vegetables. But Aisling discovered many of them had a keen wit and even if they were rather crude, at least they knew how to have a bit of a laugh.

Still Aisling found the whole place rather depressing and kept herself to herself. The one person she kept in proper contact with from her old school was Susan. All of Susan's siblings had gone to the tech, so she wasn't going to turn her nose up. In some ways, she said, she envied Aisling.

"I swear Ash," she moaned as she sucked on a Marlboro light. "You'd think we were after murdering somebody the way they carry on. I feel like saying to Miss O'Hanlon, it was only a bloody joint, it's not like she caught me trying to flush a baby down the loo. They never give me a moment's peace, they're just dying to catch me doing something else."

In contrast at the tech if you didn't turn up for class, no one was that bothered, often, Aisling didn't go in at all. Whatever tiny interest she'd still had in studying had evaporated. Her exams were in a month and her mother routinely locked her in her room to work, only letting her out to go to the toilet or to eat. Television was strictly forbidden as well as most other forms of entertainment. But her mother didn't know Aisling quite easily spent whole evenings staring out her bedroom window watching the drunks stumbling from the bar to find their way home.

Aisling had sat her exams in a kind of dream. The papers didn't seem to have any real connection to her life. She knew they didn't go well. Still even she was shocked at how bad her results were.

Her mother's lips were the thinnest she'd ever seen them. "Did you even pick up a pen when you were in there?"

Aisling shrugged. She wasn't in the mood for her mother's sarcasm. She knew her life was going nowhere, she just couldn't bring herself to care that much. She could see herself rotting in this small town forever and it filled her with panic and despair. But there didn't seem to be a way out.

But her father's anger cut through her feigned indifference. "Such a waste," he kept repeating.

Aisling didn't know if he meant she could do a lot better or if he was referring to the effort involved in bringing her into the world. He was yelling at her the way she'd only ever heard him shout at Cathal. Unlike her brother, it didn't make her feel defiant. She felt very small and afraid.

"What's wrong with young people these days? Don't you have any ambition? Don't you want to do something with your life? Instead of just smoking it away?"

Aisling tried her best not to, but she couldn't hold back the tears.

"Oh for God's sakes, don't cry," her father shouted. "I can't stand when women start crying." He walked out of the kitchen slamming the door behind him.

That evening Aisling called Jack. Since the night of her birthday party, he'd taken to ringing her now and again to see how she was getting on.

Her mother hated it when he called and would only say, "It's that man again."

But Aisling felt like Jack was her one link with the outside world. She tried to explain to him how she felt her hometown suffered from inbreeding of the soul.

"I'm telling you I go to school with people who've barely been to the next county. They've never gone to Dublin and they've no desire to. They think it's dangerous. Bloke in my woodwork class says to me yesterday, "Why would you want to spend all that money on flights when you can see all them foreign places on the telly?"

Jack laughed. The tech was mixed, but Aisling was the only girl in her woodwork class, and none of the boys would be caught dead doing home economics. Aisling didn't particularly enjoy carving up bits of wood, but she didn't dislike it any more than her other subjects. She stuck with it purely to irritate the teacher, who on her first day, was convinced she'd got her classrooms mixed up. He looked deeply puzzled as she explained that she was in the right place. She had chosen to sign up for his class.

"They're just so stuck in their thinking," Aisling continued. "It's like there's a little label and box for every situation. It's not so much that I object to how they live, it's the fact it's never occurred to them there might be any other way. They are so smug it makes me want to scream."

"I see what you're saying but you know sometimes I kind of miss that sense of certainty." Jack's voice was warm with sympathy.

"Trust me. You wouldn't feel nostalgic about it if you actually had to live here."

"Well I've been thinking," her uncle paused. "Why don't you go to school in Dublin?

Aisling sighed down the phone. "If only there was any possibility of that."

"I've made a few inquiries and there's a very good private school just round the corner from here. I'd pay your fees and you could stay with me."

Aisling was momentarily speechless. This was beyond her wildest dreams.

"My mam would never agree to that."

"Let me speak to your father." Jack was full of determination.

As Aisling anticipated, the very idea made her mother white with cold fury. "You're not even seventeen yet. You can't possibly be thinking of leaving home."

Aisling sensed her mother wondering what she did that was so terribly wrong that all her children were dying to get away from her. "It's not you, Mam, really. It's just this town, and I'm not learning anything in that tech."

Aisling didn't believe this was the tech's fault, but she knew her parents did. Her mother was under the illusion that if Aisling was still in the convent, she'd be getting straight 'A's.

Her father intervened carefully. "Well it is a very generous offer and Aisling can't continue the way she's going. She'll end up with no qualifications at all."

"You know how I feel about that man and I don't accept charity." Her mother's voice had a tremble in it.

"Pat, he's only trying to make up for the past, and I'd say he owes us, wouldn't you?"

Aisling looked from one parent's face to the other. She felt she was eavesdropping on some epic battle from years ago that she knew nothing about. Her future seemed to be dependent on a family history she wasn't privy to.

"You're not going and that's that," her mother pronounced.

Her father's voice was angry but clear. "This is an opportunity for her to get a proper education. She's my daughter too and I'm not going to let you throw this chance away just cos of bad blood between you and Jack."

"Bad blood," her mother was outraged. "Is that all you think it is?"

Her father took a deep breath. "You have to let it go, love. That's the past. This is Aisling's future we're talking about."

Aisling felt terrible that she'd suddenly become the focus of the ongoing conflict between her parents. She wasn't sure their marriage could survive much more strain. Her mother looked like she'd love to strangle her faher. But to Aisling's great surprise, she folded as easily as a house of cards.

"All right Martin. If you really think it's for the best. But I've a bad feeling about it."

Her father straightened himself in his chair adjusting his shoulders to this new burden of responsibility. Aisling couldn't quite believe they were agreeing to let her go. She could have cried with happiness. She pinched herself to make sure she wasn't dreaming. A whole new life. In Dublin.

16

WHEN AISLING TOLD SUSAN SHE was moving to live with her uncle, her friend started to cry. "I'm dead pleased for you Ash, I am," Susan sobbed. "It's just you're leaving me behind in this shit hole."

Susan could be as cutting in her comments about small town Irish life as Aisling, but it'd never occurred to Aisling that she was anywhere near as desperate as herself to leave. After all Susan had a big family, loads of other friends, and no shortage of boys following her around.

"That bunch of morons." Susan dismissed all her relatives with a wave of her hand.

"Well it's not like I won't be coming back and you can always come visit." Aisling tried to be comforting.

"Oh cheers. I'll have you know I'll be moving to Dublin the minute I finish school. To go to college too. I'm eligible for a grant and I'm not the bimbo all those bloody teachers think I am."

Aisling nodded slowly. She certainly didn't think Susan was stupid, but she hadn't quite grasped how smart she actually was. Susan was right, the only real way out was education. Without qualifications, she'd never get a job. If Aisling didn't change her attitude to school now, she was going to end up working in her father's pub. Something she regarded as one step up from tossing a pitchfork in hell. Jack was offering her a fresh start, a chance to prove herself. She couldn't blame her brother's departure for everything that had gone wrong in her life. It was time she started taking some responsibility.

She didn't feel quite so grown up though when she stepped off the coach in Busaras. Her mother had forced her to take a huge, old battered suitcase that she could barely lift. Inside was everything apart from the kitchen stove. Her mother had presented her with a big plastic bowl with homemade Irish stew inside it.

"They do have food in Dublin," Aisling protested.

But her mother was insistent. Aisling didn't even like stew, but she had to carry the container on her lap the whole way in case it spilt.

Her mother was in floods of tears when she left. "How did you get so big so fast?" she asked.

Aisling didn't know how she was supposed to answer that. She tried to give her mother a hug and her mother held her so tightly she could hardly breathe. All she could manage was, "Mam, I'll miss the bus."

She wanted to say she wasn't going to the moon, but given what had happened the last time her mother had let one of her children out of her sight, it seemed wisest to keep quiet.

Busaras was the main bus station in Dublin and an utterly soulless place. There was a vague smell of urine mixed with petrol fumes. Aisling looked around her in panic. Jack had promised to meet her and she didn't know what she'd do if he didn't show. A group of Japanese tourists was chattering excitedly and one of them took a picture of Aisling. The flash momentarily blinded her and when she could see again, Jack was by her side.

"Sure you brought enough?" he asked cheerfully, heroically struggling with her case.

She didn't know what kind of car he had but it seemed brand new. There was central locking and windows you didn't have to wind. She settled into the leather seats and thought how much her father would just love a motor like this.. As Jack turned on to the main road, Aisling felt as if she was speeding away from her old life.

She couldn't quite believe the size of Jack's house when they pulled up outside it. She'd lived all her life in the cramped conditions above the pub. Her uncle's place was over a hundred years old and built of red brick with a huge bay window. The front garden was bigger than Aisling's back yard which, admittedly, was very small. There was a neatly clipped hedge and flowerbeds in front of the window.

"But there can't be only you living here?" she exclaimed.

Jack looked momentarily embarrassed. "Well no... I do have a lodger. Her name's Claire. And of course now I have you."

A lodger? What did that mean she wondered? Aisling knew that Jack was a widow and that he'd never remarried. She hadn't thought about him being with anyone. It just didn't occur to her that men his age could have girlfriends. Maybe he was living in sin. Good thing her mother didn't know or she'd never have let her come. Aisling felt a little thrill of excitement. Everything about her uncle was glamorous.

Inside was even more impressive. The floors were all polished floorboards and the walls were off-white.

She could nearly hear her mother saying, "Now wouldn't you think a doctor would be able to afford carpets and a bit of wallpaper."

But to Aisling it was the epitome of stylish elegance. She stared at the modern art on the walls.

"Are those real?" she asked.

Jack seemed confused by the question. Of course he didn't have fakes, thought Aisling, neither did he have pictures of the Blessed Virgin or the Sacred Heart crammed everywhere. Aisling's mother had given her a fluorescent, glow-in-the-dark statue of Mary to bring with her. As a child, Aisling remembered waking up one night and being convinced the Virgin was moving. Her father told her it must've been a dream but her mother believed her. Aisling resolved to hide the statue in a black cloth under her bed where there was no chance Jack would find it.

One large painting in particular attracted Aisling's attention. It was a swirl of greens and blacks and it was only when she stepped back from it did she realise it was of a naked woman. She found herself blushing deeply and quickly turned away. She was going to have to get over her country prudery.

Her new room turned out to be three times the size of the box room she had at home. It had a huge four poster bed with a white duvet. After Jack put her case down and went to make them a cup of tea, Aisling sprawled out on the bed, feeling like a princess. The window looked out into the garden which seemed to stretch on forever. Aisling peered out. She saw a woman cutting roses with a large pair of scissors. Aisling couldn't see her face because of her sun hat. All of a sudden, the woman straightened with a rose in her hand and waved at Aisling.

Aisling was mortified that she'd been caught spying and quickly withdrew. She felt like she was in a film. It was all too beautiful and strange. She wished Susan were there. She wouldn't feel as shy and awkward as Aisling did. Aisling could imagine her laughing at the 'pornography' on the walls. A wave of homesickness hit Aisling. For a second she felt like crying, but her uncle called her and she pulled herself together. She was being silly. Wasn't this what she'd always wanted?

Aisling kept tossing and turning that night, unable to find a comfortable spot in the bed, even though the mattress was far softer than the one she had at home and didn't have the sort of dip in the middle that she was constantly rolling into. Just as the first light was creeping through the curtains and she could hear sparrows beginning to chirp outside, she finally drifted off. Even the birds sounded different from home.

Aisling was woken by knocking on her door. She sat up in total confusion.

"Good morning," cried a woman's voice.

"Hello?" replied Aisling uncertainly.

The door sprang open and a young woman stared at Aisling. She had short, cropped, blonde hair and wore vivid red lipstick. She was carrying a tea tray, struggling with the weight of it. She put it down on Aisling's bed with a sigh.

"Really sorry to disturb you," she began. "It's just that Jack had to run off to the hospital, he works all the hours God sends that man and since they promoted him again I never see him. He asked me to give you a set of keys and tell you he'd be back around seven. I've got to rush to class now. I was going to write you a note, but then I thought it mightn't be nice to wake up in a strange house with no one there and not know where the food is. So I brought you some breakfast. You don't have to get up."

The woman beamed at Aisling. She spoke very quickly like she was worried if she didn't get the words out soon, she'd lose track of them.

Aisling gaped at her. She was never much of a morning person and she was having real trouble stringing a sentence together.

"What time is it?" she managed to mumble.

"Half eight. I'm sorry I shouldn't have woken you."

Aisling looked at the tray with its bright yellow teapot and matching jug and sugar bowl and the small pile of neatly buttered toast on the plate. Her mother considered breakfast in bed slovenly, but Aisling realised as her stomach growled that she hadn't eaten since she arrived. She grabbed a piece of toast and shoved it in her mouth.

Embarrassed by her own rudeness, she said, "No, no thanks a million. Are you the lady with the rose?"

Only when the woman laughed did it occur to Aisling how silly that sounded. "Yes, sorry, I'm Claire. That garden would be a jungle within a week if I didn't look after it. Jack has no interest in plants."

Claire held out her hand to shake and Aisling took it, painfully aware that her fingers were covered in melted butter from the toast.

"And you're Aisling. Jack's told me all about you."

Aisling shifted uncomfortably. She was hoping for a fresh start and wondered if Claire knew she'd been expelled from one school and failed dismally in the other. Still Claire had a kind smile and razor sharp blue eyes that sparkled with curiosity rather than condemnation.

"Well must dash. I'm late for school."

"Are you a student?" Aisling asked confused.

Claire laughed. "Well I'm glad you think I'm so youthful looking. But actually no, I'm a teacher. History and geography. I can show you where you're coming from and where you're going to."

Aisling thought she'd never had a teacher with such a mischievous laugh. Few of the ones she'd known had laughed at all. They all seemed to take themselves deadly seriously.

A thought occurred to Aisling. "In the same school I'm going to?"

"God no," exclaimed Claire. "Don't worry, you'll be spared that. Jack is sending you to one of the best private schools in the city. Not the kip where I work. You won't have to mix with the riff raff."

Aisling was reminded of the tech. She certainly didn't feel nostalgic, but she suspected she might fit in better with riff raff. The idea of posh Dublin girls looking down their noses at her for being a bogger from the arsehole of nowhere wasn't appealing.

Claire peered at her watch. "Jesus I'm even later than usual which is saying something. Here's the keys. Help yourself to anything in the fridge. I'll see you later." Claire was gone in a whirl. Aisling smiled to herself. Even if she was a teacher, Claire seemed like she might be fun. Rather like the older sister she'd always wanted. It was a strange thing to think about someone she'd only met for two minutes, but Aisling had a good feeling. She wondered again what Jack and Claire's relationship was. She was very young for him. Aisling instantly dismissed the thought. It was the kind of thing her mother would say. If her uncle had a much younger, beautiful girlfriend – well good for him.

17

JACK RETURNED TO DUBLIN PARTLY because he was intimidated by Pat and partly because his father kept nagging him about missing lectures. Jack was on edge anyway. He had expected to feel over the moon with Troy gone, or at least a bit more confident. Instead his insomnia was worse than ever and he was gripped by an anxiety he couldn't explain.

The evening before he left he went to the pub with his father who insisted on introducing him to a friend of his who suffered from terrible arthritis. Looking at the old man's gnarled hands, twisted like the boughs of a tree, Jack knew he should feel sympathy. Instead he felt useless.

"It's incurable," he stated coldly. "There's nothing I can do for you."

The old man began mumbling on about how the piss from a cat taken at midnight was supposed to be a wonderful cure but he just couldn't bring himself to drink the stuff. Jack was bored by the superstitious nonsense. He concentrated on running his finger around the rim of his pint.

His father wasn't pleased. "You could at least have tried to say something encouraging."

"Like what? Should I fill his head full of fairy tales? Let him go to the fair and visit a faith healer if that's what he wants."

"The man's in a lot of pain," his father lowered his voice. "Since when did you get so hard?"

Jack was stung. He felt like screaming that he was suffering too. Instead he said, "Don't you remember? That's what doctors are like. It was your idea to turn me into one."

He didn't want to hurt his father's feelings, but he was bitter about the path he'd been pushed down. No one ever seemed to offer him any choices. No one had asked him what he wanted, what his hopes and dreams were. Not that he'd necessarily have had the answers if they did, but it would be nice if his opinion was called for. He didn't want to be a bit part in somebody else's drama, to be used as a social tool. He wasn't going to be like an expensive piece of china that could be dusted off and admired before being put back on the shelf. He'd hated the doctors who came to see his mother. With their neatly clipped beards and their patronising voices, shaking their heads and writing prescriptions. Coming out with smooth clichéd promises. If only his father would keep paying the bill, his wife would get better. When there was no cure for a broken heart.

His mother had said to him once, "I don't want to be back on my feet in no time, and the next person who says that to me, I'm going to shoot in the head."

The doctors droned on about her mood swings and violent outbursts being symptoms of her disease – a disease that had a name so long no one could remember it – but Jack just thought she was right. The doctors were irritating. He had started studying medicine, yet he still hadn't gained an understanding of their point in view. On the contrary he'd come to see more and more that all those big, fancy Latin words hid the fact that the vast majority of human ailments were of unknown cause with obscure and inconstant symptoms. Sometimes medicine helped, but it was more by luck than design; most people either got better of their own accord or they died.

His father was taken aback. "Don't you want to be a doctor?"

Jack sighed. If he said no, his father would ask him what he wanted to be. And he had no answer. It seemed a bit lame to become a doctor because that's what his father wanted, but the only other thing he could think of was that he needed money if he was to give Kate everything she deserved. He didn't care what he did as long as she was happy. Right now, she looked so utterly miserable and lost, but she just needed time. He would have to be patient. As much as he wanted to just grab her and kiss her and tell her that he'd take her away from all this, that she could come to Dublin with him, he knew she would just consider him mad or insensitive or both. Jack walked away from his father and went to pack. It would be easier for him if he wasn't so close to Kate right now. Just knowing she was a mere couple of minutes down the road made him feel agitated and he couldn't think straight.

His father looked puzzled when Jack went to say goodbye.

"Don't worry. I have every intention of being a doctor like you're counting on." Jack tried to say this with levity, as if he'd only been joking earlier, but he didn't quite pull it off.

"Jack... I only want you to be happy," his father replied. His face a picture of sadness.

Jack shrugged. It seemed he couldn't help his father and his father couldn't help him. Wanting people to be happy was a futile exercise.

Jack's melancholy lifted when he got back to Dublin. He set about cleaning the bed-sit with concentrated energy. Brendan came in to find Jack on his hands and knees scrubbing the kitchen floor. After his initial surprise at his cousin's burst of domesticity, Brendan was keen to know if Jack had found out why Kate stood Troy up.

"Awful shame," Brendan pronounced. "A nice fella like that getting

117

shat all over. But that's women for you. There's a lesson for you there, boy. Stay well clear."

Jack was unimpressed by Brendan's relationship advice. Instead, he began to make plans of his own. If only becoming a doctor didn't take so damn long. It was such a tedious process. Still, Christmas was nearly upon them and he'd be able to go home for the holidays. It was hard to believe that he'd known Kate for less than a year. She seemed so funda-mentally part of him – without her, he was nothing. She made him some-thing nobler, something bigger. Not just another aimless, feckless student only interested in drinking beer and getting their leg over. Sometimes the pressure of keeping his love a secret was too much to bear. He had an urge to stop people in the street and tell them that there was this girl he was sure could love him if only she'd give him a chance. She'd got sidetracked.

It was a cruel irony that somehow he was the cause of her current pain when he'd never dream of harming a hair on her head. No one else could possibly understand this contradiction.

So, even when he felt Brendan looking at him strangely, or when they went down the pub and after a couple of drinks, his cousin attempted a few sly questions he said nothing. Even when he was drunk, there was a core of him stayed sober. Like a voice in his head that spoke with an absolute clarity warning him he must keep his love to himself for now. He couldn't tell anyone, but especially not Brendan who was the only witness to what had really happened. He hoped Brendan wouldn't be too offended when he didn't invite him to his wedding. He couldn't risk him saying anything. Anyway Brendan was the forgiving sort and Jack figured he just had to keep things under wraps until he'd persuaded Kate to marry him. If she did find out the truth later, it would be so much water under the bridge, that she wouldn't be that bothered. One day when they were old and grey and in their rocking chairs, they might even laugh about it.

These were the thoughts that comforted Jack during interminable anatomy lectures. The lecturer droned on about the dermis and Jack imagined what it would be like to run his finger down Kate's neck, to feel the silkiness of her skin under his touch.

The night before Jack was heading home his cousin invited him out for a Christmas drink.

He placed a pint of Guinness in front of Jack and said, "I was thinking I might take a bit of an extended Christmas break. You know go away for a bit."

Jack was surprised. Brendan was supposed to be off home to Derry the day after, but he had never expressed any interest in going anywhere other than to the pub before. "Where you gonna go?"

Brendan paused. "Well... London maybe. Just for a bit. Till things quieten down." Meant to be a gap?

Jack stared wide-eyed. He wasn't aware of turmoil in anybody's life but his own. "You'll be all right looking after yourself. I won't be gone long."

"You're not in some kind of trouble, are you?" Jack joked.

Brendan laughed. "No, no, course not." He took a sip of his Guinness. "But like just if anyone were to come round asking for me, I'm sure they won't, but in case they did, might be best if you didn't let on you knew where I was."

"You're going on the run, is that what you're telling me?"

Brendan looked serious. "I've a few money problems, you know yourself. I just want to keep my head down till the storm passes."

Jack remembered with a lurch in his stomach that Brendan's older brother Kevin had been beaten to a pulp last year by local vigilantes for pushing drugs. They'd threatened to knee cap him, pressing the butt of a revolver into the joint and pretending to pull the trigger.

"God sakes he was only selling a bit of weed," Brendan had remarked at the time. "Be a terrible pity if they'd shot him, cos he's a great dancer Kevin."

Jack hadn't seen Kevin since he was a small child and remembered him as a big lad who'd carried him round on his shoulders. He'd probably never seen him dance. Anyway he couldn't forgive his mother's family for how judgmental they'd been. His grandmother had irritated him immensely by referring to his mother's 'accident.' They would never admit it was a suicide, but they knew it was, and being Catholics, they thought his mother must be burning in hell. Hadn't his mother suffered enough in life without them condemning her in death? All they seemed concerned about was the shame she'd brought on the family.

But Brendan wasn't like that; he didn't care about shite like that.

"You'll be careful, won't you?" Jack couldn't keep the anxiety out of his voice.

"I'm well able to look after meself. It's you I'm worried about. Fading away to nothing before my very eyes. You've gotten terrible skinny. And you've got big pockets under your eyes. You'd think you were the hunted man, not me."

Bearing Brendan's words in mind, Jack made an effort to spruce himself up before going home to his father's.

He shaved off his straggly attempt at growing a beard; he'd been aiming for a sort of goatee but the hair on his face seemed to grow in odd patches. Brendan clipped his hair short for him and he tried on the suit he'd bought himself a week ago. It was his first suit.

"A picture of elegance," Brendan informed him.

Traffic was terrible and the bus limped along. Still Jack felt a rising happiness as the houses thinned out and the narrow streets with their brightly lit shops gave way to green fields and cows munching grass. He'd grown up in a town himself, but he preferred the countryside. He didn't like the feeling of being surrounded by other people. He couldn't imagine himself in a huge city like London. Brendan had been there before apparently and wasn't particularly looking forward to going back.

"The underground is like travelling in a pack of rats and if you dropped dead sure they'd just step over your body," he informed Jack.

Jack peered out the window of the bus as the afternoon light faded, turning the passing landscape into a blur of shadows. For miles he didn't spot a single other soul. There was something about the stone walls, the rawness of the ground with the trees stripped bare, and the grass broken up by rocks, that had a comforting wildness to it. Jack could see his face half reflected in the glass. It looked as if his ghost was travelling over the fields. He felt free and excited and lonely all at the same time.

Jack had rung his father to say he would meet him in O'Rourke's. He arrived around seven and leapt from the bus grabbing his small carry-all bag. He could see in his mind's eye Kate behind the bar, serving drinks among the chaos and smiling and making jokes with the customers. The warm blast as he opened the door of the pub seemed to him the essence of what Christmas should be about.

Of course she wasn't there. He cursed himself in retrospect for having allowed his imagination to run away with him. Maybe by planning how he wanted things to go, he'd jinxed himself. Nothing had ever gone how he wished it to, why would it start to now? His father greeted him enthusiastically, but Jack's glance drank in every corner of the pub where Kate might be. Mr O'Rourke was behind the bar. He'd told Jack the last time he was home that business was so quiet these days, and with his two daughters home, he didn't think he'd need any extra help. Jack was therefore rather hurt to see a young scrawny lad he didn't recognise collecting glasses. Mr O'Rourke's eyes seemed to have sunk deep into his face and he was so busy, he barely responded to Jack's hello. Jack had to endure the whole evening with his eyes peeled, but neither O'Rourke sister appeared.

At the end of the night Mr O'Rourke came over to him. As if he could read Jack's mind, he said defensively, "I only took young Pete on at the last moment. He's just doing a few evenings when things get out of hand altogether."

"That's quite all right," Jack tried to reassure.

He wasn't interested in getting his old job back, it was more his old work colleague he wanted to know about.

"How's Kate?" he asked in what he hoped was a casual tone.

But Mr O'Rourke just ignored him. "He's not nearly as good as you I can assure you. Keeps dropping the glasses and I daren't let him pull a pint."

Jack persisted. "Is Kate not helping you out?"

Mr O'Rourke sighed and shook his head as if he'd known in coming over to Jack that he'd have to be the bearer of bad news, but he still couldn't quite bring himself to say it. "Kate's not with us any more."

He said it with such a pained expression that for a horrible moment Jack thought he meant she was dead. His heart rose into his throat. But seeing his alarmed expression, Mr O'Rourke hurried to explain. "She's been called by God."

Jack had a flash of his well-meaning neighbour trying to tell him his mother was with the angels. All he'd thought was, what's she doing with them when she should be with me?

But thankfully this wasn't what Mr O'Rourke meant. "She's decided to follow her vocation and join the Sisterhood."

"A nun?" blurted Jack, practically spitting out his beer.

He couldn't believe it. He'd never once heard Kate show even the slightest religious inclination. In fact she'd once referred to the nuns who taught her as 'dried up old penguins.'

"Since when did Kate want to be a nun?"

Mr O'Rourke fiddled with a beer mat and wouldn't look Jack in the eye. Jack was stunned. Was this really what her heartbreak over Troy had driven her to? It seemed such a cruel trick. To lose her to another man had seemed unbearable, but to lose her to an institution was just beyond a joke. He got up and strode out of the pub. He felt God was taking some kind of revenge.

18

THE IDEA OF KATE IN a convent put Jack into a complete state of panic. Not only did it mean the end of his precious hope that she would fall in love with him, but he also felt guilty for driving her into something which just so wasn't her. How could someone with so much energy, passion, and enthusiasm be a nun?

Jack even considered getting in touch with Troy, but he realised he had no idea where Troy's ship was being sent next. He didn't even know which unit of the navy Troy was in. He had deliberately absorbed as few details as possible about the American to make it easier to erase him from his memory. Tracking him down would take weeks, months even. The best idea was to go and see Kate and try to make her realise that becoming a nun was utter madness.

Jack decided to ask Mrs O'Rourke where the convent was.

She responded in cold, clipped tones. "Caitriona made her bed and now she has to lie in it. There's nothing you can do."

Surprised as he was by her sudden coldness, Jack realised that Mrs O'Rourke was very devout and had always guessed Jack's true feelings. Maybe she was delighted at her daughter's sudden discovery of her vocation and didn't want Jack to distract Kate. She refused to give him any more details of Kate's whereabouts even when Jack protested that he just wanted to visit her.

"It's a closed order," she snapped. "They're not supposed to have visitors."

Jack couldn't bear the idea of Kate shut away from the world like this. Had the loss of Troy really made her feel she had to turn her back on the rest of the world too? Jack resolved to go see Pat. She might not be any more helpful than her parents, but he couldn't think where else to turn. No one in the village town seemed to have any idea which convent Kate had joined and they seemed very reluctant to discuss the subject. For the first time in his life Jack wished people would gossip more.

Even his father said to him curtly, "I think you'd be better off forgetting about that girl."

Jack was surprised by this as he hadn't realised his father knew he had any particular interest in Kate. "I just wondered which convent she might be staying in," he insisted, trying to sound neutral.

"Plenty more fish in the sea," was his father's reply.

Jack was annoyed. If his father did guess how he felt, surely he could be more sympathetic. Hadn't he had his heart broken himself by a woman who was in love with someone else? On the bus back to Dublin it occurred to Jack that, yes, his father had managed to hold on to his mother – she hadn't run away with her soldier – but he'd held on in name only, he'd never got her back in spirit. Jack wasn't going to let that happen to him. Even if he had to tell Kate the truth and she never spoke to him again, he'd do it. He'd much rather she was with Troy than be a bride of Christ. He wanted to make her happy, not ruin her life. Troy might be poor and unreliable but at least he would take her to America. At least she'd see the world as she'd longed to. How could a girl who'd already found her hometown a prison, voluntarily lock herself up in an even smaller space?

Jack let himself back into the bed-sit and he knew at once that Brendan hadn't been back. The place was spotless just as he'd left it and it was so cold, he could see his breath in the air. He wondered how Brendan was finding London. He didn't even have a phone number for him.

The next morning Jack got the bus out to Pat's shop on the north side of Dublin. Brendan's car keys were still in a little bowl by the fridge but there was no sign of the car where he usually parked it. The bus took ages to come and Jack shivered with impatience. The morning was foggy which gave everything a slightly ghostly, unreal air. The bus moved through the traffic slowly like a ferry lumbering through rough waters. Jack sat upstairs, smoking a fag. The air inside the bus was thicker than the fog outside.

Pat stopped dead in the middle of ringing up an old woman's groceries like she'd seen a ghost. She looked alarmed to see him.

"Are you all right dear?" the woman asked.

Pat nodded and continued. Jack waited till the small queue had gone.

Once they were alone, she leaned towards him. "What do you want?" she whispered.

Jack blurted out, "I don't think Kate should be a nun."

Pat turned around and shouted into the back of the shop, "Mary, do you mind watching the till for a bit? I need to go upstairs."

The woman Jack had met before emerged. She peered at Jack curiously. "Ah your friend Brendan."

Jack was disturbed by her vivid memory, but Pat didn't seem to be listening. She grabbed Jack's arm in a vice like grip and dragged him through the storeroom and up the tiny stairway at the back, ushering him into her flat. It looked exactly the same as last time. A picture of the

Virgin Mary took pride of place over the mantelpiece. Jack's heart sank. He prepared himself for a lecture on how he was not to get in the way of her sister's call from God.

"I just want to talk her. I think she's rushing into this because she doesn't realise what she's doing." Jack's words came out in a jumbled rush. "There's something I have to tell her. She's not supposed be a nun, God hasn't spoken to her. There's been a misunderstanding. She doesn't know all the facts."

Pat laughed. It was a bitter if not unkind laugh. "You poor fool," she sighed. "You don't know, do you?"

Jack looked at her blankly.

"Kate's pregnant."

Jack's blood turned to ice.

"I take it you're not the father?"

He opened his mouth but no sound came.

"No, I didn't think so," Pat looked flustered. "You don't want to believe all that my parents say. It's just a story they made up. Kate no more wants to be a nun than the Pope wants to be a Protestant."

"So where is she?" Jack felt as if his grasp on reality was slipping. Maybe Kate had found her way back to Troy and the vocation story was just to cover her tracks.

"Oh she's with the nuns all right," said Pat. "They're looking after her till she has the baby. Then they'll take it away from her."

"So she is in a convent?" asked Jack.

"She's in a home for fallen women. A kind of prison that my parents sent her to so they wouldn't have her shame hanging over the whole family."

Pat was angry. Jack couldn't work out if it was Kate she was mad at or her parents.

"Well now you know," she stated. "So piss off."

Jack mustered his courage. "I still want to see her."

Pat glowered at him. "Why?" she demanded.

"Because I love her." Jack figured he had nothing to lose.

Pat shook her head. "I've just told you she's having another man's child."

"I don't care."

As he said it, Jack realised that he really didn't care. He already knew Kate loved Troy. That Troy had left some of himself behind was disturb-

124

ing, but it didn't change the way Jack felt. He'd still be in love with Kate if she'd given birth to ten of Troy's children.

Pat rubbed her hand across her forehead. Then she asked softly, 'And you'd still marry her?"

"Nothing would make me happier," Jack replied.

Pat wrote an address on a piece of paper and handed it to Jack. "My sister may have made mistakes, but she doesn't deserve to end up as some kind of slave to women who don't understand what temptation is. You've got to get her out of there."

Jack thanked her profusely.

Pat said fiercely, "You just make sure you take care of her, do you hear me?" Jack took the stairs two at a time and hailed a taxi outside.

19

AISLING'S NEW SCHOOL WAS ANOTHER planet compared to the tech. The first surprise was that it was Protestant. Aisling asked Jack if her mother knew and he assured her Pat had read all the fine print of the school's brochure and knew exactly where her daughter was being educated. According to him, her mother had a lot of time for God, but not especially for nuns. This was news to Aisling who'd always thought her mother had secret desires to join a convent herself.

The second and more unpleasant shock was the uniform. Not that the navy blue kilt effort of the Holy Cross was very attractive, but being at the tech had got Aisling out of the habit of having to wear a uniform. This fancy Dublin school had the most hideous one she'd seen yet. It was bottle green with an A line skirt, white blouse, and V neck jumper. But it was the tie that really upset Aisling. Originally there had been a boys' school and a girls' school, but the two agreed to merge in the seventies. Rather than choose the colour of one school's tie over the other, they simply put the two together. An egalitarian and laudable concept, but the resulting combination of brown, purple, red, and yellow was painful.

Claire pointed out to Aisling that when she was dressed for school, her eyes no longer looked blue. Instead they turned a light green. It disturbed Aisling that a uniform could change their shade. Weren't the eyes supposed to be the windows of the soul? If the colour of her soul could be changed so easily by outside forces, what chance was there of her finding her true colours?

She tried to explain this to Claire who only laughed. "Green suits you. Your eyes are like water, they reflect the light. Doesn't mean you don't have hidden depths."

Aisling didn't pretend to be Protestant to fit in, it was just she'd decided she didn't want to be Catholic any more. She wasn't sure what she thought about God, but she had very definite views on the Catholic Church – it was a repressive institution she didn't want to be part of. Still in her new school people always seemed to ask her what her religion was. Back home, no one asked if she was a Catholic because everyone was. Or if they weren't, they kept quiet about it. But Aisling discovered that as in Ireland there were so few schools not affiliated with a particular religion, Protestant schools were for Protestants and everyone else who wasn't Catholic.

Claire was amused when Aisling explained how she persisted in answering the question, "What religion are you?" with "I'm not religious." This inevitably led to the question, "Well what religion are your parents?" To which Aisling would reply, "Catholic." She felt she could see them mentally ticking the box and it really annoyed her. Why should she be defined by what her parents' believed?

Claire said, "Don't you get that it has nothing to do with God? My grandfather was a devout atheist all his life. He still died in a concentration camp. The Nazis weren't remotely interested in his personal beliefs, he was just another Jew."

Claire was the first person Aisling told she didn't think she believed in God any more. Not that she'd deliberately been secretive; it was more that God's absence crept up on her. She almost hadn't noticed that she no longer considered mass anything but a chore. But now that she lived with Claire and Jack and neither of them went to church, she couldn't think of a reason to go herself.

Several weeks went by in which Aisling was more and more convinced that Jack and Claire were a couple. She wondered if they had separate bedrooms for her sake and wanted to tell them it wasn't necessary. She never saw them actually kiss but this wasn't surprising as her uncle seemed far too reserved for public displays of affection. Claire was always teasing Jack and calling him "my thin man." Jack was in fact one of the skinniest men Aisling had ever met.

"Look at you both," Claire often cried. "A pair of scarecrows. I'm going to have to fatten you up."

Claire's cooking was so much better than Aisling's mother's, especially considering her mother put so much more effort into it. At home they had meat and veg every single night; the Brussels sprouts were often over boiled and soggy and the potatoes crumbled in their blandness. Claire made wonderful quiches, and tarts, and pasta dishes with long Italian names. Her food was like her laughter, light and airy and tasty. Maybe it was the atmosphere at the dinner table, but meals back home had always left Aisling feeling bloated and tired as if there were a solid stodge of indigestible resentment at the bottom of her stomach.

A couple of months after she moved in, Aisling was in the kitchen helping Claire make the dinner. As usual, she didn't really do much apart from stir the sauce and tell Claire about her impressions of her new school and Dublin in general. Jack never got home before eight, but that night it was getting close to nine which was late even for her uncle. When the doorbell rang Aisling ran to answer it, sure it would be him. Jack was always forgetting his keys. Instead she was confronted by a pale young man in jeans and a large, baggy jumper. He was handsome enough in a sort of generalized way with muddy greyish blue eyes. None of his features were striking and although not overweight, he gave the hazy impression he would be in a few years time.

"Is Claire here?" he asked in a high, nervous voice.

Aisling blinked, then nodded. "Who are you?" she asked.

"I'm Hugh, her husband," the man replied.

Aisling felt a strange pang in her stomach. Claire had never mentioned a husband; she didn't wear a wedding ring.

When told who was at the door, Claire turned off the gas rings on the cooker. "I'll finish this later," she said, leaving the kitchen without further explanation. A moment later Aisling heard the front door closing.

At about half nine Jack arrived home, looking exhausted. Aisling told him Claire had just left with a man who claimed to be married to her. She hadn't known whether to finish cooking dinner or not.

"Why don't I order us a pizza?" Jack said, although all the colour seemed to drain out of his face.

Aisling asked if Jack had met Claire's husband before.

"No, I haven't," he said in the kind of voice that indicated the end of a conversation.

Aisling realised then that Jack and Claire weren't any more transparent than her parents. When it came down to it, they had their secrets too. She'd thought she was allowed to look through a window into their world, but suddenly the glass had steamed up. Not for the first time in her life she had the uncomfortable feeling that just as she started to get close to someone, they turned out to be a total stranger. She might think she'd been welcomed into Jack and Claire's lives but in reality she knew very little about them.

They ate their pizza in total silence. It wasn't an uncomfortable silence. They weren't both desperately trying to think of something to say, but it was disquieting because they were straining so anxiously for the sound of the doorbell. For Claire to come back to them.

She didn't turn up till the next morning after Jack had already left for work.

"Shouldn't you be at school?" she asked Aisling.

"Why didn't you ever tell me you're married?" It came out more aggressively than Aisling had intended it to.

Claire was slightly taken aback. "Well I don't like talking about it," she said. "We're separated." Claire's eyes filled with tears.

That threw Aisling. Was it the same as divorced or taking a break or did it just mean that you had become temporarily divided through circumstances outside of your own control? She didn't know anyone who

128

was separated but she had never seen Claire look so miserable.

"So if he makes you so unhappy, why'd you spend the night with him?" Aisling could hear her mother's voice inside her head shouting, "This is absolutely none of your business," but Aisling wasn't listening to it.

Claire took a tissue out from her sleeve and blew her nose. Aisling couldn't help noticing that, even this movement, Claire managed to make look stylish. Her nose was slightly pinker and her eyes had a watery quality as if she'd been crying for weeks and had run out of tears. But she didn't have the red, patchy, smudged devastation that Aisling so disliked when she looked in the mirror after crying herself. She decided that if Claire could still look that good then her sorrow couldn't be real.

"We're trying to work things out," Claire explained.

"What about my uncle?" Was Jack just some kind of substitute till Claire decided if she wanted to go back to her husband or not?

Claire looked confused.

"Don't his feelings count?"

Claire frowned. "Has Jack said something to you?"

Aisling began to flounder. "No," she stammered. "But I don't think he was very pleased you weren't here last night."

"He's not my father you know."

Aisling thought this beside the point. "It's just that I think you two seem good together and I don't want him to get hurt."

Aisling was surprised by how protective she felt of this man who was in fact old enough to be her father.

Claire laughed. "But Aisling, surely you don't think there's anything going on between me and Jack? I mean I think the world of him, but he's a friend, that's all."

Aisling found this difficult to believe.

"Did Jack tell you something different?" Claire looked worried.

Aisling had to admit that he hadn't. Jack had said Claire was his lodger and apparently this was all she was. Aisling couldn't quite lose the feeling of jealousy on her uncle's behalf, but she was glad to discover Claire wasn't having some kind of sordid affair.

A new thought occurred to her. If Claire worked things out with her husband, she'd probably move out. Aisling didn't want the lovely balance of the three of them in the big old house disturbed. Claire was one of the most interesting people Aisling had ever met. She realised with a bit of panic that she didn't want Claire to leave.

"I'm exhausted. I think I'm going to go lie down," Claire said.

"Didn't get much sleep, hey?"

"We just talked," Claire said. "He slept on the couch." Then she laughed. "I was expecting the inquisition from Jack, not you." Claire yawned and kicked off her shoes.

Aisling watched her walk barefoot up the stairs.

The next afternoon was Wednesday and Aisling finished school early as usual. She came home for her grinds. Claire had volunteered to give her extra lessons on Wednesdays after school to help her catch up in history and geography. Aisling had wide gaps in her knowledge from where she'd missed whole sections of her education.

As the coffee she made in the big yellow coffeepot turned cold, Aisling stirred the black liquid without pouring any. She only drank black coffee because Claire did. She wasn't sure she really liked the strange, slightly bitter taste. It was more for the aroma, which was rich and full – and mixed with Claire's perfume to make a kind of spicy reassurance. It was the most delicious smell Aisling had ever known. It wasn't the same when Claire wasn't there. Instead the coffee hung in the air, heavy and dark and uncertain.

Where was Claire? She was never late. Aisling herself sometimes got delayed because she had double maths on Wednesdays and the idiot of a teacher always insisted on finishing the sums even when the bell had rung. Aisling would sit in her chair poised to leap for the door but she knew that if the teacher saw her twitching, he would deliberately take longer over the problem just to punish her. But this afternoon Aisling was on time and there was no sign of Claire. Yet Aisling felt she had no right to be annoyed as Claire was doing these extra lessons as a favour to her uncle.

Jack had offered to pay for the extra tuition but Claire had point blank refused. "I know perfectly well that you could rent my room for twice what I'm paying for it."

Jack protested he didn't need the money, but Claire insisted that wasn't the point. "Allow me to keep the illusion of my independence and assuage my guilt by doing this for Aisling."

Jack had no choice but to accept.

Aisling didn't enjoy feeling like a charity case. Her uncle did everything he could to make her feel it was a privilege for him to have her stay. But Aisling didn't rate the value of her company very highly and she felt indebted to Jack. She no longer skipped class largely because she knew Jack was paying for them. As he was forking out all that money, the least she could do was turn up.

"There's no such thing as a free lunch," her mother would have told her.

Aisling didn't hear her mother's voice as clearly in her head as she used to. It was as if of late her mother, or maybe her inner conscience, had fallen silent. With no one to set herself against, Aisling felt less sure of who she was. Of course she talked to her mother regularly on the phone, but there was a distance far greater than the miles between them.

As the light began to pale and the afternoon seeped into night, with still no sign of Claire, Aisling realised – somewhat to her surprise – that she missed her mother. She missed being told to stand up straighter, tie her shoelaces, wash her hair, and do her homework. There was something very familiar and reassuring about her mother's harassment; at least she cared about her. For some inexplicable reason Aisling began to cry. Not the elegant tears that had rolled down Claire's face, but, sort of, in little gulps like a child hyperventilating after a tantrum. She didn't feel angry, she just felt bereft – like she'd lost something and she didn't know what it was. It wasn't homesickness exactly. Nor was it the old pain of Cathal being gone. It was as if some other essential connection was about to be taken away from her.

It was just her luck that Claire chose this moment to return. She was distraught at the sight of Aisling so upset.

"What happened?" she asked with urgency.

Aisling struggled to pull herself together, but for some reason it just made it worse. Maybe because every time she opened her mouth to explain to Claire what had happened, she realised she didn't know, and she started to cry harder. Claire wrapped her arms around her and Aisling began to sob in earnest. Great waves of grief came over her. She wiped her eyes in embarrassment and began to laugh through her tears.

Claire was utterly bemused. "Tell me, what's the matter?"

"Nothing," gasped Aisling. "There's nothing wrong." Then she kissed Claire on the mouth.

It was an entirely unpremeditated act. If someone had told her five minutes before that was what she was going to do, she would've thought they were mad. Claire's lips were incredibly soft. After a moment or two, which could have been an eternity, Claire pulled away. She looked at Aisling in total shock, then slapped her hard and sharp across the face.

"What do you think you're doing?" she asked before turning and fleeing up the stairs.

20

AISLING SAT FROZEN AT THE kitchen table after Claire rushed upstairs. There was a huge roaring in her ears as if she'd suddenly plunged to the bottom of the ocean. What had come over her? Perhaps she was going insane. She was happy with Claire and Jack. At least the closest she'd ever come to being happy. She didn't see them as substitute parents, but more like an older brother and sister. Like the way she imagined Cathal would be if he was still around. She liked Claire. She thought she was beautiful and smart and funny. Aisling wished she could be more like her. She liked her an awful lot. But why had she tried to kiss her? Was she some kind of pervert without realising it?

Aisling felt colder than she ever had in her life. Her teeth were chattering. She remembered how when she was very little she'd once smeared her bedroom walls with honey. It was only when her mother screamed, "What did you do that for?" that Aisling realised she had committed a terrible crime. But her honey handprints already decorated the light wallpaper.

"I'll never get that stuff off," her mother had shouted in despair.

Aisling understood then that her mistake could not easily be undone. With time to reflect on her recent actions, Aisling forced herself to consider what Claire would do next. Would she tell Jack? Would her uncle tell her mother? The thought of this made Aisling's blood run cold. She suspected that to her mother this would be even worse than getting expelled from the Holy Cross and failing her Junior Cert exams at the tech. Far, far worse, though Aisling wasn't entirely sure why. Maybe she could plead temporary insanity. Maybe she could apologize to Claire and beg her not to tell anyone. She rubbed her cheek where Claire had hit her. No one had ever slapped her across the face before. Everything Claire did was like something out of a film.

Aisling put her coat on and slipped out the back door. If Claire was going to tell Jack, Aisling didn't want to be around for it. She wandered down the garden path and let herself out at the back gate. She wasn't sure where she was headed, but she needed to get away. Maybe she'd just keep putting one foot in front of the other and never stop. She'd walk clean off the edge of the planet.

It was a soggy evening. It had stopped raining but the damp hung in the air and seeped through Aisling's coat. She made her way, or rather her footsteps took her, to a small park about a mile from Jack's house. She'd been there the Sunday before with Claire. Claire said as she didn't go to church, she preferred to do something useful like feeding the ducks. She showed Aisling how to roll the bread into little bullets that could be flung with accuracy. They aimed to fire them at the smallest, weakest looking ducks so that the big fat ones wouldn't gobble everything down. Claire hated the injustices of the duck world where smaller ducks were always being shoved and quacked out of the way of the bigger ones. Claire did a Donald Duck voice that Aisling found hysterically funny. She laughed so much, it was as if she'd sprouted wings herself. She had felt light and airy and free.

Thinking of it now, Aisling felt like she'd swallowed a ball of lead. Her throat moved up and down like she had a large piece of bread stuck in it. She stared at the ducks and thought of Claire. She'd really blown it this time.

Soon, it was nearly completely dark and she could only see the shadows of the birds. The faint splashing of their comings and goings. She thought how nice it must be to be a duck, to feel at home in water. To thrive in the eternal rain that fell in this country. "Great weather for ducks," her father was always saying. But who knew if the ducks actually enjoyed the rain? Maybe they wished they were geese that could fly south. Aisling felt like flying south. Somewhere warm and safe and sunny.

A round park keeper waddled up to her. He had red cheeks and looked like Santa in a blue uniform. He shouted as if she were deaf. "We're closing, love. You better leave before they lock the gate."

His voice was kind and for a second Aisling considered asking him if he'd mind very much if she stayed in the park. She could sleep under a bush and look up at the stars. But it was far too cloudy for stars and she immediately heard her mother's voice telling her, "Don't be ridiculous, you'd catch your death of cold." Aisling's mother seemed to think the major cause of mortality was the common cold.

The park keeper was staring at her. "Are you all right, love?" he asked.

Aisling wanted to confess all to this total stranger, but where would she begin? How could she put into words what she wasn't even sure of herself? She pulled herself together. They'd be calling the men in white coats if she wasn't careful.

"I'm absolutely grand," she said, hurrying out the gate.

It was amazing to her that her voice could sound so normal. She wandered up a street she'd never been on before. Most of the houses had their curtains drawn tight but a few had gaps in them. She caught glimpses of glowing TVs, bookcases and children's toys. The street exuded wealth and contentment. Aisling only had 50p on her. There seemed hundreds of miles between her and the little worlds inside the sitting-rooms she passed. She would give anything to be let in. To just be able to lie by one of those open fires and bury her face in the thick shag pile carpet.

With a pang, she also realised she was ravenously hungry. Given the trouble she was in, she thought her body ought to respect the seriousness of her situation, but instead her stomach growled and grumbled. She bought a chocolate bar and forced herself to eat it slowly. She had no gloves – her fingers had turned into sticks of ice, and she had trouble removing the wrapper. She'd no idea where she could go; she only knew she couldn't face going home. She had become friendly with some of the other students at her school. She'd even been to a couple of parties, and one girl who lived near the school had invited her back for tea last week. But these were respectable acquaintances. If she was to turn up on their doorstep looking tired and wretched and cold, she could imagine their panic. They might let her in, but then what?

Aisling's legs were beginning to ache. She wasn't capable of walking forever as she'd thought. She felt tired, bone tired. She used to imagine that maybe Cathal, once he'd got going, had just been unable to stop. But now she discovered the truth is you do need to rest. She sat down on a bench. Strangers hurried past, no one looking in her direction, as though the cold had made them selfish. There was nothing for it but to go back to Jack's. Hopefully she could sneak in and straight up to bed without anyone noticing. Then in the morning she could pack and go back to her mother. It wasn't so much that Aisling believed Claire would want her thrown out into the street. It was more that she couldn't bear living there knowing that at best Claire would despise her.

Aisling headed back full of fear and dread. When she put her key in the door, her heart was banging so hard, she feared it would soar out through her rib cage.

Jack was relieved to see Aisling. "Where have you been?" he asked.

"I went for a walk," she told her uncle, relieved to realise that Jack knew nothing of her moment of madness.

"It's after midnight," Jack exclaimed.

He'd never really laid down a curfew for Aisling, but then he'd never had to. Growing up with her mother's utter paranoia had made Aisling super conscientious about saying where she was going and when she'd be back.

"I've been worried," he reproached.

"I'm sorry," Aisling mumbled and she was, more sorry than she'd ever been before. Maybe something of the despair she felt was visible on her face because Jack decided to let it go.

"Honestly," he sighed, "I don't know what's got into the women in this house."

Aisling made her excuses and crept up to bed. She struggled to get to sleep and when she did, she had a very strange dream. She was on a beach and a beautiful woman was walking towards her slowly along the sand. Her dark hair blew wildly around her head. Aisling realised with a shock that the woman wasn't wearing any clothes. Just a string of rather old-fashioned pearls. Aisling woke with the crash of the sea still in her ears and the taste of longing in her mouth. She hugged her pillow and asked God for forgiveness.

For the next two days she managed to avoid Claire entirely apart from a very hasty hello as she rushed out the door for school. When Claire failed to appear at dinner, neither Aisling nor Jack commented. The third day was a Saturday. Aisling lay in bed thinking she had absolutely no reason to get up. Her body seemed weighed down by bricks. Her head felt waterlogged and her eyes had difficulty focusing.

Eventually hunger drove her downstairs. Claire was in the kitchen making some toast. Aisling felt herself turn bright red. Then she noticed two packed suitcases beside Claire. She couldn't believe it. In her worst case scenario, Aisling had always imagined it would be her who would be shipped back to her mother. It had never occurred to her that Claire would decide to go.

"You're not leaving?" she asked in dismay.

"I think it's for the best." Claire's voice sounded carefully neutral as if Aisling were a dangerous lunatic she didn't want to provoke.

"You don't have to," Aisling said, total despair kicking her in the stomach. "This is your home. Why should you have to go because I've been an idiot? I'm the one who deserves to be thrown out."

Claire looked puzzled. "Oh I'd already planned to move on. It's got nothing to do with you."

Aisling didn't believe this for a second.

"Me and Hugh have decided to give it another go. I think the time apart has done us both good and we've realised… I mean I've realised that things can change between us."

"I'm sorry," Aisling blurted. "I'll never do it again." Her words sounded childish and stupid and she cursed herself.

"You've got absolutely nothing to apologize for," Claire said firmly. "I'm the one whose feeling guilty. I should never have slapped you. I was

135

just surprised, but girls your age often go through… I mean a phase like that."

Claire seemed to run out of words. "It's perfectly normal," she stuttered.

Aisling looked at her. Even if what she'd done had been stupid, she wasn't some kid to be patronised. It struck her with sudden certainty that what she felt for Claire was not some weird hormonal phase she was going through. She'd much rather Claire hated her than dismiss her like that. Claire had no idea what she felt. Aisling didn't even know herself.

"I think you're just a bit confused," Claire added.

Aisling's anger gave her clarity. "You're the one that's mixed up," she accused. "Go running back to your husband if you like but don't tell me what I feel."

She walked out of the room, slamming the door behind her. She didn't care if she was losing Claire's good opinion. She wasn't a kid any more and what she felt was jealousy pure and simple.

21

JACK SEEMED TO TAKE CLAIRE'S departure harder than Aisling did. They sometimes still had dinner together in the evenings but often he rang to say he was working late and would heat something up in the microwave. Aisling found it unnerving sitting at the kitchen table on her own, the only sound the rain pattering against the window and the echoing tick of the grandfather clock in the hall. She put the radio on to drown out the silence. But the songs were invariably about loneliness, or heartbreak, or love that had gone horribly wrong so she clicked it off again.

She could almost see Claire sitting in front of her, holding her wine glass up to reflect the light, her teeth flashing as she laughed at some joke she'd made at Jack's expense. Her jokes were never cruel. They were warm and funny, a combination of the witty and the silly, that made them all feel good. It was their absence that seemed sarcastic and judgmental. Aisling decided that's what love was, seeing ghosts.

With Claire gone, her absence such a hard immutable fact, Aisling understood from the drained empty feeling inside that this wasn't friendship. She thought of how lonely and awful she felt when Cathal disappeared. She should have built up an immunity to being abandoned. She had tried to adopt a somewhat cynical, worldly view that people came and went and nothing in life was permanent or could be depended on. But now the carpet had once again been whipped from under her feet, she discovered she hadn't learnt to walk on air. She felt just as bereft as she had done then, only this loss had a sharper taste. Like something vital had been removed from her diet.

The necessity of what she felt was far more shocking to her than the fact Claire was a woman. Aisling knew that God supposedly disapproved of homosexuality and it was illegal in Ireland, though possibly not for women – something to do with Queen Victoria. Still it seemed to her, looking at the daily headlines, that God had a lot bigger things to be worrying about than a schoolgirl's heartbreak. In fact Aisling wasn't convinced any more that God existed.

On the evenings when Jack did dine with Aisling, he barely ate at all. He just moved the food around on his plate morosely.

She asked Jack if he'd heard from Claire.

"She'll be in touch soon," he replied. Though as the weeks crawled by this seemed unlikely.

His words reminded Aisling of Cathal's farewell at the airport, "I'll see you very soon." There was something final and dead about them.

"Maybe we should ring her to find out if she's okay?"

"She's made her choice," Jack remarked bitterly.

Like if Claire's husband decided to strangle her and bury her body under the patio, Claire had no one to blame but herself. Aisling wished she knew more about Hugh. She struggled to recall his bland face. Admittedly he hadn't shown any outward signs of being psychotic.

She probed Jack. At first subtly, then by more direct questions: "How come she left him in the first place?"

It was like trying to get blood from a stone. Jack could be as close and impossible to talk to as her mother. "You'd have to ask her that," was all he would say.

Aisling felt like shouting, "I would if I had any idea where she was."

There were a huge number of things she wanted to ask Claire now she was gone. There was no point in taking it out on her uncle. Also just as she had wondered as a kid if Cathal had left because of something she'd done, some terrible flaw or disappointment that she couldn't see but which had caused him to want to get away from her, she felt an obscure guilt about Claire. Was it really a coincidence she'd left so shortly after Aisling kissed her? And if she wasn't upset about it, as she claimed, why didn't she call? Either she was angry or she was so utterly indifferent to Aisling that it never occurred to her to stay in touch. Aisling couldn't decide which was worse.

When Jack announced he was going away for a few days, to a conference in Bristol, Aisling couldn't quite keep the look of abandonment off her face.

"It's only three days. I'll be back on Monday." He showed her his return train ticket, guessing she would like some physical evidence he was planning to come back.

Aisling pulled herself together. "I'm perfectly able to look after myself."

Jack didn't look as if he was convinced, and in truth, Aisling wasn't sure she believed herself. Upon her arrival in Dublin, she'd felt more and more grown up, but since Claire's departure all her newfound maturity had deserted her. She felt like throwing herself on the floor, pounding it with her fists and bawling her eyes out. She wanted to express her disappointment and frustration the way she had when she was five.

The house felt incredibly empty after he'd left. Aisling had never realised how many strange creaking noises an old house makes. She wandered aimlessly from room to room. She turned on the television but couldn't concentrate on the flickering pictures and the voices irritated her. She switched it off again. She wondered what Claire was doing right at that moment. It was a habit she'd developed since her brother's disappearance, trying to imagine other people's lives when she wasn't in them. It seemed grossly unfair that yet again someone she loved had walked out of her life without even leaving a phone number. Surely there was some way of tracking Claire down?

It was these thoughts that led her into her uncle's room, the only place in the house she'd never been. It was at the very back of the house and Aisling was surprised to discover how small it was. She found what she was looking for inside the top drawer of what appeared to be some kind of writing desk. She flicked through the pages of her uncle's address book feeling like a criminal. There was nothing under C, there was nothing under S either, Claire's last name being Schwartz. Aisling felt incredibly foolish but she still looked through the entire book from A to Z on the off chance there'd be a number somewhere. Under O she noticed the name Kate O'Rourke. It occurred to her then that the address book must be very old.

As she turned the last page a photograph fell out. It was a black and white snapshot of a fiddler. It took Aisling a moment to recognise Flynn in his youth. Sitting beside him was a man with a woman on his lap. The man was Jack and he was looking up at the woman with such total adoration that Aisling couldn't help be moved. She felt a pang at how little she knew of her uncle's sufferings and thought of how a man as private as he was would not appreciate her rifling through his things. But the feeling was quickly replaced by one of curiosity. She remembered that the first time she'd met Jack he'd shown her pictures of Cathal as a baby. She wanted to see those photos again and wondered if there were any others. She was in a particularly sentimental mood and the temptation to have a quick look through the rest of the papers in the drawer proved too much.

Unfortunately there were no more photos, only bank statements that were yellowed with age. However she did find what appeared to be a jewellery box. She carefully removed the lid and inside lay two gold wedding rings. This struck her as slightly odd because she knew her uncle still wore his wedding ring even after being widowed for so many years. She picked up the rings. One of them was indeed engraved with the name Kate and a date. The other had the same date but the name was Troy. Aisling was puzzled. Had her aunt been married to someone else before Jack? She would love to know; but how could she ask her uncle without him discovering she'd been in his room?

She carefully returned the box and all the papers. Everything was so neat she was suddenly terrified her uncle would be able to tell that things had been moved. It was only because she was trying to close the drawer very gently without disturbing anything inside that she happened to glance under it. There was something tapped to the bottom. Something small and flat that didn't prevent the drawer from closing.

Aisling hesitated. If she removed the tape she might not be able to put it back exactly the same way. Still she'd gone this far. It was industrial silver tape that was not very easy to remove but she managed to unpeel the strips. Whatever she was expecting to find it was not in a million years what fell into her hand. The leather was worn but she recognised it immediately because she still had its twin. In all this time, no matter how angry or betrayed or despairing she'd felt about her brother, she'd never taken off the bracelet he'd given her. As a result his name, that was once stark against the leather, had faded till it was only a shadow of an engraving.

In contrast her brother's bracelet was less worn and she could read her own name without difficulty. Aisling broke out in a cold sweat. How had Jack gotten hold of Cathal's bracelet? She felt as if the floor had suddenly given way beneath her feet. Her thoughts stumbled over themselves in utter confusion.

22

THE TAXI DRIVER DROPPED JACK off outside the door of a large grey hulk of a building. "Not sure they let blokes in the door of that place, mate," he said as he pulled away.

Now that he had arrived Jack was unsure of what to do next. In the taxi he'd been fired by the conviction he was in the role of rescuer. But it wasn't as if he could ride in there on his white horse, pick Kate up and gallop into the sunset. Plus there was the complication that it was his fault she was here in the first place. If it wasn't for his intervention, she'd be a respectably married woman by now and no one would have been the wiser.

He rang the doorbell and a young nun with a round pale face answered it. She seemed stunned by Jack's statement that he'd come to see Kate O'Rourke. Without a word she ran away like a frightened rabbit leaving Jack standing on the doorstep unsure whether to enter or not. Just as he lifted his foot to step forward, a large nun built like a tank came bowling towards him. Her face looked as if someone had just slapped it.

"I'm afraid Miss O'Rourke does not wish to see any visitors," she informed Jack and, without even asking who he was, shut the door in his face.

Jack was left with his hat in his hand staring at the peculiar shape of the knocker, feeling like an utter fool. He hadn't quite realised Kate really was in prison. How was he supposed to get in to see her without being arrested? He could see his father's face as he read the headline in the local paper, 'Headmaster's Son Breaks Into Convent,' or 'Student Doctor In Nun Kidnap Fiasco.'

He sat down on the front doorstep to consider his next move. The cold from the stone slab seeped up through his spine. He felt a quiet fury that Mr O'Rourke could have banished his daughter to such a grim soulless place. He knocked on the door again. When no one answered, he banged louder. He felt as if the grey mass of the building was holding its breath, that the windows were eyes spying on him.

After an age the door opened. The same battle-axe of a nun stood before him, obviously disgusted to find he was still there. Jack thought with her broad shoulders and intimidating stance this woman could easily get a job as a bouncer at The Palace.

"I'm Miss O'Rourke's cousin and I've got an urgent message from her father." He lied with a fluency born of desperation, successfully concealing his Northern accent and replacing it with the pompous smugness of one of his lecturers. If he'd learnt nothing else at least he could talk like a doctor.

He held out his hand and introduced himself. "My name's Dr. O'Connell."

He held himself as straight and tall as he could. The word *doctor* had the desired effect. The nun shook his hand.

"Sister Gabriel," she grudgingly admitted. "We don't generally encourage visitors. It distracts the girls. But I suppose if it's an emergency?"

Jack merely nodded. He didn't want to push his luck by elaborating on the lie. The nun looked like she was acting against her better judgment, but she let him inside and reluctantly brought him down the corridor and into a small room. There was a threadbare sofa and heavy dark curtains that were pulled closed. A large picture of the Sacred Heart of Jesus hung over the unlit fireplace. The carpet was a thick brown and the white washed walls were more of a murky grey. Jack sat down and tried to adjust to the lack of light. He shivered and glanced up at Jesus who looked like he too was suffering from the lack of heating. The thorns around his heart were barbed wire and the drops of blood a dark musty colour. His eyes, although cast heavenward, still accused Jack.

Jack decided to study the dismal pattern of the carpet instead. Just then the door creaked open and Kate walked into the room. She was dressed in a white smock and she shuffled as if stooped by a great weight. Jack found himself staring at her stomach, but her gown was so oversized, it was impossible to tell if her pregnancy was visible or not. If anything she looked much smaller than Jack remembered. She didn't seem surprised to see him. She sat down on the sofa, but kept her eyes on the door. There was a tense nervousness about her like she was waiting for a trap to spring. All her beautiful hair had been cut off so she looked like a bird whose feathers had been ruffled the wrong way. For a moment they sat in silence.

Jack asked, "How are you?"

At first Kate didn't reply and when she did speak, her voice sounded rusty as if she was no longer in the habit of using words. "I'm very well, thank you."

Her face was pale and she looked like she was recovering from a serious illness. He knew they wouldn't be left alone together for long, but he couldn't think of a word to say. He fell back on the weather.

"It's awful cold," he muttered.

Kate stared at him as if he were a lunatic.

142

The door opened and Sister Gabriel marched in. "Well I suppose you've delivered your message."

Jack realised she must have been standing outside the whole time. Kate hadn't been with him for more than two minutes. The absurdity of the situation gripped Jack. Who did these people think they were? Kate looked half starved. He could see the fine blue veins standing out on her neck that had once been elegant, but was now emaciated like a chicken's.

"Yes," he announced. "Kate has accepted my proposal."

Sister Gabriel's eyes widened. This situation was getting out of hand altogether.

"We're getting married."

The nun stared at him.

"I intend to set right the wrongs I have done," Jack continued.

Kate was looking at the floor so Jack had no idea what her reaction to this statement was. Still there was no going back now.

"Kate will be coming with me." He put all the authority he could summon behind this declaration.

Sister Gabriel's mouth opened and closed like a swinging gate. "Miss O'Rourke's father has entrusted us with her care. We can't simply allow her to leave with any strange man that walks in off the street."

"I'm not a stranger," countered Jack. "I'm her fiancé and the father of her child."

Kate looked at him uncertainly. Sister Gabriel frowned, seemingly outraged that Kate's pregnancy had been mentioned out loud.

Jack lowered his voice. "And I think when her father discovers how thin she's gotten, how she appears to be living in building with no heating, he will be deeply unhappy."

The nun scowled at him. "This is not a holiday camp. We are trying to purify Miss O'Rourke's soul."

Surprisingly, Kate burst out laughing. Jack was relieved to hear that her laughter still had some of the old defiance in it. They hadn't turned her into a zombie after all. Sister Gabriel tutted in disgust, but didn't stop Kate running from the room. Jack nearly rushed after her, but restrained himself. If Kate didn't want to leave with him than there really was nothing he could do.

The nun pursed her lips. "You must try to understand, Dr. O'Connell. The girls that are delivered to us are in mortal danger. Our job is to wash them clean of the sin they have brought on themselves. They are weak creatures but through repentance and hard work they can be accepted back into the loving arms of our Lord Jesus Christ. We are saving them from eternal damnation."

"Damn you, you sanctimonious bitch," Jack thought. He felt a rising wave of panic.

Kate rushed back in carrying a small bag. "I'm ready," she told Jack.

She took his arm and Jack realised she was trembling from head to foot. Jack nodded to Sister Gabriel and shook hands goodbye. It took the greatest of self-control not to make a mad dash for the front door. Each step seemed to take an eternity although they moved very quickly.

When the front door slammed behind them and they were safely outside on the street, Kate threw her arms around Jack and hugged him tightly as if she'd never let him go. Jack could feel through her smock how bony she'd become. His eyes filled with tears.

23

Jack's bed-sit was cleaner than when Brendan was there, but he wished he had whisked her away to somewhere more glamorous, instead of only marginally less desolate than the convent. Still he lit a huge fire as soon as they got in. The moment they arrived Kate asked if she could take a bath. She was so long in the tub that he began to wonder if she'd slipped under the water.

When she finally emerged, her face was flushed pink and she seemed to be wrapped in steam. She'd changed out of the white smock and into a black skirt and a red blouse. Jack was glad to see her back in her regular clothes. It made her seem more real. Also he no longer felt the urge to treat her as if she were a patient. Indeed judging by the way she tucked into the simple stew he'd made for them both, her appetite was very healthy. She seemed ravenous. Jack was outraged that the nuns could half starve pregnant girls.

"How did you find me?" Kate asked.

Jack told her about visiting her sister. He left out the part about him declaring his unconditional love for her.

"Good old Pat," sighed Kate.

"I can't believe your parents put you in a place like that."

Kate shivered. "Seemed like I was there for years, but I guess it's only been a few weeks. I felt like the Count of Monte Cristo locked away on an island, everyone forgetting about me."

"I could never forget you," Jack said.

Kate nodded. "You've always been very good to me, Jack," she said with a catch in her voice. "It's just that I don't trust people the way I did. I suppose I've been terribly naïve, but I feel so let down." Her hands were shaking slightly.

Jack felt like a man confronted with the body of someone he'd murdered in a drunken rage. In the dim light of his own bed-sit, looking at her emaciated frame, the full import of what he'd done hit him. He drank up every inch of Kate sitting in front of him. From the points of her small black boots to the unbearable beauty of her tiny, sculpted shoulders. He wanted to imprint this vision of her on his memory. Like a photograph he could carry around in his soul. He prepared to make his confession, knowing that once Kate knew the truth, she would fly from his room quicker than she'd escaped from the convent. How could he have been so stupid? At least if he had let her leave with Troy, he would still have her friendship. For a second he saw himself as he was going to appear to Kate; an instant transformation from rescuing hero into calculating monster. He'd done what he did because he loved her, but it no longer seemed a valid excuse. He'd caused her heartache and pain and he deserved her hatred. He struggled to find his voice.

"Kate listen," he began. "There's something I have to explain to you. Troy…"

She interrupted him with a savage wave of her hands. "Don't talk to me about him. I never want to hear his name again." She jumped up and began to pace the room like a lion in a cage.

"You don't understand…" Jack attempted to continue, but Kate wasn't listening.

"I wrote to him you know. About the baby. I must've been really stupid to imagine that would make any difference. But I figured at least he'd have the decency to answer me."

"Maybe he never got the letter," Jack ventured miserably as he considered Troy's bad luck when it came to messages – or rather messengers.

"I thought of that," Kate said bitterly. "So I wrote again. I wrote every day for two weeks. I didn't give the convent address, but my sister's. I trust Pat. I told him I was desperate, that I thought I was going out of my mind locked up in that place."

Jack was surprised to hear Troy hadn't responded to Kate's pleas. Maybe he really didn't love her and had got over her as quickly as he claimed he would. Maybe he had a very short memory. Maybe he'd met someone else.

"And as each day passed," Kate looked at Jack intensely, "each day seemed longer than the one before. They used to get us up at six in the morning for prayers, then we had to wash clothes and pray until nine o'clock at night. I felt myself getting colder and colder. As if something inside me was dying. I know now that Troy doesn't care for me, that he never did. I was just a fantasy for him. A romantic diversion. And I don't love him any more either. I can't even begin to remember what I loved about him in the first place. Oh Jack, I've been such a fool."

Was Kate saying it had been a mistake to fall for Troy? Jack knew this was the moment to tell the truth, but the words just wouldn't come. It was as if an invisible hand had grabbed him by the throat and made speech impossible.

"Marry me, Kate," he whispered.

Kate looked alarmed by the suggestion. "I'm going to have a baby," she said slowly, like it was a concept she'd barely grasped herself. "The nuns wanted to take my baby away from me. Some of the other girls told me they make you sign a paper giving away all your rights. You don't get any say in what the child's called. Or what kind of family they're going to. It's like you're just a baby machine, a machine of sin. They were always telling us the wages of sin were death, not birth."

Jack hadn't really got his head round the fact that Kate was pregnant, he certainly hadn't for a moment considered the fate of the child she was carrying. Suddenly it occurred to him that if he raised Troy's child as his own, if he loved and cared for this baby, he could atone for any wrong he'd done Troy. Troy must've got one of Kate's letters. He must have realised she hadn't stood him up, that there had been a terrible confusion, even if he didn't realise Jack had deliberately brought this about. If he wanted to claim his wife and child, he could've done so. If he'd chosen to remain silent so far, then maybe Jack could just live the lie for as long as he could. If Troy turned up in the next few weeks and Kate discovered the truth, she wouldn't hate him more than if he told her what he'd done now. And what if he told her and Troy never did come back? Then she would leave Jack and she would still be on her own and he would have lost his chance to make it up to her. These thoughts along with thousands of fragments of other ideas roared through his brain, drowning out the little voice telling him he was kidding himself.

"If you marry me, we can pretend the baby's mine. No one need ever know any different," he said.

His words hung in the air. Kate looked at him, her eyes intense. Then she said, "I can't lie to you, Jack. I'm not in love with you. I did really like you. I mean that time on the beach, it was special. But then I met Troy and everything else just disappeared for me."

"I know," Jack responded quickly. "But I love you. I want to protect you. Maybe after a while you could get to love me back."

Kate took Jack's hand and kissed it gently. "You're too kind Jack, that's your trouble."

"I'll never leave you," he told Kate.

The intensity of his words seemed to frighten Kate. "I don't want to be on my own," she mumbled.

24

KATE WAS IN WHITE BECAUSE her parents wouldn't have it any other way. Jack had suggested they get married in a registry office but one look from Mr O'Rourke silenced the idea forever.

"This is going to be a respectable affair," he announced. Implying that even if Jack and his daughter's relationship wasn't worthy of respect, his own reputation was beyond repute.

Jack had no idea if Mr and Mrs O'Rourke believed him when he revealed himself to be the father of Kate's baby.

Mrs O'Rourke stared at him uncertainly. "Why didn't you tell us before?" she asked.

"That's young people for you nowadays." Mr O'Rourke waved her question away, looking Jack straight in the eye. "All secrets and lies and God only knows what other carry on."

Jack looked at the floor. This wasn't the best start to a relationship with his in-laws.

But then Kate's father dismissed his disquiet. "At least you're doing the decent thing now."

Mrs O'Rourke designed her daughter's wedding dress herself so that the tiny bump of her pregnancy was thoroughly concealed. Despite the fact that the invitations were just for close family and friends, half the town seemed to gather outside the local parish church.

"They just want to see if it's true I've got a bun in the oven," Kate said bitterly.

Let them look, Jack thought, let them peer with their prying eyes; it didn't make any difference any more. He was going to whisk Kate away to Dublin out of their interfering clutches. They could whisper all they liked when Jack and Kate were gone. They, and their small petty judgments, would be left firmly behind in the dust.

Jack asked his father to be his best man.

"Isn't that a bit unusual. Are you allowed to do that?"

"I thought you'd be pleased," Jack said. He didn't want to admit that while he knew plenty of medical students on his course, they were strictly for going for a pint with. There was a crowd he hung around with who probably considered themselves good mates, but in fact he'd never told them much about himself. He could hardly ask some bloke, who he'd never even discussed having a girlfriend with, to drag himself down to a small town in the middle of nowhere. It would seem too weird that he'd never mentioned this pregnant seventeen-year-old he was suddenly marrying. They would think he was being pushed into it and try to talk him out of it. How could he explain that he was the one holding the shotgun? The only person who'd guessed he was in love was Brendan, but in addition to knowing more than Jack figured was safe, his cousin had disappeared off the face of the earth. As he had no address for him, Jack didn't have to feel guilty about not inviting his old flatmate.

"I just hope you know what you're doing," his father muttered, agreeing nevertheless.

However, on the morning of the wedding he said, "You don't have to do this you know."

Jack could understand that after his own experiences his father might not have the brightest view of marriage, but his pessimism got on Jack's nerves.

"This is what I want," he insisted vehemently. "This is the happiest day of my life."

And within himself, it was. He cared nothing for the priest's words, or the church, or the crowds of people. None of them existed for him. He stood at the altar in agony that Kate would have a last minute change of heart. His nerves were shot to pieces. Every day he dreaded Kate would receive a letter from Troy promising his immediate return. Every morning he'd check the post with a sick feeling in his stomach. He'd promised himself that if a letter did arrive from America, he would pass it on. Yet every time the phone rang he worried that it was Pat to say she had news from Troy. From across the Atlantic there was a blessed silence.

Jack realised he wasn't engaged to a virgin, but he was marrying a woman he'd only kissed once in his life. He told himself just the joy of Kate's presence would be enough. And when he turned to watch her walk up the aisle on Mr O'Rourke's arm, he wouldn't have been surprised if every window in the church had shattered with the sheer force of what he felt. Her beauty was so great it might burn him.

Thankfully, the ceremony went without hitch. The only surprise was, just before the vows, the heavy church door creaked open and an embarrassed Brendan skulked into the church. Despite his anxiety about what his cousin was capable of inadvertently revealing to Kate, Jack was relieved to see him – enormously so. He hadn't heard a word since Brendan told him he was going to London. While Jack figured that Brendan was big enough and ugly enough to look after himself, a nagging doubt had formed at the back of his mind. He realised how little he actually knew about the kind of trouble Brendan was in or who was looking for him.

But his cousin looked larger than life. He beamed at Jack, and after the ceremony was over, went racing up to give him a huge bear hug. Jack thought several of his ribs would break.

"Didn't think I'd miss the big day?" he winked.

"How did you even know?" Jack asked.

Brendan tapped the side of his nose. "Ah, I have my ear to the ground, boy. Don't believe I'm not keeping tabs on you even when I'm not around. Though I have to say this did come as a bit of a surprise?"

Brendan turned to Kate. "Well aren't you one beautiful bride? Thanks be to God you decided to turn up this time."

Jack's heart came to a complete standstill. He glanced at Kate.

Kate looked momentarily confused, but before he could tell what her reaction was, another guest swamped her with congratulations and insisted on dragging her off into the crowd.

"Don't mention Troy," Jack hissed at Brendan.

His cousin frowned but nodded.

Jack knew he could count on Brendan's loyalty. He looked over at Kate who was laughing loudly with some girls she had gone to school with. Jack cheerfully poured himself another glass of champagne. Kate had put back on the weight she'd lost, her cheeks had a pink glow, and she looked the picture of health.

In a quiet moment Pat walked up and put a hand on Jack's arm. "I'm sorry if I was rude to you before, it wasn't you I'd anything against, it was that bastard of an American. I never liked the sound of him. Thank God you got her out of that awful place."

Jack felt vindicated. And there was no sign of Troy; he'd vanished back into the ocean from which he'd come.

The wedding reception was in the town's only hotel – a dingy place that had seen better days. The wallpaper had flowers embossed in velvet on it and a massive chandelier hung precariously low in the middle of the room. The glass droplets sparkled in the yellowish light. Jack remembered Brendan saying once, about a girl he'd met at the Palace, that she was the kind of bird to do it swinging from the chandeliers. Jack had a vision of a tiny swallow battering itself against all that glass and the tinkle it would make, though it probably wasn't what his cousin had in mind.

The band supposedly specialized in weddings, funerals and birthday parties and at first Jack thought they must have mixed their music sets up. They played an endless series of mournful waltzes before things got more lively with a few Elvis Presley numbers. The singer sounded like he was the King of Feedback – the mic squealed torturously at his ill-advised attempts at humour. Jack was doing his best not to drink too much. Mr

O'Rourke insisted on making a speech and though it was hard to pin down where the accusation lay, it left Jack with the definite impression that he had stolen the family silver and his only redeeming feature was that he was going to become a doctor and would one day be able to pay it all back.

Jack got Brendan to ask the band to play, 'Dream A Little Dream of Me,' a song he knew Kate loved. As Jack held her close, he was relieved to see she was smiling up at him. She looked for all the world like a happy, blushing bride. They had no money for a honeymoon, but Kate insisted she didn't mind. She said just getting out of her hometown would be enough of a wish come true for her.

"I don't care where I am," she stated. "As long as it's not here."

Jack was dismayed that Kate had trimmed her dreams, but he was in no position to take her to Hollywood just yet. So they were only booked the one night in the hotel and were going to Dublin in the morning. On the stroke of midnight he was delighted to make his excuses and lead Kate away from the crowd like she was some kind of Cinderella.

Brendan gave him an elbow in the ribs and a big wink. "The big night hey," he whispered.

Jack didn't mind Brendan talking about birds and dolls and God knows what else, but not when it came to Kate. He frowned at his cousin.

Brendan immediately seemed to sober up. "She's a lovely girl, boy. I hope you know how lucky you are."

Jack considered himself the luckiest man on earth and he was just praying his luck would hold.

Brendan thrust a package into Jack's hands. "It's for Kate. I know your mam would've wanted her to have it."

Before Jack could say anything, Brendan squeezed him in another enormous bear hug. "Take care, boy. I'm still keeping a low profile if you see what I mean. But I wouldn't have missed this for the world."

Jack was touched that Brendan had come out of hiding to be at his wedding. He wanted to ask him just how much trouble he was in, but Kate was waiting for him by the stairs and Brendan thrust him in her direction.

Their hotel room was dark and poky. The double bed was covered in a pale pink cover that had a large, unidentifiable, brown stain. Jack opened Brendan's package as soon as they had safely closed the door behind them. It was a large wooden box. Inside was a beautiful set of pearls. Jack was overwhelmed by memories of helping his mother close the clasp. It was stiff and slipped in his childish fingers. His mother always smelt of soap and some kind of light flower – lilies maybe – when she wore the pearls. It was her going out smell. He hadn't seen the necklace for years and years and had forgotten all about it. He wondered how Brendan had come to get hold of it.

"These are for you," he held the pearls out towards Kate.

They fitted her long, elegant neck perfectly. "They're beautiful," Kate gasped.

"They were my mother's."

Jack wished he couldn't remember his mother telling him as a kid that oysters couldn't cry so instead their tears formed around tiny grains of sand. That's what pearls were, according to his mother. Hardened tears. They were beautiful, but he wasn't sure if they would bring Kate luck. He didn't want his mother's sorrow rubbing off on her. But Kate looked really pleased and rushed to the bathroom to admire herself in the mirror.

Jack sat on the edge of the bed and undid his shoelaces carefully. He had absolutely no idea what he was supposed to do next. Not only was he a virgin, he didn't even know if Kate wanted them to be man and wife, in the proper sense, or if she considered their marriage a kind of elaborate cover-up. Jack wasn't expecting anything. He certainly didn't intend to put her under any pressure. He knew that marrying him had been an act of desperation on Kate's part; she'd agreed to it only because the other options were worse.

She didn't like to discuss her time with the nuns but what she told him was sobering. "Even after they take your baby away, you don't get to leave. They tell you no man would want you now you're stained. They seemed to think you could only wash away this stain by doing other people's laundry for the rest of your life. You're not even allowed talk to your fellow inmates. We'd to work in total silence. That place isn't a house of God so much as God's clothesline. They just hang you out to dry. Work you from seven in the morning till seven at night and when you drop dead, they bury you in an unmarked grave."

Kate had shuddered as she told him this. Jack had taken her hand and held it tightly. That was practically the only physical contact there had been between them since she'd escaped. He certainly didn't intend to inflict any more horror on her. He just hoped that slowly and surely he could win her trust and then her love.

So when Kate emerged from the bathroom completely naked apart from the pearls, Jack nearly fell off the edge of the bed.

She laughed. "You look like you've seen a ghost."

A vision more like, Jack thought. The only time he'd seen a nude woman before in his whole life was on the back of a set of cards that Brendan possessed. They weren't even totally undressed, they were mainly topless with strange stockings and garters. These pictures confused Jack. The women in them were smiling, but there was something totally unreal about the curves of their bodies. As though they were laughing at Jack, instead of inviting him. Kate's smile was completely different. There was something shy, magical and strangely determined about it.

"You don't have to…" Jack mumbled.

Kate silenced him by kissing him hard on the lips. As she began to unbutton his shirt, Jack wondered if she'd done this with Troy. He was also aware of the small curve of her pregnancy. But he soon forgot about the baby, and about Troy, and indeed about everything else that had ever worried him. Kate's skin was the softest silk – he wanted to wrap it around himself. He knew with absolute certainty that she was the love of his life. No other woman could ever mean anything to him. He was determined never to lose her again. Something felt so utterly and undeniably right. He felt like he was drowning inside her. But he no longer cared. He had lost his fear of water.

25

AISLING STARED AT CATHAL'S BRACELET feeling sick to her stomach. She couldn't think why the bracelet would be there. However she looked at it, her uncle had lied to her or at the very least not told her everything he knew. Maybe Cathal had sworn him to secrecy. But Jack had known how desperate Aisling had been for any information about her brother. Just to know he was still alive would have meant the world to her. Now she was confused and betrayed and felt further than ever from the truth.

She put the tape back on the base of the drawer but kept the bracelet. It had been taped so flat against the wood that it was nearly impossible to tell that it was now gone. She closed Jack's bedroom door behind her and wandered downstairs. She felt like she was going mad. Her uncle had given her the phone number for his hotel in case of emergencies. She rang it and was informed that Dr O'Connell was not in his room – would she like to leave a message? She couldn't begin to think what to say so she said no.

Maybe it would be better to confront him in the flesh. She wanted to grab Jack and shake him till he told her what the hell was going on. She wanted to be able to look him in the eye and have him try to tell her he had no idea what had happened to Cathal. She remembered how full of regret he seemed when he came to see her at the Gaeltacht. What had all that been about? She felt like a prisoner in the house. She had searched Jack's room, reading every single bit of paper for more clues, but found nothing. She wanted to scream. She couldn't bear to spend another moment in a house which had so suddenly turned from safe haven to something out of one of her nightmares. Was she dreaming? She felt like her grasp on reality was slipping. She decided to go out.

She went to the pub and then, since it was a Friday night, to a club in town. There was the familiar quickening of her heartbeat as she approached the bouncer. In a few months she'd be eighteen but the club supposedly didn't let you in till you were twenty-one. Looking round Aisling couldn't see anyone over twenty and wondered why she worried. She went there every week and had never been turned away. The club made up for its tatty appearance by having a huge glitter ball, practically the size of the room, in the centre of the floor and the extensive use of a smoke machine. It looked as if the dancing bodies were emerging from a thick fog.

"Palace, my arse," thought Aisling. "God knows when this place last had a lick of paint."

The DJ, a scrawny fellow with dyed, long, black hair that obscured his face, was playing 'Tainted Love.' Aisling swayed to, 'Once I ran to you, now I run from you...' She felt angry and bitter and rather frightened by how little she seemed to know about her own life. She decided the only solution was to get drunk. She dreaded the slow sets, having to stand against the wall like a trussed up chicken, hoping Prince Charming would ask her to dance. Then as the song played on and couples took to the floor, just some bloke who didn't have too many spots or bad breath – and then as all her friends were asked, she would inwardly scream: anyone, just anyone at all, so I'm not left standing here like a prize lemon. A lanky fella with an earring seemed to hear her cry. She bounded on to the floor relieved to escape the social rejection of the wall. He wrapped his arms around her, engulfing her in the overpowering smell of male deodorant. For an awful second she thought she might choke.

He was shouting something, but the music was so loud she couldn't hear him. He repeated himself, screaming in her ear, "What's your name?"

She thought her eardrum might pop.

"Come here often?"

Aisling felt depressed by the lack of originality of the question, but smiled when she remembered Susan's claim that she'd once answered, "No, the floor's just sticky." Susan would have the nerve to say something like that, but Aisling never could.

The conversation continued in shouts. Aisling felt she could say whatever she wanted and it would make no difference as they couldn't possibly hear each other. When the boy judged that a socially acceptable amount of chat had occurred – roughly two minutes – he stuck his tongue in her mouth.

He wasn't a bad kisser, Aisling had experienced much worse. At least he wasn't literally trying to tickle her tonsils as last week's slow set snog had. Aisling couldn't remember his name either, though maybe like this bloke she hadn't heard it in the first place.

She only discovered this week's snog was 'Jason' when he gave his name to her on a piece of paper that he'd clearly prepared in advance. Aisling quite admired this and it saved her from having to give a false number as she'd done last Friday. She made her excuses – she had to catch the last bus home. She actually had enough for a taxi fare but she just didn't feel like sticking around. She was still in shock and the alcohol was only making her feel less sure of what was real and what wasn't.

On the bus an old man tried to put his hand on her leg. She didn't feel repulsed or even annoyed. She just said, "Excuse me," very politely and moved to another seat. She stared at the scrap of paper with Jason's name on it, then tore it into the tiniest pieces she could manage. She knew she'd never ring him.

"Fuck normal for a game of soldiers," she thought angrily.

She wasn't mad at Jason. He seemed like a perfectly nice guy. She was furious with Claire for making her feel so at odds with the rest of the world. She nearly missed her stop and had to fling herself down the stairs and dive through the packed bodies and out the doors. The whole bus reeked of alcohol and sweat. She was glad to escape its claustrophobia.

On the street the rain was coming down in hard driving sheets. She could feel it trickling down her back. Like ice fingers pressing into her. She ran for it. Jumping over huge puddles and narrowly avoiding being splashed by passing cars. By the time she reached Jack's house, she was soaked. She could barely get her key in the door, her hands were so cold. She was glad she'd left the lights on. It was Jack's instruction to do so, so that potential burglars wouldn't think the place was empty. She didn't like coming back to the dark anyway. As the door swung open light and warmth swept over her. She stepped inside, breathing a sigh of relief.

Closing the door, she saw, out of the corner of her eye, a figure appear from the kitchen. She screamed in shock.

Claire jumped. "It's me Aisling, it's only me."

Aisling closed her mouth, still shaking. That it was Claire and not a knife wielding murderer was only slightly less disturbing.

Claire looked pale and very nervous, but she helped Aisling out of her wet coat. "I've lit a fire," she announced, insisting on making them both hot whiskeys.

Aisling noticed with relief that the bottle of wine on the table was nearly empty. She wasn't sober and she didn't want Claire having that advantage over her. Aisling realised she'd no idea what to say to Claire now that she'd reappeared. "I love you" seemed the only relevant thing, but she feared Claire would rush back out the door before the declaration was finished.

26

ONCE AISLING WAS SETTLED BY the fire, Claire bombarded her with a series of pointless questions about school. She answered them almost mechanically; busy adjusting herself to Claire's miraculous return. She sensed that Claire wanted her to talk so she wouldn't have to speak herself. Wouldn't have to explain what she'd been doing all these weeks and why she'd decided to reappear out of the blue. Aisling herself was scared to launch into all the hundreds of questions that crammed her mind, the most pressing of which was not: why are you back? but: how long are you staying?

Yet the little boring details of Aisling's life had a familiarity which seemed to close the distance between them. As if they were slowly walking back to that space where they had been free and easy with one another and knew the ins and outs of each other's routines. After they finished the whisky, Claire kept pouring wine. Aisling noticed how nervy and jumpy she was, like she was on the run from something or someone. But by now Aisling had soaked herself in so much alcohol that the words flowed out of her. It wasn't as if her uncle didn't ask her every evening how her day had gone or that she didn't have friends at school, but still it felt like she had been completely alone. Locked up in silence. It was a blessed release to speak to Claire – like she was the only one who really understood what Aisling was talking about.

But Aisling didn't tell Claire about what she'd found in Jack's room. Partly because she didn't want to admit why she'd gone in there in the first place, and partly because she didn't know how to explain that finding the bracelet had turned her fragile existence upside down.

At some point in the middle of some amusing tale about Aisling's history teacher, Claire laughed and said, "Oh but it's good to be back."

"Jack's really missed you," Aisling said.

"Feels like I've been away for years," Claire sighed.

It felt that way to Aisling too. "Why didn't you ring?"

Aisling feared it sounded like an accusation, but Claire didn't appear offended.

"Because I knew that if I didn't break from here, clearly and completely, I'd never stick to my resolve. Every day I thought about calling, but it would only have made things harder, not better. You do believe me."

"I don't understand…" Aisling began.

"Hugh… Hugh and I."

Aisling's heart sank. "Hugh and I" sounded so formal, so sure, so till death do us part.

Claire looked like she wanted to explain herself but didn't know where to begin. She ran her hand nervously through her hair and took a deep breath. "Hugh wanted us to try again and I agreed we should. After all we've only been married a year, it was supposed to be forever."

Forever had a death like finality about it. Like Claire had agreed to be buried with him.

"We... well I was pregnant when we got engaged."

Aisling felt slightly better. Maybe Claire had been pressurized into marrying Hugh. At the very least she had a reason for entering wedlock other than that she was madly in love with Hugh and couldn't wait to tie the knot.

"It was an accident. But when I told Hugh he was very good about it, insisted we get married straight away."

"And the baby?" Aisling asked. Hard as it was to imagine Claire as a wife, even more disconcerting was the idea of her being a mother.

Claire's eyes filled with tears. "I had an abortion. Jack... Jack helped me."

Aisling considered this new image of her uncle as an abortionist. It was still illegal for a start. A doctor wasn't even allowed talk to someone about the possibility of a termination, never mind give them one. On one of the toilet doors in Aisling's school was scribbled the phone number of an information help line in England. Underneath it someone had scribbled, 'Abortion is murder.' It fascinated Aisling that giving someone a phone number could be illegal.

Aisling thought it was reactionary and unfair. She'd once tried to express this to her mother who only said, "The unborn child has a right to life. Abortion is against God." What about the mother's right to life? It seemed to Aisling God had an objection to most of life's difficulties but he didn't offer ready solutions. The message was; don't get into trouble in the first place, but that was easy to say from the vantage point of the heavens. Didn't Jesus report back that life on planet earth was complicated and messy and that trouble was nearly impossible to avoid? Or maybe he did. Maybe that was all the emphasis on forgiveness in the Bible, but the nuns that taught Aisling had seemed more interested in condemning.

Cathal had once said to her, "You don't know how it feels to have been unwanted."

She hadn't understood at the time and wished now that she'd been able to tell him how much she wanted him around. Maybe he'd left

158

because he didn't realise how they would miss him. It seemed unfair to their parents who, whatever their faults, had certainly never neglected them. Even if her father wasn't Cathal's natural father, he'd certainly always taken a great interest in his welfare. Maybe he hadn't understood what was important to Cathal, but he'd tried to bring him up the best way he knew how. Did he love him? Aisling didn't know the answer to that. What was love anyway? Did Claire love Hugh? Enough to marry him, but not enough to have his baby? It made no sense. Aisling struggled to say something comforting. She didn't think having an abortion was wrong, but she wasn't sure she would choose to have one herself and she wasn't sure she liked the idea of her uncle performing them.

"Jack did it for you?" she asked, trying to sound non-judgemental although she was beginning to feel that she didn't know or trust her uncle at all.

Claire laughed bitterly. "No, no some butcher in London did it for me. I went to Jack when I came back because a week later I was still in terrible pain and too ashamed to tell anyone about it. Even Hugh. That's how I met your uncle. When I collapsed in his waiting room. He had me rushed to the hospital and stayed with me the whole time. I had internal bleeding and lost so much blood I nearly died. Or so they told me. I don't remember much about it."

Claire's voice was hollow. As if she'd detached herself from the whole experience. The image of Jack rushing Claire to the hospital sat far more comfortably with Aisling than him performing terminations. Sometimes she had to concede that she wasn't as liberal and open-minded as she liked to pretend she was.

In a rush of guilt and self realization, she announced, "I don't think there's anything wrong with having an abortion. Why should you be forced to have a child you don't want?"

The shadow of a smile flickered across Claire's face. "Maybe when you're older you'll realise that it's not so easy to distinguish between what you want and don't want."

"I don't get it. Hugh wanted to marry you and he wanted you to have an abortion?" In Aisling's mind there were three kinds of men: The ones that when you told them you were pregnant, fell down on one knee and promised to love you and the baby forever; the ones that offered to pay for the abortion in England and were pissed off if you weren't grateful for their generosity; and the ones that denied being the father and called you a slut that they never wanted to see again.

"Well, we were both still students, we didn't have any money. We thought we could have more kids later when the time was right. We knew we wanted to be together, it was just the timing was wrong."

The thought of Claire making babies with her husband made Aisling feel sick.

"It was a joint decision," Claire insisted. "Hugh didn't put any pressure on me at all. But, you see, because of the infection, Jack explained to me that I can't have any more children. I've blown my one chance." Claire started to cry again. "I was in hospital for a week. Hugh came every day with flowers but I couldn't look at him. Everything had changed between us. He thought I was just tired so he took me home. He had a room in a house with five other students – all boys doing engineering. They were so loud and full of energy. Always shouting and playing jokes and having parties. I just couldn't seem to join in. I felt empty. Like there was no reason to get up in the morning. I was just exhausted and drained. I was entirely detached from everyone. Nothing seemed to have a meaning any more. But Hugh believed all I needed was rest."

Aisling nodded. It was a feeling – or, rather, a lack of feeling – she recognised. One she connected with Cathal. That's what loss was – a terrible absence that filled you up from the inside. So that you didn't just miss the person who was gone, you felt as if you had disappeared as well. Like a part of you had died.

"I kept seeing Jack as my doctor and he told me I was depressed. He really wanted me to go to a counsellor but I couldn't see the point. It would just be more words. And words seemed to have lost all their meaning. I felt I was being punished. That because I'd killed my baby, God had decided not to let me have any more."

"That's ridiculous," Aisling said. "What happened was terrible, but it had nothing to do with God. Thousands of women have abortions every year and go on to have loads of kids. You were very unlucky. You can't let all the nonsense in this country invade your mind."

Claire smiled gratefully. "I know that now. It wasn't God that was punishing me. I was punishing myself. I felt worthless. Like everything I'd taken to be solid and concrete and true was suddenly made out of paper. It wasn't Hugh's fault. He thought it was a question of cheering me up. He couldn't understand that my whole comprehension of my life had been knocked off kilter. Like I still had the map but my compass had reversed poles. When I talked like that, he just looked at me as if I was mad. He started going out really late. He drank more. It's not as if he didn't ask me to go with him. But I'd no energy. I'd spend whole days just sitting in my room. When he'd come in at four or five in the morning, he'd speak to me very slowly, very gently, like I was made out of glass and he was scared he would break me." She paused. "We were far too young to be married."

Aisling agreed. Her own parents had got hitched when her mother was twenty one and her father was twenty four. When Aisling considered that this was only a few years away from her own age, it struck her as madness.

She'd once asked her mother, "Why did you get married so young?"

"That's what everyone did back then," her mother answered defensively.

Only recently had Aisling grasped that her mother must've been pregnant with another man's child when she got married. She wondered how her father had felt about that. She knew she would never have the nerve to ask him.

Claire opened another bottle of wine and poured some slowly into their glasses. Aisling knew she'd already drunk far too much but she didn't say a word. She wanted Claire to keep talking. After a moment of silence Claire said, "It wasn't that I wanted to die so much as I didn't particularly want to live any more."

A dark shadow crawled over Aisling's skin. "You tried to kill yourself?"

"It didn't seem like a conscious decision. Almost like I found myself with the glass of water in the one hand and the bottle of sleeping tablets in the other."

Aisling couldn't believe it. Claire who seemed so vibrant and full of life. How could she have thought of such a thing? Aisling realised her hands were shaking and she had to put her glass down. "Promise me you'll never do anything like that again."

"Hey, it's okay," Claire took Aisling's hand. "I'm much better now. It was a stupid mistake."

"Just promise me," Aisling repeated. She didn't have a huge amount of faith in promises, but still she wanted to hear Claire say it.

"I promise." Claire smiled.

She didn't look remotely suicidal but Aisling wished the way she said "I promise" didn't remind her of the definite tone of her brother's "I'll see you very soon."

"It was Jack who found me," Claire explained. "I'd missed my appointment to see him the day before and when he rang, I made Hugh say I wasn't there. He said he had a dream about me that night and so the next day he came round my house to see if I was okay." Claire laughed. "I'd never have thought your uncle was so superstitious. He's always claiming to be an atheist."

"What was the dream?"

"He said he was on a beach and he saw something in the water. When he went to grab it, he realised it was a body. He pulled it out, and when he turned it over, it was me."

Aisling shivered, remembering how Jack had reacted when she told him that her mother said Kate had drowned. What had happened to her aunt? That was another question she had never got a proper answer to.

"Did you know Jack's mother drowned herself?" Claire asked.

Aisling was taken aback – she'd had no idea. "He never told me that."

"Don't say I told you. He doesn't like to talk about it. He was only a teenager at the time. He said that's why he felt so anxious about me. Though it wasn't just the dream. He'd been worried about me for some time because I was refusing any support, even medication. I thought I deserved to suffer you see, I didn't want anything to take the edge off the pain. He'd prescribed me these tablets because I told him I couldn't sleep. Which was true. I hadn't slept for weeks. I'd spend the afternoons in bed but at night I'd get up and walk around the house. To check if everyone was still breathing. I used to turn all the lights on and off, one by one. I don't really know why, but it seemed vitally important at the time."

"I can see why Jack was worried."

"Yes but not many doctors would come to your house uninvited. He'd never been there before, but he had my address. He said it took ages for anyone to open the door as one of the students was blaring his techno music. When he eventually answered, he nearly didn't let Jack in because he didn't believe he was a doctor. But Jack insisted on being shown to my room. Hugh had gone away for a few days. I suspected at the time he was seeing someone else. I'm still not sure. To be honest I don't think I could blame him if he was."

Aisling felt a wave of anger at Hugh's abandonment of Claire. Surely he must have known his wife was in no state to be left on her own? And if he was being unfaithful, surely Claire felt more upset about it than she was letting on?

"He found me unconscious in the bed and called an ambulance. Apparently my housemate said, "See I told you she was sleeping," and Jack felt like punching him. His name was Mike, the student. He wasn't a bad sort. Just always stoned and not terribly clever to begin with. I could have lain there for days before it would have occurred to him there was anything wrong. Anyway, after I got out of hospital, I couldn't face going back there. It was an old house with high ceilings and it was freezing cold. It was the winter, you see, and the boiler didn't work properly. And there were always piles of dirty dishes in the sink and clothes drying on the back of chairs. Sometimes I think it might have been the smell of engineers' wet socks that pushed me over the edge."

Claire attempted to smile at her joke but didn't quite succeed. "Jack said I needed somewhere clean and quiet and that he had a spare room going. I didn't really want to leave Hugh, though that's how he saw it, I just didn't want to see him for a bit. I needed some space for myself."

Aisling realised her uncle had taken Claire in because she needed him in the same way he had taken Aisling in – two lost souls who were being slowly strangled by their home environment. Aisling looked round the sitting-room with its white walls, polished floors, and tasteful paintings. She wondered how the picture of the naked woman could ever have struck her as remotely shocking. She felt now as if it were an old friend. In Jack's house they had both found peace, a chance to lick their wounds, and become their own people again. Why on earth had Claire left this sanctuary?

Almost on cue, Claire explained, "Hugh begged me to come back. He'd bought a one bedroom flat for us to live in. He promised he'd stopped drinking and going out every night. He said he'd matured."

Aisling could imagine all these false promises of reform. In her opinion, people didn't change that much.

"We'd been apart for nearly a year. We'd both got jobs. He works for this IT company that pays a lot more than my teaching I can tell you. He said we weren't the same people any more, but he still loved me. He wanted to set things right."

"So he should," exclaimed Aisling. 'You could have died thanks to him.'

Claire shook her head. "I don't actually think it was his fault. It was more that there were a lot of things in my life I'd never really faced up to. The truth is I never felt particularly comfortable or happy in myself, but I chose to ignore it. I hid my feelings of unease underneath the trappings of a normal life. I studied, I got married... only when I lost the baby did I realise how fragile it all was. How little any of it had to do with the real me, this alien person I'd successfully kept under lock and key for most of my life. It was like getting to know a stranger."

Maybe it hadn't been Hugh's fault, but Aisling still didn't like him.

"I was a different person," Claire continued. "I always had been but I didn't realise it and neither did Hugh. But I'd married him. He was convinced our marriage had fallen apart because I'd had a nervous breakdown. Now that I was well again, we could just pick up where we left off.

163

I felt I owed it to him to try.'

"And now?"

"I kept thinking about you trying to kiss me."

Aisling was startled. In the grand narrative of Claire's past, Aisling's unfortunate act of clumsiness had paled into insignificance. Where once Aisling had worried that Claire left because of her, she now took some comfort in the fact that compared to the confusions of her life with Hugh, Aisling's actions were nearly innocent. No wonder she'd dismissed it as the phase of a silly schoolgirl. Aisling knew that what she felt for Claire was far bigger than her own limited experience. But she couldn't explain how she was so sure of it and right now the most important thing was Claire was safe.

"I'm terribly sorry about that," Aisling said earnestly. "It was such a stupid thing to do. I really regret it."

Claire peered into the depths of her wine glass. "So why did you do it in the first place?"

Aisling was at a loss what to say. Her brain was too befuddled with alcohol to come up with a plausible excuse. "Because I love you," she stated.

It was such an enormous relief to say it that Aisling didn't even care if Claire was horrified. It was like something that had been building up inside her, desperately looking for a way out.

Claire knocked back the rest of the wine in her glass. Aisling thought for an awful moment she was getting up to leave, but she pulled Aisling towards her and kissed her. The kind of slow, lingering kiss you could dive into and never surface.

27

AISLING WOKE IN THE MORNING completely confused as to where she was. Her head ached and pieces of the evening before twirled around in her brain like a kaleidoscope that refuses to fall into place. Only when she felt Claire's arm around her and the softness of her breath on her neck did she believe that the night before had been anything more than a very strange dream. She lay frozen to the spot. Her throat was sandpaper and she needed to go to the loo quite badly, but she couldn't bring herself to break the moment.

Claire's fingers rested light on her stomach, her breathing soft and regular. Like that of a small animal in its den. Aisling figured she might never be so close to Claire again and she wanted to be able to recall every detail. She noted that the hairs on Claire's arms were flecked with gold and sprinkled with tiny freckles. It was a new close up perspective that was thrilling, but she was sure it couldn't last. The only possible explanation for Claire's behaviour last night was that she was very drunk and that she'd had some kind of row with Hugh from which she was seeking comfort.

Yet a tiny little voice of hope whispered, "But she kissed me." Aisling refused to listen; it was better to be realistic. In the cold light of day Claire would be as horrified at what she'd done as the first time when she'd slapped Aisling.

Claire stirred and rolled over. She was wearing a large oversized black T-shirt that she always slept in. Part of her back was exposed. Aisling felt an irresistible urge to run her fingers along Claire's skin. Like a pyromaniac's fascination with flame, she thought, both amused and surprised at herself.

Claire's eyes blinked open and she smiled at Aisling. It was a smile so warm and open and sunny that Aisling thought her heart would break. "Morning. How's the head?"

"Not so good," Aisling replied. She felt like adding, "But I don't mind at all." Because everything else about this was so much better than when she usually woke up with a hangover. The familiar Saturday morning thumping headache and the furry taste of last night's beer, fags and often some stranger's tongue in her mouth. Normally she felt exhausted and depressed by the sordid ritual of Friday night, where now she felt strangely elated. As if her spirit was floating above any physical pain.

"I practically had to carry you to bed. You could hardly stand."

Claire was teasing her, but Aisling felt mortified. Hardly the most romantic conclusion to the evening.

"I'm sorry," Aisling muttered turning her face away, feeling awkward.

Claire put her hand gently under Aisling's chin. "I'm not," she said as she kissed her.

Aisling was flooded with relief. So much so that it took her a moment to realise Claire was taking off her clothes. She slowly removed Aisling's socks, jeans, and shirt. Aisling suddenly felt very scared. She didn't know what she was expected to do.

Then Claire kissed Aisling's neck. Soft, butterfly kisses so light they were barely there. Then she moved down to Aisling's breasts and Aisling forgot all about her hangover, her disappointing Friday nights, the entire universe in fact. For the first time her entire being was concentrated on one thing and everything else disappeared. And that one thing was how much she wanted Claire. Wanted to feel her skin against hers. Claire took off Aisling's bra and knickers and Aisling felt she'd never been so completely and utterly naked. It was a shock to her how small Claire's body was. How tiny her shoulders were and how incredibly elegant the long sweep of her back felt under Aisling's hands. She felt like someone lost in the desert, who has never known what it is to drink water, suddenly stumbling across an oasis. Like all her life something fundamental had been missing, that her body had been crying out for some essential vitamin or mineral, but she'd never realised it.

Now as Claire rocked against her, Aisling felt something falling away inside her in ripples of pure ecstasy. She knew she'd never felt so entirely alive and so entirely absent before. For a moment she couldn't breathe.

"Are you all right?" Claire asked.

Aisling felt she was more all right than she'd ever been before and it made her laugh.

That set Claire off, and the next moment they were both giggling hysterically. Neither of them could say quite what was so funny. They stopped dead when they heard a key in the door.

"I thought Jack wasn't coming back till tomorrow," Claire whispered.

Aisling realised that she'd forgotten all about Jack when only yesterday she'd felt she couldn't wait another five minutes for his return. The realisation was followed by an abject terror that he would discover her in bed with Claire. She couldn't even begin to imagine his reaction. She didn't want to. She desperately grabbed for her clothes and dragged them on, stumbling from the room as fast as possible. She scurried across the hall and dived into the relative safety of her own bed. She heard Jack

166

moving around in the kitchen downstairs, heard him whistling. He had the most mournful whistle she'd ever known.

Claire often said to him, "If you've got to whistle at breakfast time, can't it at least be cheerful? Whistling is meant to be cheerful, it's not meant to sound like a funeral march."

Jack was always surprised, as if he was totally unaware that the sound he was making was a slow sad tune full of regret and heartache. He didn't change it though. Aisling figured maybe he couldn't. Maybe that was the soundtrack that ran through his mind and they should be glad they could only hear the whistle, rather than the full orchestrated version he listened to over and over with no escape.

Aisling was struck by the thought that she'd spent the last few weeks sympathising with her uncle's obvious misery at Claire's departure, judging Claire for abandoning him, then she had hopped into bed with her the moment she returned. Why had she never thought before that her desire to have Claire and Jack back together was at odds with her desire to have Claire for herself? She supposed they had been united against the common enemy – Claire's marriage. Although Jack never mentioned Hugh's name, Aisling could sense he resented him as much as she did. But Claire had insisted there was nothing going on between her and Jack, they were just friends. If that was the case, why did Aisling feel so guilty? Like she'd betrayed the one person who'd helped her. Suddenly it seemed clear to her that if her uncle had lied about Cathal, it could only have been out of some warped idea of protecting her. But protecting her from what? Aisling wondered if she really wanted to know. Her hangover seeped back with a vengeance. She lay on her bed feeling confused and sick.

"Anybody home?" Jack shouted out.

Aisling found she couldn't bring herself to answer.

There was no denying that Jack's joy at Claire's return would be ruined if he knew what had happened between them. Suddenly Aisling had a secret of her own. She'd discovered love but also been sucked into the shadowy world of half truths that she so despised; She couldn't possibly tell her uncle what she felt, yet she knew only too well that silence was just a more elaborate form of lying.

28

AISLING DIDN'T SET OUT TO deceive Jack. It just seemed impossible to tell him what was going on. Partly because she didn't want to hurt him; partly because she didn't want to deal with his shock. Because of all those adjectives that floated in her brain just beneath her consciousness. Unnatural... sick... perverted... twisted... Words with barbs that could sink into her flesh. Jack could tell her mother. Jack could have her sent away.

That thought more than anything else kept her silent. She couldn't stand to lose Claire just when she'd found her. Maybe all this time she thought she'd been looking for Cathal, when in fact she'd been searching for Claire without knowing it. Or maybe God had finally taken pity on her, and unable or unwilling to give her brother back, had sent Claire instead. Not that they were particularly alike. Claire had none of Cathal's intense, concentrated anger; when she lost her temper it was like a summer storm, suddenly violent but quickly passing. Actually, Aisling wasn't so sure she knew what her brother's character was. Not that she couldn't remember him – some of her memories were startlingly vivid – but that's all they were, a jumbled collection of memories. Like photographs that had fallen out of an album and no longer told a story, fragments of how he might have been.

She spent hours running her thumb over her own name engraved in Cathal's bracelet. Now that her initial shock at finding it taped underneath Jack's drawer had worn off, she no longer felt so confident about confronting her uncle. How could she explain why she'd been in his room? More than her fear of his anger at her rooting through his private possessions, more than her fear that he would guess what was happening between herself and Claire, was her fear of what Jack might tell her.

She'd lived with the uncertainty of her brother's absence for so long that she was afraid to finally find out what had become of him. She'd always told herself that even her brother's body would be better than nothing. She had even said to Claire that if she knew for sure he was no longer living, she could begin to get over it. It was all the months in limbo that had stopped her from grieving. But now she felt that she would rather have the hope of his returning one day, than the finality of hearing he was dead. And he must be dead. She couldn't think of another reason why Jack hadn't told her about the bracelet. If he was alive and well and Jack knew where he was and hadn't told her that would just be unforgivable.

Every night, once her uncle had retreated to his room, she crept into Claire's bed. What had seemed so strange and impossible was suddenly absolutely right and perfect. She felt closer to Claire than she'd ever been to anyone on earth.

When she told Claire about the bracelet, she was relieved to discover that Claire was so surprised that Aisling's trespassing was passed over as a minor detail.

"You have to ask him. I can't believe you didn't jump on him the minute he walked in the door."

She was right, of course, but Aisling was used to living with secrets and being told nothing.

"Don't even bother saying how you got it," Claire advised. "Just put the damn thing down in front of him and see what he says. Seems to me he's the one whose got some explaining to do, not you."

So that's what Aisling did.

Jack turned a very strange shade, almost blue, when Aisling handed him the bracelet.

"Where did you get this?" she asked him, keeping her tone neutral even though her heart was banging inside her chest.

Claire poured them all another glass of wine.

Jack's eyes shifted back and forth between her and Aisling. He looked like a creature caught in a trap. "Cathal gave it to me."

Aisling was relieved that he hadn't pretended he didn't know what she was talking about. She thought if she had to listen to one more lie, she might kill him.

"When was that?" she asked, her voice sounding oddly hollow.

"When I went to New York to look for him."

A silence descended on the table.

"You told me you couldn't find him." Aisling could feel tears welling up in her eyes and she struggled to control herself.

"I lied," said Jack simply. "I did find him and he gave me the bracelet to give to you."

"Where is he now?" Aisling asked, aware that this, of all the millions of questions she had, was the most important one.

"I don't know," Jack replied. He seemed to have aged ten years in the last five minutes and wouldn't look her in the eye.

He lit a cigarette and Aisling noticed his hands were shaking. "You see Cathal isn't your brother," he announced.

"Of course he's my brother." Aisling was angry.

"Technically he's your cousin. He's Kate's son. Your mother just agreed to raise him as her own after her sister died."

Aisling was more confused than ever. "So you are his father! You said you weren't."

Jack shook his head sadly. "I said I wished I was. Kate was pregnant when we married."

Jack took a dip sip of his wine. "No one knows who Cathal's father is. Not even his mother. Kate was raped."

Claire looked horrified. Aisling wondered how her brother – she wasn't going to stop thinking of him as her brother – had felt when he found out his true origins. She listened with increased agitation to the rest of her uncle's tale about how he'd tracked Cathal down to a seedy hotel in lower Manhattan.

"But why didn't you tell me any of this before?" she demanded.

Claire nodded in agreement.

"Guilt, guilt and cowardice," Jack replied. "You see me and Kate had agreed we'd tell everyone the baby was mine. But after she died I kind of went to pieces, I couldn't cope. Pat offered to help me out by taking care of Cathal. Even though he was living with her and Martin and I was in Dublin, I was still meant to visit, you know keep in touch. But I couldn't. I used to send presents sometimes but then after a while I didn't even do that. Pat thinks it's cos Cathal wasn't my natural son but it was a whole lot more complicated than that. She figured seeing as I'd abandoned him there was no point in telling Cathal he'd had this kind of stepfather. She sort of wrote me out of the story. I don't blame her."

Aisling could just imagine her mother believing that it was a kindness to leave out the unpleasant details. Maybe it was.

"Then when he turned eighteen Cathal got hold of his birth cert. And of course my name was on it. So he sought me out. He seemed like a kind of mixed up kid and I thought it would be easier on him to believe I was his father. You know the truth is I had loved him like my own son. He moved in here and we got on great. I was actually happy for a while." Jack certainly didn't look happy any more.

"You never told me about this," Claire exclaimed. Now it was her turn to wonder at Jack's secrecy.

"That's because it all went horribly wrong," Jack sighed. "Cathal had some kind of row with Martin, Aisling's father. Told him he was glad he was the son of a top surgeon rather than some stupid bar man. You can hardly blame Martin for losing his temper; after all he'd been a much

170

better father to Cathal than I'd been. He told Cathal that his father was a drunken sailor who'd run off back to America abandoning his mother."

"Drunken sailor?" Claire repeated.

"Yeah, Pat thinks Kate had a fling with this Yank and that's how she got pregnant. Kate never had the heart to tell her the truth. But when I caught up with Cathal in New York I decided he needed to know what really happened. He was already pissed off with me for pretending to be his father when I wasn't and for abandoning him for all those years. But he couldn't possibly hate me as much as I hated myself. When I told him his mother had been raped, he got up out of his seat and ran out of the bar. I thought he'd calm down after a bit. But in fact he just disappeared into thin air. I went to his hostel but he'd gone. The only thing he'd left was an envelope at reception with the leather bracelet and a note saying to give it to Aisling. I searched for him for months..."

Aisling couldn't understand how Jack could have found her brother and then let him go again. If only she'd been there to show Cathal that he did have family who still cared about him.

"You could at least have let me know he was alive," she accused.

"I know but then I would have had to admit it was my fault he'd disappeared."

Aisling didn't really think it was her uncle's fault. Cathal had asked for the truth. It was just a pity he wasn't able to cope with what he found out.

29

AISLING WAITED UNTIL SHE WAS sure her uncle was asleep before slipping out of her room and across the hall into Claire's. They made love and afterwards Aisling curled her body round Claire's like a question mark and hold her close. Sometimes Aisling felt she could never hold on tight enough. Claire told her, in whispers, about her childhood in Dublin and how she met Hugh. Claire insisted that her marriage was definitely over, but still Aisling worried. Hugh had a legal claim over her and he'd loved her first. Aisling cursed the conservatism of a country that forbade divorce. How could a marriage be sacred if you hated the living sight of one another? Though, rather worryingly, Claire didn't appear to hate Hugh.

"He did try, you know, when I went back. He really had given up drinking and instead of going out with his mates, he'd insist we go see a film instead or out to a restaurant. He'd even taught himself to cook. But he didn't want to talk about the past. He said we should focus on our future. He treated me with kid gloves. It was like I was wrapped in cotton wool and not allowed to say what was on my mind. It wasn't a nice feeling."

Aisling sympathised with Hugh's desire to forget the past, to wipe the slate clean and begin again. But what had happened before was so intricately linked with what was happening now and what would happen later, that it was impossible to disentangle them. The same as when a chain becomes hopelessly tied up in knots and every time you loosen one, you only end up creating another. Or maybe it was more like trying to make a straight line out of a spider's web. The patterns were so delicate and intricate that no mere human could achieve it. So you try to sweep the past aside and end up trapped like a fly. The more you struggle, the more paralysed you become.

"You know it didn't really matter what he did," Claire added, "because the sad truth is I realised I wasn't in love with him any more. I'm not even sure if I ever was. I did love him, he was my closest friend in the whole world. I should just never have married him."

Aisling couldn't agree more. She held Claire even closer and kissed the back of her neck. She breathed the sweet soft smell of Claire's perfume and wished she could stay in that particular position forever. They talked and talked until the first fragile rays of sunlight crept through the curtains. Then they drifted into a few short hours of sleep before the cruelty of the alarm clock. Aisling felt as if her life had been reversed.

The days passed in a kind of hazy dream of teachers, corridors, homework, all floating into each other while she thought of Claire and paid little or no attention to what was going on around her. It was amazing to Aisling that no one noticed her transformation, that in fact she was no longer there, that her real existence was happening somewhere else entirely. Occasionally a teacher would remark that she looked a bit tired, but that was it.

Night was when she came alive. So awake that it felt like she'd spent her whole life up until then in a dull coma. Aisling and Claire banished sleeping; whispering under the duvet, they talked about absolutely everything. Except Jack. Not since he'd confessed to meeting Cathal. Aisling accepted that her uncle had felt a burden of guilt which he dealt with by keeping silent. It was what she was doing herself. She could never quite trust him again and she felt less inclined than ever to tell him about her feelings for Claire. Aisling sensed that Claire was just as reluctant so they were very careful not to attract Jack's attention.

Claire claimed the sleepless nights had no impact on her teaching. In fact as her students no longer got on her strained nerves; she was more patient, able to take the time to explain things properly. She'd loved teaching in the beginning. But after only a few months, the apathy, boredom, and disillusionment of her students, not to mention the other teachers, had ground her down. She used to suffer from terminal exhaustion, but now with less sleep, she'd actually gained more energy. Aisling wondered if love was a kind of fuel, rather like solar power.

Claire joked that if anyone found out they were together, she was bound to lose her job, but it was a serious threat. Just a few years ago Aisling's old convent school had fired a teacher for having a baby when she wasn't married. Or, as they put it, they felt obliged to let her go as she wasn't a good moral example to the young women in her charge. Scared as she was, Aisling was living from day to day – or rather night to night –and she couldn't deny that the need to keep her relationship a secret gave her a certain illicit thrill. Especially when she convinced herself that it was because of the prejudices of society at large – the trouble Claire's husband was likely to cause, rather than the hurt she was likely to inflict on her uncle.

At dinnertime she watched Jack carefully for signs that he was in love with Claire. But it wasn't so easy to tell. He seemed pleased that Claire had returned, he admitted he'd been very worried about her, that he thought she was better off living here, but in such a way that it could have been the reaction of a concerned friend. Only Aisling, who'd seen how withdrawn he was when Claire had left, had her doubts. She also looked for signs that he had any clues as to what was happening between her and Claire. Aisling taught herself never to touch Claire during the day. Dinners were a careful performance.

Aisling and Claire's vampire existence continued for several months. With time, they grew more reckless. Sometimes when they were doing the dishes together and Jack was reading his paper at the kitchen table, Aisling would steal a kiss on the sly. She felt they were protected by an invisible force. As if their love was a dream only they were living, The rest of the world continued oblivious.

When Aisling told Claire she loved her, she usually replied, "I'm too scared to say that."

Aisling wondered what she was afraid of. Deep down, she really didn't give a shit what other people thought. Let them say what they liked, she didn't care. There was something liberating about the feeling. Like a huge weight that had been pressing down on her for most of her life had lifted. She felt what she felt regardless of the perceptions of others. Not that this meant she wanted to go running to her mother to tell her what a wonderful thing was happening to her. Her mother's anger she could probably cope with, but her disappointment and confusion, her silent brutal condemnation was another matter. Her mother had suffered terribly when Cathal disappeared and Aisling didn't want to hurt her. She knew that, to her mother, what to Aisling felt like the best thing that had ever happened, would be a major catastrophe. Possibly even worse than Cathal going to America and never coming back.

"But how could he just vanish like that?" Claire asked. "I mean even if he was upset about his father. It's just so extreme."

"People do it all the time," Aisling shrugged. "Just pack their bags, walk out the door, and never come back. We've no way of knowing what happened to him after he met Jack."

One Saturday morning Aisling woke up late to find Claire peering at her intensely. "What's wrong?" she asked sleepily.

"I love you," Claire said.

Aisling was totally elated. Just to hear Claire utter those simple words was, to Aisling, the definition of happiness.

"We should get up," Claire sighed.

Jack had proposed the previous evening that the three of them go for a walk in the Dublin Wicklow Mountains. Something they sometimes did when the weather was fine, or at least not pouring rain. Aisling had never appreciated the countryside when she lived in it. To her it was all dripping hedges, lumps of rock and stupid cows that smelt of shit. But since moving to the city, she'd come to value space. It was great to breathe air that was pure and look down from a hill on a vast expanse of brownish, purplish heather that doesn't contain a single other person. Her parents hardly ever went for walks. They were too busy working in the pub and for them walking meant going somewhere. The idea of a stroll just for the sake of it would seem indulgent to them. Maybe that was true but Aisling was looking forward to getting into Jack's smooth car and shooting out of the city up into the wildness of the hills. She knew Jack would want to get an early start. He tended to plan these expeditions as if they were a military exercise.

As a rule Aisling always made sure she left Claire's room long before Jack was awake. Luckily he kept a rigid schedule and always got up at seven on the dot unless he was working nights. On weekends he was less predictable. But Aisling just couldn't bring herself to stop caressing Claire's cool, delicious body. She only realised Jack was standing in the doorway when Claire gave a frightened gasp that wasn't remotely sexual. For a second Aisling's eyes met her uncle's. Even if he'd wanted to, Jack couldn't possible deny what he was seeing. Neither Aisling nor Claire had any clothes on. They fumbled to pull the sheet over themselves.

Jack's expression was unreadable. After what seemed an eternity, but could only have been a few seconds, he turned away closing the door softly behind him. Aisling realised she could feel Claire's heart beating nineteen–to-the-dozen underneath her. Her own heart felt like it had stopped.

"Oh fuck," Claire said.

30

KATE INSISTED ON PAINTING THE walls a sunshine yellow when she moved into the bed-sit in Dublin. The room in its grimness had only really been suitable for two bachelor men because they spent next to no time in it.

Jack told Kate that in her condition she shouldn't be working, but she just laughed and splashed paint at him.

"I'm not an invalid," she said as she ran a roller up the wall.

Jack washed the windows which he'd never really noticed before were so dirty that very little light came through. He pulled down the sheet that had divided the room. His father had given him some money as a wedding present so he threw out the old flea bitten mattresses and bought a double bed. Yet, even with the new lick of paint, the bed-sit retained an air of dinginess. The windows rattled and, despite Jack's attempts to insulate them with old newspaper, a cold draft seeped through. It was no place for a baby.

Jack told Kate he had only another year to go till he got his internship. Then they could buy a house with a nursery for the child. They spent hours discussing what the room would be like. It was a magic, safe place they created in their own imagination.

Jack would sometimes catch Kate staring out the window with a look of infinite sadness on her face. She would jump when he asked her what was wrong. Then, smiling, she'd say, "I'm fine Jack, stop worrying all the time."

But the smile always seemed forced, like it was a physical effort for Kate to pull herself back into her body. That although she was standing there in front of him, she was very far away. After they first made love in the new double bed, Jack held her tightly in his arms, kissed her hair and stared at her. It was always a shock to him how overwhelming her beauty was.

"You're gorgeous," he said, his voice barely audible.

Kate smiled at him and kissed the tip of his nose. "I'm very grateful to you."

Jack wanted to tell her that he didn't want her gratitude, he wanted her heart. "I love you," he whispered.

"I know," was her response.

That was what she always said. She never told him she loved him and that was the one gap in Jack's happiness. But he tried not to let it weigh on him. He was extremely busy as his exams were coming up and he couldn't afford to fail them. His father had managed to pull a few strings and secure Jack work for the summer. There was a time Jack would have scorned this, but now he was grateful for his father's help.

The job was as a clerk in the post office covering for someone who was suffering from a mysterious illness. Probably boredom, Jack thought, as his duties mainly consisted of folding over bits of paper after squashing them with a rubber stamp. But Jack didn't mind the utter vacancy of this work. It gave him plenty of time to daydream about Kate. Sometimes he felt he enjoyed thinking about her more than actually being with her. Inside his own head he could enjoy her absolute perfection without having to wonder if she really was happy with him. There was still a gap between what he felt inside and what he managed to express, but he didn't resent that she was pregnant. In fact he was glad they had the baby to focus on. Also he loved to fuss over Kate, to make her put her feet up, to cook her dinner... The pregnancy just gave him an excuse.

Kate had his number at work and he made her swear that the moment she felt the slightest twinge, she'd ring him. His supervisor, Mr Davis, a pompous young man who hated Jack because he was a medical student, didn't like Jack making phone calls. He would have the whole office working in total silence if he could. Jack felt like telling him that he really was perfectly capable of stuffing an envelope and holding a conversation at the same time. It was worse than being at school.

Jack didn't want to provoke Mr Davis but every now and again he was seized by a sudden panic. He'd feel in his bones that something was wrong with Kate. He'd see her lying in agony in a pool of blood and couldn't stop himself rushing to the phone to ring. Kate always answered in a calm voice, assuring Jack that she was fine. When Mr Davis caught him, he turned a kind of reddish purple and lectured him about how personal phone calls during working hours were discouraged. This lecture always ended with the statement, "You're in the real world now, Mr O'Connell." It made Jack wonder where he was supposed to have been before.

Jack was forever asking Kate how she was feeling. He'd heard far too many horror stories of women dying in childbirth and it gave him nightmares. But the only thing Kate seemed to suffer from was boredom. Apart from Pat, she knew no one in Dublin. The bed-sit was too quiet when he was out at work and she missed the hustle and bustle of her father's pub. To compensate, Jack made sure he went home every day right after work. He never went for a few pints as was the habit of his colleagues. He wanted to be with Kate and besides they needed every penny for the baby, he couldn't go drinking the little they had.

Kate said to him once, "You're so responsible, Jack. I'm scared I'm making you old before your time."

But Jack had felt ancient for as long as he could remember. What he liked was to have a role; to feel that somebody needed him. When he put his ear against Kate's stomach and felt the tiniest of kicks, he thought of the little creature swimming inside and realised two people depended on him. He was no longer just hanging around in the shadows wondering what to do with himself.

Despite their lack of money, Jack liked surprising his wife with little presents. Sometimes he'd bring back chocolates or a scarf. He loved watching Kate's face as she opened up the package.

She would put her arms around his neck and tell him, "You're too good to me you know, you really are."

At such moments he felt his heart would burst with happiness. He'd never been interested in money for himself, but now he looked forward to the day when he could buy Kate dresses and jewellery.

One night when Kate was just over seven months pregnant, she woke Jack up with a cry. At first he thought she was having a bad dream as she often did. This time though when he asked her if she was okay, she didn't sleepily mutter, "Just a dream." She said with urgency, "There's something happening."

Jack was up out of the bed and had the lights on in flash. The bed was wet.

"I think your waters have broken," he told Kate, trying to contain his rising sense of panic.

He dialled for a taxi. "My wife's having a baby," he yelled down the phone.

Kate was walking up and down the room obviously in considerable pain. "It's too early," she gasped. There were tears rolling down her face.

Jack tried in vain to get her to sit down.

Suddenly she doubled up in agony, her eyes wide with shock. "It's coming," she whispered.

Jack hadn't ever actually been present at a birth, but he'd had the sense to skip ahead to that part of the text book so at least he knew the principles. He spread out some newspaper on the bed and made Kate lie down. Then he filled the kettle to boil. Kate was moaning, not small moans, but great, deep ones that seemed to come from a place inside her that she didn't even know existed.

There was a knock on the door. It was the taxi driver. But Kate was going nowhere. Jack could already see the baby's head.

"Jesus, Mary and Joseph," exclaimed the driver, a small fat man with a red face. He looked like he was considering doing a runner, but his good nature got the better of him and instead he took his jacket off to help Jack deliver the baby.

With one last agonizing push, while Kate screamed and cursed, using language Jack had never even known she possessed, the child emerged. Jack cut the cord with the kitchen scissors.

"A boy, Missus," shouted the taxi driver completely overcome with excitement. "You have a boy."

But the baby was a strange blue colour and showed no signs of breathing. Jack laid the tiny creature on the kitchen table and began to massage its chest. The baby's skin was so new, it was like touching a soft, damp, alien substance.

The taxi driver hurried to the phone to dial an ambulance.

"Please," Jack whispered. "Please God." He didn't know why he was so desperate for this baby, which wasn't even his, to survive but he felt at that moment he would sacrifice his own life if only the little boy would draw breath. Jack stared down at the tiny eyes and nose and mouth. They didn't look human to him, they looked like the features of some strange sea creature. A species of fish that had never been caught before.

"Do something," roared Kate. "Don't let him die."

Jack rubbed the baby's feet. He'd read somewhere this was a good idea.

The taxi driver looked doubtful.

Suddenly the baby let out a low thin wail like an alley cat at midnight.

The taxi driver burst into tears of relief.

Jack wrapped the baby in a blanket and handed him to Kate.

"Sorry, Missus," the driver was saying. "Not even my baby. It's not like me to get so worked up." Then he shook Jack's hand. "Congratulations, Sir." He insisted on staying until the ambulance arrived and refused point blank to be paid for his time.

Jack was worried the baby was premature but the paramedics assured him he was a grand size and would probably only need a short stay in an incubator.

As they wheeled Kate into the ambulance, she kissed Jack and whispered to him, "He's your son you know. You're the one that's after bringing him into the world. That's the part that really counts."

Jack looked down at the little boy and was relieved to see he didn't look like Troy. Actually he didn't look like anyone – just a sort of pink wrinkle.

31

THE BABY SEEMED TO GROW before Jack's eyes; he spent practically every second at home watching him. He'd never been responsible for something so small and delicate in his life and he was obsessed with the idea that the little boy's lungs didn't work properly. Often at night he'd wake up and listen for the gentle snuffling of his breath, and, in a panic that he couldn't hear it, rush over to his son's cot. With huge relief he'd see the tiny chest moving up and down.

The infant was a bit on the small side at first, but seemed to guzzle down Kate's milk as if her breasts were an oasis in the desert, and quickly became what Kate's mother described as 'a big, fat, bouncing, baby boy.' Only it seemed to Jack that their child didn't bounce much. In fact he hardly ever cried. He was so quiet that Jack worried he might be autistic. He had huge blue eyes, deep pools, that would follow Jack around the room. Jack waited for the eyes to turn brown like Troy's and was grateful when they didn't. People were always saying, "He looks just like his father." But apart from his serious eyes, the little boy looked just like any other baby, fat with wrinkly skin and a bald head. Probably looked like a lot of fathers too. No likeness to Troy was evident.

Kate insisted they name the baby Cathal after her father. Jack was puzzled by her sudden show of affection towards her father; Kate had always complained that her father was too strict. And since he'd sent her to the convent, she referred to him with increasing bitterness. She clearly felt he'd betrayed her so why did she want to name her first-born after him? Kate explained it was nothing to do with love or respect, it was because she wanted Mr O'Rourke to share a name with his first grandchild, the one he'd once referred to as "some sailor's bastard," before sending Kate to the convent. He'd apparently told Kate she had to give the baby away because she was bringing shame on the family name. It was her form of ironic revenge that the boy should bear his grandfather's name. From the grim look on Mr O'Rourke's face at the christening, Jack guessed he realised it wasn't a compliment. Especially as Kate barely spoke to him during the whole thing. Jack wasn't sure he wanted the family dispute inflicted on the poor child. He didn't want to dwell on the past, all he was interested in was the future. Whatever mistakes had happened were past now. Cathal was his and he cared for him with a fierce tenderness that surprised him.

Pat had spoken to him shortly before the birth, "Do you really think you can bring yourself to love another man's child?"

"He is mine," Jack had answered curtly.

He had wondered, but once Cathal was born, he discovered it was no effort at all to forget about Troy. The idea of the baby had been worrying, but the reality of a little boy who needed to be fed, dressed, and have his nappy changed, was so overwhelming that the fact he wasn't Cathal's natural father suddenly seemed irrelevant. Cathal needed his care and attention and Jack liked to be needed.

Jack found Cathal's quietness discomforting. He'd have preferred a baby that kicked and screamed and demanded. Jack had been a very quiet child himself. "Behind the door," his grandmother used to say.

Her comments had irritated Jack's mother who disliked her son being criticized in any way. "He just prefers listening to talking. The world would be a much easier place if there were more like him."

Nana was an incessant talker and peered at Jack suspiciously. "Well little pitchers certainly have big ears."

Jack hoped Cathal would be more of an extrovert.

Kate found Jack's stories amusing. "He'll be what he'll be," she declared. "Big eyes like that he's bound to break some girl's heart."

The bed-sit was far too small for the three of them. Kate found it claustrophobic. When Cathal was nearly six months old she announced to Jack that her sister needed an extra hand in the shop now she was busy planning for her wedding. Pat had recently become engaged to Martin – a small tough man from Kerry who didn't say much and spent most of his time looking up at Pat adoringly. Jack liked Martin. He made an effort to talk to Jack, in his broad Kerry accent, about the Gaelic League and how Kerry was doing in the cup. Jack listened attentively, keen to learn. He'd never been very good at sports at school and although his father had taken him to a few matches when he was small, they had stopped when Jack's mother became unwell. Jack decided that for Cathal's sake he should make an effort and took to forcing himself to read the sports pages of the local paper. At first it was all double Dutch, but it was slowly beginning to make sense. It was rather like learning a foreign language.

Jack was horrified that Kate felt she had to work. He protested that he'd be qualified soon, he'd make more money, they'd move into a much bigger place and he'd be able to buy her everything she needed.

Kate looked at him in the kind, but slightly patronising, way she had and said, "Jack, I'm bored out of my mind locked up in this little room with the baby all day long. Pat says I can bring Cathal along seeing as he hardly ever cries and won't disturb the customers."

Jack hadn't considered that Kate might find their life dull. He himself would have much preferred to stay at home than go to his studies, which he found tedious and difficult. He could watch Cathal for hours with total fascination and never get bored. He found his son infinitely soothing. Still the main thing was that Kate be happy, so he agreed.

He ignored his father when he said to him, "It's disgraceful your wife working in a shop when you're going to be a doctor. It's common. She should be at home taking care of that child."

Jack felt like saying that if his own mother hadn't spent so much time in her room with the curtains drawn, she might never have got into such a dangerous frame of mind. But since he had Kate and the baby, he no longer felt angry and bitter about the past. He had his own family to think of now and this gave him a purpose and a direction.

Jack was disappointed that Brendan missed the baby's christening. He had wanted him to be Cathal's godfather.

Kate looked sceptical. "Are you sure an alcoholic bouncer is the best choice for our son's spiritual guidance?" she laughed.

But Jack thought Brendan had done a pretty good job of looking after him when his mother had asked him to, and if anything happened to Jack, he knew he could rely on his cousin to step into the gap. His father wanted him to choose one of his college friends. Someone rich with connections who could give Cathal a hand later on in life. He seemed to have no comprehension of the fact that Jack would never have made it through his first years of med school if it wasn't for Brendan's rough and ready care.

But there was no word from Brendan. Not since the wedding.

In the end Jack decided to settle for Martin as godfather. Pat had always been Kate's choice for godmother.

He'd tried asking his father who shook his head. "I'm sorry Jack, but for me blood runs thicker than water."

Jack was furious at the rejection of Cathal, but decided not to pursue it. He didn't think his father was in any position to lecture him about his marriage. Anyway how was his father so sure that Cathal wasn't his? Jack had never admitted it. He wanted people to think he'd got Kate pregnant and that was the reason he had to marry her in such a hurry. But Jack supposed there were rumours about Kate's American sailor and that his father had heard them. Jack felt defiant. He'd lived down idle gossip before in his life and he could do it again. The tongues would eventually tire of wagging. Anyway they were safe in Dublin where everyone saw them as a lovely, young, respectable couple with a bright future ahead of them. Jack had his final exams soon and then his internship at an inner city hospital. He hadn't grown any fonder of medicine, but he was desperate for financial independence. Also he hoped that once he was actually working, making people better, he'd feel more adequate. Text books didn't interest him, but people did.

Given the choice, Jack would have liked to set himself up as a GP. Just a small practice in a quiet country place that he could run himself. He'd be happy to spend his days chatting to little old ladies about their rheumatism. He was a good listener and didn't mind hearing about minor aches and pains for hours. He wasn't required to get over involved; he just had to write a prescription, and they'd be satisfied. It was major accidents that unnerved him. On Tuesdays he had to go and work in the emergency department of St. James. The place was like a vision of hell. Hard backed plastic chairs with all forms of broken humanity collapsed in them. It was always packed with people who'd been waiting for hours and hours in considerable pain, but didn't dare complain because they could see the stretchers being rushed in with others in far more serious trouble. Jack could never get over just how much blood people had inside them. How they could scream and yell, and their bones could stick out, and they reeked of alcohol and vomit and shit.

At first Jack wondered if he lacked compassion, but then a sister said to him, "Don't look so devastated, you'll get used to it."

The other doctors did seem oblivious to the chaos around them. They clipped down the corridors in their white coats looking cool and serene, protected by the nurses who were, in effect, the front line. Jack looked around at this aching disaster of humanity and realised he didn't want to get used to it. He didn't want this kind of suffering to become in any way normal to him. Even the little he was asked to do as an intern seemed overwhelming.

One particularly busy afternoon he was asked to put ice on the face of a woman with a large bruised eye.

"Fell down the stairs," she informed him cheerfully. "God but I'm dying for a fag."

"You and me both," replied Jack.

The woman smiled at him.

Jack asked her if she had pain anywhere else.

She laughed ."You're dead cute, you are."

Jack realised on close inspection that she was probably in her early thirties, though she looked at least forty. She said she only needed to be treated for a black eye but, given that she'd fallen down a flight of stairs, Jack insisted on examining her further.

184

The woman said her name was Mrs McCarthy, but he could call her Anne. She continued to flirt with him as he discovered three fractured ribs and a dislocated collarbone. He didn't understand how she could have failed to notice her injuries and wondered if she was on drugs.

"I have a very high pain threshold," she informed him.

Jack went to get one of the consultants.

"I thought she said she only had a black eye," the doctor accused Jack.

Jack explained what he'd found and how odd it was that the woman hadn't complained more.

The older man looked at Jack as if he was an idiot. "Sure she falls down the stairs every other week, I suppose she's well used to it."

Mrs McCarthy insisted she couldn't stay in overnight. She had four kids at home with no one to look after them.

"Is their father not around?" Jack asked.

"Oh he's around all right, he's always around." Mrs McCarthy laughed but the sound seemed to catch in her throat.

She thanked Jack. "You've been very kind, Doctor."

Jack thought he'd been less than useless. He felt like he wanted to go round Mrs McCarthy's house and throw her husband down the stairs, but it wouldn't have made any difference, and under his Hippocratic Oath, he'd only have to patch him up again.

Incidents like that made Jack wonder if he was ever going to be fit to be a doctor. He envied Martin who was moving back to his wife's home-town to help run the family pub.

Martin himself seemed less than enthusiastic about the prospect. "It's the thought of Mr O'Rourke breathing down my neck morning, noon and night that worries me."

Jack tried to assure him that Kate's father wasn't so bad to work for once you got used to doing everything the way he wanted.

"Yeah well I already fucked that one up by marrying his daughter which was definitely not what he wanted."

Jack told Martin how much he'd enjoyed working in O'Rourke's.

"You weren't married to his daughter then. He's going to make my life hell. I can feel it in my bones."

Pat interrupted in her pragmatic way, "He'll be dead soon enough."

Jack didn't like Mr O'Rourke much himself but still this seemed a harsh way to talk about your own father. Kate had told him Pat was possibly angrier about her sister being locked away than Kate was, which was saying something.

Martin just looked glum. "That miserable aul bastard probably live to be a hundred just to spite us."

Pat laughed and wrapped her arms around Martin's waist. "What does it matter? Sure as long as we've each other. He didn't stop us walking down the aisle together and he won't stop us being happy."

Pat had mellowed considerably since she'd found love, but still Jack found her intimidating. There was a brutal sharpness to her honesty that scared the life out of him. Kate would say, "Her heart's in the right place," but Jack couldn't help thinking that place wasn't somewhere he would like to be.

Still at least Martin had family connections. Jack knew it would be next to impossible to set up his own GP practice as most of them were passed on from father to son. He'd never get the money together to set up on his own and even if he did, it would take him forever to build up a reputation. People preferred to go to the son of the doctor their parents went to. They didn't seem to consider that this family connection probably meant the young man had been press-ganged into a profession purely because that was what his relatives did rather than any individual vocation. Not that Jack could claim greater sincerity here seeing as he'd never felt any personal desire to be a doctor himself. He supposed he should be grateful his father hadn't forced him to be a teacher. Standing up in front of a class full of hostile students day in day out would have shot his nerves to pieces all together.

"Your grandfather on both sides was a teacher and you've got two aunts who teach primary. To be honest with you I think there's enough bloody teachers in this family. It's about time we had someone who learnt something for a change," his father had told him once when he was less than sober.

Jack had been clever at school. He didn't think this was a mark of genius the way his father did, he thought it meant he was good at remembering a great many pointless facts and repeating them by rote. He seemed in his life to have acquired a vast amount of knowledge that could never serve him any practical purpose. Most of what he'd learnt in school, he'd successfully forgotten by now anyhow. He remembered odd things like the fact William I had a withered left arm and was deaf in one ear. He knew this was somehow connected to the outbreak of World War I but he couldn't say how. Millions of people had died, but despite at one point being able to list all of the major battles and their dates, he couldn't remember why. Now he had practical day to day concerns. His father had never changed a nappy in his life, but Jack was determined to learn how to look after his own son. Maybe it was only wiping shit away, but if he didn't remember to do it often enough or if he forgot the talcum powder, the baby's soft skin became red and angry. Cathal, who never cried, would cry then. Little gulps of pain and discomfort.

One day Jack overheard an old man saying to one of the nurses, "Ah love, sure what's the point? You clean it all away but it only comes back again."

The nurse was changing bandages on the old man's leg and Jack had a glimpse of puss and blood that he quickly turned away from.

The nurse didn't seem bothered though. She informed her patient, "True enough I can't work a miracle cure for you, but when it's all wrapped and clean, you'll be in less pain than you were before."

The old man winked at her. "That's angel enough for me."

But Jack couldn't bear the idea of Cathal suffering. Kate kept telling him not to be such a worry wart. One morning Cathal was on top of the dresser to be changed and somehow managed to roll himself off. He hit the ground with a sickening thud followed by a piercing scream. Jack came running. He saw a look of absolute terror on Kate's face. She held the baby while he cleaned the small cut just above their son's eye.

"He could have taken his eye out," Kate told Jack.

Jack kissed her gently on the cheek. "It's only a small scratch. No chance of a scar," he reassured her.

Kate smiled at him. "He's lucky to have such a good father."

Her voice was full of sincerity and affection. Jack never asked his wife if she'd fallen in love with him yet, because surely this, what they had, the three of them united against the world, was what real love was about? Not some crazy, sleep-destroying teenage crush.

32

JACK WOKE WITH A START, not knowing what had torn him out of his sleep.

"The phone's ringing," Kate murmured.

As she said it, he heard the persistent insistence of the bell begin again. He sighed and heaved himself out of bed. He pulled on a T-shirt and padded down the stairs to the hall.

He never used to sleep naked before he was married, but Kate insisted. She said she liked to feel the softness of his skin next to hers, to be able to wrap herself around him in her sleep and to feel like they were the one body floating in the womb of their bed.

Jack picked up the phone nervously. He hated calls late at night. It was probably a wrong number, but he always had the awful feeling that maybe somebody had died. Even though his father was in perfect health, Jack was worried something bad would happen to him. Having lost one parent, he was terrified of losing the other.

He was surprised and delighted to hear Brendan's voice.

"Where have you been?" he demanded.

Even though his cousin had told him he was taking a risk in coming out from under cover for Jack's wedding, Jack hadn't taken him seriously at the time. But as the months had slipped by, Jack had been forced to face the fact that Brendan wasn't just waiting for some minor incident to blow over, he really was in hiding.

"Sorry for the incommunicado but I've had nothing but grief since you last saw me. Some people who I'd given the slip heard I was at your big day and didn't take kindly to the idea I was still around and out enjoying meself one bit." Brendan laughed, but his voice sounded tired and drawn.

"When are you coming home?" Jack asked anxiously. It was freezing cold in the hallway and wearing only a T-shirt, he was beginning to shiver.

Brendan ignored the question. "I heard you had a wee babbie. Congratulations, boy."

"I wanted you to be the godfather."

There was a long silence. "Sure I'm not much of a role model." Brendan's voice had a catch in it.

Jack felt increasingly alarmed; Brendan didn't sound like his usual happy go lucky self at all.

"Where are you?" Jack asked.

"Oh this little shit hole of a hostel in Kilburn. There's rats and everything."

"You know if you need anything, money or whatever, you just have to ask," Jack offered uncertainly.

"Ah sure don't worry about me, boy. Always land on me feet. I'm thinking of going to the States actually."

"When?" Jack asked alarmed. He couldn't understand this obsession everyone had with going to America. Ireland wasn't that bad.

"Couple of days, soon as I get the money together," Brendan replied. "Thought I'd give you a quick ring to say goodbye. You take care of yourself and that lovely lady, do you hear me? I hope you'll be very happy. Sure love works in mysterious ways."

Brendan sounded like he wanted to say more and for a moment Jack was worried he was going to ask him how he'd ended up with Troy's ex. At the wedding his cousin had kept giving him puzzled looks. But just then the pips started going on the phone. Jack heard Brendan shoving more coins into the payphone hurriedly.

"I'm nearly out of change. I'll call you when I get to New York. Listen just in case things don't work out..." He paused uncertainly.

"Brendan, what's going on?" Jack wanted to tell his cousin he was scaring him.

"If you see me mam, tell her I'm sorry all the trouble I've caused her." Brendan's laugh was closer to a sob.

Then the phone line went dead.

Jack tiptoed up the stairs and crept into bed, trying not to wake Kate.

She stirred. "Who the hell was that?"

"Just Brendan."

"Is he all right?"

"Yeah. He's fine. You go back to sleep." Jack kissed Kate gently behind the back of her ear to reassure her. Or rather to reassure himself.

For Cathal's first birthday they took him to the zoo. He didn't seem that impressed by the animals until they showed him the giraffes. For some reason these strange, long necked creatures made the little boy incredibly excited and happy. He kept pointing at them and shouting "Affe, Affe" and clapping his fists together. Kate took pictures of Jack holding his son with the giraffes stalking proudly behind them. Jack was enormously proud of the fact that Cathal's first word had been "Dada." Now he'd progressed to speaking his own burbling language. He was no longer so quiet since he'd discovered baby talk, and cheerfully chatted away to himself for hours. Kate insisted on buying ice creams for her two handsome devils. Cathal managed to get more on his face than in his mouth.

Jack carefully wiped the boy's cheeks while Kate nibbled his ear.

"Happy Birthday, baby boy," she murmured.

Then she dabbed some ice cream on Jack's nose. 'I love you.'

He'd been waiting so long for these words that he wasn't sure he'd heard her right.

"Don't look so shocked," Kate laughed. "It's getting late, time you took us home."

They left the Phoenix Park arm in arm pushing the buggy between them as the sun set behind the trees. Jack didn't think he had ever have felt so happy.

The next morning Jack was rushing around as he was in danger of being late for work yet again. He found it so hard to tear himself out of the soft warmth of their bed. Sometimes he buried his face into Kate's neck and thought how wonderful it would be if he could just stay there, breathing the delicious smell of her, and never have to move again.

She pushed him away laughing. "Get up, you lazy git. I've to feed Cathal and you can't spend all day in bed."

But Jack felt that after his endless sleepless nights, he needed to catch up. These days he slept like a baby.

He still checked the post in the mornings for foreign stamps but it was more out of habit than real fear. He opened them as he sat at the kitchen table shoving toast into his mouth. It was always a comforting selection of bills and the occasional letter from his father. So when he saw the American stamp he had to look twice to make sure he wasn't imagining it.

Kate was standing right behind him. "Hey, you got a letter from the States."

Jack's mouth went completely dry. Instinctively he put his hand over the envelope. At least it was addressed to him and not Kate.

"Maybe it's from Brendan," he managed to mumble. "Anyway best get going. I'll read it on the way."

Somehow he grabbed his jacket, kissed Kate and Cathal goodbye, and stumbled out the door. He knew it wasn't from Brendan. He'd recognised the handwriting at once. It had never occurred to Jack that Troy would write to him.

Jack normally cycled to work, but the rain was coming down in a fine mist so he decided to take the bus. Besides he didn't think he could wait the thirty minutes it would take him to cross the city before reading Troy's letter. He hurried up the stairs and threw himself into a seat at the very back. He drew the envelope out of his pocket and sat staring at it.

He remembered how painful it had been to read Troy's last letter and figured this one was probably worse. Had he discovered that Jack had married Kate? Did he know how he'd been duped? He had Jack's address. Maybe at this moment he was on a flight over from the States to get his revenge. Jack broke out in a cold sweat. His hands were shaking. In the weeks up to the wedding, he'd promised himself that if Troy got in touch, he'd confess all. But it had been well over a year. Why now when Jack had just begun to feel safe? As the months passed Troy had felt increasingly unreal. Like a bad dream Jack had had. Kate never mentioned his name and they both seemed to be in silent agreement to pretend they'd never met an American sailor on a beach. That their romance had been one smooth, seamless story from the moment they first kissed up to their present happiness.

Jack considered opening the window and shoving the letter out. Let the paper be carried away by the wind and rain and the words washed away forever. But he knew it wouldn't work. Troy would still be out there somewhere and Jack had to know what he was up to. He tore open the envelope.

The letter wasn't long and it was to the point. Troy seemed to have moved beyond romantic ramblings. Jack could hear the slow drawl of his American accent as he read the words, but still they seemed to come from a much older man. As if twenty years had passed instead of less than two since he'd last read a letter of Troy's.

Dear Jack,

Sorry I haven't been in touch. I meant to write before but just couldn't quite bring myself to do it. Nothing personal against you, man. Just when I left Ireland I was pretty messed up. I realised the navy wasn't for me so I left. They weren't too happy about that and I had to keep moving on from place to place so they wouldn't catch up with me. They can put you in jail for deserting. I didn't care. I never want to go near water again. I did a few odd jobs here and there but now I got me a steady job as a mailman of all things in a small town in North Dakota. Sometimes when I'm sorting through all those piles of letters I imagine that one of them might be from Kate. Crazy huh? She doesn't even have my address. It's not like I could ask the navy to forward my mail after I skipped out on them. She's probably forgotten all about me by now anyway. Weird thing is I just can't get that woman out of my head. It ain't like I haven't met a lot of other girls since then, but somehow it's just not the same. You must think I'm some fool.

Anyway I was wondering if you happened to have an address for her? Her family always hated me so I guess there's no point in getting in touch with them. I know she'll probably never write back, but I figure if I can just find out why she changed her mind, I might be able to put the whole thing behind me. I don't know if you've ever been in love, but it does funny things to a guy.

Hope life is treating you well. Keep in touch cos I'll never forget that you saved my life and if there's ever anything I can do for you, you just let me know. Even though I got my heart broken, the time I spent in Ireland was still by far the happiest in my life. I'm not bitter or anything. I was pretty angry for a while but since that's faded, all I really remember is the good stuff. If you happen to see Kate, tell her I wish her all the best whether she wants to write to me or not.

From your friend Troy.
P.S. Say hi to Brendan for me.

Jack was shivering when he got off the bus. That Troy believed Kate had abandoned him and yet he still loved her stuck in Jack's throat. The moment he got into the hospital he headed for the gents. He puked up most of his breakfast and stood with his back against the toilet door feeling like the world was about to end.

When he emerged, a young doctor he knew vaguely grinned at him. "Rough night, hey?"

Jack ignored him and splashed his face with water in an attempt to calm down. This was far worse than any hangover.

When he got home that evening, Kate had made them lasagne for dinner. He'd considered ringing to say he was working late but didn't want to act suspiciously. Still it was all he could do to force himself to eat the food.

"Are you all right?" Kate asked. "You look very pale."

"Think I might be coming down with something."

He watched Kate as she fed Cathal. She was humming "Hush little baby don't you cry, Daddy's gonna buy you a mocking bird," and Jack had to repress a desire to tell her to stop. For months he'd hardly even thought about the fact he wasn't Cathal's natural father. As far as Jack was concerned Cathal was his son and Kate was his wife. That was how things were meant to be. Why oh why wouldn't Troy just let it go?

Jack couldn't sleep a wink. He lay there looking up at the ceiling and listening to the soft rise and fall of Kate's breathing. What on earth was he going to do? Kate had told Jack she loved him. They'd built up a life together with Cathal. Jack was taking care of the two of them and they were happy. They had a great future ahead of them. Could Jack really be expected to rip his whole life to shreds because Troy still thought of Kate sometimes? Troy had said himself he wasn't bitter, he just wanted to understand so that he could move on. Deep down Jack knew what he'd done to Troy was unforgivable. If he hadn't interfered it would be Troy lying beside Kate right now with his son sleeping peacefully in the cot beside the bed. But it was too late to go back on it all. What was done was done. If it was his punishment that Troy would find Kate then so be it, but he wasn't going to help him.

Jack decided to do nothing. To act as if he'd never received any letter. He told himself that Troy would just presume he had moved on from the bed-sit and despite his protestations of love, he'd meet someone else and forget about Kate. But Jack's peace of mind was shattered. He started having terrible nightmares again and getting up at five in the morning to check the post. Kate thought he was stressed because he was working so hard. She didn't know how every time the phone rang or the doorbell went, it was like a razor across Jack's nerves in case it was Troy. He felt like a hunted man.

33

THE NEXT SIX MONTHS TOOK their toll on Jack. He felt like Troy was haunting him. He just couldn't relax. He kept waiting for the axe to fall. One afternoon he was in Arnott's with Kate and Cathal, looking at three piece suites for the house they'd finally made an offer on when he saw a bloke staring at him. Convinced the man was Troy, he grabbed Cathal's buggy and pushed it hurriedly out of the shop.

Kate ran after him. "Where's the fire?"

Jack stopped to catch his breath. He looked over Kate's shoulder but there was no sign they were being followed. Thinking about it, the man couldn't have been Troy. He had similar dark skin and brown eyes, but he was far too short.

Kate waited for an explanation.

"Just saw someone from the hospital I didn't want to meet."

"You having an affair or something?" his wife asked, only half joking.

"No, no. A consultant I used to work under. He's just a dreadful bore and I couldn't face getting into a conversation about neurological diseases – that's his specialty. Boring people I mean."

Kate didn't look entirely convinced. "You're awful jumpy these days," she remarked. But she didn't pry.

She was busy preparing for the move. She was so excited about the new house that she reminded Jack of a kid at Christmas. But it was hardly surprising when she'd been stuck in the grimness of Jack's bed-sit for nearly two years.

He had tried suggesting they rent somewhere bigger but Kate wanted them to think long term. "I want us to save our money till we can get a place of our own."

It was only after the hospital had offered him a permanent position that the bank was prepared to give them a loan. Jack had hoped Kate's father would help them out a bit.

"I wouldn't take one penny off that man if I was starving to death in the gutter," Kate was adamant.

The house was a modest affair with two bedrooms, a sitting-room, and a tiny kitchen. Jack would have liked a garden for Cathal to play in but they couldn't afford it. "When I get promoted we'll get something bigger," Jack said.

"To me this is a palace." Kate ruffled his hair and kissed him affectionately. "I've got everything I could possibly want."

Jack was looking forward to moving even more than Kate was. He crossed off the days on the calendar in his diary. Of course if Troy ever did come to Ireland to look for Jack, he probably wouldn't find it that hard to track him down. But still it would be an enormous relief to know Troy didn't have his current address. That if any more letters did arrive from America, Jack wouldn't be there to open them. He convinced himself that in the new house, they could begin again. It had been months since Troy's letter so Jack figured he was nearly in the clear. He hoped that in a new environment he'd finally be able to put the past behind him. Sometimes in the bed-sit he felt like the walls themselves were accusing him. His grandmother used to say that walls had ears – Jack was just glad they didn't have tongues.

Finally the day of the move arrived. It was early spring and the blossoms were just opening on the trees. Jack whistled as he loaded up the van he'd hired. All their worldly belongings were packed into cardboard boxes. He'd never have believed they could accumulate so much stuff in such a short space of time. He wanted to throw most of it away but Kate wouldn't hear of it.

"Cathal's outgrown all of these anyway," he said holding up another babygro. Kate looked at him. "And what if he has a brother or a sister? They might need them."

Jack had never dared ask Kate if she wanted to have another child with him. It was the first time the subject had been raised and Jack was so thrilled at the idea that all he could do was grin stupidly. He picked up the box of baby clothes and carried them out to the van.

"Well I reckon that's about it," he declared cheerfully as he came back in.

Kate was at the kitchen table, an open cardboard box set out in front of her. She was as white as a ghost.

"What's the matter?"

"I found... I don't understand." Kate seemed unable to speak.

Jack felt his stomach lurch alarmingly. But he'd burnt Troy's letter to ashes. Then Jack saw what was written on the side of the cardboard box in his own lopsided handwriting. He'd scrawled 'Brendan' in capital letters.

"That's my cousin's stuff," he said. "I'm going to send it to his mother."

There'd been no word from Brendan since he left for America and while it worried Jack, there wasn't much he could do about it. But he couldn't just chuck out his old flatmate's gear. He figured the best thing was to return it to Brendan's family so it would be there when his cousin finally felt it was safe to show his face again.

Without a word Kate put her open hand out towards Jack. In the palm of it sat two gold wedding rings. How could he have forgotten that he'd hidden Troy's rings in an old metal box that Brendan had used to hold loose change? It seemed like a hundred years ago that he'd driven up into the Dublin Wicklow Mountains to get rid of them. What on earth had possessed him to keep them?

Jack felt faint. He opened his mouth to speak but it was as if he were breathing water rather than air. The ocean flooded his lungs and he gasped.

"Where did you get these?" his wife asked.

"Kate..." Jack's voice was that of a drowning man.

"Did Troy give them to you?" Kate's tone was full of accusation. "Did you see him before he left?"

Jack nodded in despair.

"Why didn't you tell me? Why did Troy change his mind?" Kate sounded desperate.

"I love you, Kate. I love you more than you could ever imagine." Jack knew it was true, it was the one essential truth in the web of lies he'd spun around them. And Kate loved him, she'd said so. Maybe not with the same all consuming intensity, maybe the entire meaning of her life wasn't dependent on his existence, but still they were happy together. Much, much happier than the vast majority of people. He couldn't live without her, the thought of it was unbearable.

"I tried to tell you," he began. "That time when I brought you home from the nuns."

He had been on the very edge of confession back then. But not now. It was one thing to lose his vision of what a life with Kate could be like, it was another to lose the vital reality of his marriage. Troy had once said that his soul belonged to Jack because he'd saved him. Jack now thought he would sell his own soul to keep Kate.

"You said you didn't want to hear Troy's name," Jack was floundering.

"But I had no idea you'd seen him," Kate protested.

Now the lies slipped off Jack's tongue, like a foreign language he'd suddenly become fluent in. "Troy came to see me the night before your wedding. He said he'd had a letter from a sweetheart of his back in New York. They'd had a row and she'd broken off their engagement but now she'd changed her mind. He said he didn't know what to do."

"Bastard," was Kate's response. "He told me he'd never been in love with anyone else."

"He gave me the rings," Jack continued. "He asked me to tell you how sorry he was but he couldn't face you himself. He was very upset and he thought it'd be easier on everyone if he just left."

"A liar and a coward," Kate exclaimed.

Jack paused. "I should have told you. But I was scared you'd go to New York to win him back. And seeing as he didn't answer your letters... I thought it'd be best if we just tried to forget about him."

Kate stared intently at him. "You are telling me the truth?" she asked.

"On my mother's life," Jack replied. After all his mother was already dead of a broken heart and Jack was in way, way too deep to turn back.

34

AISLING FELT PHYSICALLY SICK AS she pulled her pyjamas on and hurried back to her own room. Claire had offered to speak to Jack, but Aisling thought it was better if they faced him together. Safety in numbers.

"I guess he was going to find out some time," Claire observed grimly.

Aisling just wished it hadn't been so soon. She knew it was cowardly of her. She wasn't ashamed of what she was doing, but somehow the gap between what she felt on the inside – which was so amazing and obviously right – and how she knew she would be viewed on the outside, seemed totally unbridgeable.

Jack paced nervously up and down the kitchen while Aisling and Claire sat at the table. Jack was smoking, something he never did in the morning. He always waited till after dinner these days. He had tried unsuccessfully to quit. Mainly because Claire had urged him to.

"A doctor who smokes," she had teased. "Don't you think that's a little hypocritical?"

"Fact is I'm fundamentally far more of a smoker than I am a doctor," Jack replied.

The only other sound in the kitchen was the grandfather clock in the hall. Aisling held Claire's hand under the table cloth.

"I'm in love with Aisling." Claire broke the silence.

Jack continued to walk back and forth as if he couldn't bear to stay still. The power of speech had deserted him. He was very pale.

"We wanted to tell you," Claire stood up and approached Jack. "We were going to tell you. I thought maybe you knew, that you'd guessed."

Jack stopped and stared at Claire. There was a long pause that stretched on forever. Eventually he said, "I'd never have guessed in a million years."

Jack didn't sound outraged, just deeply anxious. "She's only a child," he muttered. "I'm supposed to be looking after her. What would her parents say?"

Aisling realised that he was talking about her.

Her mother and father's reaction was what Aisling dreaded most. She suddenly felt very angry; this was none of her parents' business or Jack's for that matter. She could just see her mother casting Claire in the role of evil sick monster who'd seduced her vulnerable daughter.

"I just don't understand," Jack sucked deep on his cigarette. "I mean how long has this been going on behind my back?"

Claire hesitated. "It's only been a few months."

"A few months?" Jack looked stunned. "Look I'm Aisling's uncle, she's my responsibility. She's only seventeen, and I'm sorry things didn't work out with your husband, but I don't want you dragging her into..."

Jack ran out of steam. Into what? Aisling fumed. A life of gross perversion and decadence? She wasn't a kid any more and was sick of all this 'protection' that hung over her like a thick fog. She didn't think any of the so-called grown up people in her life were in any position to lecture her on matters of the heart. They'd thrown away their chances, and now they wanted her to throw away hers.

She was certain that Jack was building himself up to justify sending her back to her parents. It wasn't fair. She hadn't done anything wrong. She felt helpless at the lack of control she had over her own life. She couldn't bear it any more.

"You're just jealous," she shouted at Jack.

Her uncle looked like he'd been punched in the stomach. But she didn't care.

"Do you have any idea what it would do to your mother if she knew what you've been up to?" Jack lit another cigarette.

Aisling felt like crying. "You don't have to tell her."

Claire chimed in. "Jack, there really isn't any need to drag Aisling's family into this."

"I'm her family," Jack spat. "Pat's going to kill me. She hates me as it is. And now I've taken her only daughter to Dublin and she's turned into a..."

"Lesbian," Claire said. "Surely you can say the word."

"Yes, fine, lesbian, homosexual, whatever." Jack drummed his fingers anxiously on the table. "But she's not even eighteen. It's probably illegal. You could lose your job, have you thought of that?"

"Are you threatening me?" Claire's voice had a dangerous edge to it.

"No, of course not. I'm just saying I promised her mother I wouldn't let her come to any harm."

"Now I'm harmful?" Claire's cheeks were flushed red and her eyes flashed.

Aisling was glad the focus was on Claire because all this talk of her mother had taken the wind out of her sails and she was beginning to feel sick in the pit of her stomach.

"I don't think you understand how serious this." Jack stubbed out his cigarette.

"No Jack, it's you that doesn't understand. You haven't a clue." Claire spoke through her teeth.

"That may be true. But Pat wouldn't allow this to happen in her own home and Aisling is still her daughter. I can't have her blaming me for lying to her. I've told enough lies in my life." Jack slumped down in a chair.

35

THE NEXT FEW DAYS WERE torture. Jack said he needed time to think things over. Aisling imagined that he had to work out what on earth he was going to say to her parents. She considered crawling on her hands and knees and begging her uncle not to send her away, not to tell her mother. So what if it was pathetic? She'd happily swallow her pride if only she could persuade him not to wreck her relationship.

"He's doing this cos he's in love with you and he wants you for himself," she told Claire in hushed tones.

"You just assume cos you fancy me, everyone does." Claire's smile was strained. "Strangely, I think if you were his daughter, he'd have taken it better. I think he's really worried that he's let your mother down in some way."

Aisling thought, I'm the one who is disappointing my mother, me and me alone. Now she felt like maybe she understood her brother's self-ishness. She didn't want to upset her parents and she didn't want to hurt Jack who'd been so good to her, but she needed Claire the same way she needed air – regardless of the consequences.

On the fourth day Jack tried to talk to Aisling before she left for school. He sat her down at the kitchen table and made them both a strong cup of coffee. His voice was kind and gentle. "I think maybe you've been more lonely here than I realised and you've gotten a bit confused..."

"I've never been so clear about anything in my life." Aisling struggled to keep calm.

Jack sipped his coffee and frowned. "You're a very pretty, intelligent girl. You could have any boy you want. Don't you see how difficult you're going to make your life? I'm just trying to protect you."

The conversation was going nowhere. "I don't want your protection." Aisling strode out of the house and slammed the door behind her. Maybe it wasn't dignified or mature behaviour, but to hell with that. She didn't know where she was planning to go, only that she'd rather storm out than be banished like a small child sent to their room for being naughty. Jack couldn't send her packing if she wasn't actually there.

It was a beautiful morning. The early morning sunlight fell gently through the autumn leaves spinning them into shades of red and brown. At the end of the path, with his hand on the gate, was a man. He looked rather scruffy with a big bushy beard and he wore a dirty denim jacket that was too thin for the time of year. His hair was matted together into something resembling dreadlocks gone wrong. He seemed to be testing the gate as if he wasn't sure whether to open it or not. Aisling figured he was a wino. There was a group of them that hung out at the end of the road. They sat there all day with their backs pressed against the wall of a dentist's, passing a bottle back and forth between them. They weren't there every day: Aisling could find no pattern to their meetings, or why they picked a totally featureless spot by the side of the road as their drinking hole. She'd never seen one of them actually standing though. They seemed to appear and disappear by magic rather than by walking.

The man spoke. "I'm looking for Dr. O'Connell."

His voice was soft and polite with no sign of the tell tale drunken slur. Maybe he was one of her uncle's patients. He didn't look in the best of health. Aisling never thought of her uncle as Dr. O'Connell, to her he was Uncle Jack, and she always thought his professional title sounded odd. She was unsure how to reply as she seriously doubted if Jack would want to see anyone right now. Perhaps the best thing would be to say nothing at all. To just keep marching on by and let the man find his own way to her uncle. She had enough problems to be dealing with. Then again if she turned the strange man away and he turned out to be genuinely ill, her uncle would never forgive her. Although he claimed to hate his job, he was remarkably dedicated to it.

All the years her mother spent breeding good manners into her got the better of Aisling. "This is Dr. O'Connell's house. Just press the top bell."

She deliberately didn't say her uncle was at home, in case he didn't feel like answering. She opened the gate and attempted to step past the man. He smelt rather strongly of stale tobacco but at least didn't have the stomach turning stench of your typical wino. He stared at her with wild, crazy, blue eyes. Like he was seeing a ghost. For a moment Aisling worried that he was some kind of psycho. She knew her uncle had to deal with a few of these. There was one bloke who used to phone in the middle of the night and threaten to come round and murder Jack. He blamed him for his father's death.

"Go to the police," Claire had urged.

"He'll get over it," was Jack's response. "I only wish I had someone I could ring up in the middle of the night and accuse."

Aisling was never too sure if her uncle was joking or not. Still right now she wasn't in the mood to deal with some lunatic. She felt like she might kill someone herself, though she'd no idea who. She pushed past the man determinedly, thinking if he made a grab for her, she could scream. She was hardly going to be raped and murdered on her own front door step.

"Aisling," the man whispered.

She spun round. How did he know her name?

He was smiling at her now and she could see that one of his two front teeth was missing. The gap winked in his mouth."Don't you recognise me?" he laughed.

Aisling felt her heart fall through the pavement. Her head spun and she put out an arm to steady herself. "Cathal?"

36

THIS STRANGER DIDN'T LOOK LIKE her brother. She only knew it was him because although his face was obscured by the beard, his eyes still shone like two sapphires. Nobody else had that particular shade of biting blue. Cathal sat in an armchair while they stood around him, gawping like he was a ghost. Aisling put her hand out to touch him to see if he was real, but quickly withdrew it. All the times she'd imagined Cathal's return, she'd pictured throwing herself into his arms and him picking her up in a great twirl of a hug, like he'd done when she was a kid. Claire at least had the presence of mind to offer him a cup of tea.

"I didn't mean to disturb you," Cathal mumbled. He looked vaguely embarrassed as if he wasn't sure he should be there at all.

Aisling felt like laughing, except that it wasn't funny.

"We're so glad to have you back," Jack said.

"Are you?"

The question had an edge to it that struck Aisling as unfair. As if Cathal were implying they'd wanted him to leave. Before she could stop herself, she accused, "You said you'd come back soon."

The words sounded ridiculous even to her own ears. Like her brother had missed an appointment by three years. That was how long he'd been away. Three long, long years.

He looked at Aisling as if he couldn't get over the wonder of her. "God but didn't you grow up beautiful."

Claire smiled and Aisling found herself blushing.

"Where have you been?" Aisling felt like crying.

"Travelling. I went all over. Too many places. I can't believe it's been so long." Cathal sounded as if he'd only meant to go on a holiday and had lost track of time.

Aisling felt like grabbing him and shaking him. Three years without a word. Did he have any idea the agony and misery he'd put them all through? "We didn't know if you were alive or dead,' she exclaimed.

"For a while there I felt like I was dead." Cathal looked at his shoes.

Aisling had promised God that if only returned her brother, she would never torment him with a single question or reproach. But it was no longer enough just to have him back; she wanted to know how he could have left in the first place. A wave of fury came over Aisling. Instead of coming back begging their forgiveness, her brother was acting

204

like he wasn't so sure he wanted to see them. She was absolutely thrilled he'd returned, but she was also angry that he had just turned up out of the blue. The two emotions left her utterly bewildered.

"I should ring Mam. Let her know you're all right."

"Sure she's waited this long, she can wait a little longer," Cathal replied wearily. Aisling thought this callous – cruel even. She glared at him.

"I can't face her just yet, Angel. One step at a time, hey?'

It had been so long since he'd called her Angel that Aisling's heart felt it would explode. She knew she ought to be more patient. To give her brother the chance to explain himself in his own way. There was never any point in putting pressure on Cathal.

Besides he looked worn out. As if he'd been away for thousands of years. Or like in the story of Tir Na nOg where Oisin insists on leaving the beautiful Niamh and the Land of Eternal Youth to go back to Ireland because he's incredibly homesick. He begs so much to visit his own country again that Niamh lends him her magical white horse to take him there. She makes him promise that he won't get off the horse. What Oisin doesn't realise is that several millennia have passed and Ireland is no longer a land of great heroes and scholars, but a broken, impoverished place full of mumbling old men. On arriving he looks around him in dismay and sees a group of elderly people trying to roll a large boulder up a hill. He decides to help them and leans down from his white steed to push the rock. But he slips and falls off the horse. The moment his feet touch the ground, he's transformed into an ancient old man. The white horse gallops off into the distance and Oisin never makes it back to Tir na nOg or sees Niamh again. Aisling had always thought in this story what a fool Oisin had been to go back. She didn't want her brother to feel the same way.

Cathal was staying at a hotel, well more like a hostel, but Jack insisted he stay with them. Aisling understood her uncle's persistence. She didn't want to let Cathal out of her sight either. Just in case he disappeared again.

Cathal agreed to stay for a while. "I guess we've got a lot to catch up on," he observed with his remarkable gift for understatement.

At dinner, Aisling noted that the whole issue of Jack's objections to her and Claire seemed to have paled into insignificance. At least for the moment as none of them was going to mention it in front of their new guest. Jack appeared to have forgotten all about it. Aisling had never seen him in such a good mood. He kept smiling at Cathal as if he were the seventh wonder of the world. Cathal did not smile back.

As Jack poured them wine, Cathal kissed Aisling on the cheek. "God I've missed you."

Aisling wasn't sure she believed him. Now that the initial shock of his sudden appearance was beginning to recede, she couldn't help feeling like her brother had a nerve to just turn up and sit there eating Claire's lasagne as if he hadn't a care in the world. As if he hadn't completely broken her heart by running off like that.

"If you missed me so much, why didn't you come home before?"

There was a sudden silence.

"Maybe we should talk about this later," Jack said.

This only annoyed Aisling more. She didn't want to sit there making polite conversation. "I've waited three years. I don't want to talk about it later. I want to talk about it now."

Cathal smiled sadly. "You're right. There's been too much lies and bullshit in our family for far too long. I don't want there to be any more secrets."

Aisling couldn't agree more. "Jack told me about your father. I'm sorry."

Cathal stared at her with a burning intensity. "What did he tell you?"

Aisling hesitated. Cathal suddenly seemed so on edge that she wished she hadn't brought it up.

"Did he tell you my father was an evil rapist? Cos that's what he told me."

Aisling nodded and was amazed when Cathal begin to laugh. His laughter was manic and more bitter than she could ever have imagined.

Aisling wondered if the years away had softened his mind. Maybe he was suffering from some kind of paranoid delusion.

Jack shifted in his seat uncomfortably.

Claire looked like she'd no right to be hearing this conversation. Jack had introduced her as his lodger. She couldn't know how grateful Aisling was for her presence. She felt like Claire was the only proof that this wasn't all a bizarre dream she was having.

Cathal glared at Jack. "All my life I felt like I was in the wrong place. Like I was meant to be somewhere else. I can't remember a time when I didn't feel that I didn't belong. That I was this odd little kid nobody wanted. I used to wonder what the fuck was wrong with me?" Cathal's tone wasn't so much self pitying as angry and accusing.

"I never wanted to give you away." Jack looked ashamed. "I loved you like you were my own son."

"You lied to me," Cathal shouted. "All you've ever done is tell me one lie after another." Then he took a deep breath to try to calm down.

Aisling remembered that her brother had always had a certain edge to him. When she was a kid he'd seemed exciting and fun. Now seeing the way his blue eyes flashed, Aisling thought he looked unstable. She couldn't help noticing that his fingernails were bitten practically to the bone.

He turned to Aisling. "Shortly after my eighteenth birthday I went to get my first passport. Mam wanted to sort it out for me and that's what made me suspicious. I went into the big office in Dublin and insisted on looking at my birth cert. It said my father's name was Jack O'Connell and my mother's Kate O'Connell nee O'Rourke. Do you have any idea how it feels to be lied to all your life? To find out that you're not at all the person you thought you were?" Cathal lit a cigarette nervously and blew the smoke in Jack's face.

"I know all this. And I agree it must have been terrible for you. But I still don't see why you had to go and disappear off to America and never come back." Aisling took Cathal's hand and squeezed his fingers .

"I'm back now. I'm just not sure I want to be." Cathal withdrew his hand from Aisling's grasp.

This wasn't the tear filled reunion Aisling had so often dreamed of. In her fantasies, Cathal had been overjoyed to see her and begged her forgiveness for abandoning her. Just because he wasn't her natural brother didn't mean it was okay for him to have just walked out of her life like that.

"I was devastated when you left. What did I ever do on you?"

"Nothing, Angel. It was never anything to do with you. I had to find out who I was."

Aisling felt like slapping her brother. "And it took you three years to work it out?" she asked sarcastically.

"I wasn't gonna ever come back. I thought I could reinvent myself as a different person. Just start all over again." Cathal seemed to be trying very hard not to cry.

"I know that feeling," Claire said kindly.

Aisling had to repress an urge to tell her to mind her own business. She wasn't going to let Cathal off the hook so easy. "Then it was just pure cowardice," she accused.

"Please Angel. I went to America to try to find my real father. Good old Uncle Jack here caught up with me in New York. Tried to persuade me to come home and then when I told him I wasn't going anywhere till I found out who my father was, he helpfully revealed that even my mother didn't know because she was raped. And I believed him. I swallowed every word." Cathal seemed to be struggling to contain his fury. Suddenly he grabbed Jack's arm in a vice-like grip.

"But it's not true, is it, Jack? There was no rapist. My father's name was Troy and my mother was in love with him. Wasn't she?"

Jack had gone as white as a sheet.

"How could you tell me my mother was raped when you knew perfectly well she wasn't?"

Aisling had never heard Cathal sound so furious.

Anger crackled and bounced around her brother like he'd swallowed a bolt of lightning. He tightened his grip on Jack's arm till her uncle cried out in pain. Only then did he let go.

"You couldn't begin to imagine how sorry I am." Jack stood up.

"Don't you dare try to walk away from this," Cathal hissed.

Jack sat back down. "I was trying to protect you."

"Bullshit. How could making me think I was the child of a rapist be in my interest? You just wanted to stop me finding my real father."

"Why would Jack do that?" Claire asked.

Aisling remembered where she'd seen the name Troy before. "You have wedding rings with Kate and Troy's name on them in your drawer."

Jack looked like he wanted the earth to swallow him. "It was all a very long time ago," he whispered.

"Your little plan nearly worked," Cathal sneered. "I mean why would anybody want to get in touch with a father who was a rapist? I'd waited so long to hear the truth and then when I thought I'd found it, it was too horrific for me to grasp. The whole thing just made me feel sick. No wonder my family had never wanted me."

"We did want you," Aisling protested.

"I never imagined you'd be so upset you'd just disappear. I was terrified you'd killed yourself," said Jack.

"Like my mother did?" Cathal spat.

Jack began to shake and Aisling thought he was about to faint.

Cathal drained his glass and poured himself more wine. "You gave

208

me away because I wasn't really yours. And then you felt guilty so you didn't want to admit it." "What are you talking about?" asked Jack. "That's not true at all."

"How can I believe a word out of your mouth?" Cathal asked. He took a deep breath. "I felt so shit about myself. It wasn't like I decided never to come home. It was more that I kind of drifted. I went to London for a bit... That's when things got really messy."

"London," Aisling exclaimed.

She couldn't believe all this time she'd been imagining her brother in America, he'd been less than an hour's flight away.

"I started taking a lot of drugs, got into a bit of dealing, next thing I know I'm banged up for two years. I felt so ashamed and disgusted with myself. How could I tell Mam and Dad that?"

"They would have just been happy to know you were alive," Aisling protested.

"I thought they'd be better off if I was dead," Cathal said this with such conviction that Aisling didn't dare contradict him. "Anyway when I got out I was in this pub in Kilburn, completely off my face as usual, when I hear this music coming from the back room. I recognised it at once and went to have a closer listen – it turned out to be Flynn playing the fiddle. I couldn't believe it. I didn't want him to see me so I went to leave but he came running out after me. He insisted I go back to his for a nightcap and I ended up telling him my life story."

Somehow it felt right to Aisling that Flynn had been the one to find her brother. "Did he persuade you to come home?" she asked.

"He tried, God knows he tried. But I was having none of it. I'd kind of given up on myself. I told him how Jack had claimed to be my father and then I'd been told it was some sailor and then it turned out to be this unknown monster."

"It was a terrible mistake to tell you that..." Jack began.

Cathal cut him off. "Do you know what Flynn said to me? He said that my mother had been engaged to a sailor called Troy. And that he'd heard rumours that she'd gotten pregnant by him but he'd abandoned her. Flynn said it seemed like I'd been told many versions of a story but that I'd never be at peace till I found the ending for myself. That's what made me decide to go back to America."

"And did you find your father?" Claire asked.

Jack had his head in his hands. Aisling wondered what on earth could have made him tell such a horrible lie.

"No. No, I'm still searching for him," Cathal suddenly sounded very tired. "You see no one seems to know where he is. My father went missing in Dublin over twenty years ago. But I did find my grandmother. She got some surprise when I turned up on her doorstep. Turns out I'm her only grandchild. She said Troy had never even known I existed. She also said that my mother had broken his heart which seemed odd cos I'd heard it was the other way round. She'd hired this private detective to track down her son. The detective found my mother in Ireland, but Troy was nowhere to be found. So then I did a little investigating of my own."

Cathal stared at Jack. "When I checked the dates I realised my mother died less than a week after that detective came to visit her. Doesn't that strike you as a very odd coincidence?"

Jack said nothing. He was trembling from head to foot.

37

JACK THREW HIMSELF INTO HIS work to avoid thinking too much about the past. When he came home from a long hard day at the hospital, he was too exhausted and worn out for guilt. Watching Kate playing with Cathal, he felt so overwhelmed with love for them both that there was no room for any other emotion. He was never entirely sure if Kate actually believed his story about Troy or if she just chose to accept it because she had few other options. She certainly never suspected him of the treachery he'd committed. Sometimes even Jack himself wondered how he'd come to live this stolen life.

Being in the new house helped. It was possible to put some distance between his present self and how he'd behaved in the past. It was almost as if he'd divided himself in two. No one could imagine that a devoted husband and loving father could pull such an outrageous stunt. But since the discovery of the rings, Jack was no longer able to hide from the fact that everything he held most dear belonged to him because he'd lied through his teeth.

After one particularly long shift, as the sun was finally beginning to rise, Jack checked on an elderly patient. The man, who was in his early seventies and instructed Jack to call him 'Eddie', was suffering from a partially blocked aorta. His breathing was laboured and he was due for surgery the next day. The senior consultant should have increased Eddie's medication before heading off for his game of golf.

As Jack listened to Eddie's chest, the old man said, "God knows I've done some shitty things in my life and it's too late to put a lot of them right but I'm not ready to die yet." There was so much sincerity in his voice that Jack felt for him.

As he left the ward, a pretty young nurse – one of the many who enjoyed flirting with Jack probably precisely because he never showed any interest – came up to him. "There's a phone call for you, Dr. O'Connell."

He hurried over to reception to pick up the phone. Who would ring him at work so early? Jack was instantly worried something had happened to Kate.

As soon as he heard the voice on the other end, his heart stopped. There was no mistaking the mid-Atlantic twang.

"Hey man," Troy began as if they had only spoken last week. "Remember me? Troy. The guy whose life you saved."

Jack fervently hoped he was having a nightmare. "Of course I remember," he gasped.

"You sure are hard to track down," Troy continued. "There's like a million J O'Connells in the phone book. Then I remembered you said you were studying to be a doctor. So I had the bright idea to ring up a Dr J O'Connell, it wasn't you, but he put me on to some kind of medical register and they put me straight through. How you been man?"

Troy's tone was as friendly and optimistic as ever. Either he was an incredible actor or he still had no idea Jack was married to Kate.

"Where are you?" Jack managed to ask.

"I'm right here in Dublin. Just arrived last night. I woke up dead early – you know, jet lag – and I never been a real good sleeper. I'm in this bar called the White Horse, managed to find the only public house in the whole city that's open at 9am. It's full of sailors, really brings me back. I know it sounds crazy, I tried writing to you but I guess you didn't get the letter, any how I'm here to find Kate. Any idea where she is these days?"

Jack's voice caught in his throat. "We need to talk," he whispered. "My shift finishes in half an hour. Give me the address and I'll come and meet you."

Jack put the phone down feeling like a man whose just been condemned to death. Troy was back. How the hell was Jack going to get rid of him this time? His worst fears were coming true.

He didn't wait for his shift to finish. He rushed out of the hospital without speaking to anyone and drove as fast as he could to the White Horse.

The pub was hidden away in a basement on the quays and you had to descend a long steep stairway to reach it. Opening the door was like entering another world. The smoke was so thick that at first Jack couldn't see Troy. The bar was full of sailors in various degrees of inebriation, and the atmosphere was such that it felt like midnight rather than morning. There wasn't a single woman.

As his eyes adjusted to the dimness, Jack spotted Troy sitting at the bar drinking whiskey. He hadn't in fact changed that much. He'd lost some weight and had dark rings under his eyes but other than that he was as handsome and effusive as ever. He'd already bonded with the enormous barman and insisted on ordering Jack a pint. Jack wondered if his twisted guts would be able to cope.

"It's so good to see you man," Troy exclaimed.

Jack allowed himself to be hugged. He couldn't speak.

Luckily Troy was too busy telling the intrigued barman the story of how Jack had saved his life to notice that Jack was so nervous he was shaking. Troy had clearly felt no need to adjust to the local time and had

212

quite a few drinks in him despite the earliness of the hour.

"I just couldn't stop thinking about her, man. It was like the more time passed, instead of getting easier, it was getting worse. Got so bad I even ended up telling my Mom. She was like "You're a fool boy." And I thought she were gonna tell me just to move on like everybody else did. But she didn't. She said, "There's only one great love in any person's life. And if you're lucky enough to find that love, you got to hold on, hold on tight as you can in the face of everything. You don't go getting the first boat out without even speaking to the girl.""

Jack wished Troy's mother didn't give such sound advice. He wracked his brains trying to think of a way to get Troy on the next flight back to New York.

"I don't know how to tell you this," Jack began. "But... Kate's dead."

A look of great confusion passed over Troy's face. He stared at Jack as if seeing him for the first time. "So how come when I rang her father from the airport he told me Kate was a hundred times better off without me? He sounded as bitter and miserable as ever, but he sure didn't sound grief stricken."

Jack's mouth opened and closed. He'd finally run out of excuses. "Kate's married to me," he stated.

In some desperate corner of his mind, Jack hoped that Troy might accept he was too late without asking too many questions. Instead the American pulled back his fist and punched Jack so hard he sent him flying half way across the bar.

The huge barman was clearly used to troublemakers and Jack had barely risen to his feet when he was manhandled out of the pub and up the stairs. He found himself deposited on the street with an efficiency Brendan would have admired.

A few moments later a kicking and cursing Troy was thrown down beside him. Troy didn't waste any time asking Jack for details. He might not know the particulars but he'd grasped that the guy he'd asked to be his best man had somehow ended up stealing his bride. He grabbed Jack by the throat and began to throttle the life out of him. Troy's grip was incredibly strong and Jack couldn't breathe. He clawed desperately at Troy's fingers but he could feel the edges of his vision turning black. He wondered if this was how it felt to drown. It was almost a relief in a strange way.

Jack had no idea what kind of basic self-preservation instinct took hold of him, but with the last of his strength, he kicked Troy in the groin. The American reeled back, letting go of his victim. Jack gasped as the air rushed back into his lungs.

Troy, who seemed possessed by a demon, struck him a blow across the face before he could recover. Jack punched him back and Troy's nose exploded with blood.

Troy charged at him and for a moment the two men grappled with each other at the top of the quay's stairway.

Then Troy lost his footing and fell backwards down the stairs. He landed awkwardly, but he was still shouting and yelling so Jack figured he couldn't be that badly injured. He should have walked away then but somehow he couldn't. Troy was struggling to get to his feet but seemed to be having great difficulty. Jack thought he might have broken his leg, and being too drunk to feel the pain, was likely to do himself even greater injury.

"Try to keep still," Jack instructed as he descended the steps.

"Stay away from me, you bastard," Troy roared, more in pain than anger. "Why would she marry you? Why? It was me she loved. I know it was."

Jack thought someone from the bar would come out to help them but the door remained shut. When he reached Troy Jack realised the American's face was covered in blood. He must have hit his head on one of the steps. Jack put his shoulder under Troy's arm and hauled him to his feet. He'd possibly twisted his ankle but his legs were fine. With great effort Jack half dragged a limping – and rather worryingly – unresisting Troy up the stairs and into his car.

Jack decided to drive him to the hospital as fast as he could. Troy was mumbling incoherently. All Jack could make out was Kate's name. He started the engine, noting with horror that Troy's seat was already covered in blood. The red stickiness made Jack's stomach lurch. He didn't dare examine too closely but he guessed that the American had a fractured skull. Remembering the anthem singer from the night he worked at the Palace with Brendan, Jack told himself Troy would be fine.

The hospital wasn't far but the traffic was horrendous. A long snake of cars stretched bumper to bumper all along the road. Jack blasted his horn and attempted to cut through but he made ridiculously slow progress. He thought of stopping to call an ambulance but wondered if that would take longer. He looked across at Troy. The American lolled half forward, only saved from hitting the dashboard by the seatbelt Jack had secured.

Jack shouted at him to wake up. They were nearly at A&E, but Troy seemed completely unconscious. The traffic lights ahead turned red. Jack checked Troy's pulse.

"C'mon don't do this to me," he instructed the ex-sailor, slapping his cheeks.

Troy's eyes opened. He stared straight at Jack but he didn't seem to see him. "It's you," he said, smiling. "My angel." Then he gave a strange sigh.

Though Troy's eyes were still open, Jack knew with horrible certainty that he was gone.

38

JACK WAS IN SUCH AN advanced state of panic that it was as if someone else was driving the car. He just knew he had to get out of the city, away from people, away from witnesses. He found himself on one of the main roads that sped out of town and up into the Dublin Wicklow Mountains. The houses and shops got thinner and then fell away altogether. He was terrified they'd be stopped by the guards and Jack would have to explain why he had a dead man with half his skull bashed in bleeding all over his seats. He couldn't even explain it to himself.

Once they were deep in the mountains and miles from human habitation, Jack pulled over on to a narrow track that was hidden from the road. Only then could he bring himself to look at Troy. The once handsome sailor was barely recognisable. The blood on his face was still thick and wet and his skin was the colour of chalk. Jack remembered the last time he'd seen Troy with that particular shade. This time he didn't attempt to give him the kiss of life. He knew it was too late. He felt for Troy's pulse again just to be sure this nightmare was really happening. There was nothing there.

Though Jack prayed for a miracle, he sensed that God was not on his side. He sat there in the car for hours till he was as cold as the corpse beside him. They were in such an isolated spot that there weren't even any sheep in sight. It was now mid-afternoon – a beautiful sunny day – and the sky was a million times clearer than Jack's conscience.

He watched a hawk twirling majestically across the blue and wished he was any creature on earth other than himself. Kate would be wondering where he'd got to. She always had breakfast cooked for him when he came in from a night shift. She'd have rung the hospital by now and discovered he'd left hours ago. Jack realised that the only reason he had to go on living was so that Kate would never find out the truth. Troy was dead and nothing Jack did would bring him back to life. If Jack delivered the American's body to the hospital morgue, he'd be asked a thousand questions. It would probably get into the papers and it would be impossible for Kate not to find out. Even if she believed that Troy's death had been an accident, she'd guess that there was far more to the story than Jack had told her.

In a daze he dragged Troy's body from the car and rolled it into a kind of shallow ditch. It was surprisingly heavy. He tried to use a bit of old rag to mop up the blood on the seats but it had gotten everywhere. He remembered Brendan's stories of bodies buried in the Dublin Wicklow

Mountains. He needed a shovel.

Slowly he drove to the nearest town and went into a shopping centre. He was covered in blood and knew he had a wild crazed look in his eye, and yet hardly anyone looked at him. Or if they did, they quickly looked away. He bought a shovel, plastic bags, cloths, stain remover and cleaning fluid. Standing in the queue, which mainly consisted of elderly women and young mothers with their toddlers, was an entirely surreal experience. Jack kept thinking someone was bound to be suspicious, but by then he was beyond emotion. He seemed to be working on some kind of automatic pilot.

Digging Troy's grave was not an easy job. The ground was solid as rock and Jack sweated in the late afternoon sunshine. He cried with frustration, tears rolling down his face, mixed with the sweat of his labour. Eventually he had a hole deep enough and he lowered Troy into it. He wondered if he should try to say a prayer or something and then realised how ridiculous that would be. He felt a tightness in his chest that reminded him of the pain he'd felt at his mother's funeral. In spite of everything Jack liked Troy. In some other lifetime they could have been the mates Troy had imagined they were. It was an accident, Jack kept repeating to himself over and over again. He wished to God it didn't feel so much like fate.

It was getting dark as Jack drove back down into the city. He still had no idea what he would tell Kate to explain his absence. He hadn't slept or eaten in nearly twenty four hours and he felt like he'd been away for years.

As he pulled into his driveway he was alarmed to see that there was another car already present. His heart was banging as he put his key in the door. Kate was sitting at the kitchen table with a man Jack had never seen before. The man stood up as Jack entered. He was large and intimidating with an ugly scar across his left cheek. There was an authority about his presence that convinced Jack he was a police inspector. Someone had clearly seen Jack and Troy and rung the guards. Jack felt that the game was up. He was exhausted and didn't have the energy to make up any more stories. He was bound to end up being done for murder. No one would believe he'd never wanted to kill Troy.

"We've been waiting for you," the man spoke slowly, with menace.

Kate looked frightened.

"There was an emergency at work," Jack said, swallowing hard.

"I hear hospitals are like that," the man replied sarcastically. "Your lovely wife and I have been having a nice little chat. Beautiful woman you got – you're a very lucky man."

Jack just wished he'd slap the handcuffs on and get it over with.

"And from what I hear you've got a very promising career ahead of you. Be a shame if anything was to mess that up."

Jack suddenly wondered if the man was looking for some kind of bribe. It was a strange line of questioning from a police officer.

"Who are you?" Jack demanded.

"Let's just say I'm a friend of your cousin's. Your cousin Brendan, that is." Jack was startled to hear Brendan's name. He still worried about his old flatmate but his own troubles of late tended to eclipse his concern. "Is he okay?"

"Well there are a few people very keen to speak to him about some matters of considerable urgency. I don't suppose you know where he is?" The man managed to make the question sound more like a threat. Jack doubted he had Brendan's best interests at heart.

"He's gone to America," Jack explained.

"So your wife said. Leaving no forwarding address; how very inconvenient. When did you last speak to him?"

"Look," Jack said. "I've no idea who you are or what you're doing in my home..."

The man very slowly took out a small handgun and laid it on the kitchen table. The three of them stared at it for a moment. Jack's relief that the man was not an officer of the law was beginning to fade.

"We have no quarrel with you," the man eventually said. "I'll ask you again. When did you last speak to Brendan?"

"Months ago. He rang me to say goodbye."

"And where was he ringing from?"

"He said something about a hostel in Kilburn. Look if he owes money maybe I can..."

The man picked up the gun and put it back inside his jacket. He smiled at Jack. "Brendan owes a hell of a lot more than money. Thank you, you've been most helpful."

With a polite little bow to Kate, the man let himself out the back door. A moment later they heard his car engine starting up. Then he roared away.

Kate wrapped her arms around Jack and held him tight. "Thank God you came back. He scared the life out of me. What on earth has Brendan got himself mixed up in?"

Kate was so relieved the gunman was gone that she didn't ask him about his whereabouts. "The world is such a fucked up place," she said. "I'm so lucky to have you."

39

IN THE WEEKS AFTER BURYING Troy, Jack found going to work a relief. Any kind of semblance of normality came as a blessing. He couldn't sleep at all and he kept breaking out in cold sweats.

Kate could see he was deeply disturbed but she thought he was worried about his cousin. "America's a huge country," she pointed out. "They'll never find Brendan over there."

But it was who might be looking for Troy that worried Jack. He thought his guilt was written all over him.

A little over a week after Troy's death, Jack told Eddie, now recovering from successful heart surgery, that he was ready to go home.

"Shame they couldn't have given me a whole new heart, the one I got been so battered," the old man laughed. "Still I'm very grateful to you doctor. It's a wonderful thing you're doing here. There's no greater gift than life. It's only when death is staring you in the face that you realise what you'd give for a few more years, even a few more days, on this earth."

The irony of the old man's words struck him like a blow. Jack knew he hadn't set out to kill Troy, but he felt that he had blood on his hands.

Eddie suddenly gave him a warm hug. "You're a good man, Dr. O'Connell," he exclaimed. "Not like some of them in here couldn't give a shite if you keeled over in front of them."

Jack felt he'd set out to be a good person but somehow it had all gone horribly wrong. He'd never thought he'd make much of a doctor. Whoever heard of a heart surgeon who was afraid of the sight of blood? But maybe if he dedicated his life to saving others, he could in some small way atone for Troy's death.

Kate was surprised by his sudden change of direction. "I thought you wanted to be a GP?" she asked.

"I'll never get the money together to set up my own practice and besides I want to save lives, not prescribe cough medicine.'

"Well I think it's great. I'm very proud of you," his wife kissed him.

Jack's father was equally impressed by his decision to go for cardiothoracic surgery. "A heart surgeon in the family. Now wouldn't that be something," he observed with rare enthusiasm.

Jack figured there was little he could do to fix his father's broken heart or his own, but that he might do some good for others. He worked harder than he ever had before in his life and his superiors were impressed by his dedication and commitment. They also told him he had a steady hand and a calmness under pressure that were the hallmarks of a great surgeon. Somehow their professional admiration made Jack feel worse but he persisted.

Six months passed and every single day Jack thought of Troy in his unmarked grave. But now it was more with genuine regret and sorrow than complete mind shattering panic. Sometimes he found himself repeating the words 'it was an accident' over and over again in a loop in his brain. He'd once been responsible for saving the sailor's life; was he now responsible for his death?

One evening Jack came home from work, late as usual and utterly exhausted, to find his wife waiting for him.

This particular night Kate didn't even comment on Jack's lateness. "I've something to tell you," she announced the moment he walked in the door.

Jack was instantly on his guard but she was smiling at him warmly. Her smile was so beautiful it made his heart ache.

"We're going to have a baby," she announced.

Jack was utterly stunned.

"Aren't you going to say anything?" Kate asked laughing.

"That's... that's wonderful, that's the best news ever." He didn't tell her how little he felt he deserved this incredible happiness.

Still the promise of the new infant seemed a sign that life would go on after all. Kate was scared the mysterious gunman would return while Jack thought every knock on the door was the police come to arrest him. But the days slipped past without anyone hassling them in any way.

Soon his wife's small bump was visible to all. When they explained it to him, Cathal seemed excited at the idea of a little brother or a sister. Jack thought being with child made Kate more gorgeous than ever. She really did seem to glow with health and radiance.

"I hope it's a girl," she told Jack.

"I don't mind," Jack said. And he didn't. He couldn't get over the miracle of himself and Kate creating a new life together. Suddenly he wasn't so sure if he was an atheist after all. He prayed to God to forgive him for the crimes of his past, to give him the chance to be a good father.

40

WITH THE BABY DUE IN less than two months, Jack insisted that Kate take it easy. But she was as irrepressible as ever. Their son was worse. They knew two year olds were supposed to be lively, but Cathal was simply a whirlwind of energy. Jack no longer had to worry about the little boy being too quiet. Cathal's favourite refrain was "Why?" He seemed to have an endless curiosity about the world.

One Sunday afternoon they went to feed the ducks in Stephen's Green. It was a lovely day and Jack felt calm for the first time in ages.

Then Kate touched his arm. "Is that bloke following us?"

Jack looked over his shoulder and indeed there was a short man in a tweed jacket staring over at them. He turned his head the moment Jack caught his eye.

"Reckon you're being paranoid," Jack told Kate.

But two days later Jack thought he saw the same man sitting in a car in the hospital grounds. He walked over towards him but the man turned on his engine and drove away. Jack knew he had been paranoid for years and hoped to God it was only that.

But that evening when he got home, he found Kate sitting at the kitchen table staring into space. She looked like someone had died.

"What's happened?" Jack asked.

"A man came round..." she eventually stuttered.

"Looking for Brendan?" Jack thought he'd kill those bastards for frightening his pregnant wife.

"No," Kate said. "Looking for you."

She turned and stared at him. It was like being stabbed in the heart. "He said he was a private detective."

Jack wondered if the police had found Troy's body. Maybe Brendan's five hundred years was a little over optimistic. Jack felt sick and had to sit down.

"He said he was hired by a Mrs Gladys Anderson." Kate spoke very slowly, as if she were still in shock.

"I don't know anyone called Gladys?" Jack had a very bad feeling about all of this.

"She's Troy's mother," Kate revealed.

Jack remembered Troy saying that it was his mom who'd encouraged him to return to Ireland. Even if they hadn't been close, of course she'd still wonder what had become of him.

"He said…" Kate struggled to pull herself together. "He said that Troy headed off to Dublin last July to look for his ex-fiancé who'd stood him up at the altar. And that nobody had heard from him since."

Jack stared at his shoes.

"Why would Troy tell his mother I stood him up when you said he gave you the rings back?"

"I don't know," Jack whispered.

Kate glared at him with a frightening intensity. "Jack, if you're lying to me, I swear to God, I'll kill you."

"I honestly don't know," Jack repeated.

"That detective showed me Troy's flight booking. He said they were positive he'd gotten on the flight. It was for the 10th of July. I looked it up on the calendar after he left. That psycho with the gun looking for Brendan was here on the 12th of July. I remember because there were riots in Belfast over the parades and I'd been watching them on the telly. You disappeared all that day and you said it was work but you always ring me when you're stuck at work."

"Kate…" Jack tried to interrupt her.

"If Troy came all the way to Dublin to see me, why didn't he look me up?"

Jack couldn't answer. He had a terrible thumping in his head like his brain was about to explode.

"Did he get in touch with you? You have to tell me, Jack, I have to find him."

The urgency of Kate's tone made Jack realise that his wife was still in love with Troy. That the years of their happiness, the fact she was pregnant with Jack's child, meant nothing. If Troy was alive, Kate wouldn't hesitate to leave him. All this time he hadn't just been fooling her, he'd been fooling himself. The whole thing had been for nothing. Jack had thought his heart was already broken but he realised in that moment that all his guilt, all his grief, was nothing compared to finally realising Kate had never loved him as much as she did Troy, and she never would.

"I love you," Jack said. "Everything I did was because I love you."

Kate stared at him. "Troy didn't change his mind, did he?"

Jack knew his guilt was written all over his face.

"You lied to me. All this time you've lied to me." Kate's voice had an edge of hysteria to it. "You've made my whole life a lie."

"No," Jack said. "This is the life we were meant to have. This is how

223

it was supposed to be. Can't you see that?"

"What the fuck are you talking about?" Kate was cold with fury. "Where is Troy? Tell me the truth for once for God's sakes."

"Troy's dead." Jack's voice sounded to him like that of a stranger.

"What?" Kate looked as if he'd struck her.

"It was an accident, he fell. I never wanted to hurt him," Jack answered in desperation. It had all been an unfortunate accident from the beginning. He had never meant any of it to happen.

Kate stared at him in horror. "What have you done, Jack?"

Then as if she couldn't bear the answer, she turned and fled from the room.

Jack was left with the devastation of her question. He sat at the kitchen table unable to move. The early afternoon sunlight fell gently through the window. He could hear the sound of traffic passing outside. Otherwise there was total silence. Everything looked exactly as it had done before and yet his world had just ended. It had collapsed like a house of cards. Jack knew he should go rushing after Kate. Try to make her see that everything he'd done was because he loved her. But his brain was numb.

He jumped when he heard their door slam. As if he'd been jolted back to life, he tore down the stairs and threw the front door open.

Kate was getting into the driver's seat of their little Volkswagen. Jack found himself regretting having taught his wife how to drive.

"Kate, let me explain..."

At the sound of his voice she turned and looked at Jack. A look full of such hatred and contempt that his blood ran cold. "You killed him, didn't you?"

He wanted to deny it, but it was true. He'd destroyed Troy's life because he couldn't bear to give up Kate. "I just wanted to be with you," he said.

Kate threw herself behind the steering wheel and slammed the door after her. She turned on the engine. Jack tried to block her and barely managed to step out of the way in time. Kate had every intention of running him over. He watched the car as it sped off into the distance. He knew then that he'd lost her forever. She'd never forgive him in a million years.

41

JACK HAD NO IDEA HOW he got through the next couple of days. He neither ate nor slept. The only thing he managed to do was take care of Cathal who kept asking for his mammy. He didn't know where Kate was and he didn't know how he could go about finding out. He'd spent much of the previous afternoon picking up the telephone receiver and replacing it. He wanted to dial 999, to declare an emergency, for someone to recognise what a complete state of panic he was in. But what could he say? That he'd admitted to his wife he'd killed the love of her life and now she'd disappeared.

The knock on the door came as a relief even though he could see through the window that a police car had pulled up.

So Kate had turned him in. He couldn't blame her. Besides he no longer cared if they locked him up and threw away the key. His life was over any way.

The two guards were very young and polite. They shuffled their feet nervously as they asked if they could come in. They removed their hats, acting as if they were the ones under suspicion not Jack. He felt like confessing just to put them at their ease.

The slightly older one with reddish cheeks spoke first. "I'm afraid, Sir, there's been an accident."

Jack was confused. How could the police know he'd never meant to hurt Troy? "Accident?" he repeated the word stupidly.

"A car accident. Your wife's car came off the road."

"Is she all right?" Jack gasped.

"I'm really sorry to have to tell you this, Sir, but Mrs O'Connell was already dead when we found her. I'm so very, very sorry."

"She can't be dead."

The second guard came to the first's assistance. "We don't understand how it happened, Sir. Mrs O'Connell's car was discovered washed up on Dingle Beach. She was still inside."

"Are you sure it's her?" Jack knew he was grasping at straws but he couldn't begin to believe that Kate was gone.

"Her sister Patricia identified the body. She asked that you be informed. She was very upset and I don't think she felt up to telling you herself. I'm truly sorry."

Jack stared at the two guards. They did not look like they were enjoying their jobs. He could see they felt nothing but genuine pity for him.

"She drove into the sea?" he asked.

The guards looked like they had hoped he wouldn't ask. After a moment's hesitation, the older one managed to say, "We haven't found any witnesses as yet so we don't actually know what happened. Was your wife suffering from any form of depression or anxiety?"

Jack remembered the look in Kate's eyes when she'd left. This was her way of getting the ultimate revenge. Or maybe, like his mother, it was simply that her heart was broken and she had no will to live anymore. He'd killed her as surely as if he'd strangled her with his own hands.

42

Pat was the one who made all the funeral arrangements. Jack just sat in a corner like a ghost. He suspected that Pat only tolerated his presence because Martin had told her to have some pity. He'd taken one look at her and known that Pat didn't believe for a second that her sister's death was an accident.

The only thing she said to him was, "She rang me you know. I'm the last person who spoke to her alive. She was sobbing on the phone, wouldn't tell me what was wrong, just made me promise I'd look after Cathal. What the hell did you do to her?"

Jack shook his head. He didn't know how to begin to explain.

At the funeral Jack couldn't bring himself to speak to anyone. It seemed such an enormous effort, like his words had an incredibly long distance to go before being audible, as if he were on a telephone line that was very badly connected. Everything he said seemed to echo and magnify. He hated the sound of his voice. In fact he loathed the sight of himself. He cut himself shaving in the mornings because his hands shook so badly and he disliked looking in the mirror. He knew he looked like shit. That his skin was pale and clammy and that there were huge dark shadows under his eyes. He was like a zombie incarnation of his former self.

He hardly slept and when he did he had terrible nightmares. Far worse than any nightmare was the dream he had the night before the funeral. He and Kate were on the beach where they'd first kissed, where they'd first found Troy. They were having a picnic and Cathal was crawling around on the sand. In the dream Kate was trying to fix Cathal's hat back on. He kept knocking it off but she was worried his fair skin would burn under the sun.

She was laughing and she looked so beautiful in her swimsuit.

Jack walked over to her and said, "I'm so sorry about Troy."

For a moment she looked puzzled. "Troy's fine." She smiled, pointing.

Down by the water's edge, Jack could see Troy in his sailor's uniform holding a fishing rod. He turned and waved to Jack who was struck by the sun glinting off his perfect white teeth. He turned back to Kate who put her arm up and pulled Jack down beside her. Just as she kissed him, Jack woke up.

The warmth and beauty of the dream was in such stark contrast to the cold misery of reality that Jack wished he'd never have to wake up again. He looked up at the cracked ceiling and felt like screaming. But he knew that if he let the sound escape, he wouldn't be able to stop.

At the funeral Jack could hear people whispering, "Such a beautiful young girl and the child not even three years old. I heard she was pregnant too."

There was much shaking of heads and furtive glances in his direction. "Doesn't he look only devastated?"

They had no idea how totally and utterly obliterated he felt. Their public show of concern struck him as sordid and cheap. They wallowed in his tragedy, but it was he that had to live with the consequences. He wanted to throw himself into the open grave.

His father, seeing that Jack couldn't take much more of the shaking of hands and offers of sandwiches, offered to take him home. Jack took his arm.

"I never meant to hurt her," he told his father.

"Of course you didn't," his father was looking at him with such infinite sympathy that Jack nearly felt like confessing the whole story.

"You mustn't go blaming yourself," his father squeezed his arm. "What good does regret do anyone?"

Jack felt as if his entire being was drained and only the fragile outer shell of his skin remained. On the way out of the graveyard, they passed a crying Mr O'Rourke. When he saw his son-in-law, he turned away and stumbled off towards the church. Jack wondered if the old man felt any guilt, if he had any idea how he had indirectly contributed to his daughter's death. But there wasn't any point in trying to spread the guilt around. It was Jack who had killed her. He and he alone.

For a week after the funeral he lay in bed unable to move. His father fed him bowls of chicken noodle soup as if he were suffering from some severe form of flu. He protested that he wasn't hungry but his father insisted that he at least taste it, ladling spoonfuls into his mouth.

"It does get easier," he assured him.

Jack looked up into the older man's cracked face and his hair streaked with grey, wondering if it did. His father had looked like he was a hundred years old for as long as Jack could remember. Did heart break cause premature aging? Still he was grateful for his father's tender care and the fact that he didn't come out with the platitudes of other people. He didn't want to hear that Kate was in a better place. He wanted her there with him. Without her, he was in hell.

At the end of the week, he remembered Cathal. He felt terrible to have forgotten him so completely. The poor kid must be totally confused and scared surrounded by strangers.

He dragged himself from his bed, splashed some water on his face, and pulled on some clothes. His legs felt shaky and he didn't relish the prospect of going into O'Rourke's Pub, but he had to get his son back. He couldn't leave him at the mercy of Kate's family. He stumbled down the road, shaking his head from side to side, trying to move the grief that blocked his thoughts. People stared at him, but stayed out of his way. They probably thought he was drunk. In fact Jack hadn't touched a drop, not even at the funeral. He didn't want to repeat his father's performance of drowning in whisky and besides alcohol didn't dull the pain, it just made it fuzzier.

He was surprised to see that O'Rourke's was open for business. A mist hung in the air, a dampness that muffled sound and made movement difficult. The breeze tasted of salt and the threat of a coming storm. Jack pushed open the door and was shocked by the scene that met his eyes. A number of old men – regular drinkers – had gathered round the bar on which Cathal stood.

Pat was holding him up with both hands, singing, "Dance for your daddy, my little laddie, dance for your daddy, my little lad."

And Cathal was indeed kicking his legs and laughing with sheer joy. His little podgy face all red with exertion and his blue eyes flashing. The old men watched the performance with great fondness like he was the grandchild they'd never had.

Pat had a lovely voice, soft and lilting like Kate's. Jack stood mesmerized in the doorway watching his son kicking his legs on the bar. He felt like he'd come back from the land of the dead and was observing the antics of the living. Their simple happiness seemed so entirely alien and incomprehensible to him. He didn't begrudge them it, or feel offended by it, he just knew it was lost to him forever.

Pat glanced up and saw him standing there. "Jack," she said surprised.

Everyone stopped. Even Cathal peered at Jack as if he was a Martian that had landed. Pat ushered Jack into a chair. She clearly thought he looked like he might pass out. She asked him if he wanted anything to drink.

He gestured for her to pass Cathal over. He suddenly felt too tired for speech. As soon as the little boy was placed in his arms, the familiar smell of milk and soft skin overwhelmed him. He buried his face in Cathal's neck and began to cry. He hadn't shed a tear at the funeral. Even in his own bedroom, he'd thought of shouting, yelling, smashing the furniture, but not crying. Now holding Cathal, his sorrow came unfrozen and rivers flooded from his eyes. Cathal looked surprised by the sudden wetness of his father's tears, but he made no sound.

Pat gently prized the baby from Jack's grasp. She didn't think a grown man's tears were good for a child. Instead she put a pint of Guinness in front of Jack. The old men had retreated into the far corners, embarrassed to be seen to be intruding on such pain. They were old enough to know what heart break looked like and that there was nothing to be said that would offer any consolation.

Pat let Jack cry himself out. She didn't touch him or even look at him "Poor Kate," she sighed. She clearly wanted Jack to know where her sympathies lay. She hadn't spoken to him at all since the funeral. Jack didn't care any more if she blamed him; she couldn't possibly hate him as much as he hated himself. Still at least she'd given him a drink and seemed to be making a determined effort to be civil.

"Look Jack, I've talked it over with Martin. We both know Cathal isn't really your son. Why don't you leave him here with us? We could bring him up as our own and put all this horrible mess behind him."

Jack was shocked. He hadn't considered that Pat would want to take Cathal for her own. The little boy was all that Jack had left of Kate. Without him, he really did have nothing.

He said forcefully, "Cathal is my son."

To demonstrate his point, he held out his arms to the little boy who happily clambered into them. Pat seemed to consider snatching the child back, but decided against an unseemly tug of war. Instead she stood up and stalked out of the bar. Jack sat shivering in the frosty air of her hatred.

Jack decided to get himself and Cathal out of Pat's clutches as quickly as possible. He ignored his father's pleas that he needed more rest, that he wasn't in any fit state to go back to work so soon. Jack thought throwing himself into his job would help. The last thing he needed was time to think. Having Cathal back gave him a reason to get up in the morning. Whatever Jack felt, the little boy still needed to be fed, changed, and washed. Through the routine of caring for his son, Jack hoped to achieve a certain numbness.

So he was surprised by just how upsetting going back to the house was. The place was full of Kate's things. Her hairbrush by the bed, her dressing gown hung on the back of the door. Jack rubbed it against his face and smelled Kate so vividly it was as if she was standing behind him. How could all the signs of her still be there and yet she wasn't? The very air he breathed seemed proof of her existence. She felt so much more alive than he did.

He remembered his Nana telling him, "The angels have taken your mother away." And he couldn't understand why they hadn't taken him too. Did they forget? Had he been accidentally left behind? Then he remembered that angels were nonsense. He didn't hold with ghosts and spirits and all that superstitious rubbish. He didn't believe that his mother was haunting them even though he saw her at the foot of his bed every night for two weeks after she died. He screwed his eyes tight to make her go away and told himself he was dreaming, or going mad, or both.

Now though as he shivered in the bed he'd once shared with Kate, he prayed that he would catch a glimpse of his wife. He kept watching for her expectantly. Even her ghost would be better than nothing. But Kate didn't seem to want to visit him – and who could blame her?

Jack felt completely alone. There was no one he could talk to. Maybe if Brendan had been there, he'd have confessed all to him. He had hoped his cousin would turn up for the funeral as mysteriously as he'd showed up for the wedding. Surely the grapevine he was always boasting about would have told him of Jack's troubles. But there was no sign of Brendan. Not even a card. Brendan wasn't a great one for casual correspondence, but in times of crisis he could always be counted on. Maybe he hadn't heard. Jack brushed other possibilities from his mind.

Staying in the house was too much for him. All those echoing rooms full of the ghosts of regrets. He moved himself and Cathal into a small one bedroom flat. Even the flat sometimes seemed to deafen Jack with the oppression of silence. He kept the TV or the radio on at all times. The quiet at night did him in completely. His insomnia, which had receded since Kate had told him she was pregnant, now returned like an old enemy who knew where his weaknesses lay. He'd sit by Cathal's cot and listen to him breathing. The baby's soft breath seemed the only real sound in the universe. Everything else was just noise. Listening to his son was like a thin rope that linked him to sanity. He watched the little boy's chest move up and down in the half shadow of his night-light. He looked so peaceful and perfect, his hair now a halo of curls.

"My little angel," Kate used to call him.

At first Jack couldn't bring himself to tell Cathal his mother was dead. He told him she'd had to go away for a while. But naturally the little boy kept asking, "When's Mammy coming back?"

Eventually Jack had to explain that she wasn't. He tried to say she was in heaven, but he lacked conviction, and he had the distinct impression Cathal didn't believe him.

Jack hired a child-minder, a large, donut-shaped woman with huge breasts called Mrs McKiernan. She had a loud, booming voice and was unstoppably cheerful. She treated him as if he were another of the children in her care and told him he was wonderful to be bringing up his son on his own. She insisted on cooking Jack dinner and leaving it for him in the evenings. Jack knew he'd never have managed without her. At the hospital, his colleagues expressed their sympathies before turning back to the more pressing problems of their own lives. Jack had always been quite reserved, but now he withdrew into himself.

What was there he could possibly say? He was surrounded by pain and suffering, disease and death. When he lost a patient, he felt a certain depressing sense of failure, but that was it. He was contained within the thin envelope of his own grief. Like he was floating along in a bubble. A bubble of ice that no one could cut through. He felt cold, cold in the deep marrow of his bones, and he couldn't imagine that he would ever feel warm again. He didn't mind. He didn't want to have to deal with the burning pain of thawing out. He preferred to keep himself protected. Clenched tight like a fist. If he was to let go of his self control, even for a second, he would fall apart all together. He didn't want the burden of emotions. He just wanted to survive. To get through the day to day and to make sure that Cathal had everything he needed. He was living for his son now. His own soul had died. Or wandered off to a land so far away that Jack didn't believe it would ever return.

He had no ambition even though he found himself being offered yet another promotion. He wasn't there to save people any more, he was there to patch up the wounds. Life was a battle they were all destined to lose.

So when Brendan's mother rang him one bitter January evening, he wasn't surprised. He asked questions in a calm, even tone of voice. Found himself echoing all the platitudes he'd learnt at funerals over the years. Took down the details of this one. Only when he hung up the phone did the full horror of what Brendan's mother had said, in short, sharp sentences that gave away the rawness of her own pain, hit him. A body had been dragged from the Thames. It had taken some time to identify as it had been in the water for quite a length of time. The victim hadn't drowned. Death had been by a single gunshot to the back of the head. Someone had caught up with Brendan before he got the chance to leave for America.

43

DEATH IN JACK'S HOMETOWN, WHICH he hadn't been back to in nearly four years, had a unique flavour. Particularly violent death. It was a whispered, hushed affair riddled with rumour and horror. Jack was relieved to see there were no men in balaclavas. He dreaded the possibility of the tricolour draped over the coffin and the sinister sound of guns being fired into the air by men whose faces you couldn't see. Whatever his cousin's Republican connections, they had deserted him now.

Jack wasn't keen to catch up with Brendan's family, an assortment of tough looking men with closed faces and harsh women old before their time. Relatives he hadn't seen since he was a boy. The same ones who had judged his mother so completely that they had refused to attend her funeral. People without pity or mercy. Jack wondered if the hostile glances cast in his direction were because he was his mother's son, and therefore somehow tainted, or if they naturally looked at everybody they didn't recognise in this way. Screw them, thought Jack, nursing his whisky in a remote corner of Brendan's mother's tiny front room. He tried to be as invisible as possible, but he didn't really care whether he was welcome here or not. He hadn't come for them. He'd come because he thought Brendan would have wanted him there.

For a Catholic funeral, it was remarkably small. The world and his mother had turned up for Kate's. People love a good tragedy. But maybe there was a world of difference between a beautiful young mother drowned in what everyone told themselves was a tragic accident, and a ginger bouncer dragged from a river with a bullet in his head.

The only person who'd attempted to speak to Jack at the graveside was a pale thin woman with wispy hair. So thin you could snap her in half. "You lived with Brendan in Dublin?"

Jack thought she must be Brendan's older sister. The one with the little kids that his cousin was always going on about. He wasn't sure, but he nodded.

The woman seemed to want to say more. Eventually she managed to gasp, "Brendan was always very fond of you."

She turned away before Jack could respond. As the clods of earth hit the coffin, Jack thought, I was very fond of him too. He felt cursed. As if everyone he ever cared about was destined to die in some grim and violent fashion or end up like his father. Broken inside. Jack felt he was suffering from a very slow form of internal bleeding. He'd left Cathal with Mrs McKiernan and without his son's face to reassure him there was some good in the world, Jack felt utterly desolate.

Brendan's mother at least had the grace to thank him for coming. "You knew what he was really like," she told him grabbing Jack's hand so tight he thought his fingers would break. 'He wasn't an informer, I know he wasn't.'

Jack was left to ponder this until a man he didn't recognise stepped up to him. "Are you Mary's son?" he sneered.

Jack realised how long it had been since he'd heard his mother's Christian name. He looked up at the man who was a good six foot six and towered over Jack. He had a blunt, raw, cruel face and Jack thought about making an excuse about needing to go to the bathroom. Then he remembered what Brendan had told him the night Jack had worked as a bouncer. "Never let them see you're afraid. Once they see the fear in your eyes, you're done for."

The advice clearly hadn't saved his cousin, but still Jack lit a cigarette and was amazed that his hands didn't shake. He offered one politely to the ugly man who stared at him as if he'd just insulted him.

"I'm Brendan's brother," he snarled.

Jack wondered which one. Brendan had four brothers plus three sisters. When he was growing up Jack hadn't known any other children like himself who'd no siblings. He'd often wished he'd had a bigger, older, tougher version of himself to look out for him. Yet Brendan, who was the baby of the family, had often referred to his brothers as 'cunts' who'd beat the living crap out of him when he was little.

"Suppose it taught me to look out for myself," Brendan would say looking at Jack from under his funny, reddish blond eyebrows. He clearly didn't think Jack was able to take care of himself. Now Jack was alive and Brendan wasn't. There was no justice in the world.

Brendan's brother leant in close, his breath sour. "My brother never had any problems till he fell in with you."

Dear God, was he to blame for everything? Jack was already torturing himself with the idea that the information he'd given the gunman had directly led to Brendan's death. He'd only said his cousin was ringing from a hostel in Kilburn but Jack could still remember the chilling way the man had told him he'd been most helpful. Why had he opened his big mouth?

For a terrifying moment, Jack thought Brendan's brother was about to punch him. But he stumbled away in search of another drink. Jack sympathised. He felt like hitting something himself. He had another whisky. He was in that artificially crystal state of mind where no matter how much he drank, he'd never feel drunk. I'm the traitor, he thought, not Brendan. I'm the one who has let everyone down. I'm the one who deserves a bullet in the back of the head.

He wondered if Brendan had heard his assassin creeping up on him or if he had been taken unawares. They would've had to take his cousin somewhere quiet to shoot him. Down some dark alley. He wondered if Brendan was scared then. He'd never known him to be afraid.

Jack drove back to Dublin in driving rain that slapped against the windows and made visibility difficult. He could just about make out the cat's eyes on the road in front of him. Winking lights embedded into the tarmac itself. He no longer felt numb. Brendan's funeral had caused the anaesthetic to wear off. He felt as if his skin was crawling with maggots and there were ravens swooping through his head.

The first thing he said when Mrs McKiernan opened the door was, "Birds. There's birds everywhere."

The poor woman looked utterly confused but pulled him inside. She tried to persuade him to go to bed, but he insisted on seeing Cathal. It was past midnight and the little boy was sleeping peacefully. Jack looked at the child and started to tremble. Mrs McKiernan thought he had a fever. Again she urged Jack to go to bed, but he was having great difficulty concentrating on what she was saying. Her words seemed to fragment and split and he couldn't quite grab hold of their meaning. He told her he needed to keep watch and insisted on sitting in the armchair. If he was cursed, if everything he loved was to be taken from him, then they would be after Cathal next. He resolved never to let the child out of his sight.

Jack forced his eyes to stay open till they were red raw and burning, but he must have drifted off eventually. When he woke it was daylight and a man in a dark suit was bending over him. For a confused moment he thought it was an undertaker.

"I'm not dead yet," he told him.

The man smiled, a smile that didn't reach his eyes. "I realise that. I'm Dr. O'Neill. Mrs McKiernan rang me. She said you didn't seem very well last night when you came in."

Jack didn't trust or like the man. "I don't want to be a doctor," he informed him.

It seemed important that the man should know this.

The next few weeks were a blur to Jack. He knew he was in hospital and that the drugs they gave him made him feel like he was a piece of driftwood at sea. He floated through the ward like a ghost. Sometimes he felt like he was being crushed by a great weight and he couldn't breathe. He'd call out in panic. There'd be a rush of footsteps, hushed voices, and a needle in his arm that plunged him into a black dreamless sleep. Rather how he imagined death to be.

But he wasn't dying after all and slowly he began to return to his own body. He felt weak and shaky but increasingly lucid. The psychiatrist told him he'd had a nervous breakdown following the loss of his wife and that he was in a psychiatric hospital for his own safety.

"You had a great shock," the shrink explained in his soft, slimy voice. "It's quite normal for the mind to crack under such pressure."

Jack imagined his brain with a hairline fracture running down the middle of it. Like a cup that had been dropped. Nothing about Kate's death had been remotely normal, but Jack didn't mention this. Instead he concentrated on convincing the medical staff that he was well enough to go home. He had to get out of there. He had to make sure Cathal was okay. He was informed that his son was being cared for by his aunt and uncle. Apparently Pat had even been to visit Jack shortly after he was first admitted. Jack had absolutely no recollection of this, but he could imagine her telling the doctors he'd always been a bit unstable. To make sure they kept the medication up.

When Jack was deemed well enough to go home, he was astonished to find that three months had passed. He'd lost all track of time. He rang Pat the moment he got out.

Her voice was cold on the phone. "Cathal is happy with us," she kept repeating as if she'd an ice cube stuck in her throat.

Jack asked when he could collect his son.

"You're not his father," Pat hissed. "Kate asked me to look after him. She killed herself rather than be with you. She wouldn't want you anywhere near him."

Her cruel statement hit Jack between the eyes. He'd never questioned how Kate would feel about him raising her child before. He'd just thought he'd let her down, but he'd make sure Cathal had everything he needed. But maybe what the boy needed was a normal family. Solid, respectable people like Martin and Pat. Not a father driven mad by grief. Not to be raised in a house where all the joy had been sucked from the marrow of its bones.

"I'll go to court if I have to." Pat said threateningly.

Jack felt infinitely tired. He thought he might faint. He didn't have the strength to fight Kate's sister, to face what accusations she might throw at him in court. She wasn't one to be messed with and she wouldn't stop until she'd stripped Jack of everything.

"Can I at least see him?"

Pat didn't even pause. "Over my dead body will you get anywhere near him. I never want to see you again as long as I live."

With that she hung up on him.

Jack sat for a good fifteen minutes cradling the telephone receiver as if it were a baby. He knew Pat had won. That she'd got her revenge by taking the one thing that still mattered to Jack. He knew he'd lost his only son and he didn't have the strength left in him to do anything about it.

44

CATHAL STOOD OVER JACK AS Jack struggled to light a cigarette. Jack's hands were shaking so badly that he couldn't get the match to strike.

"What do you mean he's dead?" Cathal demanded.

"I'm sorry," Jack said. "So many times I've wished I could have my life over. If only I could go back to certain moments..." His words trailed off.

"I couldn't give a fuck how sorry you are," Cathal kept his voice low but Aisling could see her brother was very close to the edge. "You killed my father?"

"I never meant to, I swear. We had a fight... Things got out of hand, it was an accident." Jack sounded almost relieved to be telling them.

Claire stared at him in horror. "What are you saying, Jack?"

"I was in love," Aisling's uncle replied. "That's all it was."

Suddenly Cathal swung back and punched Jack in the face so hard that he went flying back in his chair.

"Cathal, stop," Aisling shouted.

But her brother was completely out of control. He had Jack on the floor and was kicking him repeatedly in the stomach and in the head.

"You bastard, you fucking bastard," he roared.

Jack groaned as Cathal kicked him viciously in the guts but made no attempt to get up or defend himself. Aisling tried to pull Cathal away. There was a sickening crunch as her brother's boot made contact with Jack's face. Her uncle was being beaten to a bloody pulp.

"Cathal, please," Aisling begged.

Her brother stopped. He was crying now. His face wet with tears. Aisling wrapped her arms around him. Jack lay unmoving.

It was Claire who called the ambulance. Aisling was still in a state of utter shock. Cathal just kept repeating the word 'bastard' over and over to himself. He seemed incapable of any other comment. In spite of everything Aisling felt maybe she should go with her uncle to the hospital but she also didn't want to let her brother out of her sight. He seemed in a fragile and dangerous state of mind.

Jack was semi-conscious as the ambulance men moved him on to the stretcher. 'What happened?" Aisling overheard one of them ask him.

"I don't know; I'm sorry," Jack replied.

As the ambulance men wheeled Jack out, Cathal suddenly stalked out of the room slamming the door behind him.

Claire could see Aisling's anxiety. "I'll go with Jack," she said. "You look after your brother."

Aisling caught up with Cathal before he'd even opened the garden gate. For a moment he looked at her as if he didn't know who she was. Then he said, "I need a drink."

They went to O'Flaherty's, the pub on the corner. A local, full of people who looked like they'd been drinking there for the best part of fifty years and had forgotten how to go home. Cathal ordered two pints of Guinness and headed for a table at the back. Aisling remembered that the last time she'd shared a drink with her brother was at the picnic before he left.

"I hope I've killed him," Cathal said defiantly. "I hope the cunt's got internal bleeding and he dies slowly in great pain."

Aisling was still in shock. She couldn't believe that her uncle, who seemed the kindest, gentlest man in the world, could have killed someone. She could totally understand Cathal's anger, but his bitterness upset her.

"How could you have stayed away for so long?" she asked carefully.

Cathal looked uncomfortable. "I wanted to come back. All this time I've wanted to come back but I couldn't admit it to myself."

"I don't get it," Aisling replied. She still felt like she understood nothing.

Cathal was looking into the depths of his pint. "After I finally found my grandmother in New York I had some confused notion that I needed to confront Jack before I could face going home. She convinced me that Troy must indeed be my real father. She said that he was obsessed with my mother, that she was all he talked about before he left. But after he went to Dublin to find her, she never heard another word. She told me how painful not knowing what had happened to him had been and it made me feel terribly guilty. I thought if I could just get Jack to tell me how I could contact my father, I could start to put everything right again. I didn't expect you to be living with Jack. I guessed Jack had some jealous grudge against my father, but I never in a million years thought he murdered him."

"He did say it was an accident." Aisling just couldn't believe her uncle capable of murder.

"And you believe him? Every word out of that man's mouth is a lie. He told me he was my father. For months I believed him. Then he told me my mother was raped. What kind of sick fuck makes stuff up like that?"

Aisling felt sorry for her brother. But it hurt her that he'd come back to confront Jack, not to see her. She preferred the story she used to tell herself when he first went missing: That he'd gotten a knock to the head and was suffering temporary but total amnesia. One day something would jog his memory and it would all come flooding back. But Cathal hadn't been suffering from memory loss. He knew perfectly well that he'd a sister who loved and adored him, wondering where the hell he was.

Aisling felt tears pricking her eyes. Her throat constricted painfully. The atmosphere of the pub was smoky but that wasn't what was making it difficult for her to breathe.

"Are you all right?" Cathal asked.

Aisling could feel her face was flushed but inside she felt cold and furious. "Just because I'm not really your sister doesn't make it okay for you to have left like that."

"I know it must've been awfully hard for you."

"No, you don't. You haven't a clue what it was like for me. You don't know anything about me."

As she spoke, she realised how true it was. It wasn't just that Cathal had come back a stranger, it was the fact she'd turned into one. She couldn't ever again be that innocent girl who'd worshipped her big brother. She'd become another person entirely. Someone Cathal had never met. It wasn't just a question of forgiveness, it was all the time he hadn't been there. Time that neither of them could get back.

They sat in silence until Cathal spoke. "I'm sorry Angel. I wasn't very well in my own head when I left. I felt like I'd no idea who I was, where I was going, what I wanted to do. It was like something inside me had been cut adrift. After Jack told me my father was a rapist, I just went to pieces. I couldn't cope with anything; I just lurched from one day to the next. I thought I was useless and you were better off without me. It was never anything to do with you."

"I know that now. But I used to wonder all the time what I'd done that was so awfully wrong you'd never want to speak to me again. It was selfish Cathal, it was selfish and cruel."

Cathal looked like she'd punched him. "Yeah it was," he admitted. "And then as time went on, knowing how I'd let you down, I just couldn't face you. I thought at least if you thought I was dead, you wouldn't hate me, you wouldn't know just what a shit brother I really was. I was so ashamed of being in prison, I thought you were all better off not knowing.'

240

"We love you, you know. As far as I'm concerned you're still my brother no matter what. And Mam and Dad have always seen you as their son. They were trying to do the right thing in adopting you."

"But why they didn't tell me? You shouldn't lie to the people that you love."

"Oh stop feeling so sorry for yourself." Aisling, having said what she thought, was feeling a bit better. She'd rather have her brother back, flawed and wrecked as he appeared to be, than have him lying dead in a ditch somewhere.

Cathal grinned at her sheepishly. "You've grown up to be some woman. Mam and Dad must be dead proud of you.'

Aisling laughed. How could she begin to explain to Cathal that she'd been expelled from school, flunked her exams, and that Jack had been about to inform their parents that on coming to Dublin, she'd turned into a dangerous homosexual? She might blame her brother for the pain he'd caused his family, but she wasn't doing so much better herself.

"What's funny? What have you been up to all this time?"

So over the course of several pints, she told him.

When she got to the part about Claire, her brother sat open mouthed. "Jesus fucking Christ. So you're gay? That puts everything I've ever done in the shade."

They both started to giggle uncontrollably. They laughed till they cried. After all this time it felt good to be united once more in the face of their parents' disapproval.

Cathal put his arm round Aisling as they stumbled back to Jack's together.

As Aisling struggled to get her key in the lock, her brother leant against the porch wall and lit a cigarette. He offered her one. "You know something," he said. "It feels good to be home."

Once inside Aisling rang the hospital. She wanted to find out if Jack was all right. She certainly didn't want her brother to have beaten her uncle to death even if he wished he had. In spite of everything, she was very fond of Jack and it was hard to suddenly switch that off. There could be no justification for what he'd done, but still she wanted to hear his side of the story.

She got put through to Claire.

"He's going to be fine. Several broken ribs and severe bruising but nothing serious," Claire sounded on the edge of tears. "He's insisting he wants to make a full confession to the police."

That night Aisling lay in bed with the Guinness and a thousand thoughts twirling through her brain. The sheer depth of her own ignorance amazed her. Nothing in her family was how she'd supposed it to be. All her life, she'd had the uncomfortable feeling that they were tiptoeing around unmentionable truths, but the extent to which they had contorted their lives to play out some fantasy of normality was crazy. Cathal said he didn't really blame their mother any more. She belonged to a generation where the most important thing was to belong, not to stand out from the crowd. She thought she was doing him a favour by pretending he was her own child, although plenty of people who'd known Kate must've been aware that he wasn't. She'd relied on the fact that people might whisper behind his back, but would never dare tell him the truth to his face.

Aisling wondered if her brother's sudden reappearance would make her mother so happy that news of Aisling's homosexuality would barely register. But she knew it was more likely that she'd despair of the two of them and disown them both; a criminal and a pervert was hardly what she'd hoped to raise.

The next day Aisling went to visit Jack in hospital.

Cathal was not impressed. "He killed my father. Why do you care what happens to him?"

Aisling wasn't sure she was up to hearing all the gory details, but still she needed to understand. She just couldn't grasp how Jack had turned out to be such a monster.

When she arrived, Claire left Jack's bedside so Aisling could talk to him alone. Jack looked a fright. One eye was completely closed and his entire face was swollen and bruised.

"Is Cathal okay?" was the first thing Jack asked.

Aisling stared at her uncle. "Of course he's not okay," she said, sounding harsher than she meant to.

"And what about you?"

Aisling had no idea how to reply. She felt such a strange mixture of emotions, she couldn't even say if she'd enjoyed the evening with her brother or not. Underneath her anger there was a huge joy at her brother's return, but she wasn't ready to let him back into her life with open arms just yet. He'd have to prove that this time he intended to stick around.

It would be easy to blame Jack for everything that had gone wrong in her and Cathal's life. The idea was particularly appealing because it offered the opportunity to stop blaming her mother. In the last few days Aisling had been forced to face up to the real reasons behind her terror that Jack would tell her mother about Claire. And it wasn't that her mother was a conservative, reactionary, fundamentalist Catholic who in her ignorance and prejudice was bound to do her utmost to ensure Aisling never saw Claire again. It wasn't her mother's shock or her anger or even her contempt that Aisling most feared. The truth was she loved her mother so much that her voice was always inside her own head. A voice she violently disagreed with, but still a solid, reassuring presence that gave her a centre of gravity.

What she was most scared of was that her mother wouldn't love her any more. That this fundamental fact, all her mother's worrying and fussing and generally harassing her, would be withdrawn. She needed her mother, even if it was only to be able to disagree with her. Just like you shouldn't go on a journey unless you've got a place to return to.

Jack had caused her brother to wander into the wilderness and he had the power to cast her into exile. Because when it came down to it, if her mother made her choose between her family and Claire, she would pick Claire. It wasn't even a choice. Her mother couldn't possibly understand and neither could her uncle. Maybe she'd tell her mother one day when she was older and stronger. But she wanted it to be her choice, she didn't want to be handed over like some kind of criminal

Jack was staring at Aisling. "I suppose you hate me?"

He caught Aisling off guard. Much as she was horrified by what he'd done, it had never occurred to her to hate him. It was easy to pass judgment, but life took you on strange paths and until you'd been down that particular road yourself, who were you to say you would have fared any better? That was her main problem with organised religion. It always seemed to be pointing out what you'd done wrong in the abstract rather than the concrete, lived reality.

So all Aisling could say to Jack's question was, "I don't hate anyone."

And she didn't. Maybe at times she was angry, bitter, cynical, but deep down she didn't mean it. Maybe that wasn't good enough, but it was a start.

Her uncle seemed to draw courage from her words. "I've done some really awful things in my life."

Aisling nodded. She wanted to say something to make things better, to ease Jack's obvious pain, but she couldn't think of anything. The past was what it was. There was nothing she could do to change it.

"All I wanted to say," Jack cleared his throat, "is that I don't pretend to understand, in truth there's a great deal I've never understood." Jack paused.

Aisling felt she knew exactly what he meant. Her own ignorance had hung around her like a dense fog for such a long time.

243

"I'm really not trying to destroy your relationship with Claire. I'm not jealous. I'd like to think I've learnt something from my past mistakes."

"Did you kill Troy because you were jealous?" Aisling asked.

"You know, maybe I did. I just didn't see it that way at the time."

"But you didn't mean for him to die. It wasn't murder," Aisling wanted her uncle to defend himself.

"No I didn't, that's true. Technically his death was an accident. For years I've tried to ease my conscience with that thought. But you know the truth is there's worse things than murder."

"You said it was because you were in love?"

"Love is no excuse," Jack smiled sadly. "Do you love Claire?"

"Yes I do," Aisling said. "I really do."

"Well can't say I blame you. She's a wonderful woman." Jack paused. "Don't worry I'm not in love with her myself. She's far too young for me. Besides the only woman I ever loved was your Aunt Kate. There's never been anyone else. I managed to destroy the one person that meant the world to me."

"What do you mean?" Aisling asked.

And Jack told her the whole painful story. Aisling listened to his confession and felt for the first time she understood that her uncle was the loneliest man alive. Whatever wrongs he'd done, he'd certainly paid for them.

She found it hard to believe he could have told so many lies and she told him so.

"I can hardly believe it myself," Jack sighed. "But as my mother used to say "oh what fine webs we weave when first we learn to deceive". I just got myself and everyone I cared about trapped in my own web. I've caused so much pain where there should have been happiness. And yet, you know, I always meant to do the right thing."

"What are you going to tell the police?" Aisling asked.

"The truth for once," Jack smiled. "I doubt they'll believe me. Why should they? I almost hope they don't. I deserve to go to prison for what I did to Troy. I've been a terrible judge of character, most particularly my own. Troy was a much better man than I ever was or ever will be."

"Are you going to tell my mother about Claire?" Aisling ventured.

"I guess if I've learnt anything it's not to stand in the path of true love." Jack laughed when he said this. A laugh that was unbearably light, a laugh that floated above them and hung shimmering in the air. A genuine laugh, the laugh of a man who realises that he has not forgotten how to laugh after all.

Suddenly Aisling took Jack's hand and squeezed it hard. It wasn't just gratitude, she felt they understood one another.

"Are you really going to turn yourself in to the police? Is there any point after all these years? I'm sure I could talk to Cathal, try to make him see…"

"Don't do that. Cathal has ever right to hate me." Jack grimaced. "It's time for me to face up to it all. I've been imprisoned in my own head for years. I was so terrified I'd be found out. That's why I went to America and told Cathal that terrible lie. You see people respect me and look up to me as a surgeon, a man who saves lives. I couldn't bear the idea that the world would know who I really was. I wanted to bury the past in a shallow grave, like I did with Troy."

Aisling thought of all the pain Jack had caused her brother. She doubted Cathal would ever be able to forgive him. But even sadder was that Jack would never be able to forgive himself.

Jack stared at her intently. "It doesn't work you know. Life is full of ghosts. There's only so long you can keep running from the truth."

Jack looked to Aisling like a man who was drowning, a man who'd been swimming against the currents for a thousand years and had finally given in to the waves.